Eena

-The Dawn and Rescue-

Thank you for your
interest in my books.
I truly hope you
enjoy this reading adventure!

Richelle E. Goodrich

Eena

~The Dawn and Rescue~

The First Book in the Harrowbethian Saga

By
Richelle E. Goodrich

Dedicated to my Father in Heaven,
without whose blessings this adventure
would never have developed.
I thank Thee for Thy hand in my life.

TABLE OF CONTENTS

Life is a valuable and unique opportunity
to discover who you are.
But it seems as soon as you near
answering that age-old question,
something unexpected always happens
to alter your course.
And who it is you thought you were
suddenly changes.

Then comes the frustrating realization
that no matter how long life endures,
no matter how many experiences
are muddled through in this existence,
you may never really be able
to answer the question....
Who am I?

Because the answer, like the seasons,
constantly, subtly, inevitably changes.
And who it is you are today,
is not the same person you will be tomorrow.

~Sha Eena
87th Queen of Harrowbeth

PROLOGUE

The final red tinge of another sunset was fading, sinking behind a distant sagebrush-dotted horizon.   In a matter of minutes the sky would be filled with the soft lights of a million stars. Sevenah watched the performance as faithfully as she did every night from her grassy seat beneath the old weeping willow tree where she could see across her father's cornfields and beyond. This hill was her favorite place to be, evenings her favorite time of day, almost always spent with her very best friend, Ian.

The two usually rode her horse, Paka, up the hill to watch the sunset, but her beloved pet had been fitted with new shoes and was struggling to adjust to them.   Her mother had suggested leaving him in the barn.

Sevenah glanced at the silhouette of Ian seated beside her— tall, lean, and slightly slouched.   He was staring up at the first star of the evening, which wasn't really a star at all but the bright reflection of the sun off the nearby planet, Venus.

"Do you think people will live there someday?" she asked him.

Ian turned his head to find her staring at the same celestial light he had been contemplating.   His fingers brushed away the dusty-brown bangs that hung in his eyes.

"You mean Venus?   Doubtful.   I can't imagine the atmosphere ever changing enough to sustain life—at least not our kind of life."

She laughed.   "What other kind is there?"

"Oh, species that require alternative atmospheres to survive," he said matter-of-factly.

She laughed even more.

"You disagree?"

"I think you read too many sci-fi books," she smiled.   It was true, he usually had a book or two in his possession to thumb through when there was nothing else demanding his attention. Even homework didn't take priority when it came to an off-world adventure story.

"I'm still right," he insisted.

Sevenah resumed staring up at the darkness. The sun had set entirely, giving way for the appearance of a speckled night's sky. It seemed the more she stared, the greater the number of stars. She pondered the immensity of the universe and how it resembled an artist's black canvas peppered with a haphazard splattering of white paint.

"I think there probably is life out there a lot like our own. I can't imagine so many suns—so many planets—and not at least one of them being something like ours."

She could sense Ian nod in agreement beside her.

Her eyes searched for the big dipper, one of the few constellations she easily recognized. It wasn't within view. She twirled around and pulled her long, red-brown hair over one shoulder before lying back on the grassy slope to see past the droopy limbs of the willow tree. It was only a matter of seconds before Ian copied her move, a habit of his. As soon as his head lay beside hers, she pointed directly up.

"There it is," she announced, "the Big Dip."

Ian pointed off to the right. "And there's Arcturus and Virgo and Leo…"

"Show off," she muttered, slapping him lightly on the shoulder. Her head turned sideways to catch a twinkle in his green eyes as he chuckled. They were a shade darker than her own. He smiled his usual warm smile when she stared at him a little too long.

"What?" he asked.

"Nothing." She rolled her eyes to divert attention from her blushing cheeks.

Ian's lips slipped crookedly to one side. "Maybe someday you and I will visit another world."

Sevenah laughed out loud, causing a frown to erase his grin. Apparently he was serious. To spare his feelings she chose to play along.

"Okay, okay, how about I'll fly to Orks Nation while you go visit the little green men on Zeeksville?"

"Oh come on!"

She turned up a questioning palm. "What? You're the one who believes in aliens."

"Yes, I do, but that's not what I'm groaning about. Orks Nation? Zeeksville? Those are horrible names! Could you at least *try* to be creative with your planets?"

Her body rolled sideways to face him, elbow bent, hand cupping her cheek. Lengths of reddish hair fell straight behind her shoulder.

"I suppose you have better names?" she challenged.

"Oh, definitely yes," he insisted. He rotated to face her, copying her move again.

"Lay 'em on me then."

Ian glanced up at the darkness for a moment. "Okay, how about….Rapador of the Paegus Solar System. Or even better— Moccobatra of the Alaheron System."

"Did you pull those out of one of your sci-fi books?" she asked suspiciously.

"No."

"You just made them up?" Her eyebrows lifted, a little surprised and impressed.

"Well…..no."

The same eyebrows scrunched together in confusion. "Then where'd they come from?"

"Okay, I got them from a book," he admitted.

"I thought so," she smirked. "You're not so terribly clever either."

Ian sighed as he watched Sevenah's pink lips curl into a wide, triumphant grin. "No fooling you, is there," he muttered.

"No—but nice try."

Sevenah fell on her back again and stared at the heavens silently for a while. Ian remained on his side, watching her scan the universe with wonder. They listened to the remote chorus of crickets and tree frogs until Sevenah's arm shot up, tracing an arc overhead.

"Did you see that?" she chirped. Her eyes glimmered with excitement. "A falling star! Did you make a wish?"

Ian dropped onto his back and looked up. "No—no wishes. I don't believe in superstitions."

She laughed. "But aliens *you do* believe in. You're so weird."

"What did you wish for?" he asked, ignoring the playful

insult.

She grinned big. "I wished for all your wishes to come true."

"Really? You wasted a wish on me?"

"Of course. You're my best friend." Her hand reached to squeeze his.

"But I thought if you told your wish it wouldn't come true."

"I thought you didn't believe in superstitions," she retorted.

"Okay, okay."

Their conversation was interrupted by the muted beep of a cell phone. Sevenah reached into the pocket of her Levis and pulled out a small, pink, touchscreen device.

"Your mom?" Ian asked, seeing her frown at a glowing text message.

"Ugh, yes. Who else would it be?" Her eyes flickered over at Ian before returning to the text she was quickly typing in response. "You're so lucky no one hounds you like this."

He grinned, amused. "What are you telling her?"

"That I'll be home as soon as you're done molesting me."

Ian quickly reached for the phone. "Sevenah, don't you dare…"

It dinged—message sent—as she avoided him, shrugging innocently. "Ooops, too late."

"You are so rude to your mother," he chided. "Ruth is going to hate me now."

It was always strange to hear Ian refer to her mother by name. Sevenah sighed, complaining. "Well, if she wasn't so darn overprotective. It's annoying."

"She cares about you."

"I know."

"Which is a good thing."

"I know."

The phone was shoved back into her front pocket before she sat up and crossed her legs. Ian did the same, slumping a bit.

"I guess it's time for you to go," she announced. "Walk me home?"

"Don't I always?"

Ian shed his J.D. jean jacket and tossed it over Sevenah's shoulders as she started down the hill in front of him. They skirted the browning cornstalks at the bottom before heading for a distant white fence that encircled her house. He would drop her off by the gate tonight instead of going in to visit with her parents as usual.

"I might not see you in the morning, Sevenah. My uncle's got plans."

"Really?"

That was odd. Ian hardly ever mentioned his uncle, let alone did anything with the grumpy, old guy. She had never actually met the man but had heard about his ornery character on occasion.

"Yes, but it shouldn't take all day. I'll be here as soon as I can be."

"Okay," she shrugged. It was the weekend, so they would still have plenty of time to hang out even if he wasn't there first thing in the morning. She would have to remember to tell her mom not to make any breakfast for him.

"Hey, Ian. Jackie mentioned at school today something about the whole group going back to Sun Lakes one last time before winter sets in. Maybe you could join us there when you're done with your uncle."

"It's a little chilly for swimming isn't it?"

"Oh, we're not planning to swim. Just a barbeque-picnic sort of thing."

She caught the disapproving look on his face when he glanced at her. "I'd rather you wait for me."

"Why?"

"Actually, I'd rather not go at all if you don't mind. I had other plans."

"For us?"

"Yes. Is that so hard to believe?"

"Well, um…uh, no," she stammered, "I guess not." Truthfully it did surprise her. She was used to him going along with her plans and her friends. Very seldom did he suggest an alternate activity. Curious, she asked, "So, what did you have in mind?"

He lifted both shoulders undecidedly.

"I thought you said…" she started. Then her eyes pulsed wide and she poked at his arm accusingly. "You just don't want me hanging around Erik!"

His head shook in denial. "That's not it."

14

"Don't tell me you're going all 'Ruthy' on me. Are you getting my mother's overprotective gene?"

Ian laughed with amusement. "I'm not going 'Ruthy' on you, but I could probably one-up her if I wanted." His laughter halted when he turned a serious face on his friend. "Just promise you'll wait for me. I'll take you to the lake if that's where you really want to go, but wait for me, alright?"

Her hand batted at the air. "Whatever."

"Promise me," he insisted.

She looked up to see if his expression was as stern as his voice. It was.

"Fine," she agreed, her brow creasing with puzzlement. "I promise." She crossed her heart as if swearing it.

"Thank you."

Sevenah wondered at his sigh of relief.

Surprisingly, they had made it to the main gate, just outside the reach of a porch light. Ian held the wooden entry open for her.

"I'll see you tomorrow then," he said.

She handed back his jacket before starting down the cement path for the front door. "Okay, but don't be too late. I'm not going to sit around and waste my entire Saturday."

"Hey!" he called out behind her. "You promised you'd wait for me."

"Yeah, yeah, yeah." She grinned impishly, glancing back at his troubled face. Great. He *was* going "Ruthy" on her.

CHAPTER ONE
Who Are You?

What on earth am I still doing here? she wondered.   Why is this taking so darn long?

Sevenah had been sitting in the doctor's office for hours, slouched on the edge of a cold examination table.   This was the second time they had recalled her to the clinic for tests.   That alone was enough to make her stomach ache.   She hadn't expected to combine the anxiety with an entire day of fasting.

"What time is it now?" she muttered to herself.

Not having developed the habit of wearing a watch, Sevenah pulled a glossy, pink cell phone from the front pocket of her faded Levis and glanced at the digital display again.

5:38pm, it read.   Only ten minutes past the last time she had checked.

Her arrival at the clinic had been just after 11:30 that morning at Dr. Tracy's request, with his assurances it was nothing more than a follow-up appointment.   But the way those worry lines had deepened around his white eyebrows made her wonder.   Even more disconcerting was his agitated and distant behavior, so uncharacteristic of the warm and friendly doctor she had come to rely on over the years.

The old man was an icon in Royal City, having practiced medicine in their small, desert town for over three decades.   He had been the Williams' family doctor since before Sevenah could recall.   Her mother had brought her to see him as a child, and still the young lady was a loyal patient at seventeen years of age, able to drive herself to the clinic.   Growing up, Dr. Tracy had treated her numerous bouts of strep throat and given her several sports exams, never forgetting a lollipop on the way out.   She trusted him.   She liked him—especially the way he welcomed her with a friendly pat on the shoulder and the kindest smile.   Today, however, those affable gestures were missing.

Sevenah tried to convince herself the anxiety she felt was

nothing more than the product of an overactive imagination.   She had even spoken to her father about it that afternoon, seeking his common-sense reassurance there was nothing to worry about— advice reliably offered over the phone.   *"Relax, honey, the lab's probably busy.   Doc said it's just follow up tests.   Results take time; be patient."*   But six hours in a sterile room enduring ultrasounds and blood draws and repeated x-rays was torturing her tendency to fret over imagined what-ifs.

"I thought this place closed at five," she groaned.

Alone, listening to the grumbling complaints of an empty stomach, her fingers found their habitual place coiling lengths of her hair into ringlets.   She was blessed with her mother's thick strands that draped over her shoulders like copper corn silk.   Her other hand tapped on the metal table in an attempt to calm agitated nerves.   The pattered rhythm proved somewhat hypnotic.   Her hazel eyes disappeared beneath apricot eyelids as she breathed out a long, heavy sigh, releasing a portion of the built-up tension in her chest.   A shiver traveled down her spine, and her muscles stiffened in response.

It was chilly in the clinic, despite the unusually warm autumn breeze that blew across irrigated farmland outside.   Sevenah rubbed her arms briskly, wishing she had thrown on more than a t-shirt and jeans that morning.   A sweatshirt would've been wise; she almost never felt warm enough.   Why she didn't carry a jacket with her more often was a puzzle, especially with the days growing shorter.   Just absentminded perhaps.   If her best friend, Ian, had been there, he would have offered his by now.   She smiled, realizing he was probably the reason she never brought her own.   Ian routinely looked out for her.   He was always in her company, always prepared like a boy scout.

Except for today.

Sevenah had assumed he would eventually meet up with her at the clinic.   He would have gone to her house when finished with whatever responsibilities were his at home.   Then her mother should've directed him to town—explained that Dr. Tracy had called, personally requesting her presence that morning for follow-up tests.   She had texted her other friends a dozen times already, but no one had admitted to seeing head-nor-tail of her best friend.   Four calls to her mom had received no answer.   That was typical.

Her mother's phone usually sat buried in a purse or a pocket if it wasn't just plain lost altogether, a fact that proved a constant irritation to Sevenah. She couldn't understand why a person bothered owning a cell phone with no intention of ever answering it.

Admittedly, a portion of her agitation was due to Ian's absence. It was rare for the pair to spend one day apart. They had become attached at the hip after first meeting a little over a year ago when the young man had moved to town. He had seemed shy and quiet at first, but had opened up to Sevenah with little effort. Since then, they were nearly inseparable.

Their initial meeting had occurred shortly after her first excruciating attack—the one Dr. Tracy now claimed required a second follow-up. The chest pain had been debilitating, radiating throughout her upper body and across her back. Her mother had rushed her to the clinic on that cold autumn day in a worried frenzy.

Sevenah recalled crying nonstop, arms folded over her chest, squeezing against the agonizing internal pressure. It had mattered little what position she assumed—lying, sitting, or standing—each had been equally insufferable. Dr. Tracy had ordered x-rays, but after a while the pain had subsided as quickly as it had come on— miraculously vanished. It was bizarre.......and embarrassing. Her mother had taken her home, feeling both relieved and confused, before any diagnosis was rendered. Sevenah had insisted.

A couple months later, Dr. Tracy had called requesting another set of x-rays and additional tests. "*Just a follow up,*" he had explained. Ian had accompanied her that day, only weeks after meeting him. Everything had tested "hunky-dory," as the old doctor liked to say. So why another call back more than a year after the fact? Had something critical been discovered?

Sevenah fidgeted on the elevated medical bed, her feet dangling over one side. She stared down at her white Nikes, now a worn and faded vanilla color. Trying to pass the time, she examined how the side seams had begun to unravel.

"Note to self—I need new shoes."

She hopped off the table and raised both arms toward the ceiling, reaching to stretch out her spine. Waiting was one of her stronger points, usually.   Biding time was merely a fact of life in Sevenah's world.   She expected delays; to say "no problem" even when it was inconvenient; to compromise; to wait her turn; to calmly keep the peace.   She found it difficult to complain under normal circumstances, but this was getting ridiculous.   Couldn't the nurse just call with test results?

Her brow tightened trying to decide whether to track someone down or just quietly slip out and head for home.   After all, they did know where to reach her.   A squeak sounded from her sneakers with every swivel on the linoleum as she paced indecisively, searching for the courage to defy authority.   No doubt her father would hear about it if Dr. Tracy found her missing.

"That's it, I'm leaving," she finally announced to herself. Enough was enough.

Headed for the door, her fingers reached for the knob.   It twisted beneath her touch, and she quickly withdrew her hand.

"It's about time," she breathed.

Through an opening, she spied an angry face on Dr. Tracy. His white eyebrows were pulled low, creating a deep vertical furrow in his forehead.   The frown he wore couldn't have appeared grimmer.

"Sevenah!" he gasped, clearly shocked by her nearness.   The door closed to only a small crack through which he spoke.

"I uh....I apologize for the wait, but I need you to be patient— just for a while longer.   Not much longer, I promise.   Just, please.....stay here."

"But, Dr. Tracy," she began.   She leaned forward meaning to speak through the opening, but he hurriedly shut the door in her face.   She heard the click of a locking mechanism.   No, no—he couldn't have.   She tried the knob to confirm what her ears had told her.   The door was locked!   But why?

"Dr. Tracy?" she called out, twisting uselessly at the handle. "Wait!   Wait, come back!"

A surge of fear chilled her to the bone as she slipped into fretful overdrive.   What possible, sane reason could there be for locking her inside a room?   The question was valid.   The answers, frightening.

Her mind sifted through every potential "what if," taking only seconds to imagine a variety of rare diseases and excruciating ends she might face in the near future.   It had to be an illness—a highly contagious one.   Why else would her kind, old doctor try to quarantine her?   But she had experienced no further pain!   No other attacks!   No additional symptoms!

Sevenah dug out her phone, wishing she could call Ian. Unfortunately, his uncle didn't allow him to have a cell phone, and she didn't know his home number.   There had never been any need to call him before, seeing how he was always at her house.

"Mom."   She muttered the word while her fingers tapped a habitual three-button sequence that led to her mother's number. It rang once…twice………five times.

"Hi there!   You've reached the phone of Ruth Williams. Most likely I'm screening my calls, so if you're feeling lucky today leave your name and number and…"

"Darn it, mom!   Where are you?"

Sevenah cut off the message and then immediately tapped another memorized sequence.   It rang and rang.

"You've reached the phone of Roger Williams.   I'm sorry I can't answer your call right now, but if you leave your name and number I'll get back to you as soon as harvest ends.   Maybe sooner, provided I don't plant another cell phone with my tractor…………Beep!"

"Dad!   Pick up will you?   Why don't you guys ever answer your stupid phones!   I mean what good is having a cell phone if you never keep it with you!"   She realized she sounded frantic, probably too much so, and tried to calm herself.   "Okay, Dad, I tried to call mom, but, um…….look, I'm at the clinic still. I…I'm a little worried.   I know, I know, you'll probably tell me there's nothing to worry about, but I've been here for six hours now, Dad.   Six hours!   And, well, um……Dr. Tracy has locked me in one of the examining rooms.   Dad, that's not normal procedure……is it?   Am I okay?   Um…….please, call me.   I love you, bye."

She stared at the black screen on her phone, concerned that her message might either cause a great deal of unnecessary worry or not excite quite enough.   She could see her father laughing at her, figuring she was overreacting again much like her mom did on occasion.   But this whole thing certainly didn't feel right.

She wandered over to the furthest corner and leaned against the wall. Sliding all the way down to the floor, she curled up below a large diagram of the inner ear. One free arm hugged both knees to her chest as she redialed her mother's number. Again no answer. She didn't leave a message, knowing how her mom would certainly panic. It would be better for her father to say something. He seemed to take things more evenly. Why she hadn't been born with *his* genes rather than her mother's….

Sevenah laid her head on her knees, resigned to the fact that all she could do now was wait. And worry. More than ever, she craved the comforting presence of her best friend, Ian. Anxious for his company, she recalled the first day their paths had crossed.

Ian was a handsome boy. His build—tall and skinny yet muscular. His dusty-brown hair he wore short, except for long bangs that framed the most striking green eyes to ever reflect sunlight. He was quiet, his shyness emphasized by the way his shoulders slouched forward.

Ian had moved to Royal City just over a year ago. It seemed he just fell from the clouds one day. The boy behaved like an orphan—no curfew, no one to report to, never in a hurry for home, and nothing much to say.

Sevenah had noticed him at school, leaning against a gold brick wall, watching her. The minute their eyes had met, his gaze had dropped to the ground. After that, she spotted him numerous times during and after school. He was never with anyone—just hanging solo, staring in her direction. He showed up in most of her classes aside from phys. ed. and art, and he made an appearance at the library the same time she normally studied there—probably a coincidence—seated three tables away. After catching him looking at her from behind a copy of *The Lord of the Rings,* her friendly smile had caused him to bury his head in the pages.

That brisk, autumn evening her horse, Paka, nearly trampled him on the edge of her father's cornfield. She thought she had scared the new kid plumb to death.

"Oh my gosh! Are you alright?"

Sevenah slid down from her saddle, offering a helping hand to the long-legged fellow on the ground. He had stumbled and fallen backwards when her horse had cleared the cornstalks. As soon as he managed to scramble to his feet, his eyes dropped. He froze in a slumped pose, looking as guilty as a child caught where he was told not to be. She recognized the boy at once.

"It's you," she said. Her gaze traveled up and down, giving him a good once-over. He stood well above her; she guessed over six feet tall. "You're new here, aren't you?"

The young man said nothing, continuing to stare at the soil around his shoes. He seemed afraid to speak.

Sevenah tried a different approach, offering her hand for a friendly handshake.

"Hello, my name's Sevenah. What's yours?"

He looked at her palm for a moment, hesitant, stealing a glimpse at her face before finally speaking. His answer was scarcely audible.

"Ian."

"What was that?" she asked.

"My name—it's uh…Ian," he mumbled again.

She could hardly hear him. "Spell it out for me."

His shoulders appeared to droop even more as if he was unsure how to perform her simple request. She thought it curious. He seemed to sound it out.

"Uh…..I…A…N."

"*Ee-un?*" she asked, pronouncing the name as most would read it.

He shook his head. "No, *I-un.*"

"Oh, with a long I."

He nodded and glanced at her again, this time for more than a brief second. It struck her how evergreen his eyes were up close, like a mesh of pine needles.

"I like your eyes."

He lowered his face, hiding behind long bangs.

Sevenah reached to take his hand and slipped her fingers between his. She shook it firmly. "I'm very pleased to meet you, *I-un.*"

He looked up tentatively and smiled the nicest, warmest, most enchanting smile back. He was endeared to her from that moment on. Not like a boyfriend, but a good friend. A best friend. For some reason he felt like a long-lost companion—comfortable to be around and easy to talk to. It didn't take much time for him to warm up to her, and the two became near inseparable. They were buddies, confidants, study partners, teammates, periodic accomplices in spontaneous practical jokes, and always one another's convenient and reliable alibi.

Sevenah recalled the day she had asked to see where Ian lived. She was growing strongly attached to him, though he was still very much a mystery.

"I'd sure like to meet your parents. Would you introduce me to them?" Ian never offered personal news voluntarily, so a visit to his house seemed like a good way to learn more about him.

Ian didn't respond right away. He seemed busy concentrating on lining up a pebble at the toe of his boot. When he kicked it, they watched it travel down the dirt road leading home from school.

"My parents aren't around," he finally muttered. He hopped and struck the same pebble another yard. "I live with my uncle right now, but he's not all that friendly. I don't think you want to meet him."

His tone had been so somber that Sevenah never again suggested a visit to his house, figuring it was a personal hardship he didn't care to share. Not yet anyway. She always wondered if he actually had a home. Or parents. Had they abandoned him? Were they even alive? She never asked these questions; it was like an unspoken agreement between them. But she felt confident he would reveal his secrets to her one day.

Whenever school wasn't in session, the pair usually hung out at the Williams' farm. Ian hardly ever left Sevenah's side. He never mentioned a curfew, which meant she had to tell him when it was time to go. It was obvious he didn't care for his own home, a fact that earned her sympathy. Every now and then she would ask her parents to allow Ian to sleep on their couch, especially if the evening had grown late. Of course it was a habit her mother was wary of encouraging. It just seemed to her the young man was constantly shadowing their daughter. Not that they minded; he was a well-mannered, helpful, and kind soul. But the fact was.....he was a *boy*. A handsome, hormone-driven, teenage boy spending the night in their house while their only daughter lie in bed just a few silent tiptoes down the hallway. Sevenah recalled her father advocating the very first sleepover.

"Sweetheart, they're clearly just friends. Even I can see that."

"Exactly how it starts out, honey, but the next thing you know they're kissing under the mistletoe!" Sevenah groaned at her mother's exaggeration. She was sure where her overactive imagination came from.

"Come on, Ruthy. Ian's never given us reason to question his intentions. He's a perfect gentleman. It's late; let the poor boy crash on the couch."

"Even so, what about appearances? What will the neighbors say?"

"Appearances? Seriously? Our closest neighbors are a mile away!"

"Alright," her mother sighed, giving in to her husband's judgment. "But mark my words, Roger, this is not going to become a regular occurrence. Understand?"

However, the more Ian won them over, the less resistance Sevenah's mother gave. Soon, his periodic sleepovers became a normal part of life. The boy was quick to lend a helping hand with farm chores in appreciation for their kindness.

Every weekday Ian walked Sevenah to and from the goldbrick high school. On the nights he slept at his own house, he would show up at the Williams' front gate bright and early. He hung out on their farm on the weekends and assisted with the cows, goats, and chickens. Mr. Williams even convinced him to drive a combine during harvest since Ian was "practically living there anyway."

Nightfall was the best part of everyday. When the sun began to sink behind a rolling horizon, everything came to a halt. If Ian didn't ride up the hill with Sevenah and Paka, he would be there waiting when she arrived. There they sat and watched the sunset, a ritual shared faithfully every night, settled side-by-side below the drooping branches of her favorite weeping willow tree. Sometimes they discussed the day. Sometimes they simply stared out at a fiery sky and said nothing at all. Regardless, Ian was always at her side.

Always.

Except for today.

"Where are you, Ian? I could really use you now."

It had grown quiet in the clinic, enough that every little hum and click sounded amplified. The murmur of conversing voices had completely ceased, leaving a sense of exile in its place. Sevenah lifted her head to glance at the phone in her hand, wondering perhaps if the lack of return calls was due to an inconvenient dead battery. Not so. Her fingers started into the same sequence to dial her mother, but stopped short at the echo of footsteps down the hallway. They seemed to be drawing nearer.

She got to her feet and remained pressed against the wall, troubled by a churning in her gut. Dr. Tracy had never been one to fear, but the sound of his approach was filling her with dread nonetheless. What sort of bad news would he deliver? When the lock released with a click, she swallowed hard. Maybe the doctor had contacted her parents. Maybe they were with him now and she wouldn't have to bear the awful news alone.

Sevenah jumped when the door swung wide open and two strangers looked in. It wasn't anyone she expected, but a couple of tall, burly men with tight eyes and tangled scowls. They scanned the room before focusing in on her.

The first man to step inside was baldheaded and dressed entirely in black from his broad shoulders to the polished shoes sticking out from beneath a pair of slacks. His partner, sporting an airman's jacket, ducked in next. He had a full head of raven hair so heavily oiled it glistened under the ceiling lights. Both were intimidating characters who headed straight for Sevenah.

"Stop!" she shrieked, thrusting out a halting palm. "Stay back!"

The men froze in their tracks as if they shared a concern she might be a legitimate threat. Sevenah took advantage of their hesitation and darted sideways, putting the examining table between them. The scowlers exchanged a chary glance before continuing toward her.

On her phone she pressed a redial button and prayed someone would answer.

"Get that bloody cell phone from her!" the bald man barked.

His partner swiped at her hand over the table, just missing the mark. Terrified of his clawing, she tossed the device across the room, making a perfect basket in a small garbage can beside the sink. The baldheaded scoundrel scooped it up and shoved it in his pocket, grinning slyly.   Meanwhile, his companion managed to reach across the examining table and catch his victim by the wrist.   Sevenah fought to pull away, using her body weight like a sinking anchor, but her captor held on tight, squeezing to the point of bruising.

"Ouch!   You're hurting me!   Let go!"

He struggled to climb over the table, but Sevenah twisted her arm like a water valve, freeing herself and tumbling to the floor in the process.   She scrambled to her feet and ran to an unguarded wall, pressing her back against it.   The exit was blocked.   There was no way around these thugs.

The frightened girl demanded to know what was going on. "Who are you?   Where's Dr. Tracy?   What have you done with him?"

No information was volunteered.   The men spoke only to each other.

"Grab the little monster.   Braxton's waiting."

"No!   Stay away from me!"   Sevenah tried to appear brave despite the trembling in her voice.   She took a step away from the wall and fisted her hands as if she would fight.   "I demand to see Dr. Tracy!"

For a second she bravely stood her ground, but soon enough she was hoisted off the floor and sandwiched between one man's bare muscular bicep and the other's cold leather jacket. Adrenaline coursed through her small frame, and she kicked at her abductors, screaming at the top of her lungs until a large hand covered her mouth.

With arms restrained, she flailed her legs in self-defense.   A successful dig into the bald man's ribs had her ankles constrained as well, snatched up by another, thick arm.   The men carried her down the hall in this manner until they reached a back door marked EXIT.

It was opened from the outside.   Sevenah spied the culprit as soon as they stepped into the alley—none other than her trusted family doctor.   Her mind flooded with incredulity.   How could he be helping these two thugs?   Why?

She bit down hard on the calloused fingers covering her mouth.   When the big man pulled his hand away, cussing her for the deed, she begged Dr. Tracy to rescue her.

"Help me! Stop them! Please, help me!"

But he was already gesturing denial of his assistance.

"Dr. Tracy!" she implored further, unwilling to believe what the scene suggested. "Don't let them hurt me, please! Come on, you know me!"

The once kind and caring old man scrunched his eyes into a hard, unfeeling stare. His reply was saturated with revulsion; it nearly stopped her heart.

"I don't know who you are, and I don't care. But I do hope you get exactly what you deserve."

He turned his back on an act of abduction and shut the door behind him, leaving her in the hands of two aggressive strangers.

Her eyes pooled with moisture as she felt her will to fight dissolve. Did she deserve this treatment? Why would he say that?

Her captors forced her into the back seat of a long, black limousine and then climbed in the front. The vehicle started forward. She blinked back rising tears as the car moved from the shadowed alleyway into a sunlit street. With tinted windows, Sevenah assumed no one could see in to recognize her.

The sound of shuffling papers made her aware of others in the car. Twisting her neck, she found a big, grizzled character in a dark overcoat sitting on the other end of her seat. He bore no real expression, but his gaze was as fixed on her as the gun he held aimed at her chest. On the bench directly across the way, a short, stout man in a white lab coat was concentrating on a clipboard gripped within his stubby fingers. Sevenah noted his irritated countenance, magnified by thick spectacles that rested partway down his nose. Though his smaller stature seemed less of a threat, there was something about him that reeked of authority. Eventually he spoke, his eyes never shifting from his paperwork.

"Don't even think about doing something stupid or I assure you, my friend here will not hesitate to shoot. He's done so on several other occasions without much provocation at all. With that said, would you mind telling me exactly who you are?"

Still grappling with the reality of her doctor's betrayal, it took a minute for Sevenah to register the stranger's words. All she could manage was a timid, "Excuse me?"

Her peep was enough to grab the man's full attention. His

fierce gaze shifted to study her through thick spectacles. The look communicated both impatience and disgust. Sevenah instantly loathed the man.

"I am not playing games," he growled, sounding much like her father at the very moment you knew to come forward with the truth or pay severe consequences.

She glanced nervously sideways at the barrel of a gun. "My name is Sevenah. Sevenah Williams."

The little man narrowed his stare as if attempting to read her mind. It was hot and stuffy inside the car and his rudeness only made it more unpleasant. During the long moment of silence, she began to wonder if maybe he *could* read her thoughts. At length, he spoke up again.

"So, Sevenah Williams—who are you?"

His persistence frightened her. She wondered who he thought she was—who they all thought she was. A sidelong glance passed the question to the large man beside her, hoping he might have an answer. It seemed preposterous for anyone to feel a need to point a gun at her. What kind of threat could they possibly imagine her to be? Who in their right minds would consider her a danger? Her musings were rudely interrupted.

"It would seriously benefit you to answer the question. We have unpleasant ways of drawing out information if you choose not to cooperate."

"I am cooperating!" she gasped, shocked he would threaten her. "I…I don't know what you want to hear!"

He leaned forward as if expecting her to divulge some great secret. His voice escalated. "I want to know exactly who you are and what you're doing here!"

She began again, afraid she might cry. "I already told you, my name is Sevenah. I live here in Royal City, on a farm with my parents. I go to school here. I'm seventeen, I'm a junior and…"

He had stopped listening.

"*Ah-hmmm,*" he interrupted, "I know you're lying."

Sevenah closed her eyes, aware that tears were spilling over, running down her cheeks. I'm not crazy, she told herself. Everyone else has gone mad.

"We've been watching you for months now, ever since the

first set of unusual x-rays."

Her eyes flashed open, stunned.   The man kept right on talking.

"I have to admit, the second set was rather convincing.   You had Dr. Tracy fooled, that's for certain.   He was sure it was all a curious mistake.   But *I'm* not so easily deceived.   We've monitored your activities very closely since then, and I daresay you've done an excellent job of hiding out among us.   You've managed to copy our routines perfectly.   I'm surprised you let your guard down today.   Or did we catch you at a bad time perhaps?   Did we step in before you had a chance to alter your medical results like in the past?   Or were you relying on accomplices who failed to come through?"

"What?   What are you talking about?"   She was trying to follow, but it was all nonsense he was spouting.

She flinched when his clipboard slapped against the seat. Her eyes followed his stubby hands down to a leather briefcase where he pulled out a folder of thin, gray sheets and what looked like prints of ultrasounds.

"These are yours," he informed her.   He held up a series of ultrasounds, adjusting his glasses as he spoke.   "These are the images we took this afternoon."

Sevenah scrutinized the man's face more closely.   That's when she realized she had seen him before—in the lab with Dr. Tracy when her x-rays had been repeated.   She hadn't paid attention to him then, figuring he was just another technician.

A thick finger pointed to the first picture.   "This is your heart.   From what we can tell, this here is a second heart."

"Wha—what?"   Sevenah squinted at the ultrasound.   Had she heard him say *second heart?*

He continued his outlandish allegations, holding up an x-ray sheet this time.

"This is your ribcage, but you can plainly see how its form is unlike any normal human ribcage.   The upper section appears to rap around the first heart while the lower portion bends slightly beneath, protecting the other organ, the one I'm sure acts as a conjoining heart.   These ribs are designed like a partially-woven shield to surround both vital organs.   I find it interesting that both hearts have two chambers and beat at exactly the same rate—

29

totally in sync.   It sounds like one strong, steady pulse.   That's probably why it was difficult to detect more than one."

He immediately held up another image.

"Your lungs are unusually formed as well.   From what I can tell, they're layered to some extent, maybe three or four walls thick, increasing the surface area greatly.   I can imagine advantages to these differences in your anatomy, but what I don't see is how you could possibly be who you say you are.   You are definitely not human.   So, in light of this information, would you now like to come forward with the truth?"

Sevenah's mouth gaped.   Her head shook in tiny, quick jerks as she stared in bewilderment at the pictures.   His declaration echoed in her mind...... *You are definitely not human.*

"No, no, this is crazy.   That....that can't be me."   Her words were barely breathed, but overheard.

"Make no mistake this *is* you.   I'm sure the next set of tests will support and clarify these findings."

"Next tests?" she squeaked.   Once again her thoughts turned to Ian, wishing he were there.   How would he know what had happened to her?   And her parents—what would her mom think when she didn't come home?

"Mom..." she panicked.

"That's being handled.   I've plenty of questions for your parents as well."

Sevenah's eyes bulged wide.   Was her family in danger too?

A complaint from her stomach lingered audibly in the car.   It had been irritable for a while—grumbling, empty, and nervous.   Strangely, she no longer felt any hunger pains.   In fact, everything was numb.   She was certain her body had gone into shock.   Her fingers had no sensation, yet she was aware of how they balled into fists.   It was a purposeful action, an attempt to tighten her muscles and stop the shivers caused by a sudden onset of paralysis.

Her eyelids closed, and her head fell back against the leather seat.   There was no sane way this could be happening.

Breathe in.   Breathe out.

The man asked no further questions, perhaps allowing her to think it over.   Regardless of his claims, Sevenah kept coming to the same reasonable conclusion: he was wrong.   This was all a huge, ridiculous mistake.   It had to be!

They drove in silence for minutes on end. It was difficult to measure the passing of time. Maybe an hour had transpired. Maybe more. A muted conversation traveled from the front seat—the two thugs joking about personal matters. Sevenah didn't pay attention to what was said, preoccupied with mulling over every detail of this living nightmare. It was preposterous! Unreal! An invented fantasy! That didn't stop genuine tears from flowing. She didn't bother wiping them away. Reacting to their existence meant facing a reality she refused to accept.

When the limousine finally came to a stop, Sevenah remained still—eyes closed, head resting on the back of the seat. She tried to convince herself that at any minute daylight would shine upon her face and draw her back into consciousness. Everything would return to normal. Ian would be waiting at the front gate to walk her to school, and they would share a laugh over her crazy dream.

The company waited in the parked car for five minutes. Maybe ten. Again, it was hard to say. Eventually, the door creaked on its hinges beside her, causing her eyelids to flutter open.

Nothing had changed.

The baldheaded man who had originally carted her to the limousine was standing just outside the vehicle. The white coat who seemed in charge of the operation grabbed his clipboard and briefcase before exiting the car. The other backseat occupant waved his gun once in Sevenah's direction, motioning for her to get out as well. She slowly slid to the seat's edge. As she stood up next to the man in black, she whispered a word of warning.

"Don't touch me. I will walk myself this time, thank you."

He cracked a wry grin.

When all five occupants had exited the limo, the men escorted Sevenah across an extensive stretch of blacktop toward a large jetliner with no visible markings. A small group had congregated beneath the plane—men and women apparently waiting their arrival. It was obvious by the way arms flailed in the air, hands animating every word, that an intense conversation was taking place. The debate was distracting enough to keep participants from noticing Sevenah's approach. It didn't take long, however, for someone in the company to finally spot her. One by one, heads turned until all eyes rested on the young woman. An eerie

31

hush accompanied their curious stares.

A cold breeze whipped at Sevenah's hair and caused her to shiver. It was hard to tell if the reaction was due to the chill or her circumstances. She was prevented from continuing forward at a few strides from the small assemblage.

No one said a word until the man in charge introduced himself.

"Good evening, colleagues. I am Dr. Braxton. I'm looking forward to briefing you further on our unique situation." He gestured to Sevenah with his clipboard. "This is the subject. She calls herself Sevenah Williams and so far has been unwilling to cooperate."

"I am cooperating," she objected out loud.

Someone from behind struck the back of her shoulder.

Dr. Braxton went on, but his words drowned out for her. She wondered what in the world she could do to convince them she was who she knew she was—a normal, regular teenager. A simple, ordinary girl. *A human being!*

As the briefing continued, someone reached across Sevenah's shoulder from behind and held a rag firmly over her nose. There was no time to squeal or struggle. She passed out instantly.

CHAPTER TWO
Friends or Foes

The room was cold and dark when Sevenah awoke. It was most likely her mother's fault for leaving a window cracked open in the house again. The nights were getting too chilly to do that anymore. Her head felt heavy trying to raise up. She let it fall back, swirling with muddled thoughts indicative of oversleeping. It was a strange sensation, like emerging from a ghostly pit of disconnected dreams. She was eager to shake it off and head outside to exercise Paka. Then, after a quick breakfast, Ian would meet her at the front gate for school.

As the grogginess started to dissipate, strange and frightful images took clearer shape in the forefront of her mind. "What a nightmare," she yawned, assuming it could be nothing more.

Her hand went to brush stray hairs from her eyes, but failed. It seemed oddly unwilling, as if weighed down with numbness from lack of circulation during the night. No, no, that wasn't right. She tried again, able to wiggle her elbow, but her wrist remained fixed. Panic set in as she struggled unsuccessfully to lift either arm—something snug and abrasive held her wrists firmly beside her. She tugged defiantly against the restraints, discovering both ankles secured as well. Her legs fought fiercely, tugging and yanking, unable to break free. This didn't make any sense, unless....

The nightmare was real.

An avalanche of events rushed back to her memory: Dr. Tracy's betrayal, the lying x-rays, the frightful abduction, Dr. Braxton's implausible claims, the unmarked jet....

She couldn't recall getting on the plane or how she had ended up wherever she was now. Her final memory played out as a moment of terror—a strong hand pressed over her nose and mouth, smothering her. They must have knocked her out with something. A drug or chemical fumes.

Her body shivered uncomfortably in the dark. There was little she hated more than the cold, and it was goose-bump chilly in

33

this place.   Silence permeated the room, excepting a low and steady mechanical hum that murmured in the blackness.   A dim light flashed tiny, red numbers, blinking on and off and on in a constant rhythm.   More than one line flashed its scarlet readings on the wall, their faint glow providing the only source of light.

Sevenah continued to fight her restraints, desperate to slip free.   Friction marked her skin where it rubbed repeatedly against abrasive bands, and soon both wrists stung as if chafed by rug burns.   She gave up, deterred by the pain.   Despair wet her cheeks in the form of tears.

"I can't even scratch my stupid nose!" she bawled into the darkness.   "Where are you Ian?   Where are you?"   Why had he not come to meet up with her at the clinic?   He was always with her—*always!*   Why not this time?

Moisture streamed along her temples, damping her hair and the cushion beneath.   She couldn't wipe her eyes and thus had to suffer the swamping moisture.   Each shallow gasp that escaped her throat echoed off the surrounding walls, every sob sounding forlorn and miserable.   No one responded to the weeping.   Perhaps she had been abandoned.   Perhaps her misery was simply being ignored.   Eventually, the grieving waned and she slipped back into calm unconsciousness.

It was impossible to tell the duration of her sleep when murmuring voices woke her.   This time the restraints and the darkness came as no shock.   Crying had done some good, easing earlier feelings of distress and despair.   Such devastating emotions were now replaced by determination to escape her situation.   She was her father's girl, and he had never been one to give up without a fight.   Neither would she.

The buzz of conversation grew increasingly louder outside the room.   It was easy to pick out two distinct tones in the dialogue.   One was female, loud and prominent with a troubled quality about it.   The other she recognized as Dr. Braxton's smug responses.   Bits of the conversation were audible from Sevenah's location, and she strained to hear what they were saying.

"You have no idea what effect……..you're not being reasonable…."

Too much competing noise from humming machines drowned out every lowly-spoken word.   Sevenah strained harder to listen as the discussion drew progressively closer. It seemed to stop and linger just beyond the door.

"I know they want answers; I'm aware of their pressure tactics. But to take unnecessary risks simply to appease a self-serving mob of paranoid politicians is foolish! The procedure you're proposing has never been tolerably tested, not to mention the fact that we don't know enough about her biology to safely attempt this."

It was Dr. Braxton's voice to contend. "We've performed sufficient examinations and gathered analyses that suggests it's worth the relatively minor risks."

"Minor!" exclaimed the female.

"We have six highly-competent doctors on staff ready to jump in at the slightest sign of a problem, Stefanie, and I have full confidence…"

"What if you kill her? Tell me, what good will her death do our research?"

This last comment hit Sevenah hard. Intuitively, she understood their argument was about her. Mention of some risky procedure conjured up awful imagery; still, Dr. Braxton's next remark was even more terrifying.

"Quite frankly, an autopsy might prove enlightening."

"I cannot believe you just said that!"

Sevenah felt the blood drain from her face as she sided whole-heartedly with the woman.

"She's not human, Stefanie. Keep your perspective here."

"She's no lab rat either."

The door swung open and Sevenah twisted her neck to stare into the blue eyes of her lady advocate. Dr. Braxton appeared from behind. The two were identically dressed in white lab coats with identification badges clipped to their front pockets. They stopped and gawked at the young woman as though shocked to find her awake. Sevenah wondered exactly how long she had been unconscious. Apparently, long enough for some extensive exams to take place. Luckily, her body still seemed to be in one piece.

The woman approached, and Sevenah read the badge on her jacket: **Dr. Stefanie Mikiska, M.D.** The lady smiled—a genuinely warm gesture. She was tall and as thin as a twig, with

35

long dark hair clipped in a loose bun behind her head.   Her blue eyes were the color of forget-me-nots framed by rectangular glasses that slipped gradually down her gently-sloped nose.   An index finger pushed the frames back into place every so often. Olive-toned features were naturally highlighted with very little makeup.   Sevenah caught the subtle scent of vanilla perfume.   It was enough to stir her empty stomach.

Dr. Mikiska greeted her patient with a cheerful "Good morning."

"Morning," Sevenah rasped.   It was shocking how weak her voice sounded.   She swallowed at the rawness in her throat.

"I'm actually glad to find you awake.   I've been anxious to talk to you."   The doctor pulled up a metal stool and retrieved a pen and a small notebook from the inside pocket of her lab coat.

"I'm thirsty," Sevenah complained.   She tried to clear her throat, but the dryness burned.   "I'm hungry too."

Dr. Mikiska smiled pleasantly, resituating her glasses.   "I understand you're hungry, and I promise you'll get something to eat and drink soon.   But first, I want to ask you a few questions, okay?"

Sevenah gave a whispered consent.   It was impossible not to like this woman; her presence was naturally pacifying.   Perhaps it was her gentle voice, or the warm and friendly smile, or possibly the sweet smell of vanilla that lingered in her presence.   Or maybe it was just the fact that she had acted so protectively while contending with Dr. Braxton.

"Good, good.   Alright, let's begin.   Will you tell me why you're here?"

"Because you won't let me go."   The obvious reply was less sarcastic than honest.

"No, no, I mean, why are you here on our planet?   Are there others living among us like you?"

Sevenah screwed up her face, confused by the question.

The doctor tried again.   "How did you get here?   Did you come to Earth alone?   Are you the last of your kind?"

"I was born here.   I'm the same as you—only I'm starving." She swallowed again, wishing for something to soothe her irritated throat.

The lady doctor pursed her lips.   "Look, Sevenah, we know

you're not like the rest of us.   You do realize your anatomy differs from that of any human being."   Dr. Mikiska raised one eyebrow and held her palm open as if everyone in the world understood this.

"I was born here," Sevenah insisted.   "Ask Dr. Tracy, he knows."   She was still clinging to the reasonable conclusion this was a dreadful mistake.   How could she possibly be what they were suggesting without being aware of it herself?

"Okay, okay.   Let's try something else."   The tip of a pen tapped against the doctor's lips as she stared out over the rim of her glasses, thinking.   "Alright, Sevenah.   What is the earliest thing you can recall from childhood?   Think hard.   How far back do you remember?"

That was easy.   She was often haunted by a frightening incident from her youth.   It was a recurring nightmare that seemed to evolve over the years.

"I was little," Sevenah started.   "I remember sitting on the ground, in the dirt.   There were trees all around.....and snakes."

"Snakes?"

"Um-hm."   She cleared her throat before continuing.   "I was scared of the snakes.   They covered the ground.   I don't know where they came from, but I couldn't get away from them.   I called for my mom, but she never...."   Her eyebrows pulled tight, straining to bring the past to mind.   "I don't know why my mother never came.   I can't remember anything else."   Then she quickly added, "No, no, wait—there was a boy.   He was young, but older than me.   I think he was with me, trying to help me."

The doctor's face tangled up uncertainly.   "Are you sure this is a memory?"

Sevenah nodded.

"Could it have been a dream?   Or a story you heard as a child?"

She shook her head.   "I'm sure it happened; I know it did."

"Huh.   Can you recall how old you were?"

"I think I was five or six."

"Okay, then.   Try to remember something before that.   Can you recall an event when you were four?   Or even three?"

Sevenah sighed heavily, "No."

"Try."

The interrogation was getting annoying.   What did memories have to do with anything?   "I can't.   I was a baby, I don't remember that."

"You can at least try.   People recall events as far back as two years of age, sometimes even earlier.   I remember the songs my mother use to sing to me when I was a toddler.   I have fond recollections of a yellow blanket I took naps with when I was two, three, four years old.   It's common to have simple memories of younger experiences.   Now think.   Concentrate.   Can you recall anything at all?   Even a trivial piece of information—like a color? A familiar smell?   A favorite toy?"

"No, nothing!   Why are you doing this to me?   Why won't you let me go home?"   She was through with the pointless questioning.   Her stomach felt knotted and queasy and tight with anxiety.

Silence took over for a long moment.

"I'm so thirsty," the girl whispered.

The ink pen went back to resting on Dr. Mikiska's lips, her blue eyes lost in thought.   Sevenah wondered what the woman was thinking.

A glance in the background found Dr. Braxton planted at a corner desk ignoring the interrogation.   A writing utensil in his stubby fingers bobbed back and forth, scribbling on the clipboard that seemed his constant companion.   Sevenah felt a sickly stir of hatred towards the man.   She wished for a fat venomous rattler from her nightmare to slither over and sink its fangs into his calf.

Dr. Mikiska finally gave in.   "I'll go get you some breakfast. Please, concentrate on your childhood while I'm gone.   Maybe you'll remember something more.   I'll be right back."

"Thank you."

Sevenah watched the woman leave, observing how her I.D. badge was swiped through a scanner beside the exit before the lock released.   It appeared the badges were literal keys to getting around the facility.   Most likely it was the same procedure coming and going.   She noticed how the door never completely closed but pushed open again, allowing another white coat to enter the room.   This one was worn by a short, wiry female carting a box of medical supplies.   The woman stopped at a table to rummage through the contents of the box.   It made Sevenah nervous.

"I've got to get out of here soon," she worried.

Her attention returned to Dr. Braxton who continued to pay her no mind. And why would he when in his opinion she ranked lower than the animals? Sevenah took note of how he disregarded the new attendant, not even casting a glance in her direction. It crossed Sevenah's mind that if by some fantastical chance she was actually......not human......then at least she wouldn't be related to that rude, heartless excuse for a person. Thank goodness for Dr. Mikiska and her civility.

Recollecting Dr. Braxton's earlier remarks sparked a sense of urgency for Sevenah to find a way out of her predicament. Her parents and Ian were probably worried sick, having no idea what had happened—why a simple trip to the clinic had resulted in her complete disappearance. Unless.........unless Dr. Braxton had fed them some convincing lie, like a horror story of her demise.

Oh crud! If such was the case, then no one would be looking for her!

She needed to call home; there had to be a way. If her parents were to hear her voice over the phone for even a second they would know the truth, that she was alive and in trouble. Then they would search for her!

Twisting her neck to look over her shoulder, Sevenah scanned what was visible within the room. No windows divided the walls, and nothing resembling a telephone stood out. Large cardboard boxes, canisters of medical instruments, plastic containers marked with supplies, and a collection of cylindrical tanks stacked the shelves behind her. White, printed labels were too small to read clearly. Nothing but noisy electronics lined the adjacent wall.

Preoccupied with her task, Sevenah didn't notice when the new visitor approached her bedside. It was startling sensing a looming presence. With wide eyes Sevenah gasped, but the lady calmly shushed her.

"It's okay, it's okay. I'm just here to check your vitals."

Sevenah exhaled raggedly, and her jarred pulse settled. She didn't resist a blood pressure cuff tucked beneath her arm. Glancing at a pocket badge, she read the printed name: **Leisha Morroway, LPN**. The woman was a nurse. That explained Dr. Braxton ignoring her presence. He was the kind of conceited jerk who wouldn't give anyone the time of day unless he considered the person an equal.

The nurse went about her task, swabbing a cold, clear liquid over the natural crease in her patient's arm.   Short, black waves fringed her high cheekbones, framing brown eyes that sparkled with unfitting enthusiasm.   Her tomboy mannerisms had been evident upon entering the room, but those rough and confident gestures didn't diminish her natural beauty in the least.

Sevenah envisioned the woman as a Roman warrior with strong, pronounced facial features and an athletic body.   She wasn't as tall as Dr. Mikiska, but stood sturdy and confident nonetheless.   It seemed a sure bet that Nurse Morroway could hold her own with any condescending doctor.

A hushed question interrupted Sevenah's thoughts.   "Are you feeling alright?"

Noticing how the nurse had her back turned to Dr. Braxton, the girl whispered a reply in case they weren't supposed to be talking.

"I feel weak.   My throat hurts."

"I know.   I'm so sorry."   Leisha's brown eyes expressed their own apology as she moved in a little closer to Sevenah's ear. "This wasn't supposed to happen to you.   I promise you won't be here much longer.   We'll have you out soon."   She winked, and that sparkle of enthusiasm flashed again.

Sevenah was stunned by both the nurse's behavior and her words.   Had she heard correctly?   Her heart pounded a little faster, hopeful yet puzzled.

"Who are you?"

Leisha smiled, a sign of reassurance.   "Don't worry, we're taking you home.   You'll be fine, and you'll feel better soon." Then she grabbed her gear and headed for the door.

"Wait!" Sevenah called out wanting to know more.

This outburst caused Dr. Braxton to finally look up from his paperwork.   He watched the nurse step toward the exit.   Then his beady gaze shifted to Sevenah.

Thinking quickly, she announced aloud, "No one listens to me."

Dr. Braxton returned to his work without a hint of concern.

Sevenah let her head fall back as thoughts of the whispered

conversation consumed her.   Was this too good to hope for? Someone was actually on *her side* and plotting to help her escape! There was nothing she wanted more than to shed the immobilizing bands—to be free and headed home.   Her pulse thundered at the prospect of evading the arrogant and pitiless Dr. Braxton who couldn't care less if she lived or died.

As hope swelled in her heart despite no known motive, it occurred to her she was already experiencing renewed vigor—a substantial wave of strength and wellbeing that was more than the result of good news.   Nurse Morroway had never taken her blood pressure, having left the cuff on the bed, unused, as a cold liquid was rubbed on Sevenah's inner arm.   This had all transpired during their brief verbal exchange.   Whatever drug the liquid consisted of, it was working wonders on her aches and nausea.

Breakfast arrived moments later with Dr. Mikiska.   A warm serving tray was set on Sevenah's lap before the constrictive wrist bands were unlatched.   It was hard to decide which was better, the chance to feed her griping stomach or the simple opportunity to freely move her arms once again.

The food smelled heavenly: eggs, toast, bacon, a small carton of milk, and a cup of water.   She went for the paper cup first, discarding the provided straw to gulp down every last drop of soothing liquid.   Under her present circumstances she had expected a meager offering of bread and water—rations for which she would have been grateful.

"Thank you," she uttered at the end of what seemed like the tastiest meal of her life.

"You're welcome," Dr. Mikiska replied.   The woman had patiently sat by, watching every crumb disappear.

Sevenah brought both hands up to her cold nose and cheeks, taking advantage of the chance to warm her face.   It was humbling to feel gratitude for such a small thing.

"Would you like to take a walk, Sevenah?"   The question received an immediate answer.

"Yes!   Yes, please!"

Dr. Mikiska stood up from her stool, grinning at such eagerness.   "Well then, let me get your legs down.   One......and two… and here we go."   Repositioning her glasses, Dr. Mikiska moved toward the door, gesturing for her patient to follow.

41

This irregularity in protocol grabbed Dr. Braxton's full attention. The man with no real expression other than sheer disgust appeared baffled for the first time.

"What in the world do you think you're doing, Stefanie?" he asked.

"Don't worry, we won't go far. It's healthy to get a little exercise—keeps the muscles from wasting away." With perked eyebrows she extended her colleague an invitation. "Feel free to accompany us if you're concerned."

Dr. Braxton's features contorted with skepticism. "You ought to have her on a tight leash." He shook his stubby finger in warning. "If it were anyone else, I'd never allow this."

"Well then, shall we?" Dr. Mikiska swung open the door and waited for her patient to step outside. She flashed a big grin at Dr. Braxton before exiting.

It seemed unwise to attempt an escape without a plan. Chances of success were minimal, and any consequences might prove disastrous. It was a blessing in and of itself to simply be on her feet, free to maneuver. Sevenah decided to concentrate on scoping out the place, or at least every inch she could observe on this impromptu stroll.

The hallway was nothing much—rectangular and bare and seemingly endless in length. Dim lighting fell from above in a florescent blue that turned their skin and the white walls a dingy gray. It didn't feel as if the halls were heated.

Keeping in step with her guide, Sevenah's thoughts naturally returned to the curious encounter with Nurse Morroway. It seemed possible that Dr. Mikiska might be a collaborator with the nurse. She did come across as a caring enough person. Sevenah dared imagine the possibility, but wouldn't mention it at the risk of giving away a potential rescuer. With the tomboy nurse dominating her thoughts, she asked a vague enough question.

"Do you know everyone who works at this place?"

The doctor shook her head. "No. I'm familiar with a number of people here, mostly physicians. But too many others come and go."

"What about the nursing staff? Are you acquainted with them?"

The doctor shrugged. "Only a handful."

42

Sevenah tempted her with a name. "Leisha Morroway?"

Dr. Mikiska looked sideways at the young enquirer. Her blue eyes squinted as she considered the name. "No, I don't believe I've met a Ms. Morroway. Why do you ask?"

"No reason." Sevenah tried to dismiss the matter, but the doctor pressed for a better answer.

"Where did you pick up that name?"

"Oh....the nurse took my vitals earlier. She reminded me of you.....very kind. And she smelled good."

Dr. Mikiska appeared flattered.

Sevenah quickly asked a personal question to change the subject. "How did you end up here—working in a place like this?"

"Oh.....well, I suppose you could say it was my reward for years of hard study and persistence. I was actually a student of Dr. Braxton's for several years. As a graduate student, he challenged me with a variety of difficult and strange medical puzzles to solve. I spent a great deal of time assisting him, but never made much sense of the things we were doing. Of course I asked questions; he didn't readily offer information. I was intrigued with the work, though, so I struggled to solve the mysteries he presented to me. Finally, one day, my hard work paid off. Dr. Braxton brought me here." Dr. Mikiska held up her hand gesturing at the facility they were in. "I was astounded by the things accomplished here—incredible breakthroughs in science, technology, and medicine. It's remarkable the advancements that have come to light in this place. Wonders I never dreamt I'd see. Few people are aware of this facility and what goes on inside these walls. It's highly confidential and tightly monitored. I'm fortunate to be a part of it all."

"It sounds like you and Dr. Braxton spend a lot of time together." Sevenah dared a very personal question. "Are you a couple?"

"Oh dear, no!" the doctor chuckled. Her cheeks flushed a rosy shade of red. "No, no, we're just colleagues. We've worked together for years, yes, but there could never be anything between us." She smiled at an amusing thought. "I'd hate to have to compete with that precious clipboard of his. I don't think I'd win."

Sevenah grinned at that. "What exactly do you do?"

"I can't tell you—top secret, you know." The doctor looked over the rim of her glasses, a slight smirk on her lips. "I will say that *you* are the most interesting subject I've yet encountered. I sure wish I knew your purpose for being here."

Sevenah dropped her gaze to the floor. What good would it do to repeat the same answers? No one believed her.

The appearance of larger vents caught her attention while looking downward, and she wondered if a smaller person might manage to squeeze through an opening. The complete absence of windows was also noted, leaving no means to glimpse at the outdoors, not that there was any sign the world outside even existed. An eerie absence of familiar sounds—no patter of raindrops, no whistling wind, no chirping birds, not even the hum of traffic or the roar of passing planes—made the silence palpable. She wondered how far from civilization they were or if the facility was buried underground.

The hallway remained empty as their footfall tapped lightly against shiny, gray tiles arranged like crossword puzzles. Periodically, a fire extinguisher appeared at waist height, hung behind glass. These red canisters provided the only color. Every metal door was positioned yards away from the next and had a matching I.D. scanner mounted beside it. Sevenah suspected no room ever remained unlocked.

Eventually, their path came to a 'T' and Dr. Mikiska turned left. A set of stairs led further down another dreary hallway.

"How big is this place?" Sevenah asked.

"Oh, it's sizable. You'd get lost rather quickly if you didn't know your way around. Every hallway resembles the next one."

Sevenah frowned at this news. Curious about their distance from civilization, she asked, "Do you live here or do you go home every night?"

"I stay for weeks, if not months, at a time. Usually, I'm so preoccupied with a project there's really no sense in leaving. Besides, I haven't much to go home to anyway."

"Oh, I'm sorry."

"Don't be. I enjoy my work immensely. You can't imagine the things I've seen or the brilliant people I've been privileged to work with. I'm spoiled actually. I've had access to the greatest technologies and the most interesting projects you could dream of."

The slightly condescending manner in which Dr. Mikiska spoke caused Sevenah to glance up, catching a hint of defensiveness in the doctor's eyes. She wondered if the woman considered her anything more than an interesting project.

Their walk came to a halt beside a gray door that looked exactly like a dozen other metal doors they had passed. Dr. Mikiska swiped her I.D. badge through the scanner. As the latch gave, Sevenah took an anxious step backwards. Her instincts warned against placing much trust in anyone, despite a show of kindness. Entering another locked room just seemed like a bad idea.

"Why have we stopped? What's in there? I thought we were just going for a walk."

Dr. Mikiska continued to hold open the door, smiling pleasantly enough. She motioned for her patient to step inside. "It's fine. Go on in; we won't be staying long."

Believing she had no choice, Sevenah followed the doctor's orders and entered. What she found inside made her want to turn and run, but the click of a locked door resounded behind her, declaring it was too late.

"What's going on? What are *they* doing here?"

Sevenah pointed a nervous finger at the same two thugs who had not-so-gently carted her out of Dr. Tracy's office at the onset of what was now her living nightmare. She backed away from everyone, keeping a close eye on the men positioned against the far wall.

This new room was half the size of the other. Cupboards lined one end, mounted above a double sink. A computer, a large flat-screen monitor, and a variety of plastic boxes were scattered across a low counter. The longest wall held the same kind of machines that hummed in the previous room, only fewer. Center floor stood a medical chair, a stool, and a silver sliding table that supported a handful of instruments. Sevenah noticed an item in particular—a needle. The sight of it made her shudder. Whatever they had planned, she would not cooperate.

Dr. Mikiska didn't act surprised by the observed reaction. "I suppose you could call these fellows my 'tight leash.'"

The frightened girl narrowed her eyes. "You're no better than Dr. Braxton. I should never have thought otherwise."

"Now, now, Sevenah. You may not believe me, but I'm doing this for your benefit."

A nervous laugh echoed in the room. "Forgive me if I don't appear grateful!"

The doctor acted earnest as she tried to explain. "Listen to me. Dr. Braxton has far worse plans in store for you. What I'm attempting to do is prove that those other measures aren't necessary. I'm doing this for you."

"None of this is for me! If you want to help me, let me go home!" Sevenah made her desires known keeping as far from everyone as possible. "I want to go back to my parents and my friends! I want my normal, regular, *human* life again! Let me go home! Please, just let me go home!"

"You know I can't do that. I'm sorry, but there's no way to be certain you're not a threat to humanity."

The girl's eyes widened with disbelief. She pointed down at herself as though visual proof should suffice. "Do you honestly believe I could be any sort of threat?"

"Are you?" the doctor asked, poising her eyebrows in question.

"No!" Sevenah shrieked.

Dr. Mikiska looked like she wanted to believe the girl, but faith alone wasn't enough.

A pair of latex gloves slid easily over the doctor's thin fingers before she picked up a syringe filled with clear liquid. Sevenah stared at the tip of a needle, terrified.

"What is it you people think I'm going to do?" she asked. Her voice shook with fear, growing increasingly defensive. "I've lived here for seventeen years! I haven't caused any problems— not one! If I were a real threat to humanity, don't you think I would have done something by now?" Her whole being wanted to explode—to shake someone until they believed she was telling the truth.

Fueled by a desire for self-preservation, she made a desperate attempt at escape. In one swift move, she lunged at Dr. Mikiska and ripped the badge from her front pocket. The needle fell to the floor. Sevenah hit the scanner, swiped the badge, and jerked the metal door open.   Ducking through the opening, her skinny body was yanked back in, arms grasped by the men who had reacted as quickly as she had.   Once again, her feet were lifted off the floor as they carried her to an empty, waiting chair.

"*Nooooo!*" Sevenah screamed.   "*Let me go!   Don't do this! LET ME GO!*"

She kicked and fought with every ounce of strength, but her captors were too powerful.   The baldheaded man grabbed her by the waist, slamming her down in the chair.   The other man kept a secure hold on her arms, attempting to prevent any scratching. Her limbs were secured within a couple minutes, but not before she dug a heel into someone.   She noticed how the bald man rubbed at his hip when he backed away.

Sevenah twisted her wrists, tugging against cuffs she knew were impossible to escape.   Her only option now was to plead.

"Stefanie, please, please don't do this to me, please!"

"That's Dr. Mikiska to you," the woman huffed, pushing her rectangular frames back into place.   "You've left me no choice, Sevenah.   Our government wants answers that you haven't provided.   They want to know who you are, where you came from, if there are more like you roaming about our world.   They want to know what kind of threat your race poses.   You've told us nothing.   And, if you *are* a threat to humanity I would expect you to tell us nothing."

"*I've told you the truth, I swear!   I've always lived here just like everyone else!   I don't know what you're talking about!*"

"Then apparently, you need these answers as much as we do, which is all the more reason to continue.   I can help you remember who you are."

"There's nothing to remember!" Sevenah insisted.

"On the contrary, there are five early years you don't seem to recall, aside from one unclear, nightmarish incident.   Whatever we can dig up before that might give us the answers we're all seeking."

Sevenah eyed the syringe being tapped by the doctor's finger. "And how are you planning to do this?"

"It's painless, I assure you.   I'll put you to sleep with a light sedative and then…"

"No!" Sevenah objected.   "No needles; I hate needles.

Can't I stay awake?"

"The process works much better if you're asleep. You'll be fine. Do you see the screen over there to your left?"

Sevenah turned her head. There was a flat-screen monitor powered up, but the display showed only pepper and fuzz.

Dr. Mikiska went into an explanation. "I'll be using a memory marker to unbury subconscious memories." She held up a C-shaped metallic device and turned it over. "This is an amazingly useful apparatus. I'll place it over your ear and it will adhere to the side of your head. A few thin needles extend from this device and slowly push their way through to the brain where a chemical is released that stimulates memories. These memories as you see them will be displayed on that monitor, transferred from this device to the computer. Basically, we see what you picture in your mind's eye. It's absolutely incredible. The only difficult part is piecing the random images together to make reasonable sense of them. But despite the drawbacks, we've been able to attain a great deal of useful information using this procedure on a few other individuals."

"But you claim I'm not like you. How do you know this will work on me?"

"It's true your chemistry is somewhat different, but so far the tests we've performed show that you have a high tolerance for our medicines. I'm ninety-nine percent sure this will be a walk in the park for you."

"What if you're wrong? What if something bad happens? What then?"

"Listen, Sevenah. The procedure Dr. Braxton has proposed is much riskier, and it's still in its theoretical stages—never having been tested on a living subject. He plans to perform open-brain surgery, probing for information using electric shock and chemical treatment to rouse your memories. You'll be conscious for the entire operation. He believes he can activate the parts of your brain that will force truthfulness. Plus, the memories will show up on his monitor, transferred by the device he'll be probing with. Basically, he'll steal your memories, and under his influence you'll answer his questions with complete and total honesty. He believes this process will *guarantee* the answers we seek."

"I swear I've told you the truth," Sevenah whined, desperate for someone to believe her.

"Perhaps," the doctor sighed, "but Dr. Braxton doesn't think so. He's determined to go through with this. I personally feel he wants to test his procedure on you specifically for a couple of reasons. First, to find his answers without having to decipher memory images, and secondly, he knows that since you aren't human, you have no legal rights. Using you as a test subject won't interfere with ethical guidelines. If it doesn't work, he's lost nothing. But you, on the other hand, will be awake for the whole painful operation. If something goes awry, you run the risk of suffering brain damage or worse......death. Not to mention the fact that you'll lose all your pretty red hair. I've tried to tell him it's risky and unnecessary, but I can't get him to listen to me."

Sevenah felt cold and numb. The weight of utter helplessness pressed on her chest as she realized how dire her situation was. Her eyes fell closed wishing the nightmare would end and her world would return to normal. All she wanted was to sit beneath her willow tree and watch the sunset with Paka and Ian again. She had never asked for any of this. She had never wished to be different.

"Sevenah. I'm honestly trying to help you, please believe me. If I can piece together how you came here, why you're here, then perhaps I can convince the rest of the board that further, riskier procedures aren't necessary."

Sevenah lifted her lids and stared into Dr. Mikiska's blue eyes. She nodded as if her permission were required. Maybe, she thought, there were memories she had forgotten. Maybe this would work. Exhaling nervously, she tried to relax.

"You'll feel a little sting, but that should be all you feel. Now count with me......ten, nine, eight...."

Sevenah let her head fall back. Her eyelids dropped. She was out by seven.

She was dreaming again. It was the same nightmare she had suffered all her life. Sometimes it altered slightly, but it always started out the same.

She was five. Her reddish-brown hair was long for a five-year-old, braided and secured with a pink ribbon. A spirit of

49

dread accompanied the dream, looming over her childish form. Naturally, she wished for her mother, but she wasn't alone. Someone else was with her, an unclear personage off to the side. He was a boy; she was certain of that. A young boy, maybe ten or eleven. She couldn't make out his face but accepted him as a friend. He had been with her entering the forest. Yes, that's right—the boy had brought her with him.

They were running and had already traveled deep into the woods, sprinting long and hard. The little girl began to drag her feet, wishing to rest. The boy allowed it. She sat on the forest floor while he backtracked to check on something. In his absence, a circle of crooked trees appeared to hunch over, huddling around the girl, darkening an already gloomy environment. It was eerie the way their limbs reached, some dropping low to the ground, disturbed by every gust. The wind flitted the spindliest twigs, giving the illusion of grabbing fingers.

That's when the snakes came. From every direction they pushed up through the soil, slithering and writhing as they made their way toward the girl. She cried out for help.

"Mommy! Mommy!"

The snakes slid across her skin, wrapping around her arms, around her legs. They were too strong to deter.

"Mommy! Mommy!" she cried. But her mother didn't come. Only the boy responded. She reached for him, and his fingers grasped tightly around hers, tugging against the pull of coiled snakes.

She screamed as the creatures ripped her fingers from the boy. That's when she blacked out.

CHAPTER THREE
Take Me Home

Sevenah woke to a pounding headache and nausea. Her body felt weak and drained. She had experienced migraines before, but this intense throbbing behind her eyes was worse. Darkness surrounded her again. She made a feeble attempt to move her arms, but failed; they were tied down along with her legs. From the hum of electronics, she assumed to be back in her original room.

Trying to bring to mind the latest events, she recalled her nightmare with the snakes. If that bizarre memory was all she had given Dr. Mikiska, then surely they had found no promising answers. What did snakes have to do with anything? Perhaps the boy from her dream was a clue to the past, but she could never clearly envision his face.

A moan crossed her lips, and she listened to the sound bounce back from the ceiling—a morose echo in her ears. The memory-recall procedure may not have killed her, but it certainly made her wonder if death wouldn't have been preferable.

You do not want to throw up, she thought to herself, swallowing in an attempt to heed her own warning. With no one around to clean up the mess, the idea of lying in vomit for an indefinite period of time was unappealing.

She tried to relax her queasy stomach by breathing slowly in and out, concentrating on the steady whirr of machines. Nothing was visible in the darkness except for strings of red numbers flashing over and over in a faint glow.

Lying there, feeling helpless and discouraged, her thoughts turned to Nurse Morroway. She contemplated this stranger who had offered the only bit of hope she felt for a possible escape. Leisha had said *they* would get her out of here. But who were *they?* And why the concern for her predicament? Regardless, she prayed the nurse and her companions had a plausible rescue plan. The way things were unraveling, she couldn't imagine getting out alive without someone's assistance.

Her concern shifted to Ian as she dared to imagine returning home. How was he coping with her absence? Did he suspect foul play? Was he looking for her? Or had Dr. Braxton delivered a lie to explain away her disappearance? Did Ian and her family believe she was dead? The thought made her shudder, imagining the grief her parents must be suffering. Sevenah agonized over what to do.

Deep in worry, she nearly missed the sound of a door cracking open. Someone was coming. She panicked, unsure of whether to attempt a glance or feign unconsciousness. When the lights switched on, her eyes automatically closed. Two arguing voices paralyzed her.

"I'm sorry, okay? I'm sorry, already! It's been days; I'd think you could get past this."

"You had no right to go behind my back, Stefanie."

"Why are you still upset about a simple scan? It wasn't a major deal. I've apologized every day since! Can't you see, I was simply trying to find the answers we're looking for in a humane manner? Quite frankly, it was worth a try because I *did* learn something."

Sevenah felt her stomach turn. Were they talking about the memory-recall procedure? Was it true that days had already passed since then? But how was it possible to feel so horribly sick after all that time? What more had they done to her?

"You are purposefully sneaking behind my back and defying me!" Dr. Braxton roared. Sevenah could hear him stomp across the room. Something slammed down on the corner desk—most likely his clipboard.

"I am not defying…"

"You took it upon yourself to scan her memories, and now I come to find out you're bothering Dr. Davis, seeking his support against my proposed course of action!"

There was a heavy, conceding sigh much closer than expected. A presence brought with it the strong scent of vanilla. "I just wish you would hold off for a while. Just a short while."

"I'm aware of your feelings, Stefanie."

"And I maintain that this whole thing is unnecessary. You have no idea how it will affect her."

Sevenah felt a hand rest gently on her forehead. She

struggled to keep still, knowing this would be a bad time to be found wide awake.

"She's a person, Dr. Braxton. A young woman. And as such, she has some God-given rights."

"Well God can save her then."

"Dr. Braxton!" Stefanie snapped.

Tensions amplified as the hand on Sevenah's forehead tightened. It ran over her scalp a few times—four skinny fingers combing through her hair—before moving to rest on a shoulder. It reminded Sevenah of her mother's anxious and protective touch.

"If this alien is really so important, why hasn't one of her kind come to retrieve her?"

Dr. Mikiska answered from right above. "Maybe she's part of a dying race, one of the few remaining left."

"Good. Then let them die."

A gasp sounded so near her ear, Sevenah nearly flinched.

"You can't really mean that!"

"Oh, but I do. What? You would have them take over *our* world?"

"No, of course not, but I hardly think one teenage girl poses a serious threat."

"That's what they *want* you to think!" Sevenah could hear the scoundrel draw near, closer to his associate at her bedside. "They're hoping you feel so confident and secure you won't look any further and see the *real* danger."

Dr. Mikiska groaned, clearly frustrated with the obstinate refusal of this man to see any other possibility. "What if those memories of hers *are* what we're looking for? What if she's already told us everything we need to know about her?"

"You don't have concrete answers, Stefanie, you have theories. Guesses. It's what you *think* you saw in some chaotic, nonsensical images."

"No, no, it's more than that," she argued, her voice suddenly optimistic.

Dr. Braxton harshly disagreed. "No, it's not! You saw a child's ridiculous nightmare! Images of running through some forest with a boy, the two of them overtaken by odd-looking snakes? Then visions of her dead parents, miraculously resurrected! Childhood memories of a forest, and then all of a

53

sudden she's on horseback, riding through the open desert. You say she dreamt of walking through space. Walking through space? What is that? I'll tell you what it is—it's impossible! What you have is a bunch of meaningless images and nothing more. You've learned nothing useful about her, Stefanie; that scan explains *absolutely nothing.*"

"They're memories, Dr. Braxton, and they do mean something. Just think about it for one minute. Put the pieces together. She was a young child, okay, living somewhere with lush, forested terrain. Somehow she ends up in the woods with that boy, both of them obviously frightened. They were running away, trying to escape some type of danger. She calls out for her mother, but no one comes. Maybe there was a tragedy and her parents......well, maybe they died. Perhaps the snakes were to blame. I don't know, but it makes sense that a serious enough incident occurred to warrant her being taken from her home and relocated. Her memory of walking through space obviously means she traveled on a spaceship, I'm guessing on her way to Earth. We know she's alien and she definitely came from another world, so it makes sense she was brought here from her planet."

"Oh please," Dr. Braxton groaned, but Dr. Mikiska ignored his irritated objection and continued.

"Her parents are different people when she sees them alive again because they're human substitutes. We know this to be true from the results of the Williams' tests. They're both conclusively human beings. Somehow, though, they believe that Sevenah is their real daughter, and she believes they are her real parents. It must have been set up that way on purpose. Her people must have wanted her to fit in here. So now she lives on Earth with her new family in the desert. It all makes sense." Dr. Mikiska held up her palms as if it were plain as day. "That's why she doesn't know who she is. That's why she can't remember anything before five years of age. Whatever happened on her home world happened when she was very young, and it must have been traumatic. Her people could have planted her here to keep her safe or to give her a second chance. I honestly believe she has no idea where she came from. She thinks she's human, and I don't see her as a threat to us or to Earth."

Dr. Braxton laughed out loud and clapped his hands

derisively, clearly amused. "It's a very creative story, Stefanie, but that's all it is—a crazy, highly-imaginative story. You're playing connect the dots and who's to say your picture's right? She could've been exiled here for all you know. And if something did happen on her home world, there may be others like her hiding out as well. Who knows? She could be the start of a total world takeover! You can't guarantee your interpretation of her memories is correct."

"We could try it again. Please!" Dr. Mikiska was begging—an unmistakable edge of desperation in her voice. "We know *this* procedure is safe, and I'm sure we can unlock more suppressed memories. You'll see, we'll find the answers." She was trying hard to convince her superior, but he had grown impatient.

"No. The subject is closed."

"You *can't* cut open her brain, Dr. Braxton!"

"I'm going to do exactly that, Stefanie, and I'll be moving forward with the process today before *you* have the opportunity to attempt any more alien-saving schemes. Then we'll see who holds the real answers!"

"*Why?*" The question came out in a shriek. "There's no reason for us to put her life in danger! We have a viable explanation for why she's here; give that to the bureaucrats in Washington. It's a solid, plausible theory and it very well *may be the truth!* It would at least buy us time to learn more about her through humane methods."

"*I will* learn more about her—today." His tone was insistent.

Dr. Mikiska kept pleading, shocked by the horrible turn of events. "Come on! You don't need to do this! Not yet, not now!"

"As of this minute, you're off the project. Pack up and go home."

There was nothing but silence as the shock of his orders sank in. Then Dr. Mikiska panicked.

"No! No, you can't dismiss me!"

"Pack up and go or I'll have you escorted off the premises. I will not be bothered by any further interference in this matter. You've lost your perspective and hence you're of no use to me."

Having nothing else to lose, the woman turned hysterical.

"You don't even care about this project! It's all about getting around the ethical guidelines for that *stupid* experiment of yours! That's what this is really about isn't it? *Isn't it!* You've found a way to test your invention on a technically non-human subject so you're going to *whether it's really necessary or not! You are so arrogant and selfish and contemptible and...*"

"*That is enough! You will leave immediately!*"

The sudden hush was frightening. It was hard for Sevenah to keep her eyes closed; she fretted for herself and for Dr. Mikiska. Then she heard a quick swipe and the door click open. It slammed shut, the sound of heated protest lingering in a resonance. With her lady advocate gone, Sevenah realized she was on her own, alone with the enemy.

It was hard to breathe knowing time was up. Something had to happen today or else....

She didn't want to think of the possible consequences. It couldn't be true that the foggy memory of her last sunset would prove to be the final performance she ever witnessed. It couldn't be that the ones she loved were gone forever.

Her parents.

Ian.

Paka.

She would never see any of them again—never look into their beautiful faces, or hear their kind voices, or feel their warm touch against her skin. Her heart pounded wildly at these thoughts, but her body remained stiff and frozen, fearing to be found conscious—fearing that Dr. Braxton would put her to sleep a final time.

His footsteps tapped across the floor as he moved from one spot to the next. She wondered what he was up to yet lacked the courage to peek. He might see. The rustle of paperwork hit her ears, and she pictured him flipping through pages on his clipboard. Then his voice carried across the room.

"Christopher, I want you to arrange a team for surgery. Prep room eight-thirteen. Call Dr. Fancher and Dr. Davis—let them know we're moving forward today. Yes, it's a go. At ten-hundred hours. We'll meet in the blue room first. I want my equipment there and ready on schedule."

More footsteps echoed in the air. Finally, the door clicked

and fell shut.   Sevenah opened her eyes and exhaled in a quivering gust.

"Oh crud, oh crud, this can't be happening!" she panicked. "What am I going to do?"   It seemed she would have to free herself.

She began fighting her restraints, desperately tugging, hoping for some give in the cuffs.   Perhaps by a miracle she could wriggle one hand free.   With adrenaline-enhanced strength she pulled and twisted, wrenching against the straps until the chafing action cut into her skin.   She didn't care.   The sting would be worth it if just one arm broke loose.   She yanked and squirmed until her wrists were raw and burning.

"*No, No, No!*" she finally cried.   Her effort was producing zero results.   She would have to face facts—the bands were too strong to break, too tight to slip through.

Her mind raced, searching for another way, some other possibility of escape.   But with all her limbs so tightly secured, it seemed bleak.

"Okay, okay," she breathed.   A deep inhale was meant to calm the heightening anxiety.   "There's got to be a way.   Think, think, think…"

A lurch in her stomach reminded her of its empty and sick condition.   She closed her eyes and allayed a wave of nausea. Lying perfectly still, her mind worked on a plan—a scheme to potentially get her bands removed.   Then, at least she might stand a fighting chance.   Perhaps by offering them the truth—an actual lie—they would listen.   A creative enough story might satisfy Dr. Braxton and make him give up the brain surgery madness.

A click echoed across the room, and Sevenah froze. Someone was coming.   She pretended to sleep again, fearing the return of Dr. Braxton.   A man called out but with a deeper and more authoritative tone than the snobbish one she had come to despise.   In a foreign language, he vocalized what sounded like direct orders.

"Rhoen, loamma lan naash.   Co, loamma ee, meeah Sha Eena.   Marguay, ahntaa."

"Ruha, tanee," replied a husky voice.

"Ruha," repeated the lighter tone of a female close by.   This one sounded vaguely familiar.

She heard a fourth—another man. "Ruha, cu ahntaa."

Sevenah felt someone grab her upper arm. Her eyes opened automatically.

"Leisha!" she exclaimed. It was Nurse Morroway. All at once there was hope. She attempted to sit up in her excitement without success.

"Are you alright?" Leisha asked.

"Yes....I mean, no! They're planning something absolutely awful for me today! You have to get me out of here!"

"We know. It's going to be okay. We weren't prepared to move you yet, but there appears to be no other option. You'll be going home today, but you must do everything we tell you, understand? If you want to get out of here alive, you must follow orders."

"Okay, I will, I will, I promise!" The words were hurried and desperate.

Sevenah yanked on the bands that held tight to her wrists, motioning for Leisha to release her. Two accompanying men stepped in to help. They had the restraints removed in seconds. Sevenah felt an immediate desire to run with her freedom—a self-preserving impulse to flee—but curtailed the urge.

She surveyed the strangers around her, dressed alike in white lab coats. The men were large-statured and able-bodied. One wore tinted glasses; he behaved like the person in charge, seeming more alert and edgier than the others. Closest to Leisha stood a baldheaded man with a thick, five-o'clock shadow darkening his face. His eyes were fixed unwaveringly on Sevenah, making her nervous. The third man guarded the door. He resembled a military soldier—stiffly postured and clean-cut, staring ahead while awaiting his next order.

"What now?" Sevenah asked.

"Lie down and don't move," Leisha told her. "Don't open your eyes. Don't do anything unless we tell you, no matter how tempting, understand?"

"Yes, I understand."

Sevenah knew that these people were her only realistic chance at escape. She had come up with nothing on her own. Having no idea who they were or why they wished to help her, she determined to follow orders regardless. It crossed her mind they might be rivals of her present captors, and once outside they might not allow her to go home either. She would have to deal with that possibility afterwards. Dr. Braxton seemed the worse threat at the moment, making her best option to get out now and face the unknown later.

Leisha helped Sevenah lie down. They tossed a white sheet over her body, covering her up to the neck, but not before swabbing a cold, clear liquid over the crease of her arm. It was the same stuff Leisha had applied to her skin before. The migraine and queasiness disappeared almost instantaneously. Sevenah whispered her gratitude.

"Thank you."

"Don't forget," Leisha reminded her, "you must do as we say. You cannot move or open your eyes until we give you the word—no matter what."

Sevenah assured her rescuers she understood.

The tomboyish female then turned to her associates, addressing them in the same strange tongue they had used upon entering.

"Neerai cu. Iee?"

"Iee," they all replied.

Leisha turned to the man in sunglasses. "Nahpai lan."

He nodded to the bald man with gritty whiskers who then swiped a badge through the scanner. The soldier yanked on the metal door and held it wide open.

Sevenah could hear Leisha breathing above her while guiding the hospital bed through the doorway. An echo of tapping footsteps seemed extra loud as they hurried down the hall. The walk felt endless—traveling one long passageway, a right turn, down another hallway, a left turn, and so on. Finally, they stopped. The sound of automatic doors hit her ears.

Sevenah sensed her bed being guided into an enclosed space. An elevator. One man stepped inside with the ladies while the other two stayed back and prevented the door from closing. There was a short, foreign conversation, but even without an interpreter it was evident they were splitting up.

It took a moment for the elevator to budge after the company parted ways. No one spoke while the heavy sliding-cables whirred, dropping them a number of floors. Sevenah wasn't sure if a camera showed their every move to a viewer by monitor. Whatever the case, she refused to stir until Leisha told her otherwise.

When the elevator came to a stop, she was rolled down another long hallway. The swipe of an I.D. badge preceded a brief click followed by the sound of an opening door. Sevenah sensed being passed through the frame. She felt the foot of the bed hit something yielding—swinging doors. The air buzzed with the familiar sound of machines again, suggesting another medical room. A shiver of dread traveled down her spine, but she cautioned herself to keep still. She trusted Leisha. These people had a plan, she was sure of it. When the strict, insensitive voice of Dr. Braxton carried across the room, however, it delivered a cold sting of betrayal. Just then a reassuring hand squeezed on her arm.

"You're late," Dr. Braxton complained, "and she isn't even prepped. Her head was supposed to be shaved."

"I'm sorry, doctor," Leisha said. "There was some uncertainty as to whether…"

Dr. Braxton interrupted in a grumble. "Stefanie." He assumed it was his associate's interference that had caused this inconvenience.

"Yes, sir," Leisha agreed. "Dr. Mikiska's orders were…" Again she was cut off.

"Dr. Mikiska is no longer involved in this project. She has been dismissed, and you will take no further instructions from her. Understood?"

"Yes, doctor."

"Get her prepped."

"Yes, doctor."

During this conversation, Leisha's companion slipped on a pair of latex gloves and made his way to the furthest end of the room where a short, white-haired surgeon stood busily skimming over medical charts. Dr. Davis was preoccupied enough not to notice the man behind him with one hand hidden in a coat pocket. Leisha, meanwhile, fumbled through a box of utensils searching for a razor. Sevenah could hear the clunking stir of small items.

The nurse purposefully positioned herself beside the third surgeon, Dr. Fancher. He was also middle-aged with peppered hair combed perfectly into place. He towered over his associates by at least a foot. Leisha rummaged persistently through her supplies—stalling.

"Is this going to take all morning?" Dr. Braxton finally asked, his tone grouchy and impatient.

"No, doctor, I'm working on it."

Leisha sighed, exposing a note of irritation. She moved to the top of the bed and gathered up the patient's lengths of hair. Sevenah could feel a tug as the strands were bunched into a ponytail, nervous fingers brushing through the ends. It was obvious Leisha was stressing, waiting for something. Despite how petty, Sevenah genuinely feared losing her hair.

Dr. Braxton's intolerance seemed to build by the second until at last he slammed his clipboard against a silver tray. His determined strides stamped against the floor, but before he growled a word, the swinging doors pushed inward to allow Leisha's other associates inside. They wheeled a bulky piece of equipment in front of them.

"Ah, here it is!" Dr. Braxton exclaimed. He held his hands out wide, admiring his own invention. As soon as the men entered, the soldierly figure approached Dr. Fancher. Leisha was at that point closer to Dr. Braxton.

Their leader belted out an order. *"Kahei!"*

All at once the surgical staff was jabbed with tranquilizers. Three white-coats fell to the floor, unconscious.

"Get up! Get up!" Leisha ordered Sevenah.

Finally, permission to open her eyes! She was off the bed and standing on the floor in a heartbeat.

"You have no idea how hard that was. I really thought you were going to shave my head!"

Leisha kept her focus. "You need to change quickly."

Sevenah grabbed the bundle of clothes handed her. It was her favorite faded Levis, pink t-shirt, and discolored Nikes. "I can't believe you found these!"

She proceeded to dress beneath her hospital gown, thrilled to have something of her own again. As soon as she finished, Leisha helped her slip into a lab coat.

"Put this surgical mask and cap on too. You won't be recognized so easily. Lucky for us, your presence here is top secret, so few people know about you."

She did as ordered, twisting her hair up under the cap. "Okay, I'm ready."

As the group turned to leave, the echo of footsteps traveled their way. All three men quickly took position on either side of the swinging doors while Sevenah stepped behind Leisha and stared ahead.

They heard a female voice exclaim out loud, "Hurry, they're in here!"

Sevenah recognized it was Dr. Mikiska. But what was she doing?

As soon as the leading staff cleared the entrance, they were pounced upon and pricked with tranquilizers. Dr. Mikiska stood frozen in her tracks, her mouth gaping at the sight of her colleagues passed out on the floor. She looked up, questioning the scene, when a strong arm wrapped around her neck.

Sevenah hollered before the doctor was put to sleep. *"No, wait! Wait!"*

The man paused, but kept his hostage secure.

Dr. Mikiska addressed the only person she recognized. "Sevenah, what is all this? What's happening? Who are these people?"

Sevenah removed her face mask. "I'm going home. Why are you here? I thought you were kicked off the project."

"You heard." The doctor frowned. "I came to help you. I found associates who agree with me, and I thought perhaps they could stop Dr. Braxton from going forward with this procedure today. I didn't want to see you get hurt."

Sevenah smiled, a truly grateful expression. "Thank you. I take back what I said before; you're nothing like that awful man."

Dr. Mikiska pleaded for the girl to stay. "Please don't do this, don't leave. You don't have to go. There's so much we haven't learned about you, and you could learn from us in return. Don't forget, the mystery of your childhood. Stay and we can figure it out together. Please, Sevenah, don't act so hastily."

It was hard to watch her lady advocate beg. "I can't. Even with your support I would still be in harm's way."

The doctor sighed ruefully. "You're right. We should've treated you better. We were wrong. I'm sorry."

"We need to go," Leisha whispered. "Time's wasting."

Dr. Mikiska was knocked out and left unconscious on the floor.

Sevenah and the others stepped around the bodies and rushed to the nearest elevator. One last look behind brought a warm swell of appreciation for what Stefanie Mikiska had attempted to do. She would never be forgotten.

"Leisha, how long will they be out?"

"Only for a while. We should be far gone by the time they come around."

As all five fugitives disappeared behind sliding doors, Sevenah voiced her greatest desire. "Take me home."

CHAPTER FOUR
Why Didn't You Tell Me?

Dodging the operating room and Dr. Braxton's plan for alien torture gave Sevenah new energy and greater hope, but she realized they weren't clear of the woods yet. Breaking out of this guarded facility would prove to be the real challenge.

She couldn't understand a word her associates were speaking as she listened to them converse. The language sounded strange to her ears; nevertheless, the gravity in their voices was easy to detect. Their hushed, somber tones reminded her of a conversation someone might have following a tragedy.

One by one, buttons lit up on a broad panel as their elevator climbed multiple levels. This facility was turning out to be even bigger than she had imagined. Most likely there were additional, confidential floors few knew existed outside of those with priority clearance. If it wasn't her life on the line, she may have found the situation exciting. But at the moment it was just plain frightening.

The elevator came to a stop on the main floor. Sevenah held her breath, anxious someone might appear when the doors parted—a staff member who could recognize her.

There was no one.

"Curo, neerai cu," the man in sunglasses ordered.

Sevenah followed her rescuers into a long hallway where the walls remained windowless and the same dull, gray tiles stretched out of sight. Someone swiped a badge through a scanner when they approached a metal door, curiously not gray but beige in color. They entered an extra-large room unlike the rest of the facility. This area actually appeared inviting.

Ginger carpeting softened half the floor while the other half was white vinyl—no gray tiles. On the carpeted side, cushioned chairs encircled four card tables, all of them front row seats before a widescreen television. A selection of movies lined the shelves above. On the adjoining wall hung three coordinating watercolors depicting a seaside landscape, the very center reddened by a fiery sunset that appeared to melt into the ocean.   It was a refreshing scene to behold.

Opposite the sitting area stood two extended tables topped with piles of folded laundry.   A line of vending machines rested against the furthest wall, reminding Sevenah she hadn't eaten in nearly forever.   Her stomach reacted immediately to the sight of food, and she pressed on her tummy to quiet the groans.   The very back length of the room harbored washers and dryers, double stacked in a long row.   To the right of the machines, laundry baskets were organized in clusters, most overflowing with soiled lab coats, cloths, and sheets.

Leisha led Sevenah behind the cluster of square baskets and down a narrow passageway that opened into an attached warehouse.   More hampers of dirty laundry waited there to be transported to an offsite facility.   Parked side by side were two trucks with trailers big enough to haul a few oversized bins.

After thoroughly checking the warehouse for unwanted company, Leisha turned to Sevenah and proceeded to give explicit instructions.

"Listen.   We need you to hide inside this laundry cart." Leisha gripped the edge of a basket filled with heavy carpet pads. "I know it won't be very comfortable, and I do apologize, but you must stay as deeply buried as you can.   Remain absolutely still and silent.   It's the best chance we have of sneaking you out quietly."

Leisha pointed to one of the two rigs.   "We'll load your cart into that truck there.   Then Jerin and Marguay will drive you outside the gates.   They almost never check the goods going out, just the drivers.   In the off chance the load is searched, it's usually only a quick peek at the contents.   Keep quiet and everything should go smoothly.   Jerin's in charge."   She pointed to the man in sunglasses.   "He'll be driving with Marguay."   Leisha touched the arm of the baldheaded man, and Sevenah caught a brief, tender exchange between them.

"I'm going to leave you in their hands for now, but Rhoen and I will meet up with you on the outside.   Don't worry about us, we've been on staff here for a while and shouldn't have any trouble getting around.   We'll catch up with you soon."

Sevenah nodded her understanding.   It all sounded

straightforward and simple.

Leisha squeezed the girl's arm encouragingly. "Don't worry, you can do this." Then she motioned to Rhoen who joined her in chiming "Sha Eena" in their native language. They bowed their heads before turning to leave.

Sevenah wondered at the unusual farewell.

Jerin and Marguay had already shed their disguises, exchanging lab coats for coveralls and baseball hats. Sevenah removed her facemask and cap as she watched the men switch I.D. badges, tucking the old ones safely away in their boots. When the men were ready, they helped her into a laundry basket partially filled with throw rugs. She maneuvered herself as far down as possible, instinctually curling into a ball and holding onto her knees.

"Are you ready?" the leader asked.

The man's English surprised her. She had assumed he spoke only in his foreign tongue. "Um….I think so," came her muffled reply.

Sevenah brought her forehead to her knees and closed her eyes. The weight of more carpeting was felt before the basket was lifted and shoved into the trailer's deepest corner. The men hoisted five additional baskets after hers, making a full load.

Sitting in darkness she tried to calm her anxieties, slowly drawing in air and then exhaling deeply despite the dirty smell. Her heartbeat drummed so strongly she feared it might be audible. "Relax, relax, relax," she chanted to herself. It helped a little.

The truck's engine started up and roared defiantly as the trailer shifted into drive. They jerked hard once, and the wheels rolled forward.

It was difficult to hear over the noisy engine. The ride was bumpy but tolerable so long as it meant getting far away from this prison. Sevenah missed her family and longed for the simplest joys in life—to kiss her mother, to hug her father, to watch the next sunset with Ian and to sleep in her own soft bed under warm, downy covers. Her yearning for home felt powerful enough she could nearly discern the natural scents of the farm.

It didn't take long for the truck to come to a stop at the first of three checkpoints, separating them from the final exit a mile and a half up the road. Jerin pulled up to a white line on the pavement and then shifted the truck into park, leaving the engine to idle.

A young man in military garb stepped out of a glass booth. Two armed guards stood at the gate about twenty yards behind him. The young officer approached the truck—a clipboard in hand, firearms attached to either hip.

"Mornin'," he greeted both drivers. Sevenah could barely overhear their muffled conversation.

"I.D.'s and driver's license please."

"Yes, sir," Jerin said. "Here you go, sir."

"What ya haulin' out? More laundry?"

"Yes, sir."

"Mind if I take a peek?" The guard was already headed toward the back of the trailer.

"Be my guest," came the reply from the cab.

Sevenah recognized the sound of footsteps. She listened intently as the officer walked alongside the truck, rounding the back. Squeaky hinges groaned when the heavy trailer doors were pulled open. Then there was silence. After a few long seconds, the metal doors slammed shut and the same footsteps tapped the pavement returning to the cab. The young officer seemed satisfied that all was as it should be.

With a chuckle he commented, "Ain't nuthin' like airin' out other people's dirty laundry, eh?" He must've amused himself because he laughed aloud at his own pun.

The gate was ordered open, and the truck rolled on, clear of the first checkpoint.

So far, so good.

Sevenah felt the tension in her shoulders noticeably soften as she sucked in a greedy, stale inhale. Without realizing it, she had held her breath almost the entire time the truck had idled. This wasn't anything close to her idea of fun. She had never been the adventurous type, not without some heavy encouragement from peers. While her friends often enjoyed the rush of adrenaline that accompanied a dare, Sevenah didn't. She craved the familiar, the secure and dependable things in life like regular routines, everyday faces, and reasonably harmless activities. It made her feel safe— a feeling she earnestly longed for at the moment.

They traveled on toward the next checkpoint, passing a number of domed buildings and a long hangar surrounded by planes and helicopters.   Military personnel passed by in camouflaged jeeps, headed in the opposite direction on the winding stretch of blacktop.   Jerin didn't slow down until the second gate came into full view.

Inside the trailer, Sevenah held tight as they jolted to another stop.   The engine roared its own complaint before dropping into a low idle once again.   Everything transpired much like the first time, with I.D. checks and a request to examine their cargo.

"Be my guest," Jerin told the new officer.

This second security guard wasn't as young as the previous one, or as friendly.   He didn't seem as easily satisfied either.   On his way to the rear, he examined each tire and tapped beneath the trailer, squatting to take a peek at the undercarriage.   Sevenah listened to the hinges protest when the rear doors were yanked open.   The floor leaned and rocked, and she understood that the officer had pulled himself up into the trailer.

One by one he rummaged through bins, turning over piles of dirty laundry to check the contents.   Sevenah could hear the slight echo on steel flooring as the officer stepped, halted, and then stepped forward again.   She dug deeper beneath throw carpets, pressing herself flat against the bottom.   Soon, he was standing above her.

For the first time in a long time she found herself mouthing a prayer.   The words were mentally spoken but earnest and heartfelt.   "Please, please, God, don't let him find me.   I can't go back there, I can't, I just can't…"

All at once, the load on her back lightened as a handful of carpets were shoved aside.   Not knowing what else to do, she squeezed her eyes shut and quit breathing, resorting to the child-like idea that if she couldn't see him, he couldn't see her.   It was a ridiculous notion, but her prayer nonetheless.   His hand nearly grazed her cheek as he dug deeper, peeling away at her hiding place.   The next thing she knew, everything was tossed back in a heavy heap.   She had miraculously gone unnoticed.

"Thank you, Lord," she mouthed, hands clasped in sincere gratitude.

Finding nothing out of the ordinary, the officer finished his search.   His footsteps clunked more rapidly on his way out, and the truck rocked as he hopped out the rear.   Sevenah breathed a

68

huge sigh of relief when the doors slammed shut. Then she maneuvered herself into a ball again, finding it a more comfortable position.

A few minutes later they started forward, safely past the second checkpoint.

Only the final gate remained, a mile ahead.

Away from the main facility, they passed fewer personnel patrolling the area. For half a mile nothing significant came into sight, only endless blacktop cutting a solid trail through red desert sands. A few small hills and flat-topped mesas appeared in the distance while desert flora crept up here and there, mostly cactus and sagebrush sparsely scattered across the terrain. A lizard or two scurried overland, headed for protective brush.

Sevenah concentrated on the hum of the engine, allowing its steady drone to have a hypnotizing influence. Her thoughts drifted. She wondered about these new people—about their true intentions. What plans did they have in store after successfully stealing her away? They seemed friendly enough, but it was hard to imagine them risking their lives merely as an act of kindness. She was sure they expected something in return. Something significant. She refused to trade one prison for another and would do whatever the situation required if it turned out their motives were devious.

Contemplating a successful getaway, her thoughts naturally wandered home. She missed her parents terribly, and Ian equally as much. Wouldn't they all be surprised to see her walk through the front door! Despite the ordeal and her prolonged absence, Sevenah refused to accept that life could never return to normal. Her only goal was to get home. She was positive that reaching Royal City would make everything okay; her father would make it so. No one needed to know about her hidden differences. She didn't even want to know.

The truck rolled on steadily until they neared a large, cement warehouse. A sharp bend in the road veered around the structure, located less than a quarter mile to the final gate. Sevenah was jolted from her thoughts when a blaring siren pealed through the air. It rang out so loud and shrill that even beneath the carpeting she had to cover her ears.

"They know," Sevenah gasped. This was bad.

The truck jerked to an abrupt halt behind the cement warehouse. Jerin jumped out of the cab and ran to the rear, yanking open both squeaky doors. He hopped into the trailer with Marguay right on his heels.

"Sha Eena!" they cried.

The words sparked a vague sense of familiarity, yet Sevenah didn't grasp the meaning. She did, however, recognize great urgency in their tone, and quickly dug her way up through the carpets. The men lifted her out as soon as she surfaced.

"The place has gone into lockdown, which means they may be looking for you. If so, they'll be checking all these hampers thoroughly. It's not safe for you to remain back here any longer."

While the man in charge spoke, his friend undressed. He handed over his hat and coveralls to Jerin who then offered the clothing to Sevenah. She looked up uncertainly.

"Put them on," he ordered.

"But they're way too big," she complained, holding the garb up to her.

"We'll have to make it work. These soldiers will be searching for a female. We're going to make sure they don't find one."

"You've got to be kidding me," she groaned. This had to be the worst idea, but she lacked a better one to offer. After stepping into the outfit, Jerin did his best to fold under both pant cuffs while she rolled up the sleeves. The excess material was bunched behind her to make the outfit appear somewhat fitted.

"This is crazy," she breathed, rolling her eyes at the ceiling.

Jerin ignored her qualms. "Pull your hair up under the hat."

She did so, trying her best to twist the long locks on top of her head. The baseball cap fit snuggly with all the stuffing. She ran her fingers along the brim, tucking in shorter hairs around her face.

Meanwhile, Marguay had redressed in a white lab coat, switching the identification badge on his front pocket. The men briefly swopped words in their own language while Sevenah worried about their plans.

When the exchange ended, Marguay nodded once in Sevenah's direction, respectfully uttering, "Sha Eena." Then he turned and hurried out.

"Yeah, bye," she waved after him.

Jerin handed over his sunglasses, ordering her to put them on. She stood before him, ready for inspection.

"Do I look okay?"

He didn't smile.

"Let's go," he ordered, heading outside. "You must remain silent. Don't speak. Follow my lead. And don't take off those glasses."

"Sure thing," Sevenah agreed.

Jerin hopped off the edge of the trailer, and then reached up to help her down. He slammed the metal doors shut and headed for the driver's side of the cab. She almost followed him, but changed her direction to head for the passenger's side. If they were to take much longer there would be a suspicious time gap between the second and third check points. Someone might demand an explanation.

Sevenah glanced at the glaring desert sun as she pulled herself into the cab. It felt like an eternity had passed since her last day outside. Even behind tinted glasses the sunshine appeared glorious. The warm tingle on her face inspired an intense appreciation for the open air. Drawing in a deep breath, she wondered exactly how long they had locked her away.

The decision not to buckle her seatbelt seemed reasonable in case a quick exit were necessary. Jerin revved the engine and steered them down the road. Within minutes the third and last checkpoint came into view. Sevenah pushed the sunglasses up her nose and flickered a glance at Jerin, thinking to herself how grim their chances were of pulling this off.

"You do have a backup plan, right?"

"Yes," came a cool reply.

"Good." It seemed likely they would need one.

The sirens had stopped blaring after the first couple minutes. It was only the incessant flashing of red lights that now communicated a high-alert status. That and the attentive conduct of the guards.

"Stop right there!" commanded a tall, redhead in uniform. He held up the palm of his hand as the truck rolled up to the final gate. "Kill your engine!"

Jerin did as ordered. Sevenah wiped a layer of sweat from her forehead, attempting to hide her face from view of the fast-approaching officer.

"Hand over your identification."

Jerin reached into the front pocket of his coveralls and pulled out two badges. "What's all the noise about?" he asked. "Some kind of fire drill?"

The soldier answered sternly. "This is no drill. And for now, no one leaves or enters the place." He reached through the open window and snatched the badges from Jerin's fingers.

"You think maybe that doctor there knows anything about what's going on?"

The officer turned to face the direction in which Jerin pointed. A jeep had nosed up to a human barricade of soldiers, and the driver, wearing a white lab coat, was ordering the guards to allow him immediate passage. He seemed in a frantic hurry.

"Be right back," said the redhead. "Stay here." He tucked both I.D. badges into his front pocket. Sevenah watched him hustle over to the disturbance—a distraction that, for the moment, was working in their favor.

The exchange grew heated as the driver insisted he be let outside the gates. Sevenah watched with great interest, her stomach churning. She wondered if the commotion had anything to do with her disappearance. Whatever the problem, neither side was backing down. A minute into the conversation had the redheaded officer speaking into his radio while at the same time ordering a determined medic to back off.

"If a faculty member can't get through, there's no way we're ever getting through," Sevenah breathed in discouragement.

"Just wait," Jerin told her.

A second vehicle pulled up just then. Sevenah's jaw dropped when she recognized the driver. "It's Leisha!" she exclaimed.

"And Marguay," Jerin pointed out.

With his back turned to them, Sevenah hadn't noticed that the man in the jeep was their friend, Marguay. He had been quick to react after leaving the truck, confiscating the nearest vehicle to create a disturbance. He was doing his best to convince the guards that the sirens were, in fact, a false alarm—insisting they allow him through for what he deemed a *genuine* emergency. They weren't buying his story, however, until Leisha presented the man in charge with a legal slip of paper. After reading it over, the officer handed it to another guard and proceeded to call out on his radio again.

"He's checking up on them," Sevenah guessed.

"If Rhoen's done his job, they'll be fine," Jerin assured her.

And he was right. It appeared Rhoen did intercept the call, because the gates were immediately pulled open for Marguay and Leisha. They were allowed to leave. Then the redhead jogged back to the truck and handed over Jerin's I.D. badges. He hadn't bothered to glance at them.

"It looks like all's clear. You're free to go."

"Mind me asking what the problem was?"

"False alarm, I guess. Some idiot set off the sirens for an off-premises emergency." The officer waved them on.

"Good day," Jerin called as they slipped safely through the final gate.

Sevenah shook her head in utter amazement. She couldn't believe it; they were free!

"I thought for sure we were trapped—how in the world...?"

"We're not home yet," Jerin reminded her. He looked sideways and cracked a slim smile. "But it does look promising."

She couldn't help but smile back. It was such a relief to be outside the gates and driving away from Dr. Braxton. Far, far away.

They continued down blacktop until it ended at a random point, converting into dirt road that pushed straight ahead for miles. Sevenah removed the borrowed sunglasses and set them on the dash. She squinted until her pupils adjusted to the brightness, peering out at an endless sea of red sand.

Jerin sped up after the final checkpoint, knowing time was their enemy. The ride felt rough and consistently bumpy. In order to keep from being tossed around, Sevenah held tight to the armrest. With a free hand she clumsily removed the baggy coveralls, not caring to wear the disguise any longer than necessary. Eventually, she questioned Jerin about their plans.

"Are Leisha and Marguay very far ahead of us?"

"No. We'll meet them at the rendezvous point just over that hill." He pointed to a steep mesa behind a rolling hill in the distance.

73

"What about Rhoen?" she asked. "He's still back there, isn't he?"

"He'll be following soon."

She asked the next question with some hesitancy. "What happens when we all get to the rendezvous point?"

Jerin didn't answer. She knew immediately why not. In the background, sirens blared out their warning cry again. Sevenah held on tight as Jerin pressed the gas pedal to the floor.

"No, no, no," she exhaled, fearful their victory had been short lived.

"We're not that far away. We'll make it, just hold on." But Jerin's troubled face wasn't reassuring.

They swerved off the main road and onto a wide dirt trail. The rendezvous point inched nearer as the truck was steered on the shortest, direct course. Sevenah gripped at her seat and held onto the dash as the terrain jarred them around. She monitored her rearview mirror, copying Jerin, nervous that a pursuer might appear in their dust. She prayed they had a great enough lead to keep them safe. It was a moment of wishful thinking.

The truck swerved recklessly to the left when a blinding spotlight glared through the windshield. Sevenah screamed, grasping at the interior, while Jerin steered wide to avoid an unexpected, low aircraft. He quickly corrected the vehicle, skidding back onto the dirt trail. A helicopter hovered overhead, its propellers a furious buzz, but Jerin kept his focus on the hill ahead.

"Pull the vehicle over now or we *will* shoot!" The warning sounded across the desert, amplified by intercom.

Sevenah's big eyes spoke to Jerin before she breathed a word. "I can't go back there."

He had no intention of stopping. He kept the pedal to the floor and continued forward as fast as their rig would move. She watched him reach into his pocket and pull out a tiny red box that he attached to the dashboard. He then retrieved a small communications device and spoke into it with great urgency.

"Una! Una! Pahrta lo ahmannay keea pii naash. Sha Eena lo kii me. Una!"

"Krono shema. Nay!" came the reply.

"Ahntah lo pahmm!" Jerin spoke into the device.

"Ruha! Nay!"

"Jerin!" It was Leisha's voice now coming over the device. "Jerin! How many are following you?"

"Just a helicopter so far…" He stopped talking when Sevenah screamed. They both ducked at the sound of gun fire. Warning shots.

"Are you okay?" Leisha shrieked.

"Yes," Jerin said, "but we're being fired at!"

"Just hurry!" she urged loudly.

Sevenah was terrified they would be caught or, worse, killed only yards from their destination. How just her luck. As if that weren't bad enough, she groaned at the sight in her rearview mirror when Jerin commented, "We've got more company."

A half-dozen military vehicles were distantly chasing them. It wouldn't be long before they caught up. The jeeps were smaller and faster than the bulky truck Jerin had already pushed to its top speed.

"Get down and stay down," he barked. She didn't have any trouble following orders.

Scrunched below the dash on the passenger floorboard, her arms protectively sandwiched her head in case this pursuit ended in a crash—a strong possibility. Then the loudspeaker sounded up again.

"Pull over now! We will *shoot if you continue to run!"*

They were so close to the rendezvous point.

Seconds later, another round of shots were fired. Bullets ricocheted off the metal exterior of the truck. Sevenah screamed again with her head still buried in her arms. From the rearview mirror Jerin watched military jeeps continue to gain on them. He decided they were close enough.

He slammed on the brakes and the truck spun sideways, throwing the trailer across the dirt path and positioning Jerin's door toward the oncoming vehicles. Sevenah was grateful for the arms protecting her head when she knocked hard against the lower dash.

"Get out and run!" Jerin hollered.

Sevenah obeyed without delay, jumping out of the cab and sprinting for the hill. It wasn't an easy task trying to run through sandy soil with any speed. Jerin slid across the seat and took off right behind her. He kept looking over his shoulder, waiting for a safe distance to separate them from the truck.   About sixty yards away he pointed a palm-sized device behind and pressed on it.

An explosion shook the air, ripping apart the truck in a violent ball of fiery scarlet.   It was enough to swerve the jeeps off course and force the helicopter to veer up and backwards, buying them a little more time.

The thunderous detonation startled Sevenah, but it didn't slow her sprint.   She hadn't noticed any weapons on her rescuers up to that point, so the destructive explosion came as a shock.   The red box Jerin had set on the dash must've been one volatile bomb.   A warm hand pushed on her back and she tried to run harder in response.   Jerin stayed right with her, matching every pumping stride.

The hill was almost within reach.   They were only yards away when Sevenah heard her name bellowed over an intercom.

"Sevenah Williams!   Stop now or I will shoot you!"

She recognized that horrible voice.   In her worst nightmare she was sure to shudder at the malice in Dr. Braxton's tone.   Her head automatically turned to see if it was him, but her legs continued to race forward.

Jerin urged her on.   "Don't stop; keep going!"

Gunfire followed them.

That was too much.   Terrified by the nearness of the shots, she tripped over her feet and rolled flat into the red sand.   As Jerin reached down to help her up, she turned her wide eyes on Dr. Braxton.   Billows of black smoke and hot flames outlined him like a menacing, supernatural beast.   He held up his gun and aimed.   She knew the brute would kill her given the chance.

Another shot rang out.   Jerin reacted before she heard the sound, falling on top of her and forcing her back into the hot sand. He was hit in the process.

"Jerin!   Jerin!" she screamed.   Blood ran down his arm. He winced when she touched the wound.

She could hardly believe it when he pulled her up with his good arm and pushed her to get to safety.   "Run to the hill now! Go, *GO!*"

It was adrenaline that took over, giving her the ability to continue on.   Her feet automatically obeyed his command, sprinting ahead despite how bleak their hope of escape appeared.

76

There seemed no logic in believing the hill would offer any protection. Surrender looked like the only realistic hope for survival. Even if it was temporary survival.

"You can't get away!" Dr. Braxton yelled after her.

Two more shots hit the air and she twisted her neck to find Jerin still running with her, his wounded arm held protectively against his chest. No one had been hit this time. When additional gunfire failed to pop off, Sevenah turned her head to find out why.

Dr. Braxton was on the ground, tackled by a man who was grabbing at a gun fallen loose. Sevenah watched her hero confiscate the weapon, shoving it in his back pocket before starting into a sprint in her direction. She recognized the man as Rhoen.

"Keep running!" Jerin ordered. They were just about at the foot of the hill. What now? Was she supposed to climb?

Then, as if a hundred firecrackers had been lit at once, the air exploded with the piercing discharge of heavy gunfire. Sevenah dropped to the sand and covered her head. She was sure they were dead. Every soldier had been told to shoot to kill.

This would be the end. Death by firing squad.

When Jerin's shadow crept over her, she looked up in amazement. Something impossible was happening. Deafening shots were ringing out as if a large hunting party had fallen across an open field of deer, but no one was hitting the standing targets. All the gunfire, and yet they remained unscathed? That's when she noticed it—the image that altered her life forever. Undeniable evidence of her new reality.

From behind the nearby mesa, an enormous black-and-silver ship rose to hover above the ground with a long, pointed nose and outspread wings. It was like nothing she had ever set eyes upon. An honest-to-goodness alien spaceship!

The vessel was emitting a force field, surrounding itself and Sevenah as well as her companions. She understood why Jerin and now Rhoen were standing above her, impervious to gunfire. The bullets couldn't harm them now.

She laughed out loud, not sure if it was hysteria or pure ecstatic gratitude. Either way, it was painfully clear that everything she believed about herself up to this point was a lie. She really *was* alien, and so were her rescuers. They had saved her life.

Rhoen took an immediate interest in Jerin's wound and the two men headed toward the belly of the ship floating just above them. A stairway descended from the bottom of the vessel, ending near their feet. Sevenah glanced at the top steps when she heard Leisha's voice.

"Come on, we need to go! It's alright!" Leisha motioned for the girl to follow them aboard.

"No." Her soft reply wasn't so much a refusal but a statement of incredulity. She didn't trust her legs to stand just yet. All she could do was stare. Her eyes followed the men up the steps until they disappeared into the ship. Jerin probably needed immediate medical attention. Why had he jumped in front of a bullet anyway? Why risk his life?

Then an angry voice cut through all the mystery, threatening her again.

"You'll never get away! We'll follow you and hunt down every last one of your devious kind!"

Sevenah whipped her head around, focusing narrowly on Dr. Braxton's portly figure. He was stuck behind the eerie force field, desperate to push through it. No more shots disturbed the air. The gunfire had ceased when it became obvious nothing could penetrate the alien barrier.

As Sevenah glared at the man she had come to loath, anger welled up in her chest. She understood she was safe now, but nothing would ever be the same. This was *his* fault. Her life had been normal. It had been wonderfully normal until he screwed it all up! Her fingers curled into tight, pale fists as she rose and began to march toward him.

Leisha called out urgently to the girl. "Sha Eena! Sevenah, no! *Come back!*" But she wasn't ready to go just yet.

Dr. Braxton spoke first when she stopped mere inches from him, separated by a film of invisible wall.

"I should've killed you when I first found you. Believe me, as soon as we track you down I'll not make that same mistake.

"You have no way of following me. And you're lucky I don't control that ship or I'd have their weapons fire on you and do every life form in this universe a favor. No one deserves to be treated as miserably as you treated me, human or otherwise. I will never forget what you've done. Never!"

She wanted to reach through and strangle him, as hurt as she felt. It was *his* fault she had lost her parents. It was *his* fault she had lost her best friend. It was *his* fault she wasn't really going home. *It was all his fault!*

Smug arrogance spread across Dr. Braxton's face. "I don't fear the likes of you. You're not human. You're not even an earth-born rat, which makes you of less worth to me than those filthy, disgusting vermin."

That was more than she could take. Her temper flared, and she forgot about everything else but the arrogant jerk standing before her. Fueled by deep-seated hurt and resentment, she threw her clenched fist at him. To her great astonishment she penetrated the eerie barrier. Her punch landed squarely on his jaw, effectively knocking him to the ground. She fell forward herself, drawn ahead by her own momentum.

Someone grabbed her from behind, pulling her to her feet before she completely slipped through to the other side.

"Rhoen," she breathed gratefully. He had returned when she failed to follow them onto the ship. Shocked and yet relieved, she hugged the man. Apparently, the force field only kept things out, not in.

Glancing sideways, she caught the furious look on Dr. Braxton's face as he recognized a missed opportunity to snatch her. Her hand automatically made another fist.

"Ouch, that hurts." Her punch had landed fairly hard.

Rhoen turned her toward the waiting ship, and squeezed her shoulders in a gesture of encouragement. "It's time to go home," he said.

Sevenah understood she had no choice. It wasn't the home she had hoped to return to, but it was the only place left to go. Earth was no longer a safe option.

She nodded her willingness to follow. Rhoen walked her to the open stairway, ignoring a barrage of threats from Dr. Braxton in the background.

They disappeared into the belly of the ship, the steps rising behind them. The force field dissolved, and then nothing remained but a gathering of human onlookers staring up at a clear desert sky.

Inside the ship, Sevenah sank into a shiny, black seat across from Rhoen. Straps whooshed across her lap and chest, holding her in place. It was startling, but she could see Rhoen and Leisha strapped in the same way. A long aisle ran down the center of the ship, dividing them from four seats set up identically on the opposite side. The interior was dark, a combination of black furniture and dim lighting. Jerin and Marguay were nowhere to be seen, but it was reasonable to assume Jerin's bullet wound was being tended to.

"Rest your head back," Leisha instructed. "You'll feel some strong forces as we exit the atmosphere. It'll be fine once we leave this planet."

Sevenah let her head drop against the chair. Her eyes were drawn to a skinny window spanning her side of the ship. Clouds blocked the view at first, but soon they dispersed, revealing a glaring sun. Sevenah squinted at the sudden brightness. Then, as if someone tossed a blanket over her head, it turned as dark as night. Not pitch black, but a darkness infested with millions of sparkling dots. Stars. They were irregular stars unlike those she and Ian had gazed at nightly. These distinct celestial lights glowed with more clarity than she had ever observed. At the same time, her body lifted from the chair only to be instantly pulled back down.

"Artificial gravity," Leisha explained. "It always takes a second to kick in."

The seat belts retracted, disappearing into the cushions. That too was unexpected and startling. Free of restraints, Sevenah scooted up to peer more closely through the skinny window at her side. The entire planet was now visible. Earth's bluish image looked beautiful. Never in her lifetime had she imagined being a firsthand witness to something this incredible. The globe seemed to float in a vast, black sea—a wispy, sapphire marble existing solo. How could it be she wasn't from that world? Her eyes closed with a deepening sadness, understanding she was never to see the place again, or any of her loved ones.

"Would you like to meet our pilot?" Rhoen asked, gesturing toward the aisle as he stood.

She agreed with a nod, still dazed by the mind-boggling experience.

Rhoen led the way while Leisha took up the rear. At the end of the aisle a large control room appeared, separated from passenger seating by a dividing wall. Sevenah caught sight of two pilot's chairs, the high backs toward her.

Once on the bridge, she noticed how everything was labeled in foreign script—from display monitors to posted instructions to gauges lit up in a variety of colors. Electronic switches and buttons covered every panel and counter. It was truly an awesome sight. The pointed nose of the ship was visible through a front windowpane that swept clear from one side of the bridge to the other. She awed at the immensity of the moon as they seemed to duck under its rocky surface.

"This is unbelievable," she breathed.

Rhoen dismissed himself, leaving their guest with Leisha. Sevenah continued to stare into space, mesmerized by absolutely everything.

Leisha spoke into her ear, "Sha Eena." That was the umpteenth time she had heard those words.

She had to ask, "Will you please tell me what Sha Eena is?"

The answer came from the pilot's chair, a quiet and familiar utterance. "You are," the voice told her. "*You* are Sha Eena."

"No way," Sevenah gasped, not because of the answer, but because of the voice. She knew that voice. The chair slowly swiveled until the pilot faced her. Ian, her best friend, rose from the seat—a miracle standing before her eyes.

"*Ian!*" she screamed, jumping into his arms. He had to grip the chair to keep from falling backwards. They hugged like reunited family. After a few seconds, Ian carefully pushed her back. She was puzzled by his behavior but too overjoyed to care.

"I can't believe it's you!" she exclaimed, elated to be reunited with her best friend. "I never thought I'd see you again!" She hugged him once more, overcome with joy.

Ian patiently allowed her to hug him.

When her arms relaxed, she stepped back and stared up at his face, disbelief swimming in her eyes. Not knowing whether to laugh or cry, she did both.

Wanting to fill him in on what had happened to her since being separated, she delved into a brief account of the frightening adventure she had somehow managed to survive.

"I don't even know how much time has passed since I was locked up in there!"

"I'm so sorry," Ian said. "None of that should've happened. Forgive me, Eena." His face wilted—pained and apologetic.

"It's not your fault." But his request for forgiveness made her think. Her face scrunched up, puzzled. "Is it?"

His shoulders slumped as his eyes dropped to the ground. The familiarity of his conduct made Sevenah feel better in a way, but his response didn't.

"It is my fault. I should've been with you. I should never have left you alone, not even for one day."

Then Leisha spoke up supportively. "He was the one who found you, though. I still don't know how, but he found you. That's the only reason we were able to pull this off."

Sevenah was beginning to think now, her mind piecing things together, realizing there was only one reason Ian would be among them. She glanced questioningly at Leisha and then back at Ian.

"How long have you known?" she asked him.

He didn't answer right away.

"You've been my best friend for over a year, Ian; we've done everything together. How long have you known about me?"

He looked into her troubled eyes and admitted, "I've always known."

She was hurt. How could her best friend have kept something this big, this important, from her? "Why didn't you tell me? Why didn't you tell me the truth about you—about me—about us?"

"I couldn't." His reply was sincere, pleading for her to understand.

"No, no," she said, unwilling to believe that he couldn't. *Wouldn't*, maybe, but he *could* have told her. And as far as she was concerned this entire nightmare might have been avoided if he had said something.

Her voice trembled as she lashed out at him. "If you knew, you should've said something to me. I had every right to know who I was….who I am! You should've told me, Ian!"

"But I couldn't."

"Yes, you could have!"

"And if I had, if I had come to you with the truth and said,

'Oh, by the way, Sevenah, guess what? You and I are aliens from another planet far off in the galaxy somewhere, and furthermore, your real name isn't Sevenah. It's Eena.' If I had said those words to you, would you have believed me?"

He waited for her answer.

"I don't know—probably not……but you could have convinced me, proven it to me. If I had known, I would never have gone to see Dr. Tracy; that I'm sure of! Then all of these horrible things would never have happened to me!"

Ian's shoulders sagged more than usual, burdened by guilt. "I'm sorry, but I really couldn't tell you. My orders were not to disclose anything, Eena."

"My name's not Eena! It's Sevenah!"

She didn't want to hear his excuses. The whole thing felt like a cruel conspiracy. Her best friend was turning out to be someone she really didn't know, pretending to be someone he wasn't, pretending she was someone *she* wasn't.

Sevenah stormed out of the control room and down the aisle, throwing herself into a passenger seat. Ian and Leisha followed. Leisha sat beside her while Ian took a chair across the way. She refused to look at either of them, staring out into space instead, trying hard not to cry.

"He was under orders to keep silent," Leisha tried to explain. "All of us were. The council and Derian…..they gave strict instructions to protect you at all costs but to say nothing directly to you. Ian had already been reprimanded for violating those orders and befriending you a year ago."

Sevenah continued to look out the window, shaking her head back and forth in tiny gestures of denial.

Ian tried again. "I wanted so much to tell you, I truly did."

She turned abruptly to face him. "You *should have* told me, Ian! I had a right—my *parents* had a right to know my real identity! And all along you knew. I thought you were my best friend." Her eyes began to tear up, so she turned to the window again.

Ian fell back in his chair. He understood her anger. And for the moment, no explanation would be good enough.

CHAPTER FIVE
Harrowbeth of Moccobatra

"We've reached the Kemeniroc. Prepare to board."

It was Marguay's voice resounding over the intercom. They had traveled beyond the orbit of the moon and were approaching their mother ship. The starship Sevenah currently occupied had appeared huge to her at first sight, but compared to the massive spacecraft outside her window, this present ride seemed to shrink to a mere fly on the wall.

The Kemeniroc was a first-class military transport that held hundreds of smaller battleships like the one Marguay now piloted. Enormous by anyone's standards, it provided ample accommodations for an entire army and all immediate family. The exterior appeared a rusty copper color with black script painted across each side. This strange writing indicated its designation: the *Kemeniroc*.

Sevenah continued to peer outside her window, partly to divert her attention from Ian but drawn more now by curiosity. Never had she seen a vessel of such massive proportions. Never had she imagined an alien ship so near Earth.

They maneuvered slowly toward the stern, sailing between double wings with blunt tips that spanned each side. The nose came to a point, somewhat resembling the smaller ships; however, this spacecraft appeared antique—worn and faded by years of active combat. The closer they drifted to the hull, the more an abundance of battle scars became visible. Soon, they were near enough to create the illusion that brushing fingertips along its metal exterior was a feat within arm's reach. When docking-bay doors parted open, a sizeable hangar quickly swallowed them up. Their tiny ship came to an easy halt just inside.

A minute later, a stairway descended to the floor, leading into the bay. Rhoen and Jerin were first to exit, emerging from a private back room. Jerin's shoulder was wrapped in bandages, held protectively by his other hand. Marguay exited next, hustling down the aisle from the bridge. Ian and Leisha rose and motioned for Sevenah to go ahead of them.

"After you," Leisha encouraged.

Sevenah slowly walked the aisle before stepping down onto an open step.   She froze near the top, overwhelmed by a vast expanse that unveiled itself before her eyes.   Two massive levels stretched as far off as she could see, sheltering hundreds of ships that looked exactly alike—black-and-silver hulls, pointed noses, wings stretched thin for finer maneuvering.   She glanced below to find Marguay, Rhoen, and Jerin lined up at the foot of the stairway, standing at attention like soldiers in the presence of a superior.

While descending a few more steps, her eye caught sight of a tall figure approaching from another area of the bay.   She stopped to observe the man—broad-shouldered with solid arms swinging back and forth at his sides, one large hand wielding a heavy tool in its grasp.   Confident, determined strides brought him quickly near.

Sevenah found his features attractive, appearing slightly Grecian in a square jaw, a prominent nose, dark brown eyes, all topped off with short, chocolate waves.   But despite the handsome face, his expression was stern and daunting.   It looked as if the man had been called away from mechanical repairs, his clothing soiled and scruffy.   Yet the way he carried himself suggested a status of greater importance.   Something about his demeanor was especially intimidating and seemed to demanded respect.   Sevenah felt her pulse quicken at an inexplicable rise of anxiety.

She descended to the last step with Leisha at her side and Ian remaining in her shadow.   The dark-haired stranger stopped directly in front of them.   His interest fell first on his men—the three on the floor still poised at attention.

He spoke in their strange foreign tongue; it sounded as if he were asking blunt questions.   Jerin did most of the responding. Sevenah glanced back and forth between the men during the exchange, eerily certain she was the main topic of conversation. She understood only the mention of names, including the newest in her vocabulary, "Eena."   Their chat came to an end with an unmistakable command from the formidable figure whose deep voice was even more commanding than Jerin's.

"Cohme naash.   Shii don heiguay keeah Neeraida.   Co

nahrma kahei," he ordered.

The men saluted their captain, replying in one respectful chorus, "Mrii, tanee!"   Then they turned to the newest arrival with lowered heads and chimed, "Sha Eena."

Sevenah followed them with her eyes until they disappeared at the far end of the docking bay.   She felt immense gratitude for their sacrifices on her behalf.   Sacrifices she couldn't quite understand.

Her attention then returned to the intimidating man who had shifted his stance to face her.   As their eyes met, the frown on his face deepened.   His fixed gaze narrowed into a scrutinizing stare. She had to look away; the anxiety he evoked was debilitating.

"So this is Eena," he said, sounding mostly annoyed.   He continued to look her up and down.

Sevenah felt a swell of defensiveness in response.

"What is this?"   He swiped the cap from off her head.   Long strands of hair fell loosely over her shoulders, framing her face in reddish highlights.

Sevenah swallowed hard, feeling distaste for his aggressiveness.   With everything that had happened, she had forgotten about the baseball cap.

Leisha stepped in to explain.   "We had to use a temporary disguise."

"Hmmm," the man grumbled.   "Get rid of it."   He tossed the hat at Leisha.   "So, I assume everything went well?"

"Yes sir.   Mostly, anyway."

"What went wrong?"   His focus remained steadily fixed on the new girl who was obviously uncomfortable under his scrutiny.

"We were followed, and Jerin was injured," Leisha reported. "We had to reveal our ship in order to protect Eena."

"Sevenah."   It was a softly spoken correction.

The man gruffly questioned her whispered interruption. "What did you say?"

Unable to look him in the eye, she turned to Leisha who answered for the girl.   "She's a little overwhelmed with everything, Derian.   It's going to take a while for her to feel comfortable with all these new revelations.   She'll need you to explain things."

Sevenah reacted immediately to the man's name, wrinkling

her nose and squinting at him for a long moment.

So this was Derian. This was the Derian whom Leisha and Ian had mentioned—the man who had kept Ian from telling her the truth. It was becoming evident why they were hesitant to disobey him. Perhaps she had been a little hard on her best friend.

Derian focused on Ian next, who was still standing in the shadows of both women.

"I thought you were certain she's the one."

"I am," Ian affirmed.

"She clearly doesn't agree." The remark essentially accused Ian of securing the wrong person.

"She *is* Eena," Ian growled defensively.

"And your proof is…?"

"I told you before….I know who she is."

"So you say."

Leisha broke in, cutting off a developing quarrel. "Derian, I'm sure she's hungry and tired. It's been a long day."

The hangar fell silent—a vast, uneasy stillness. No one said a word as Derian observed their new arrival, eyes tight as if he were perturbed at having her on his ship. Eventually he spoke.

"My name is Kahm Derian, or as you would say, Captain Derian. This is *my* ship. The people here are *my* crew."

Once again he fell silent. Sevenah tried to look him in the eye, only managing to glance up at his unwelcoming stare for brief moments.

"Take her to the medical bay," he finally ordered.

"No!" The outburst was automatic, triggered by fear of further abuse at the hands of more curious physicians. She was through playing guinea pig to the medical profession.

"What?" Derian barked. His entire being stiffened, appearing irritated by her outright defiance.

She managed to meet his gaze with the same intensity this time. "No more doctors. I refuse."

Leisha put an arm around the trembling girl. "Derian, please. She was mistreated by the doctors on Earth. She's just afraid."

The captain's countenance actually softened a few degrees, and he offered a word of assurance. "You have nothing to fear here. Jinatta is the best doctor in the entire galaxy. She'll check you over to be sure no damage was done while you were gone.

That's all." He sounded sincere, almost kind that time.

"I'll go with you," Leisha offered.

Sevenah glanced back at Ian, making sure he intended to follow. He nodded. Reluctantly, she agreed to go.

The captain swiveled about and started off, intending to return to his repairs. He shouted an additional order over his shoulder. "And get rid of those ghastly clothes!"

"What? Why?" She was dressed in her favorite attire; what was wrong with faded jeans? Sevenah looked to her companions who merely pursed their lips and groaned behind their captain's back.

Leisha led the way to the medical bay with Sevenah and Ian trailing in a line. They marched through a well-lit corridor painted bright apricot. The flooring beneath was smooth and soft, barely giving with each step. Here and there paintings adorned the walls—framed works of art that shifted in appearance after a moment of scenic stillness. The pictures were like short animations brushed onto the wall, playing for about five seconds before freezing, only to repeat the same movements again. The unusual images immediately grabbed her attention.

She stopped to examine a colorful tree, its leaves rustled by a gentle breeze. A mass of tiny white blossoms lifted off the branches and were carried away in the wind like a swarm of moths. Then the picture froze in a still-life pose, nothing but a thick, naked trunk. After five seconds, the branches bloomed again, abounding with clusters of white petals. The wind stripped away every last one, carrying them off as before. It was a repeated cycle.

"This is incredible! I've never seen anything like this!" Sevenah exclaimed. She stayed to watch the sequence repeat itself—two, three, four times—before Leisha finally pulled her along.

"Come on. You'll have time to study them all later."

They continued on through three separate corridors. Sevenah noticed how each one had a control panel located somewhere on the wall flashing lines of bright green script. She wondered why the lettering didn't spark some familiarity. If she was truly from their planet, why was their language such a mystery?

Leisha came to a stop at a wide door and put her hand up to a small box beside it.   The box glowed, leaving a lingering shadow of her handprint.   Then the door slid open.   They entered a tiny space that proved to be the equivalent of a very fast elevator.

Sevenah didn't recognize the symbols on the controls inside, but she counted up to the one Leisha touched. Two…three…four.   There were twelve symbols altogether.   It didn't seem enough levels for such a large ship, unless other routes led to higher levels.

They climbed four decks in a blink.   The elevator settled with a sigh and opened up, revealing another long corridor.   This one was painted white with a continuous red stripe traveling clear along the upper edge of each wall.   Just a few feet beyond stood a pair of white doors striped red through the center.   There they stopped.

"Here we are," Leisha announced.

She held her palm flat against another mounted box.   It glowed exactly as the previous one had, leaving her hand-shadow lingering again.   The doors parted allowing access to a sizeable medical bay—an open room lined with beds on either side.

Sevenah followed Leisha clear down the center aisle, then off to the left around a dividing wall that concealed a smaller private area.   This secluded space housed only two medical beds and a glass-partitioned office on the far side.   Behind the glass sat a pretty woman with blonde curls.   She was slouched over a desk, immersed in reading.   Her long hair was pulled away from an ashen profile, secured by crystal combs that sparkled like sapphires in the light.   She was startled when the three stepped into her office.   After flashing wide eyes that gleamed the same blue as the gems in her hair, her lips thinned in a warm and friendly manner.

"Cohme ahtee!" she squealed, jumping up to embrace Leisha with welcoming arms.

"Rahntaco," Leisha replied, returning the same warm hug.

Ian nodded when the woman glanced his way.   "Eena lo ahtee kahei."

The doctor then noticed their newest arrival.   She stared for a moment.   Sevenah experienced the same uneasiness she had felt meeting Derian, like her soul were being critically scrutinized. She glanced at Leisha for reassurance and received an encouraging

89

smile.

At last, the woman spoke. "Sha Eena." She tilted her head the slightest bit and then addressed Ian. "So, this is Eena?"

"Yes," Ian said assuredly. He cast a stern look at his best friend to discourage any protest. Though uncomfortable with the idea of taking on an unfamiliar name, Sevenah kept her silence.

"Well then…" The woman smiled kindly and introduced herself. "My name is Jinatta. I'm the primary medical provider on this ship. Kahm Derian asked me to give you a checkup to make sure all is well. Would that be alright with you?"

"I guess." Sevenah glanced nervously at her best friend. She honestly didn't care for another examination.

"Ian, Leisha, you two don't mind stepping outside for a while, do you?" Jinatta motioned toward the exit.

"No, no, we don't mind," Leisha said.

Ian nodded his consent.

Sevenah watched her friends disappear behind the wall. She was nervous about being left alone with a stranger, but she trusted Ian.

"Why don't you step behind that screen. Remove your clothing and put on this gown." Jinatta held up a white frock. It looked like a simple nightgown, silky to the touch, not anything like the ugly cotton wraps she had worn for medical exams in Dr. Tracy's office. The thought of him made her wonder what the old doctor figured had become of her.

"Eena?" Jinatta's gentle voice pulled her from her thoughts.

"Right. Um…okay."

She disappeared behind a thin partition and changed. The gown slipped on easily, feeling soft against her skin. She folded up her jeans and t-shirt and laid them neatly on a bench, placing her Nikes on the very top.

When she reappeared, Jinatta had her lie down on a padded table and proceeded to perform a thorough checkup. A monitor overhead was flipped on, beeping once before silently displaying detected vitals. The doctor made use of a variety of medical instruments during the examination, items that were strange and unfamiliar to Sevenah.

"What does that do?" she asked as a rectangular plate drifted across her abdomen.

"This? Oh, it helps me see things inside of you. I can view all your major organs on this screen." Jinatta held up the flat board. A grayish blob filled the display, unrecognizable to Sevenah.

"Your lungs seem to be in good shape," Jinatta commented, thoughtfully studying the blob. "Yes, everything appears normal."

"Well, I'm glad you know what it is," Sevenah sighed.

The doctor chuckled and traded the board for a cubed instrument. An impressive three-dimensional image lit up the inside when she turned it on.

"This contraption allows me to examine your bones. I can calculate their strength and density as well as pinpoint any weak spots. She passed the cube over her patient's chest. "Your ribs look beautiful."

Jinatta moved down the legs, across the feet, and so on, but when she passed the instrument over her patient's right hand, she squealed, "*Eeooww!*"

"What?" Sevenah asked with concern. It certainly didn't sound good.

"Don't your fingers hurt?"

"Well, yes, actually." She cupped them with her other hand. "They've been throbbing a little."

"I would imagine so. You have two fractures there!"

Sevenah laughed to herself. It figured. In the act of assaulting Dr. Braxton she had managed to break her own hand. "I guess I've been too preoccupied to be bothered by the pain."

"Don't worry. I'll fix them up as good as new." Jinatta turned over the girl's wrist and added, "I'll repair those abrasions while I'm at it."

She walked over to a long counter and pressed one of several buttons displayed across the front edge. This triggered an opening where a hand-held instrument emerged shaped something like a screwdriver with a thick stem. The doctor squeezed the contraption while passing it slowly over both broken fingers.

"This will feel warm and possibly numbing." It tingled and heated her skin like a tanning lamp. After a couple minutes the doctor finished.

"Move your hand now."

Sevenah wiggled the fingers of her right hand. There was no pain at all. She was amazed. "You healed the bones that fast?"

"Oh yes," the doctor smiled. "Bone fractures are easy. Tissue damage, that's a little trickier." After putting away the instrument, Jinatta turned back to the exam table. "Go ahead and sit up, Eena. Let me take a quick look at your back."

Both legs lifted as the girl swiveled to drop her calves over the edge of the bed. She mumbled a correction to her name. "I prefer to be called Sevenah."

"Really? Why?"

"Because it's my name. It's the name I've responded to all my life. At least as far back as I can recall."

"You don't remember your childhood or your real mother?" Jinatta asked.

Sevenah shrugged; her body hunched with emotion. "I remember my mother from Earth—Ruth Williams. She seemed very real to me."

"You've been gone for such a long time. Far too long. They should've brought you home much sooner."

Sevenah twisted her neck to look at the doctor. "Why didn't they?"

"I can't say."

"Can't or *won't*, like all the others," she murmured, still upset that her real identity was more a mystery to her than anyone.

But the doctor's attention was diverted by an interesting find. There was a note of triumph in her next announcement. "Ah-hah! Here it is!"

"What?" Sevenah attempted to look over her shoulder and see, but Jinatta turned the girl's head back around.

"It appears they left something embedded under your skin. Give me a second. I'm sorry, this will sting just a bit. Okay......almost.............got it!"

"Ouch," Sevenah winced. "What was that?"

She peeked over her shoulder again and this time caught a glimpse of a teeny-tiny gizmo held between the pointed tips of a pair of tweezers. It was a small chip about an eighth of an inch square. The doctor held it up to the light to examine.

"This is a tracking chip. Your captors didn't want to lose you." Jinatta placed the microchip in her patient's open palm.

92

Sevenah looked it over musingly.   A tracking device.   No wonder that helicopter had caught up so quickly.   They had known exactly where to find her.   The thought brought to mind how Jerin had taken a bullet with her name on it.

"How is Jerin?   Is he going to be alright?"

"Jerin?   Oh, he's perfectly fine.   I removed the metallic fragments from his arm and repaired the damage.   He left here just before you arrived."

"You mean he's already healed?"   Their obviously advanced medical capabilities were astounding.

"All you need are the right tools," the doctor said, snapping her fingers like it was elementary.

Jinatta returned to the counter and pressed another button.   A circular instrument with a handle appeared.   She slipped her fingers beneath the strap and then held the device over Sevenah's scarred wrists, demonstrating its function.   After a few moments of concentrated regeneration, the red abrasions were gone, leaving only clear, peachy skin.

"This basically accelerates the cell-division process, enabling tissue to quickly rebuild itself.   Without this instrument it would take days, maybe even weeks, for surface wounds to heal."

The doctor repeated the same procedure on Sevenah's shoulder, mending the tiny incision where the tracking chip had been removed.   When she was done, Jinatta offered the device for inspection.   Sevenah turned it over, contemplating its inestimable value.

"This would be worth a fortune on Earth," she said, "not to mention the money it would save in shortened hospital stays."

Jinatta took back her instrument.   "I don't think Earth is ready for interplanetary trade.   Perhaps someday."   She rested her hip against the table, fingering the circular device as she spoke.   "Everything looks good so far.   I've seen nothing of real concern.   I'd like to do some blood tests, though, just to be thorough."

"Okay," Sevenah agreed.

The doctor smiled at her patient, but the expression looked unnatural, contrary to the disquiet swimming in her blue eyes.   She sighed uneasily, brushing a curtain of blonde curls over one shoulder.   Things fell quiet.   Sevenah watched the regeneration tool pass from hand to hand, juggled in a contemplative manner.

Eventually, the doctor asked the question weighing on her mind.

"Why exactly do you object to being called Eena?"

"I told you, it's not my name."

"Ian seems absolutely sure that it is."

"Maybe at one time it was, I don't remember. But I've spent the majority of my life on Earth. Everyone there calls me Sevenah. Sevenah Williams. Everything I've ever done has been with that name. Now you ask me to change it, because you say so? I won't. I don't know who Eena is, but I *do* know who Sevenah is."

Jinatta nodded understandingly. "You should know that Eena…..Sha Eena…..is a very important person. Every living creature on our home world is waiting and hoping to see Sha Eena return." Jinatta looked up, focusing directly on the young woman. "It's been a very, very long time, but you will come to realize you are more valuable to our people as Eena than you could ever have been on Earth under any other name."

Sevenah leaned forward and begged the doctor, "Then please, please will you tell me who I am?"

"Has Derian said nothing?"

Sevenah breathed a gust of desperation while shaking her head. She kept perfect eye contact hoping to earn an ounce of sympathy.

Jinatta nodded. "Okay. I'll tell you what I can. But it's really Derian's place to explain certain things."

Sevenah's face soured. "So I've heard. I'm not sure he's the one I want to talk to. He seems a little……..mean."

Jinatta laughed. "No, no, he's harmless. He's a good man, Eena. Oh, um, sorry, I mean……*Sevenah*. Derian's a hero, really. Every person on this ship owes his life to the captain."

"Why is that?"

"You don't know?" Jinatta looked surprised. She threw her hands up disgustedly. "Oh for crying in the night! This isn't right at all! They should've explained some things to you."

Sevenah was sure now that she had found a willing and sympathetic voice.

"We might as well start at the beginning."

Jinatta put away the medical instrument she was handling, then pulled up a chair and took a seat beside the exam table. She brushed her long, blonde locks behind her ears and prepared to tell an eager listener a long, true story.

"All of us, including you, are from a planet called Moccobatra. The name means *'everlasting.'* Our people have always believed that our world would thrive forever. That is until recently. At present, our planet is suffering. Dying."

"Why?" Sevenah asked.

"I'll get to that. You should know first that we are but one of many nations living on Moccobatra. Our land there is called Harrowbeth which means *'land of living origin.'* We've dwelt in harmony with our neighbors, mostly because we all, generally, keep to ourselves. It's not exactly like Earth. On Earth I noticed they have many nations but only one species—humans. On Moccobatra each nation is comprised of a different species. Each group basically stays with their own kind, but we've managed to share our planet's resources with minimal hassles.

"Our history records how people came from various worlds long ago to escape destruction and persecution on their home planets. I suppose you could say Moccobatra is a galactic sanctuary of sorts. Unfortunately, history didn't record where our people originated."

Jinatta sat up tall, head inclined, eyes intent on her patient as she divulged the next bit of information. "Your father's name was Laynn. Shen Laynn. He was a very good man. He loved your mother dearly. Your mother's name was Tashi. Sha Tashi. She was a beautiful, caring woman. You are their daughter, their only child. You are Sha Eena."

There was a momentary pause. "Sha means *'queen.'* Your mother was Queen Tashi of Harrowbeth. You are Queen Eena of Harrowbeth." Jinatta stopped again as if expecting a reaction.

Sevenah didn't breathe a word. She kept looking at her storyteller, hoping she would go on—and so she did.

"Our people have lived in relative peace for hundreds, even thousands of years. I suppose that might seem remarkable to some, but in our society such a state is normal, even expected. If problems or difficulties arise, the Shen and Sha or the council step in and resolve them.

"Our citizens have managed to work together, every family assuming responsibility for a necessary trade, passing those duties along from one generation to the next. Each family in Harrowbeth has become quite expert in the area they oversee. For instance, my family has always cared for the medical necessities within our population. Leisha's family has been in charge of engineering and integrating new technologies. Lately, she's assisted me more and more with medical matters, however. Our people aren't as healthy as they once were, and her knowledge of science and technology has come in handy. Derian's family has directed our national security for ages. He can pilot a battle cruiser better than anyone I know. Ian—his family has always served as protectors of the Shens and Shas. That's why he follows you everywhere. In fact, my bet would be he's standing right outside the medical bay doors at this very moment. Would you like to go look?" Jinatta grinned good-humoredly with the question.

"No, please go on." Sevenah didn't want anything to stop this voluntary outpouring of information.

"Okay, where was I? Harrowbeth has largely been at peace for as long as history records. Now and then we've had a problem with a nearby neighbor, but nothing major. Fourteen years ago, however, that all changed."

Jinatta shifted in her seat. She leaned forward, placing the tips of her fingers together in front of her. She seemed to talk to her hands at this point.

"A man named Kahm Vaughndorin began to cause trouble for your parents. They had always considered him a friend. In fact, your families did many things together, but Kahm Vaughndorin often voiced his desire to see changes made to our 'old worn traditions' as he called them. He tried to influence your parents, to convince them that change was necessary and inevitable. I know he was a cause of worry for them, but no one foresaw what Vaughndorin would eventually do."

Jinatta frowned while speaking down at her hands. Her facial muscles tensed.

"One evening, he uh……he asked to see your parents privately to discuss his concerns. A heated debate ensued. Ian's father was there watching out for your mother. He never saw it coming. No one did. Vaughndorin……he uh…" Jinatta paused, finding it hard to spit out the words. Her voice lowered with the next announcement. "Vaughndorin killed your parents that evening. He beheaded them both."

Sevenah saw the doctor's eyes flicker up, but they fell just as quickly. The story continued, hushed and somber.

"After that, he and his followers tried to take over Harrowbeth. They failed. Ian's father stopped him and killed him on the spot. Those few responsible for helping Vaughndorin were captured and imprisoned. The council took over after that."

Jinatta ran both hands over her lap and drew in a deep breath, finally looking up at her listener. "You were to be the next queen, but at the time you were too young—only three years old. Ian's family adopted you into their home and took care of you. I imagine that's where Ian grew to know you so well. Why he knows you now."

"I was three," Sevenah uttered. No wonder she couldn't remember anything.

"Yes," Jinatta sighed, a pitying sound. "For two years our nation struggled to recover from the shock of losing your parents. Such a thing had never occurred in all our history. But this peace was short-lived. Vaughndorin's eldest son decided to assume his father's quest. He was a young man at the time—only seventeen. But as young as he was, he still managed to gather a large group of supporters. He claimed he would fight for the freedom his father had died pursuing, for a society where all could choose their own path instead of keeping to the old Harrowbethian traditions. His speeches were extremely flattering and convincing. He is a man, as you say, with a silver tongue. His name is Gemdorin."

"Gemdorin," Sevenah repeated. "His cause doesn't sound so terrible, Jinatta. Freedom of choice is a desirable thing, isn't it?"

"That's why he was able to attract so many followers. But his cause is not as it appears. If you knew him as many have come to know him, you would realize his true intentions are to gain control over Harrowbeth and set himself up as king. He may allow some freedom of choice, but he will ultimately be the one in charge. He's a vile and power-hungry man. Under his rule it will be chaos. He'll destroy centuries of valued and respected traditions. Our people have taken great pride in upholding the commissions handed down from our fathers. We've functioned effectively for thousands of years this way. Besides, it's not as if we don't have the freedom to pursue our own interests and talents beyond our responsibilities."

"That's not at all like the society I was raised in," Sevenah pointed out.

"I know. It's ironic really, but I suspect there wasn't much choice. Harrowbeth may be unlike your home on Earth, but when you see how well our people work together, you'll realize our ways are worth protecting. We don't lack freedoms because we honor tradition. Gemdorin is using this idea to lure people into helping him gain power. He will not allow them the freedoms he promises, believe me. His intentions are far from noble. He's a monster—a true demon."

Jinatta's warning was harsh. The anguish in her eyes painted a picture of someone tormented by years of distress and struggle. The doctor swallowed back her hatred before going on.

"Exactly two years after your parents died, Gemdorin and his followers attacked Harrowbeth and killed hundreds of innocent people. He'd convinced these extremists that it was for the greater good. Ian and his family feared he would try to kill you as well, erasing any possibility of a new Sha and thus leaving our nation vulnerable and in need of a ruler. That would clear the way for Gemdorin to take over as Shen himself, King of Harrowbeth. When he attacked, Ian fled into the forest with you, against his parents' wishes. Ian insisted *he* was your protector. He wasn't about to see his family held responsible for losing another Sha. His father had suffered much harsh criticism for allowing your mother to be killed; people blamed him for letting Vaughndorin get near her. I'm sure he did all he could, but you know how ruthlessly people can judge. Ian took the criticism personally. He hid you in the forest for days. I'm not sure how the two of you managed, but Gemdorin never did find you. They searched and searched but Ian kept you perfectly hidden."

The story sounded much too familiar, like the beginning of her recurring nightmare—running through the forest, afraid, accompanied by a boy, wishing for her mother. But where did the snakes come in?

"I think I remember something like that."

"You do? Really?" Jinatta straightened up with a wide-eyed look of hope.

98

"I think so. I remember the forest. I remember running with a boy and being overtaken by snakes."

"Snakes?" Jinatta shook her head. "We have no such thing on Moccobatra. There are no snakes. You must be remembering something from Earth."

"Oh, but it sounds so familiar…" She shrugged it off, unwilling to waste time over a bad dream. "Please, just go on."

"Alright. Well, the sad thing is, some people wanted Vaughndorin's sons locked away after your parents were killed, fearing they might take up their father's cause. But Gemdorin effectively put those concerns to rest. It took a while, but he convinced the council his father had acted alone and that none of his family had sympathy for his cause. Of course, he was lying. Once again our people were taken off guard. But a hero arose shortly after Gemdorin overthrew Harrowbeth. A few days following the initial attack, Derian took it upon himself to hunt down Gemdorin. People were shocked, to say the least. He was only thirteen years old at the time."

"Thirteen? That's so young!" Sevenah's face tangled up at the thought of a boy attempting such a daring feat.

"True, but he had something to prove."

"What? Why would he try to stop Gemdorin on his own?"

"He knew your mother well, and he was furious over all that had happened. His own mother died when he was quite young. Sha Tashi had stepped in, somewhat filling her shoes. He thought as much of her as he did his own mother. He hates Gemdorin and blames him for the destruction of his family and our society. Anyway, it's really Derian's place to tell you more."

"But wait! What happened next? What happened to Gemdorin?"

"Well, Derian nearly killed him that day, managing to bypass his guards and confront him face to face. He challenged Gemdorin to a sword fight, and as arrogant as the traitor is, he accepted, positive that Derian's age would prove him an ineffectual match. But Derian was always good with a blade. Gemdorin received a crippling wound in the fight and was almost defeated. Almost. When others learned of what Derian had done on his own, it gave our men the courage to take up arms and fight back. But Gemdorin and many of his followers managed to get away with help from a sneaky Mishmorat."

"A Mishmorat?"

"One of the species that co-exist on our planet. Anyway, when Gemdorin realized he was losing the battle, he and his followers commandeered one of our great battleships, much like the one we're on now. They left Moccobatra. Of course, their escape had been planned in advance."

"I'm sure," Sevenah agreed.

"After that, the council knew you were in danger so long as Gemdorin was free. They came up with a plan to hide you away until either he was caught, or you were old enough to assume your rightful position as Sha. Truthfully, everyone thought you would return years before now, but Gemdorin has managed to elude us in every confrontation. He doesn't fight fair, if there is such a thing. And he uses his powers of persuasion to convince armies from other worlds to stand with him. I'm sure he promises great rewards in return, which I guarantee they'll never see. We've faced more foes than I ever dreamt possible. Luckily, we've also made a few allies of our own out here. Derian has led us in countless battles in the Kemeniroc and has saved us from destruction more times than I care to count. He's a very good man, Eena. You'll see."

Sevenah pursed her lips into an uncertain frown, but didn't disagree. Perhaps everything their captain had been through gave him the right to be grouchy. She asked, "Why did the council choose to send me to Earth?"

"It was one of the few planets where they knew you would easily fit in and not be recognized for who you are. Of course, a thorough medical exam would show that your insides are not as human as your outside appears. For this reason the council sent people to watch over you and to intervene when necessary. You've had guardians keeping you safe and protected for the majority of your time on Earth. And…well……..you weren't the only girl planted there."

Jinatta rose from her seat. She began pacing as the next part of the story unfolded, flickering a periodic glance at Sevenah who was hungrily taking in every unbelievable word.

"What do you mean I wasn't the only one?"

"The council was afraid that if Gemdorin discovered the world on which you were hidden, he'd have no trouble tracking you down, considering you would be the only Harrowbethian child on the surface. So the council chose seven other girls about your same age to plant as decoys. All with red hair, and all taking on the name, Sevenah."

The news was shocking. "Their parents didn't object?"

"They weren't happy about it," Jinatta admitted, "but they weren't forced to comply either. Each family had a choice. In the end, they felt your safety was worth the sacrifice. They knew there would be guardians watching over their daughters as well. They also knew that once you returned to Harrowbeth, so would their daughters. Like I said before, no one ever dreamt this war would drag on for so many years."

Sevenah suddenly found it hard to breathe. The thought of such immense sacrifices for her sake was overwhelming.

"They should never have done that," she whispered. "What a stupid idea."

"Every family affected would disagree. You underestimate your importance to our world, Eena."

It was hard to imagine anyone being significant enough for parents to justify yielding up their daughters. Doubting eyes squinted to ask, "Why would one person matter so much to Harrowbeth?" But the doctor's sharing was cut short.

"Jinatta, are you busy?" The captain's voice carried over a knock on the wall.

"Derian! No, no, please come in." Jinatta hustled to meet her captain as he poked his head around the corner.

Sevenah was disappointed by the interruption, yet thankful to have learned so much about her home world and why all these strange things were happening. She focused on the floor while the doctor and captain talked. When a blood sample was drawn, Sevenah hardly felt the sting, absorbed by thoughts of Jinatta's story.

She couldn't wait to learn more about this Harrowbeth of Moccobatra.

CHAPTER SIX
Remember Yaka

The captain laid a firm hand on Jinatta's shoulder. "So, doctor, what's your diagnosis?"

"Overall, our patient appears to be in sound health. I found a tiny tracking device embedded beneath her skin, and there were a couple of hairline fractures along two fingers. Easy repairs."

Derian's jaw drew taut, mimicking a rigid rise throughout his frame. He turned to the young woman, questioning her directly. "How did you manage to break two fingers?"

Once again the man's presence heightened her anxiety. She stammered over a reply. "I uh, I guess it probably happened when I hit Dr. Braxton."

This news was clearly upsetting to the captain. "Tell me— why in the world were you hitting anyone?" The answer to his demand came from behind.

"It isn't like the creep didn't deserve it. She socked him a good one too, right in the jaw."

Sevenah's countenance brightened in the presence of her best friend who had followed Derian into the medical bay. The captain turned around to face her bright-eyed protector.

"So tell me, Ian, where were you when this happened? Where were the others?"

Sevenah cut in, wanting to defend her friend. "Rhoen was with me. I hit Dr. Braxton without thinking. He made me angry; it was an impulsive reaction. Really, it's no big deal, your doctor fixed everything."

"It *is* a big deal!" Derian barked. "My men were responsible for your protection!" A rigid finger aimed straight at her and then quickly turned on Ian. "This will *never* happen again!"

"None of this would've happened in the first place if you hadn't ordered us all to return to the ship! It's *your* fault she was left alone. If you had allowed me to stay with her, those despicable humans wouldn't have laid one hand on her!"

Derian's tone rose to match Ian's defensive outburst. "We

were preparing to bring her on board! It was necessary to organize our efforts, especially with Gemdorin's forces spotted in the area. You knew well in advance she would be alone for a few hours. *You* should've prepared for that, Ian. That's the problem with your family, none of you possess the capacity to think far enough ahead to take preventative measures!"

"Oh right, and what about your reputable bloodline? What's your excuse for…"

"Stop it! Just stop it!" Jinatta stepped between the two combatants, flashing them both a look of dismay. "When are you going to get past this? This quarrel is over fourteen years old— let it go! You need to….*we* need to work together. Now, find a way to get along or I'll sic Eena on the both of you."

Sevenah's eyes widened. What good would that do?

Their little display, though uncomfortable, was also enlightening. Apparently, a lasting grudge existed between both families. Derian obviously still blamed Ian's father for the deaths of Sha Tashi and Shen Laynn.

The men complied with Jinatta's wishes and dropped the issue; however, neither was willing to forgive. Derian insisted on reiterating his point.

"It will *not* happen again, Ian, understand?"

Ian replied through gritted teeth. "Yes…sir."

The captain turned his attention back to Sevenah, speaking to her with renewed courtesy. "Are you hungry? Tired?"

She held her stomach knowing she had adjusted to the hunger pains. Still, her thoughts were, "*Are you kidding? I haven't eaten for who knows how many days! I'm Famished! Ravenous! Starving!*" But, all she dared say was, "Yes…um, a little."

"Come on then, I'll get you some food." He motioned for her to follow him.

"Could I change first?" she asked, scooting down from the examining table. But he was already headed toward the exit.

"You're fine. A meal and a decent night's sleep will do you good."

Sevenah left her things behind in order to keep up with the captain, feeling awkward in only a thin medical gown. It was comfortable and all, but she preferred her jeans. Glancing back,

103

she raised a tentative brow at Jinatta who offered a smile of encouragement. It was a relief when Ian followed, a few steps behind. All three exited the medical bay and headed for the express elevator where the captain stopped to scan his hand for access. It created a lingering shadow of his handprint, exactly as Leisha's had.

It was dead silent on the lift. Tensions increased when Sevenah sighed audibly and Derian's harsh gaze flickered down at her for a moment. She considered holding her breath after that.

When the platform came to a full stop they entered a short hallway, gloomier under meager lighting than previous decks. The walls were cocoa, rough and neglected. Just around the corner, tucked snugly away in a lonely recess, stood an oversized door. The surface resembled rough, old mahogany—the wooden panels carved with detailed etchings of wild, unfamiliar creatures. Sevenah loved it at first sight. It reminded her of a slighter version of a castle's great entrance.

She noticed the absence of a fancy grip as would normally be found on such a door. Derian placed his hand flat against the surface, just above where no knob existed. Following another bright flash, his handprint lingered as a white aura on wood.

"Very cool," Sevenah breathed.

The door unlatched and swung inward, and the captain held the way open.

"Come inside."

Sevenah hesitated before stepping across the threshold, noticing how Ian took position standing guard in the corridor. It seemed strange this entry was more old-fashioned than other doors on the ship, not only in appearance but in function—being pushed open and shut rather than mechanically separating. She jumped at the heavy thud when it locked her inside.

"Have a seat over there."

The captain pointed to a square table at his right. It was small but bulky, constructed from a dense, red wood. Two chairs sat at opposite ends of the table. Sevenah reached for the nearest one and sat down. Her nerves were doing an adequate job of suppressing her appetite.

Glancing over the room, her eyes were drawn to a display of weaponry mounted from end to end clear across the back wall.

Swords, shields, daggers, hatchets, guns, odd-shaped lasers, and things unrecognizable hung in related clusters.

"Are all of those yours?" she asked, both in awe and a little leery of the precarious collection.

"Some are.   A few belonged to fallen comrades.   Others I acquired here and there.   We've made a lot of friends, and some enemies, in space."

Derian disappeared into an adjacent room, leaving Sevenah alone to survey his quarters.   Opposite the square table, two shabby chairs and a cushioned couch were arranged in a sociable cluster.   The extra-large seats appeared well worn, upholstered in a heavy, dark material.   A few frayed pillows and blankets draped across the furniture.   In the center of everything stood an old, flat-topped trunk that acted as a small table.   It was piled high with papers and scrolls, some resembling star charts.   An oddly-spotted fur rug supported all the pieces.

Derian emerged in a short time with two full dinner plates. He set one in front of Sevenah.   She recognized the food immediately: a red baked potato, sliced tomatoes, and a wheat roll.

"This is food from Earth," she said, surprised.

"Yes."   He handed over an eating utensil and then took the chair across from her.   "We replenished our food supply while we were there.   Provisions were running low.   It's not what my crew is used to, but it'll do."

She was more than happy to have familiar food to eat, and dug right in.   It was hard to keep from sighing sounds of relish over every mouthful.   After a few swallows, she realized just how starved she was.

Derian watched her eat, picking at his own plate.   When she finished, he left the room again and returned with two tall, slender glasses.   He handed her a drink.

"Something to wash it down."

"Thank you," she mumbled, swallowing the last bite of bread.

The captain reached to hold up his own hardly-touched plate in offer.   "Would you care for more?"

She politely declined.   "No, no thanks.   It was good, though. I can't remember how long it's been since I've eaten something."

"Sixty-eight days," he said for certain.   "You were held at that facility for sixty-eight days."

She was shocked. "I didn't realize......I've completely lost track of time."

"We're just glad to have you out alive."

Derian took a drink. He left his plate of food on the table near Sevenah and moved across from her, leaning with his back against the wall.

"I suppose you have some questions."

"A few," she nodded. Her eyes glanced at his abandoned plate, tempted. She was still a *little* hungry.

A dark eyebrow lifted as the captain asked, "What would you like to know?"

She decided to give in and take the untouched roll from his plate. Breaking off a piece of bread, she gave him her answer. "I want to know everything."

"Of course you do." His troubled gaze turned toward the ceiling. "Where to start?"

"I already heard about the war and how my parents died. I know about Gemdorin, and I know about the other girls hidden away on Earth. Did you find them all? You are taking them home, aren't you?"

Derian dropped his eyes to stare at her, shocked and displeased. Mostly displeased.

"Who told you all this?"

She had forgotten how Leisha and Jinatta both mentioned it was the captain's right to talk to her first. Now she feared her words might get the doctor in trouble.

"Oh, um…uh…" Her mind raced for an explanation that wouldn't anger him. Luckily, he didn't wait for one.

"I suppose it doesn't matter, you should know what happened. Did Jinatta tell you anything else about Gemdorin?"

It figures he already knew who spilled the beans. Perhaps he had overheard their conversation in the medical bay. Who knew how long he had been standing behind that wall? She tried to hide a sigh of relief, swallowing before saying anything more.

"Jinatta told me that Gemdorin was the son of Vaughndorin, the man who killed Shen Laynn and Sha Tashi, your king and queen. She said he's been difficult to hunt down."

"Far worse than difficult," Derian grumbled. His expression hardened while the heel of his boot kicked absentmindedly against

106

the wall.

"You mentioned earlier that Gemdorin's forces were spotted close by. Is that why you came to get me? Were you afraid he'd find me?"

"Actually, he's already found most of you."

"You mean the other seven girls?" Sevenah guessed.

Derian lifted an eyebrow again. "Jinatta told you that too?"

"Um.....sort of. She said something about the council feeling it would be more difficult to find Sha Eena if there were decoys from your world placed on the planet too. Is that right?"

"Yes, that's right, only it worked against us. You see, a little less than two years ago Gemdorin somehow found out our Sha was living on Earth. He went there prepared with a great number of battleships, mostly comprised of gliders from a world called, Hrenngen. Those are some vicious, ugly looking aliens." Derian scowled while speaking of the natives from that planet. "Gemdorin somehow convinced these creatures to fight his battles for him. I can only imagine what kind of empty promises were made for their loyalty." His heel continued stabbing at the wall as he went on.

"Anyway, the council had set a group of men and women to live on Earth and act as guardians for you and the other girls. The idea was for everyone to return home as soon as the war ended. No one foresaw things getting as bad as they have. Gemdorin attacked our orbiting mother ship. Everyone on the planet was recalled to fight, except for you girls of course. There were at least two dozen ships hidden on the planet and they all responded to battle against Gemdorin and the Ghengats."

"Ghengats?"

"Yes, those hideous allies of Gemdorin's." Derian pushed away from the wall and approached the table, setting down his empty glass. He stood over his eager listener while finishing the rest of his story.

"Almost every ship we had in the area was destroyed. There were just too many gliders and our people weren't prepared. There'd been no warning. One soldier managed to survive and get a message to Moccobatra. By the time I arrived with additional backup, our forces had been demolished and Gemdorin had begun his search for you."

Sevenah swallowed hard, learning how she had been hunted without knowing.

The captain went on. "Gemdorin located and captured five of our girls. Once the Kemeniroc arrived in the Sol System, I demanded he hand over every last young woman he was holding prisoner."

"And did he?" Sevenah held her breath awaiting an answer.

Derian replied in a heavy exhale. "Yes, he sent them all back. Dead."

She covered her mouth in horror. Her eyes watered at the thought. This was a nightmare! How could anyone do such a monstrous thing?

"We fought one of our most successful battles that day. We destroyed his mother ship and most of the Ghengats who fought with him. A few gliders escaped, but not many. To tell you the truth, I wasn't sure he survived. I thought just maybe... I even dared to hope, until recently; my lookouts say they've spotted him again."

Sevenah was hesitant to ask the next question, but needed to know the answer.

"What about the other two girls?"

He turned his back on her for a moment, returning to the wall. She got the feeling his answer wasn't going to be good news.

"Honestly, with most of your guardians killed in battle, it was impossible to know the exact locations of the three of you. All we knew for certain was that every girl went by the name, Sevenah, and that you all looked similar."

"That doesn't narrow it down much," she realized.

"No. But, there was a man who survived Gemdorin's attack. He was certain he knew the whereabouts of our Sha. In fact, he assured us his information was flawlessly reliable." Derian made the last comment with a hint of inexplicable anger behind the words. "This man told us you were in a country called the United States, positioned in their royal city. Our assumption was that the main capitol of the land had to be what you'd refer to as a royal city—anyone would assume that. And as luck would have it, we found one of our girls right there in Washington DC. Unfortunately, it turned out she was *not* Sha Eena."

Sevenah noted his bitter tone.

"This meant there were only two of you left who could possibly be our Sha.   And honestly, the likelihood seemed dismal. Most of us had begun to accept our queen as dead—murdered at Gemdorin's hands.   We contacted the council regarding the situation.   That's when we received word that Ian was hounding them, claiming he knew you were still alive.   He was so sure of it, the council allowed him to come look for you.   And he found you, in *Royal City*.   If we had known it was the name of a town, well…."   The captain's eyelids closed as he trailed off.

"We tracked down the final girl in a providence called Canada.   The council wasn't sure what to do with either of you. Ian insisted *you* were the real Sha Eena, but the council wanted proof.   We've been waiting for over a year for them to make a decision, afraid to interfere too much in your earthly routine.   Ian has been your guardian for the most part.   When word came that Gemdorin had been spotted again, the council voted to bring you home.   That was the same day you disappeared.   Heaven only knows how Ian tracked you down at that military facility.   I think you know of the rest of the story."

"You don't believe I'm Sha Eena."   She voiced the words boldly, sharing her observation.   His behavior, his despondent speech—it all seemed to convey a continued loss of hope.

"Ian says you are.   He knew exactly where to find you on both occasions.   I don't know how or why…..but he seems very sure about you."

"But you don't believe him.   As far as you know, the real Sha Eena could be dead, couldn't she?"   It was hard to read him, his stoic face unwilling to show emotion.

"I have no idea.   We all assumed that she…..you….were dead.   But now I…..I don't know."   He smiled feebly, and then went to clear the dishes.   Both plates were empty, thoroughly cleaned during their conversation.

"I have something for you." he said, changing the subject to a lighter tone.   "It's something I know you'll like."   He disappeared into the adjacent room with the dishes.   Half a minute later he reemerged with a treat.

"I've been told this is a cure-all for Earth women."

"Chocolate!   *Dark chocolate!*" she exclaimed, noticing the label.   "That's my favorite!   Thank you—how'd you know?"

She was smiling from ear to ear.

The captain actually chuckled. "Ian," he admitted.

Of course. Ian knew all her obsessions. She broke off a piece of the chocolate bar and placed it on her tongue, savoring its rich, bitter-sweet flavor. "Mmmmm."

The captain wrinkled his nose. "I don't know what you see in that stuff. It tastes awful to me." He ran a hand over his scalp while backing up to a door located behind the sofa. Stopping short of it, he made an announcement. "You can sleep in this room tonight. It's not anything special, but it's comfortable. I'll sleep out here on the couch."

"But……uh, aren't these your quarters?" Sevenah glanced around uneasily. "Isn't there another room for me?"

"I feel better having you nearby for the moment, given that Gemdorin's location is unknown. I don't want to scare you, but I think it's safer if Ian and I watch over you fairly closely."

"Well, okay," she conceded, but her uneasiness with the arrangement was obvious.

"Would you like to have Jinatta come sit with you until you fall asleep?"

She jumped at the opportunity to have the doctor continue her storytelling. "Yes, please." Jinatta seemed more willing to talk than anyone.

"Alright then, just let me grab something out of this room first."

The instant the rear door slid open, a monstrous-looking fur ball sprang out and jumped up on the captain's chest. On hind legs the animal stood near identical to the man's height. One sniff at the air turned the creature's attention onto Sevenah. The beast went right after her, bounding to the table on lion-like paws. She screamed and scrambled to the top of her chair.

The animal had a body shaped something like an earthly buffalo—a bulky chest, heavily-hunched shoulders, a thick neck— but on a smaller scale. The frightened girl screamed again, climbing onto the tabletop just as the hairy creature perched its front paws on her empty chair. It stretched its neck to examine her.

With nose in the air, it made a loud, awful howl. "*Hhhrrroowwww!*"

Dark eyes as big as saucers stared up from a face that was nothing but a thick mass of fur. The same long hair draped over the creature's entire body, patched in browns and ivory with shadows of black and maroon. From the top of its head protruded two tiny horns positioned behind ears that spiked rigid with every curious sound. An oversized mouth spanned the width of its face, baring a lion's share of sharp teeth. The creature howled once again and then scrambled after its target, following her right onto the table.

"Help me!" Sevenah screamed, jumping down and dashing toward the captain. She escaped just as the hairy beast took over her abandoned spot. Luckily, her discarded candy bar provided a momentary distraction. One sniff had the animal turning up its nose.

By this time Sevenah had taken cover behind Derian. That's when she realized……he was laughing!

"What is that thing?" she shrieked. "And stop laughing; this is *not* funny!"

"It's okay, it's okay," he chuckled, struggling to suppress his amusement. "The animal's tame. This is Yaka. Yaka, meet Eena."

The creature howled again and then jumped off the table to approach his master. Sevenah clung to the captain's shirt.

"Help me!" she demanded, pressing herself against his back.

Derian tried to assure her she was in no danger. "Think of him as an earth dog, only bigger and harmless. That is if he likes you."

"I hate dogs—keep that thing away from me!"

The captain laughed again. Yaka was trying his best to squeeze a wet nose in between his master's legs, hoping to give the girl a proper welcome. The animal was whimpering, frustrated. Derian turned around slowly, careful not to let Yaka get past. He scooped Sevenah up in his strong arms, holding her well above the perceived threat.

"Better?" he asked.

"Make him stop!" she demanded.

"Yaka, kahei nrahk!"

The animal immediately set his rear on the floor. He sat perfectly still, except for what appeared to be a short, hairy tail that wagged wildly behind him. Derian placed Sevenah on her bare feet facing the creature. She clung to his arm, untrusting.

"Yaka, nrahk," he repeated, making sure the animal would stay. "Eena, this is Yaka."

"Hi," she peeped, giving a tiny wave with her free hand.

"You don't remember him?"

She glanced uncertainly at the captain, and then returned her wary gaze to the oversized beast. "No. Should I?"

"I'd hoped you would," he admitted a little disappointedly.

"Derian, I don't remember anything from Harrowbeth. And I certainly don't recall ever meeting any animal as unusual as Wanyaka."

The captain was stunned. "What did you just say? What did you call him?"

"Wanyaka," she repeated, still afraid to take her eyes off the animal. "Isn't that its name?"

"Yes, but…..that's not what I told you. I said his name was Yaka. He was your mother's and she named him Wanyaka, but you were so young you couldn't pronounce the name, so *you* called him Yaka. He's been called by that nickname ever since."

Sevenah's eyebrows wove tightly together. Just then there was a loud knock at the door. Derian went to answer it, his wary guest clinging to his arm.

Ian stood in the doorway looking them both over. "Is everything alright? I heard screams."

"Everything's fine. She just met Yaka. She *remembered* his name."

"Really?" Ian entered the room. He approached the animal, greeting Yaka with a welcomed ear scratch.

"I don't know," Sevenah said. "I don't remember him at all."

"Ian, why don't you sit with her while I go get Jinatta." Derian stepped through the doorway and then turned back.

Ian gave him a questioning look.

"Jinatta's going to stay with her," the captain explained, "until she falls asleep."

"Sure," Ian agreed. He continued scratching Yaka's ears.

Even though she was more relaxed in her best friend's company, Sevenah still wasn't willing to take a chance on being

mauled by on overgrown fur ball.   She made her way to the
furthest chair in the sitting area and sat on the high back, watching
how Ian continued to spoil Derian's pet.   The animal appeared to
be in heaven.

"Ian," she finally said, "I'm glad we have a moment alone.   I
wanted to talk to you.   I…I owe you an apology."

He shook his head.   "No you don't.   You owe me nothing."
Yaka followed Ian to the sofa and sat down at his feet.

"I was much too hard on you back on the ship.   I was
confused and upset.   I mean, you're my very best friend and
I…well…..I just didn't realize how difficult things have been for
you too.   Expecting you to go against your captain and an entire
council…..I can see now it would be asking a lot.   I understand
why you didn't tell me anything."

Ian flashed his usual, warm smile.   "I wanted to tell you.
I've fought to bring you home from the very beginning, but the
council disagreed with me.   I had my orders, Eena, and if I had
disobeyed, they might've sent me home.   I couldn't take a chance
on that happening.   Protecting you is my life—it always will be."

She wasn't sure what to say; his words were overwhelming.
All she really wanted from him was his friendship, but she felt
immense gratitude for the loyalty and dedication he had sworn to
her.   She felt ashamed for questioning his actions earlier.

"I just want you to know I'm sorry."

"No need to be."

Feeling more comfortable with her relative safety now that
Yaka had been lulled into snoring at Ian's feet, she moved down
from her high seat and scooted to the cushion's edge.   Her eyes
considered a pile of papers lying on the chest between them.   She
commented on it.

"Derian sure has a lot of paperwork."

"It's not paperwork.   These are galactic diagrams: maps, star
charts, other things like that.   Most are antiques worth a fortune to
the right buyer.   He's really into old relics and lost treasures.   He
looks over them a lot.   Sometimes I think he's trying to hunt
down Gemdorin.   Other times, I wonder if he's just searching for
a place to run and hide."

She dared a more personal question.   "Ian, why don't the two
of you get along?"

113

Ian made a scoffing sound and rolled his eyes. "Like any sane person can get along with him; he's an unreasonable, demanding brute! Derian expects far too much from everyone, and if he holds anything against you at all he expects absolute perfection! He can't even give that himself." Ian sneered distastefully while shaking his head. "That jerk was so angry with the council for sending me here aboard *his* ship. If I had been here earlier, you would already be home—safe and sound."

"But…" she started.

"No, it's true! He blames my father for not protecting your mother, and he blames me for your disappearance when the truth is, all of this is more *his* fault than anybody's!"

Ian cut himself off abruptly, a look of regret in his eyes.

"Sorry," he uttered, quickly calming down. "No, we obviously don't get along. But he is the captain of this ship, and for *your* sake I'll do my best to work with him."

Sevenah wondered about his slip of the tongue. Why did he feel Derian was so much at fault? She wanted to know more but didn't dare ask; Ian was upset enough already. She watched her best friend quietly scratch behind Yaka's ears. Every muscle in her body felt tired, yet not half as exhausted as her mind. Resting her head against the arm of the chair, she let her eyelids fall closed. The next thing she knew, the world had distorted—transformed into shaded woodland. It was her recurring nightmare….

She was five again, her hair long and braided, tied back with a pink ribbon. Her big eyes shifted about, fearful. She longed for her mother who was nowhere to be found. A young boy stood beside her, maybe ten or eleven years of age. They had entered the forest together fleeing something or someone. He had brought her here by himself. Just the two of them. She trusted him. Her gaze lifted to see his face, as it had in many repeats of this dream, but this time he wasn't a blur of features. His expression was clearly worried—his face entirely familiar.

"Ian?" The boy in the woods—it was Ian!

Voices echoed off the trees from close by. Ian reacted immediately, grabbing her hand and tearing deeper into the woods. They traveled swiftly, as fast as she could run, but she tired within minutes being so young. She begged for a moment's rest.   Ian allowed her to sit while he backtracked to check on their pursuers.

Trees surrounded her—tall, dense, and crooked.   They seemed to crowd from all sides.   Their branches hung low like huge, arthritic claws that swayed in the wind, appearing to reach for her.

That's when the snakes came.   They rose from the ground, as usual, but on this occasion they were void of facial features—no eyes, no mouth, no hissing tongue.   They burrowed up from the soil, faceless!   What were they?   As the threat slithered toward her, she cried out in fear.

"Mommy!   Mommy!"

She struggled futilely against them, her legs wrapped and constrained.   Her arms flailed, fighting to stay free of the faceless snakes.

"Mommy!   Mommy!"

Only Ian responded to her cries.   She reached for his offered hand, feeling his fingers grip tightly around her own.

"Eena!" he called as snakes coiled around his legs as well. "Eena!"

Sevenah woke in a cold sweat, her pulse a frantic thundering. She was blind, caught in a silent, pitch-black environment.   For a second, she imagined Dr. Braxton waiting to harm her.   Quickly, she brought her hands to her face and realized they weren't constrained.   The bed was soft and wide.   She could feel heavy, thick blankets layered overtop her legs.   Then she remembered this was Derian's room.   She was safe.

A light snore caught her ear and she reached in the darkness, finding Yaka asleep beside her.   His coat felt warm and silky soft. Her fingers combed through the fur—an act of comfort for herself.

As soon as her anxieties calmed, she drifted off to more pleasant dreams.

115

CHAPTER SEVEN
The Necklace

Four crew members sat together in the captain's quarters formulating a plan for the morning, which was shortly to arrive. Leisha rested on a dark couch, hugging a throw pillow to her chest. Jinatta sat beside her with arms folded. Across from the women, Ian slouched on the edge of a chair with his elbows on his kneecaps. Derian stood in the midst of them all, holding a weathered, wooden box about half the size of a briefcase. It was beautifully decorated with intricate, detailed carvings. He cradled it in one arm like a newborn.

"Tomorrow the necklace comes out," he said in a hushed voice. He wanted to be sure the occupant asleep in the next room didn't overhear their conversation. The captain held up the wooden box, suggesting the necklace he referred to was inside. Then he placed it on the flat-topped trunk used as a table, now cleared of its previous clutter.

"Have you told her anything about it?" Jinatta asked. "She has a right to know the risks before you put it on her."

Derian's reply was emphatic. "No, and I don't intend to. Our world and our people are depending on this; it must be done. I can't give her a choice."

"What about the last time?" the doctor worried. Her eyes, filled with fret, locked onto his. "What if we're repeating the same mistake? Derian, I can't live through that again."

"If Ian's right, you won't have to."

Every head turned toward their slouching friend. He straightened up at the attention, glancing from one troubled face to the next. His wide eyes came to rest on the captain's dour stare.

"I *am* right. She *is* Sha Eena. Everything will be fine, you'll see."

No one appeared convinced.

"You'd *better* be right," Derian grumbled lowly, "because if anything happens to that girl, I swear I'll kill you myself."

"Derian!" Leisha gasped. The pillow in her lap hit the couch.

Regardless of old grudges, threatening Ian's life was crossing the line.

Ian immediately rose from his chair, pointing an accusatory finger at the captain. "*You* killed the other girl, not me! Had I been there, that tragedy never would've happened! If you and that cursed council would just let me do my job…"

"That's enough!" Leisha was fast to put herself between both men, one palm pressed against each challenger's chest. "If you don't keep it down, she'll certainly hear you."

They backed off, and Leisha continued in a cool manner. "Now look, there's nothing we can do about what happened last time. There was no way to know we hadn't retrieved the real heir, nor could we have anticipated fatal consequences. Ian, it's not Derian's fault you weren't here. The council agreed you were too young to accompany Sha Eena on Earth and were better off remaining in Harrowbeth."

"But you could have called on me when Gemdorin killed the others," Ian argued. "I would have found her right off; I told the council that."

Leisha looked doubtful. "You'd been separated from her for years. Why do you feel your chances were any better than ours?"

"Because I know her," he insisted.

"Better than the guardians who watched her grow up?"

Ian didn't respond. His eyes hinted at a desire to explain, but he took his seat, defeated by his own refusal to speak.

Leisha went on. "We had every reason to trust the man who survived Gemdorin's attack. He insisted he could recognize our queen. He'd been entrusted with that information as a guardian, so there was absolutely no reason to doubt him."

"But he was wrong," Jinatta broke in gravely, "and his mistake cost a life." The doctor's voice quivered, reminding them of the senseless death three had witnessed. "That poor girl died on the table—under *my* care in *my* medical bay. I couldn't help her. I tried, but I couldn't get it off of her."

Derian took a seat beside the doctor. His hand rubbed gently on her shoulder. "It wasn't your fault. You did everything you could."

"It was *no one's* fault," Leisha proclaimed. "It was just a mistake. A dreadful mistake. One I don't care to repeat." She cast a severe glance at Ian, causing him to reiterate his claim.

"She is Eena, I *know* it.   I would recognize her thirty years from now or even a hundred years from now.   I know her better than I know myself."   His last remark was mumbled aside.

"I want to believe you, Ian, really I do.   But how can you be so sure?   Despite all the lab tests Jinatta has run, there's still nothing to prove she's any different from the rest of us.   No solid evidence points to her being Sha Eena."

Jinatta supported Leisha's objection.   "I thought the Shas possessed a variation in their chemistry—an aberration passed down from their mothers to make them strong enough to withstand the severity of the necklace.   I've searched and tested and analyzed every sample, and there's nothing!"   Jinatta's palms turned upward, conveying her doubt.   "There's supposed to be something unique about her, right?"

"Yes," Ian agreed.

"Then where is it?   What is it?"

"I really don't know," he muttered.

"If only we had a DNA sample from her mother, it would make this easier."   Jinatta shook her head regretfully.   Then she implored the captain.   "Derian, please let me do a few more tests before you go through with this.   Another blood panel, perhaps. I must've missed something—a tiny detail."

"And I'll help her," Leisha volunteered.   "Between the two of us we may find it."

The captain granted their request.   "You've got until tomorrow afternoon and then the necklace comes out.   I want it on her before we encounter Gemdorin again.   I know he's close; there have been reports of gliders very near us.   This necklace offers her greater protection than we can."   He inhaled deeply, and then exhaled with an adamant declaration.   "No one else is to know about this.   You will all be present, and you will not discuss it with anyone.   Have I made myself clear?"

"Yes, sir," Leisha and Ian chimed in unison.

The doctor wasn't quite satisfied.   "Even with the necklace, Gemdorin can kill her."

"I know," the captain admitted, "but she stands a far better chance of survival with it than without it."

"Derian, I still feel you should tell her first.   She has a right

118

to know the truth."

"No! That's my final decision. If I were to inform her that the last girl died wearing this thing, do you think we'd ever get her to put it on? Not likely. If she *is* Sha Eena, as Ian insists, then it's imperative she wear this necklace. We need the powers it offers our world. Otherwise, Moccobatra will continue to die. And if it turns out she's not Sha Eena—" Derian cast a narrow glance at Ian while finishing his statement. "—then our world will die right along with her."

Ian stuck with his claim. "She *is* Eena."

They hoped very much he was right.

All but Derian left the room. Ian didn't go far, settling in a chair situated outside the captain's quarters.

"You ought to go get some sleep," Jinatta told him as she and Leisha stepped past.

"I'm fine here," he mumbled. The captain wouldn't allow him a direct watch over Eena, but he was determined to stay as close as possible. He would manage well enough in the armchair.

"Suit yourself," Jinatta shrugged. She stepped onto the elevator behind Leisha and disappeared.

Eight decks down, the two women headed for the medical bay where they would likely spend the night. They had only hours to find what they were searching for. Not wanting to waste time, they began retesting blood and tissue samples taken from their subject earlier in the day.

Back on the empty lift, a strange thing was happening. A button on the control panel engaged independently, causing the platform to descend without any occupants. When the doors parted, allowing access into the docking bay, the compartment appeared empty.

Not so.

A familiar figure materialized inside the elevator, appearing from out of nowhere. Rhoen tapped on a gold band encircling his wrist, a clever device that when activated gave him the ability to stand invisible. He had been an uninvited guest to the captain's secret meeting, entering and exiting sight unseen. It was something he had done many times before. Now he knew exactly what they were planning.

Rhoen peeked into the hangar, checking to be sure he was

119

alone.   Satisfied there was no one else present, he hustled to the furthest corner of the bay and climbed into one of hundreds of similar battle cruisers.   He reached down alongside the furthest passenger seat where a tiny communications device was tucked away—a perfect hiding place.   This undersized ship didn't see enough activity to worry about someone finding it.   The device was small enough to sit in the palm of his hand, but he placed it on the counter before pressing the surface to activate it.   Then he quietly spoke in his native tongue.

"Setta Nii keeahma,"

Hearing no immediate response, he repeated the message. "Private One reporting."

Again he received no reply.   A third attempt, "This is Private One.   I have new information."

Continued silence.

At last, a deep, strong voice sounded from the device.   "Go ahead."

"They have the necklace.   Derian plans to put it on her tomorrow."

"Are you certain?" the voice asked.   Authority resonated in those three short words.   The tone alone was formidable.

"Yes, Kahm Gemdorin, I am certain," Rhoen replied.   "Ian believes she is Sha Eena.   The others aren't convinced, yet Derian has ordered them to go ahead with the joining."

Rhoen held his fists tight against his stomach.   He was anxious, even without the owner of the voice physically present.

"Then tomorrow we shall see if Ian is correct.   Either way......tomorrow she dies."

Gemdorin's statement caused an immediate reaction in his spy.   Rhoen's eyes enlarged—his unseen expression one of trepidation.   He was guilty of spying for the enemy, that was undeniable, but he had no desire to see their Sha killed.

Rhoen dared to protest.   "But, sir!   If she dies, our world will die with her!"

"It's already dead!" Gemdorin growled over the com. "Derian destroyed your world the day he chose to rebel against me!"

"But, sir," Rhoen hesitated, "I mean....well, sir....why not take advantage of a rare opportunity to control the necklace?

She's been gone so long, she knows nothing about our world. Convince her to join you; she would be easily influenced. That kind of power must be worth prolonging her life!"

There was a long, silent pause.

Rhoen's knuckles paled, waiting. A nervous sweat dripped from his forehead.

"Sir?" he uttered, wondering if his words had had any persuasive effect.

"Maybe there *is* a more satisfying revenge than the death of Derian's precious queen. It would be a just reward for him to cower in defeat as his beloved Sha Eena stood loyally at my side, fighting for *my* cause, her powers at *my* command. That would crush him. Perhaps she could serve me alive—for a while."

"Yes, sir. Right, sir," Rhoen agreed, trying to hide any sound of relief. He was mildly comforted.

At the end of their conversation Rhoen hid the evidence of his treachery. He hurried from the hangar, but not before retrieving a palm-sized metal disk from the pocket of his uniform. He pressed gently on the top, switching on a miniature hologram. It was a tender image of a woman cradling a tiny baby in her arms. A young boy hugged tight to her leg. The child looked up adoringly at his mother while the lovely woman smiled at Rhoen in the same manner. He stared at the image with sad eyes and then tapped it off, returning the disk to his pocket. Using the gold wristband, he made his way out undetected.

Sevenah awoke to a dimly-lit room. She was happy to be snug and warm beneath two layers of heavy blankets, unable to remember the last time she had felt so rested. A blur of sideline movement made her twist her neck to look. Lounging comfortably against the high back of a mahogany sitting chair was her best friend. When their eyes met, Ian smiled warmly.

"Good morning, sleepyhead."

"Good morning, Ian. How long have you been here?"

"Not that long."

She yawned, stretching her arms toward the ceiling. Rolling to the side, she pushed herself into a sitting position and scooted back against a magnificent wooden headboard.

"I assume this is still Derian's quarters. He sure has a taste for old, dark things, doesn't he?" Her eyes roamed the room, observing a pair of brown lampshades, a heavy sable comforter, and several items of furniture fashioned out of umber wood. On the wall hung a huge poster-photograph of a galaxy, complete with charted stars and planets. A large portion of the poster was black space which made the already dim room appear even gloomier.

"It fits him," Ian remarked in a low grumble. "Are you ready to get up?"

"Oh, do I have to?" She snuggled her pillow and sighed contentedly. "It feels so good to lie in a real bed."

"I have my orders. Jinatta wants to see you again in the medical bay."

"Ugh, not again." Sevenah made a miserable face. "I thought I was done with doctors. Jinatta said I was in good health yesterday. Why do I have to go back there?"

Ian shrugged cluelessly. "I have my orders."

"Fine," she groaned, knowing he wouldn't let her get out of it. After scooting to the edge of the mattress, she slid from beneath the covers onto the floor. "Would it be okay if I freshened up first?"

"In there." Ian pointed to a back room.

She was eager to clean up. Along with eating a real meal and sleeping in a real bed, taking a real bath was another thing she hadn't done in the past two months of confinement. Even if it forced the entire ship to wait, she was determined to relax in a tub for a while. After entering the small restroom, however, first observation told her things were set up a little differently.

Ian heard the door reopen. He glanced up to find Sevenah's head peeking out, embarrassment rouging her cheeks.

"Um......I'm not really sure how things work in here."

He grinned and pushed himself up from his sitting chair. "Don't worry, my lady. I'm here to rescue you."

She feigned a swoon. "Oh, a hero! Thank heavens!"

Ian gave a quick demonstration on how to start up the ionic liquids meant for cleaning hair and skin. He showed her how to activate a wall of heating elements that warmed a gentle breezeway for drying off. Most things required the simple push of a button and knowledge of which button to push. He singled out cleaners meant for teeth, for skin, for the face, or not to be used at all.

122

Given her unfamiliarity with their written characters, it was impossible to recognize labels.

"Don't you have a mirror somewhere?" she asked, wanting to see for herself how poorly the last couple months had treated her. There were no reflective surfaces anywhere.

"Sorry, no mirrors. But you can use this."

Ian picked up a small round item that resembled a shrunken version of a ladies compact case. He pressed its top center and then attached the device to his shirt. As soon as he did so, a life-sized hologram appeared—the mirror image of himself staring back with the same twinkling green eyes.

"What do you think?" he asked.

Sevenah's mouth fell wide open. "Can I have one of those?"

"Sure you can," he chuckled. "It creates an exact copy of anything you touch too. See?" He picked up a hairbrush to demonstrate. As he did so, the same brush appeared in his hologram's hand.

"And of course your image moves as you move." He demonstrated this with a slight finger wave.

"Thank you, Ian, I think I can handle it from here." Her open palm waited, requesting the hologramming gadget. Then she opened the door, communicating he could leave.

"Okay, okay, but be quick. They're expecting you in the medical bay soon."

She groaned and all but shoved him out, locking herself inside.

It was shocking when she finally saw her mirror image. Lack of food had thinned an already slender frame. There was no bath in the captain's quarters—not exactly surprising; he didn't strike her as a man of luxuries. The ionic shower proved a pleasurable substitute. Sevenah melted under its caressing liquid for a long while. When she finished washing, another stretch of time was spent standing before the heating elements, letting a mild breeze dry her. With eyes closed, it was easy to imagine the warm winds of a hot desert rushing past her skin, reminding her of home.

Once her hair was free of moisture, she ran a brush through the red strands. This wonderful clean feeling was long overdue. Refreshed and invigorated, she redressed in the same white gown from the previous day.   It was the only piece of clothing available at the moment, which was one good reason to return to the medical bay, if only to recover her own clothes.   Glancing one last time at her hologram image, she wished for a little color to paint her eyes and lips.

"Oh well," she sighed.   "Good enough."

She went to step into the bedroom but halted abruptly.   Ian was gone.   In his place stood the intimidating Kahm Derian.   With arms folded across his chest, he appeared more annoyed than he had at their first meeting.

"One more squandered minute and I would've come in and dragged you out," he informed her crossly.   "People are waiting."

She dared to point out his lack of consideration.   "Yes, I do feel much better, thank you."

Her remark didn't faze him.   "Let's go," he ordered, turning to leave.   He made it all the way to the front door before realizing she wasn't at his back.   *"I said, let's go!"* he hollered across the room.

She stood in the bedroom doorway, feet planted apart.   "I heard you, but I'm not ready yet."

"Oh yes you are!"   He started toward her like a bull, as if he would toss her over a shoulder and haul her to the medical bay.

She backed up in response to his heated approach.   "Stop it! You don't have to be so mean!"

That effectively halted his steps.   "I am not being mean!" he snapped, refusing her assessment of his behavior.   With resentment in his face, he lectured the young woman, speaking to her like a stubborn child bent on compromising the functional arrangement and stability of his ship.

"You don't seem to grasp how vitally important it is for people to follow orders around here!   This is *not* a game, Eena! I know you're new here, but you need to get it through your head that when I give someone an order, I expect it to be obeyed!   If you fail to follow commands, people get killed; do you understand that?"   His face had progressively moved closer until their noses were practically touching.

She uttered a quiet surrender.   "Yes....sir."

The captain swiveled about and returned to the front door, opening it with a motion for her to exit the room.   He followed her out. Sevenah vowed to think twice before challenging the man again.

They made their way to the medical bay in uncomfortable silence. Along the way, the same artistic images from the previous day danced across corridor walls. Most of the paintings were of natural settings—meadows and forests and picturesque skies. These beautiful images were heartening. Sevenah yearned to stop and study them more closely, but as swiftly as the captain was moving, only a brief glimpse at each scene was possible. Before long, they were standing outside the familiar red-striped doors.

Derian earned admittance by placing his hand over the mounted security box. It flashed bright, recognizing him. Sevenah wondered what would happen if she placed her own hand in the same spot, imagining sirens alerting the ship to an intruder attempting to maneuver between rooms. Wouldn't the captain just love that!

As soon as they entered the medical bay, Jinatta hustled over to meet them.

"Eena!" she exclaimed. "Finally!" The doctor looked at Derian with accusing eyes, turning up her palms as if to ask, "Where in the world have you been?"

He responded to her gesture sarcastically. "She wasn't ready yet." And with that snide remark he left the bay.

From their small interaction, Sevenah got the impression she had held up something pressing.

"Is everything okay?" she asked warily.

"Oh, yes, yes….of course," Jinatta replied. She led her patient to the rear room where they found Leisha busily jotting down notes, observing slides under extreme magnification.

"Oh good, you're here," Leisha sighed with relief. "Come, come, sit down."

Sevenah did as instructed, but wondered about their urgent behavior. She fished for an explanation.

"I thought you said I was fine yesterday."

The doctor stopped what she was doing, realizing her haste had given a bad impression. She and Leisha were tired from lack of sleep. They were discouraged, having spent all night repeating tests without any conclusive results. Jinatta had hoped to have her subject in the medical bay earlier, feeling a sense of urgency now that the morning hours had arrived. She forced herself to slow down in order to ease apprehensions.

"I'm sorry," she said, forcing a smile. "We've been very busy. Really, you are fine. It's just that yesterday I only had time for preliminary tests. Leisha and I would like to run a few detailed scans to make sure all's well on a cellular level too. We don't expect to find anything wrong, but it's good to be thorough." She patted her patient's hand and then proceeded to get to work.

Sevenah didn't buy the doctor's story, but she didn't question it either. Chances were she had no choice in the matter anyway. But why the rush if they were simply running additional tests? It made no sense. Her accommodating and patient nature prevented her from saying anything.

The exam began with non-intrusive scans. Jinatta and Leisha worked nonstop into the afternoon. They repeated tests on a fresh draw of blood, sampling tissues and bodily fluids, performing comparison assessments. They shot chemicals into the girl's bloodstream and required her to lie still while recording images of internal organs. They worked as quickly and as efficiently as two very good medical professionals could, and still they found nothing significant.

By late afternoon they were exhausted and had resorted to arguing in Jinatta's office over trivial differences. Sevenah listened to their conversation, not understanding a word of the foreign language, yet recognizing stark disharmony as the discussion grew progressively louder. A sense of helplessness began to gnaw at her insides, churning an empty stomach. She was growing desperate for an explanation as to what was really going on.

It was Dr. Tracy's office all over again.

Cross-legged on the exam table, Sevenah lowered her face into her hands. The tears spilt, unpreventable. Now more than ever she longed for home. Her entire being ached for the only safe haven she had ever known—back on Earth.

Sorrow swept through her like an arctic front, making her shiver and curl up. The grief was overwhelming. Her thoughts turned to her parents back on the farm. She couldn't help but weep for the loss of her family. Worse was imagining their heartache over her disappearance.   Silent tears rained at first until the sobbing grew audible and uncontrollable.   Absorbed by emotion, she forgot about everything else.

The argument taking place nearby halted when Jinatta and Leisha realized what they were overhearing.   Both turned to view their patient through the office window—curled up, back quivering.   They ran to her side.   Jinatta tried to comfort the girl.

"Eena, it's alright.   You're alright."

"No!" she cried, "no, I'm not!   I'm not Eena!   Don't call me that!"   All the bottled-up pain and frustration erupted, targeted on her would-be comforters.   She wiped the tears from her eyes and jumped off the table, retreating against the nearest wall.

She screamed her assertion for all ears to hear.   *"My name is Sevenah!   I'm Sevenah Williams!   I know who I am, and I am not Eena!"*

Holding her hands up as a signal to stay away, she laid into them.

"I'm not doing this anymore!   You think I'm stupid, but I'm not!   I know you're lying to me!   You're looking for something; you have been all day!   But you can't find it, can you?   You're trying to prove that I'm Eena, but I'm not!   I'm not her and *I don't want to be her!*   I'm Sevenah, and I want to go home!   I want to go back home where I belong—back to Earth where I know who I am!"

Her eyes pleaded as strongly as her words.   "Have you any idea what it feels like to lose your identity?   To lose your home, your life, your entire family?   I want to go back.   Please, please can't you take me back home?"

Her hands moved to cover her mouth, and she wept.   Jinatta and Leisha approached with caution.   When she didn't fight them, they wrapped her up in consoling arms.

"We're so sorry," Jinatta apologized.   "Please come sit down."

"I'm getting Derian," Leisha declared.

Jinatta stopped her.   "Don't.   She just needs to get it out. Derian won't tell her the truth anyway."

"Jinatta!"   But it wasn't Leisha's scolding voice.   It was the captain's.   He had entered the medical bay soon enough to catch the last half of Sevenah's desperate speech.   No one had

127

seen him listening from the other side of the partitioning wall.

Jinatta glanced at the man with unapologetic eyes before returning her focus on the crying young woman. "It's going to be alright," she reassured her.

When offered a hug, Sevenah held on tight, wishing it was her mother calming her fears. She embraced the doctor for a long time while Leisha rubbed her back.

Derian stood by, silently watching.

"You okay?" Jinatta asked when Sevenah finally slackened her hold.

"No." It was an honest response.

The doctor tried another question. "Are you hungry?"

Sevenah nodded, having eaten nothing all day.

"Well, I can do something about that."

Jinatta disappeared into her office while Leisha remained as a support. Derian approached the bedside and placed an old wooden box on the edge. He kept his hand on it.

"Your mother was a strong woman," the captain began. "I can tell you've inherited that same quality."

Sevenah squinted at him, her eyes red from crying. For a moment she thought he was being his usual mean self, but his face seemed to be in earnest.

He continued, "I don't think any member of my crew could handle what you've been forced to endure with the same patience and long-suffering. I'm surprised you didn't put us in our place sooner."

She said nothing, but felt better about his initial comment.

Jinatta emerged with an armful of apples and offered one to Sevenah. All three women took an apple. Derian declined. They ate quietly, no one really knowing what to say. Sevenah eventually broke the silence.

"I'm sorry. I didn't mean to scream at you."

"No, no, please don't be sorry," Leisha insisted. "You have nothing to be sorry about. I agree with Derian completely; it's impressive how well you've handled all of this up to now. I would've lost it a long time ago."

"You don't believe I'm Eena, do you?" Now that they felt some sympathy for her, she was hoping the truth might be more forthcoming.

Derian answered the question. "Ian says you are."

"But you don't believe him, do you?" Her eyes scrunched, seeking honesty.

"Yes, I do believe him." Everyone looked surprised by the captain's words.

"Then why all of this testing?"

The doctor jumped in to explain. "Leisha and I were the ones who wanted to do this. I just have a hard time understanding how Ian can be so sure it's you after years and years of absence."

"But Derian's right," Leisha cut in. She spoke as if making up everyone's mind on the matter. "We should have faith in Ian. If he's sure, then he's sure. He would never put your life in danger; he cares far too much for you."

"Whoa, wait—" Leisha's words were seriously troubling. "How would he be putting my life in danger?"

Leisha looked to her captain who sighed resignedly and then started in with the truth.

"Gemdorin has been spotted nearby. Actually, his allies, the Ghengats, have been sighted numerous times. And wherever they are, Gemdorin isn't far behind. We've been altering our course to try and avoid them, but our scouts keep sighting their ships. Eena, he's looking for you."

"But what if I'm not really Eena? What if it's the other girl?"

"She's being highly guarded as well; however, Ian is adamant that you're our Sha, and so you're the one we're desperate to protect. Our world's future depends on you."

She didn't say a word. She didn't want this calling or the immense pressure that came with it.

"This belonged to your mother." Derian handed over the wooden box. He placed it in her lap.

She looked at him and then down at the pretty lid. Moving her fingers across it, she felt at the intricate carvings covering every side. She hesitated opening it.

"Eena, only you can wear this."

She slipped her finger under the latch when Jinatta exclaimed, "Wait! Ian's not here."

"Where the criminy is he?" Derian hissed, clearly irritated.

"I'll go get him." The doctor hustled around the corner.

Sevenah held onto each side of the box and questioned its contents. She wanted to know what was inside before looking.

"It's your mother's necklace. This heirloom has been handed down from Sha to Sha for centuries. It's meant only for the next in line, the eldest daughter of the previous Sha. That would be you."

She stared at the lid for a few moments, contemplating the weight of accepting this valuable treasure. Then she handed the container back to him. "I don't want it."

"But it's yours," Derian said, refusing the box.

"I don't care. I don't want it."

"It's yours nonetheless." It wasn't the captain's voice, but Ian's soft words that time. He appeared from around the wall, having been out in the corridor waiting.

"I don't want it, Ian," she repeated. "I can't do this."

"There's no choice in the matter," Derian said.

Ian stepped in front of Sevenah and placed his hands over hers, setting the box back down in her lap.

"I don't want it," she insisted in a whisper. "I can't be anyone's queen; I don't have it in me, Ian."

He responded to her in the same quiet voice, as gentle and sincere as their friendship. "Yes, you do. You're naturally perfect for the job. You *are* Sha Eena. It's your calling; no one else *can* do it." His warm hands fixed her fingers securely to the container, making her grasp her fate.

"No, Ian, I'm not strong enough. I can't…..I *can't* do this." Her tone grew more desperate as she argued. "I'm not brave or wise or experienced or anything a queen should be. I'm not ready for this."

She tried to push the burden away, but Ian wouldn't allow it. He kept their eyes locked and talked her gently through her fears.

"You are everything we need in a queen, Eena. You're compassionate. You're patient, kind, and sincere. You genuinely care about people and give so much of yourself to make others happy. I know you, and you're stronger than you think. It's okay to be afraid, but we need you. No one else can take your place." He took her face in his hands and tenderly urged, "Take the necklace. Only *you* can wear it. I promise it will be okay. Trust me."

She liked Ian.   He had been a perfect friend to her over the past year on Earth, even if he had concealed his true identity.   He was being a good friend now.   She didn't want to let him down, but this was too much to expect from anyone.

Curious about the necklace's appearance, she flipped the latch and carefully lifted the lid.   Spread flat inside was a lavish neck piece formed from a mix of metallic bronze and copper.   It wasn't by any means a small item of jewelry.

The top portion was formed to sit high on the wearer's neck, with thick arms meant to hug the throat and latch in the back. The front resembled a slightly curved plate, shaped like an inverted pyramid with the tip pointing toward the chest.   It was six inches along either side, covered in elaborate designs set in ruby red. Four black pearls separated a mirror-image pattern while a border of tiny green gems glimmered along the very edge.   Every detail was outlined in gold, making it richer in appearance.   Molded into the front plate were two oval grooves.   These depressions measured three inches in length, coming to a point on either end. The entire piece seemed much thicker than a normal piece of jewelry.

She went to pick it up, and the arms hung limp in her hands. It felt unusual—not metallic at all but like flexible putty.   Her fingers ran along the green gems that met in a 'V' at the tip. There was something hauntingly familiar about the piece.

"I've seen this before," she breathed as something very strange happened.

The arms began to wiggle as the front plate expanded.   It constricted and expanded again, appearing to….breathe?   The putty stirred as if it were alive.   Without warning, the piece wrapped itself around Sevenah's arm, winding its way up to her shoulder.

She screamed and shook her arm violently, trying to remove the active ornament.   It held on tight.   With her other hand she swiped the necklace down her arm and onto the floor where it fell still and motionless; all signs of life vanished.   Desperate to get as far away from the thing as possible, she stood up on the medical bed and pointed down.

"It's alive," she shrieked.   "You saw it!   It grabbed me!" Her big eyes glanced over a group of stunned faces.

131

"I don't believe it," Derian muttered. "It knows you." He stared with incredulity at the woman standing atop the table. His queen. "You really *are* Sha Eena."

She yelled at him. "You didn't tell me that thing was alive!"

Jinatta stepped forward, explaining, "It never behaved that way before, honest! We had no idea it would respond to you. If we had known…." Jinatta closed her eyes and shook her head, thinking of all the misfortune they could have avoided. "Oh, if we had only known."

"I'm tired of this!" Sevenah hollered, standing above them all. "You say I'm supposed to be a queen, but you treat me like a child! You've kept me in the dark about everything! I'm no child, Derian, I need to know the truth. If I'm Sha Eena, then you listen to me. No more lies. No more secrets. I want to know everything….right now!"

Every eye turned to the captain. Jinatta gave him an "I told you so" twitch of the brow.

"Alright," he agreed, still under the influence of shock. "Okay, the truth. Sit….sit down."

First he retrieved the discarded necklace from off the floor. He chuckled lightly as it draped motionless across his hands, amazed by how she had brought the thing to life with a mere touch. Then he placed it inside the wooden container and closed the lid. The others started out of the medical bay when Sevenah stopped them.

"I want you to stay, please."

They obeyed. Jinatta and Leisha rested against the second bed. Ian took a chair. Derian stood center stage, holding onto the wooden box.

"It's hard to know where to start," he began. "If your mother were still alive she would be the one to guide you through all of this. But she's not, and to tell you the truth we aren't very familiar with the process. I can only tell you what I *do* know. I know that you are undeniably Sha Eena." His eyes focused intently on her, a newfound respect in them. "I wasn't absolutely sure until now.

"I told you earlier about the girl we assumed to be our Sha. It wasn't until we placed the necklace on her that we realized she wasn't the one. It didn't respond in the least to begin with.

Nothing like it did for you right here, right now. In fact, it just draped limply around her neck for minutes, motionless. Then all at once, it began attaching itself to her. Of course, that is supposed to happen."

Sevenah rubbed her neck. The thought gave her goose bumps.

"You're right too—it does seem to exhibit signs of life. I don't know much more except that the necklace has existed for over three thousand years, passed down from Sha to Sha. The catch is, only a direct descendant can successfully wear the necklace. Only a true Sha can withstand its powers. There's something in your genetics that allows you to have a symbiotic relationship without suffering any physical consequences. In other words, anyone else who tries to wear it......well......they don't survive the joining."

"You mean......the last girl died?"

"Unfortunately, yes," Derian sighed. "We had no idea she wasn't.....you. When it became clear that her life signs were fading, we tried to remove it but couldn't. Jinatta did everything in her power to help. Nothing worked. The only consolation, I suppose, is she died in her sleep. Then the necklace simply fell off."

Sevenah glanced over at the women. Their faces were both pained and sorrowful.

"That's why Jinatta and Leisha were trying so hard to find something unique in your blood. They wanted to be sure not to repeat what happened the last time."

"Why use the necklace at all? Why is it so important?" Sevenah noticed how everyone smiled at the question. She waited for Derian to explain.

"It has special powers. For example, it can protect you from harm."

"It didn't protect my mother. Vaughndorin killed her, and she was wearing the necklace, wasn't she?"

"Yes. Well, it can protect you from most things, not a beheading apparently. However, it will provide you with perfect health. You won't suffer from illness and your wounds will heal quickly. For instance, if you were to be shot or stabbed, the necklace would repair the injury within moments. You would

133

survive such a thing."

She shuddered at the thought.

Derian continued, "The necklace is also the key to life on our world. Through its power things grow on our planet. Every plant form depends upon you and this necklace to survive. And since that is the essence of our food source, we, in turn, depend upon you to survive. That's why our world is dying, because you've been absent for so long. There's been no one to care for the vegetation."

She didn't understand. "What about water and soil and sunlight? Those things aren't enough to make the plants grow?"

"Not on our world. The water and sunlight help, but they're not enough. We've had no fruit or herbs for the last four or five years now. Once our food reserves were emptied we were forced to look elsewhere. We've resorted to gathering stores from other planets. The worst part is how it's affected every nation on Moccobatra, not just Harrowbeth. Needless to say, they're all very upset with us for your overextended absence. We've shared our rations, but I'm afraid if we don't get you home soon we may find ourselves warring with more armies than Gemdorin's."

"So....how exactly does it work? I mean, what do I do with it? What will it do to *me?"*

"I'm not certain of the details. I only know that it permanently attaches itself to its host and makes use of your energy to heal the plant life on our world. In return, you receive perfect health and strength. Not only that, but it appears our people benefited with improved health as well. Disease and sickness have become rampant on Moccobatra these past few years. Perhaps our own herbs strengthened our immune systems more than we realized. Jinatta and our finest doctors have been busy searching out cures for ailments we've never encountered before." Derian's eyebrows pulled together, emphasizing a serious regard as he approached the young queen. "We need you, Eena. Our entire world needs you."

"This is crazy," she said, swallowing back a healthy case of angst. "I've never heard of anything as bizarre as this. And I'm not sure I'm okay with having that thing permanently attached to me."

"I'm sorry, but there's no choice here," Derian insisted.

She looked to Ian who'd been gauging her reactions.   He smiled in a comforting manner, a gesture she couldn't return.

The captain's stature seemed to grow as his voice turned more authoritative.   "Eena, understand that I must put the necklace on you tonight.   I want it secured before we encounter Gemdorin again.   It's added protection for you."

"Can't it wait for a while?"

"No."

She sat quietly for a moment, trying to process everything— all the strange, unbelievable news.   It seemed far too much to ask of anyone.   To heal a world?   To be their queen?   To allow some living, alien thing to attach itself to her neck and never ever, ever.....

Her head began to shake in small, rapid movements.   "No," she whispered, "I can't do it."

"Eena, listen…"   Derian's tone grew gruff, but Ian took over before he could finish, quickly moving in front of his best friend again.

"Sevenah, look at me."   He could read genuine fear in her eyes when she looked up.

"Ian, please no.   I can't do this—I won't."

He held onto her arms and spoke softly.   "I'm not going to let anything happen to you, I promise.   But you need to trust me. *You are* queen of Harrowbeth, and no one can change that.   Not even you."

"No," she breathed.   Her head shook frantically.   She wanted to slip down and run away, but she was positive the captain would stop her if she tried.

Ian's warm, tender eyes begged for her trust.   "I need you to do this.   My world will die without you.   My parents are back there…"

"No, Ian, please no."   The tears began to fall, trickling like raindrops.

"My parents are waiting for your return.   I told them I'd bring you home, safe and sound, and I will.   Look at me.   We all need you.   Our world is desperate for your help."

"No, no!" she insisted, "I can't!"   She wriggled her arms free of his grasp, free from the fate she wanted to flee.

Her cheeks glistened with tears that Ian wiped away.   She

was sure she heard Derian's frustrated sigh beside her, but she didn't care to look at him. Why was he even letting her protest? Surely, he wasn't going to allow her to leave without that dreadful heirloom secured to her neck. It was clear her destiny had been decided. Fate had spoken. No choice. No escape.

As it hit her there was no way out, the flow of tears increased and she found herself balling up like a frightened child. Ian's sympathetic hands naturally moved to stroke her back.

"Ian," the captain growled, but his protest was hotly challenged.

"Can't you just give her a minute? For crying out loud, she's not going anywhere!"

The air tensed until Derian finally yielded. "We'll be around the corner." He left with Leisha and the doctor.

Ian lifted himself up on the table to sit beside his best friend. He continued to rub her back as she wept. When the intensity of her sobs subsided, he began to talk to her again.

"Eena. Sorry, I mean…..*Sevenah*," he corrected himself. "Do you remember the trip we took to Sun Lakes last summer? The day your friends invited us to go swimming?"

She nodded, wiping at her tearstained face.

"You were so excited to show me the park and the high cliffs bordering the lake. Remember how we climbed up that trail to the very top and looked down over the edge?"

She recalled the hike. "Yes. Erik, Joe, and Jackie followed us up there. Jackie was really into you, and you wouldn't even give her the time of day."

His mouth pulled down to one side. "I remember that."

"Jackie liked you……*a lot*." Picturing it made her lips grin faintly.

"She wasn't my type."

"You mean, human?"

Ian shrugged. "If I recall correctly, Jackie wasn't the only one trying to get someone's attention. I think Erik was showing off quite a bit for your sake."

"I know, I was watching." A ragged inhale and exhale sounded mournful in a way.

"He wasn't your type either," Ian insisted.

"He most certainly was. I was hoping he would get around

136

to asking me to Homecoming.   And he very well might have if you hadn't broken his nose."   Sevenah gave Ian a weak shove, still unhappy about the unfortunate accident months after the fact.

"He *was* planning to ask you," Ian admitted.   "That's *why* I broke his nose."

His confession only earned him a harder shove.

"You've missed the dance anyway, and besides, he was never the guy for you."

She wondered about Ian's comment, aching for that simple, ordinary life again.

"I'll never forget the look of horror on your face when Joe and Erik both took a running leap off the edge of that cliff."

"It was incredibly stupid and dangerous," she declared. "They had no idea if the water was even deep enough."

"They'd done it before.   And, besides, they weren't about to let a little danger get in the way of impressing you."

"I wasn't impressed."

Ian chuckled.   "I remember how terrified you looked when I asked if you wanted to jump.   I thought you couldn't hug that back wall hard enough."

"It was awfully high up," she reminded him in her defense.

"Jackie jumped."

"Only to impress you."

"Rachel, Wendy, and Dawn climbed up there and jumped altogether when they saw the others."

She scrunched her glistening eyes at him.   "What's your point, Ian?"

"You were afraid, remember?   No matter how I tried, I couldn't get you away from that wall.   You were so terrified someone would push you off the cliff.

Her eyes turned downward.   "They would've found it funny."

He nodded, recalling how her fear of heights had amused her friends.   "Remember what you did when I offered to hold your hand and jump with you?"

"I said no."

"Until I stood there on the brink and threatened to jump on my own.   You finally stepped away from the wall when you thought I was really going to do it."

137

She looked sideways at her best friend. "I didn't want you to leave me up there alone."

"I would've hiked back up for you."

A tiny smile admitted she knew it was true.

"But you took my hand and, with a little prodding and some faith, you made the leap."

A deep breath calmed her stomach's memory of the fall.

"You trusted me then, and we made it. If I recall correctly, I held your hand as we jumped off the same ledge half a dozen times after that."

She choked on an unexpected chuckle.

"It turned out to be okay after all, didn't it? Even kind of fun."

"Yes. It was exciting in a *scary* sort of way," she confessed. Her head began to nod as she realized where he was going with this.

"Eena….Sevenah…..please trust me now like you did then. I'll hold your hand again, and I promise everything will be okay, just like it was that day we stood on the cliffs at Sun Lakes. You only need to trust me."

"I do trust you," she uttered.

"Then you'll do this?"

Her hazel eyes glistened as she stared at her best friend. Ian could see willingness behind the fear. He took her hand and squeezed it tenderly. "I won't let go, I promise."

"You promise?"

"Yes, I promise."

She breathed in and out. "Okay."

"Okay," he repeated.

She wasn't at all surprised to see Derian reappear. No doubt he had been listening expectantly on the other side of the wall.

"Ian," she said quickly, "you do it. You put it on me."

Ian turned immediately to the captain who seemed momentarily stunned. Both men appeared hesitant to act.

"Derian," Ian began, "I didn't mean to…"

"Just get it on her," the captain grumbled. He shoved the box into Ian's hands and then stepped back. His face was hard. Sevenah wondered if she had upset him with her request. What did it matter who did the deed? He was getting what he

138

ultimately wanted.

Ian placed the box on the table and removed the necklace, holding each end limply in his hands. Sevenah breathed in anxiously as she eyed the piece.

"You'll be fine," Ian assured her. "Trust me."

As he leaned in, draping the heirloom across her upper chest, she whispered to him. "It's okay for you to call me Eena, if that's who I am."

He whispered back, "You are; I've always known it." Then he latched the collar in place. It gripped onto its host immediately.

"Ian, it's tight," she complained.

"It'll be alright," he said, helping her to lie down.

"Don't leave me," she begged, holding fast to his hand. "Promise you'll stay with me."

"I promise."

The others quickly made their way over to observe what was happening. Jinatta turned on a set of monitors above the bed, still concerned something might go wrong. They had never done this before, at least not successfully. It was a tradition performed within the family of Shas, never a public ritual.

"Ian it feels weird. It's so tight." She wanted to pull it off but knew it was too late to reverse things.

Ian squeezed her hand. "Just hold onto me. It'll be okay."

She nodded, feeling her neck stiffen.

Derian found his way to her other side where he stood and watched.

"Get her a blanket," the doctor ordered. "Her temperature's dropping fast."

The captain grabbed some covers from a lower drawer. He wrapped them snugly around the young queen as she started to shiver, but then things got worse.

"Ouch!" she cried. "Aahhh! It hurts! It's digging into me! *Aahhh!*" She released Ian's hand and grabbed onto the necklace, trying futilely to rip it off.

Ian pulled one hand away from her throat and held fast. Something resembling thin vines traveled in every direction below her skin. She screamed in agony.

"Aahggg! You didn't say this would hurt!"

Derian stood by and grabbed her other hand, holding it securely. "I uh, guess I forgot that part," the captain muttered.

"*Aaahhhh!*" she screamed again. Her back arched as she fought to endure excruciating pain. "*I hate you, Derian!*"

"I know, I know, just squeeze my fingers as hard as you can. Keep squeezing. It'll be over soon."

They watched her break out in a sweat. Derian wiped a hand over her forehead as something burrowed up the sides of her face underneath the skin.

"Her temperature's rising; get the blankets off! Get them off!" the doctor ordered.

Jinatta was fraught with worry. This same point was where the last girl had developed serious problems. A growing red column on the monitor registered a rapidly increasing fever. Her patient's body temperature had exceeded the normal Harrowbethian 99.7 degrees.

"104 degrees. 105.5…..106….. We need to cool her down, Derian!"

Ian tried to reassure them all. "She'll be fine. Trust me, she'll be fine."

Jinatta stared at the monitor, anxious. "107 degrees. It's still rising!" Her blue eyes flashed wide at Ian.

"She can handle it," he insisted.

Eena was screaming in agony the entire time. Then she passed out, her grip on both men slackening. The room fell dead quiet. Derian placed her limp hand on the table, but Ian continued to hold onto the other.

The captain pointed out a blessing. "At least she's no longer in pain."

"108 degrees," Jinatta informed them, her voice quivering. "Ian, that's way too hot for anyone."

"She's fine," Ian maintained. "She's not just anyone, she's a Sha."

Derian took Jinatta by the arm and pulled her away. "There's nothing you can do, you know that. It's up to her now." He placed his hands on the doctor's shoulders as they all watched to see what would happen next.

For twenty minutes a burning fever inched higher. It peaked at 113 degrees. Fifteen minutes later it dropped rapidly and settled at 102.   That time seemed like an eternity.   102 degrees Jinatta could live with.

The company continued to monitor Eena's vitals, watching the display map out branching tendrils within her body.   Movement centered in the brain at first, wave activity increasing substantially. In time, irregularities shifted to other organs.   For a while her heartbeat quickened and became erratic.   Then her breathing hastened and slowed.   It seemed like the necklace was taking over every function of her body, testing organs one by one. Eventually, all systems stabilized.   When an hour passed with no major changes, Derian dismissed the ladies.

"Jinatta.   Leisha.   You two go get some sleep."

They tried to protest, wanting to stay by Eena's side, but the captain insisted.

"You haven't slept in two days.   Go.   I'll watch over her."

"*We'll* watch over her," Ian corrected.   He wasn't about to leave.   Not after his promise.

As the women headed out for some much deserved rest, Ian and Derian settled in for a long night.

CHAPTER EIGHT
Gemdorin

Ian and the captain were seated on opposite sides of their sleeping queen. She was resting peacefully at this point, covered in a warm blanket that Jinatta had provided before heading off to seek some sleep herself. The monitor overhead continued to chart vital signs, steadily tracking the growth of the necklace. Both men sat in silence, lost in their own thoughts. Neither was much for conversation.

Derian leaned back in his chair, frowning, arms folded across his stomach. He watched Eena's chest rise and fall as she breathed in and out a little more laboriously than normal. He thought about all she had been through: abducted from home, learning of her alien origin, surviving Dr. Braxton's intrusive tests, risking escape, being shot at during the attempt, only to find herself on a spaceship surrounded by expectant strangers. And now the harshest test of all—enduring an invasive union with some foreign entity.

The more he thought about it, the more he admired her courage. He felt a pang of remorse for not having shown her greater kindness, although truth be told, he had been less than thrilled about her arrival. After Gemdorin's murderous act, slaying five innocent girls, and with the sixth dying under Derian's care, he had given up hope that their queen, Sha Eena, still lived. On some level he had convinced himself that Moccobatrans would have to find a way to survive without her.

Ian's admittance onto the Kemeniroc hadn't helped any. The captain had placed no faith in the unproven protector. Maybe that wasn't entirely true. It was less a matter of faith. More a matter of resentment. He had wanted Ian to be wrong. The council's insistence that the meddling know-it-all join his crew in search of Eena had left the captain irate. This, after the news of their disastrous attempt to attach the necklace to one who had been recognized as the rightful heir. Derian had told the council it was utter foolishness to believe Ian could have any clue as to the

142

whereabouts of their young queen when the man who had lived six years on Earth as a guardian had failed. He had also told the council that placing the necklace on any other girl would be no better than allowing Gemdorin to murder her. One senseless death on their hands was enough! But Ian had stubbornly insisted and somehow convinced the council to let him try.

Derian's eyes moved past the sleeping queen to rest on her protector who was slumped forward in his chair, head hung. The guy had been right all along. Perhaps he deserved a bit more trust. He had definitely earned it. Derian looked on Eena and smiled. Now that she was back and undeniably real, everything would change.

On the edge of his thoughts he sensed Ian watching him. His gaze shifted, and they stared at each other for an awkward moment, neither knowing what to say. Ian broke the silence first.

"You know, Derian, she doesn't really hate you."

The captain chuckled once. "Oh, I think she might. It's okay."

"No, it's not. She doesn't know anything about you or about the…"

Derian cut him off. "Ian, it's fine. I haven't exactly made a grand first impression. But I plan to fix that. I'll tell her the truth—the truth about everything—when she wakes up."

Ian gave a half-hearted smile before diverting his eyes.

Derian continued to share. "I thought I was protecting her, not burdening her with too much information. I thought it would scare her and she would run the other way. And truthfully, I wasn't sure I was even talking to the right girl. I'm sorry, Ian; we should've had more faith in you."

Ian glanced up. He hadn't expected anyone to believe him. With no solid proof, he wasn't sure he would have believed himself had their roles been reversed.

"You know, I honestly thought I would recognize her. I was sure I'd know her, that I'd sense something familiar, see it in her eyes, but…." He let the thought trail off. His focus shifted, zeroing in on Eena's protector. "You recognized her, though. You knew for certain."

Ian shrugged it off as nothing.

The captain exhaled long and low—a dismal sound. He

didn't press for an explanation. "It's remarkable to me how trusting she is. I shared the truth about the necklace and she still went through with it. I know she was scared, but she did it. Maybe I need to show a little more faith in both of you." Derian shook his head, amazed at how well things had worked out. It wasn't easy for him to voice his feelings, especially to Ian.

"She's a lot like her mother," Ian said. "She whole-heartedly believes in people."

"Yes," Derian agreed, sitting up taller in his chair. "Unfortunately, there are individuals undeserving of such confidence."

Ian didn't offer another word. The fact that these two were able to hold a decent conversation without quarrelling was miraculous. They sat in extended silence, hearing only the soft whistle of Eena's labored breathing.

"Derian! Derian, are you there?" Both men jumped when a voice of alarm transmitted over the captain's personal communicator or PCD.

Derian touched a small, oval object attached to his vest and spoke. "Yes, Jinatta, what's the problem?"

"Gemdorin's on the ship! He's here! Don't let him get to Eena, Derian! You have to protect her!"

The men hopped to their feet, each withdrawing a concealed weapon.

"How do you know this?" the captain asked, pointing his firearm in the direction of the only obvious entrance to the room. Ian did likewise.

They could hear Jinatta sobbing over the PCD. "She's dead, Derian! The other girl—she's dead!" A report came out rapid and incomplete, like she wanted to tell him everything in one breath. "I went to check on her—the guards were gone—I tried the doors but had to pry them open, and—she was dead, Derian! He killed her! *You can't let Gemdorin get to Eena!"*

"Eena's fine. You need to calm down, Jinatta. Contact Rhoen and Jerin. Let them know we could use their help."

"Okay, okay," she said, still in a frenzy. "Okay, I will. I'll do it now."

Derian approached the partitioning wall and placed his hand against an inactive control panel, letting it scan his print. The station immediately came to life.   He ordered the entire crew on highest alert, announcing their enemy was somewhere on board. All hands responded, dividing up decks to be searched from top to bottom.   The captain tried to convince himself Gemdorin would be hard pressed to stay hidden for long.

Meanwhile, he and Ian remained at their queen's side, ready to defend her at any cost.   They were unprepared for what happened next.

She vanished right under their watch.

"No!" Ian gasped.   "Where'd she go?   Eena!   *Eena!*"

The captain saw it too, but he could hardly believe his eyes. His fingers swept over the empty bed, grasping for anything material.   It was no mystery who was behind her disappearance. Derian shouted out the villain's name.

"Gemdorin!   Gemdorin, show yourself, you coward!"

They waved their weapons across the room, turning anxiously in every direction, scanning for any sign of the enemy.

"Gemdorin!" Derian growled fiercely.   *"Bring her back now!"*

From out of nowhere a solid blast of blue light shot across the room, hitting its target dead on.   Ian fell to the floor.   Derian returned fire in the vicinity the shot had originated but with no apparent luck.   A low, mocking snicker rose in volume until it was nearly a cackle, taunting him.   The voice he recognized all too well.

"You should be more careful shooting that thing.   Unless you want to be the one responsible for killing your precious queen."

Gemdorin's figure took shape in the middle of the room— from ghost to mortal terror.

Derian's worst nightmare smirked at him, emerging from nothingness a mere ten feet away.   The captain and his enemy were identical in height and build—both tall, broad-shouldered, highly-intimidating figures.   But unlike Derian's dark features, Gemdorin had fair blonde hair falling a little past his shoulders, combed away from a wide forehead.   Striking blue eyes twinkled under dark eyebrows, the left one bearing a two-inch scar.   He shared the same square jaw as Derian, but with a scruff of unshaven whiskers.   A heavily-decorated belt hugged his waist, supporting shiny black pants with the legs tucked into fancy, knee-

145

high boots.   A long, ornate vest-jacket hung open over a pleated white shirt, making him appear as someone of means.

Gemdorin hugged an unconscious Eena against him, a phasor in that hand.   His other arm was wrapped around her neck, a dagger lined at her throat.   For the first time in ages Derian felt a jolt of genuine fear.

The captain pleaded with his enemy.   "Don't do it, Gemdorin.   Killing her will gain you nothing, and it will destroy our entire world."

The blonde intruder seemed pleased with the elicited reaction. "Now, Derian, you act as though I care.   What does it matter to me?   There are more worlds out there to be had.   Haven't you noticed?   Some harboring impressive treasures too, like this marvelous little wristband here."

Gemdorin pressed once on a flexible gold strap encircling his arm.   He and Elena vanished, reappearing a second later.

"Quite interesting, don't you think?"

Derian didn't react.   His weapon remained fixed, eyes locked on his enemy.   "What do you want, Gemdorin?"

"Oh dear, are we seriously going to play this silly game? How about foregoing the pointless questions so we can entertain a little reunion instead?   What do you say—for old time's sake? You.   Me.   Eena.   Ian.   Oh wait!   Ian can't participate.   Too busy lying down on the job."   Gemdorin smiled wide, a devious and gloating reminder of how he had caught both men off guard.

"Well, it'll have to be just the three of us then."   Gemdorin's lips moved close to his captive's ear.   He pretended to converse with her, showing off with dramatic vocal flair.

"So, Eena, how have you been the past twelve years?   Good, huh?   Really?   Derian, what do you think?"   He lifted his eyebrow, spiking the scar above it.   "She's looking quite lovely after such a long absence, wouldn't you agree?   All grown up and pretty."

Gemdorin used his dagger to brush away stray hairs from Eena's profile.   He appeared to consider her attractive features. Then his eyes dropped lower, resting on her upper chest.

"Oh my.   That certainly is an interesting necklace you're wearing, Eena.   I'd love to take a closer look at it.   Actually— mind if I borrow it?   What's that?   Well, Derian, she doesn't

146

seem to mind at all. Now let's see. How do I remove it?" He paused, pretending to check for a clasp around her neck. Then his face brightened as if he'd had an epiphany. "Oh yes, I remember now. I have to *take your head off first!*"

Derian took a step forward, raising his weapon to where it pointed straight at his enemy's snickering face. Gemdorin pressed his cheek to Eena's, a sharp blade still crossing her throat.

"Uh, uh, uh! You shoot me, I take her head. It's that simple." Then he gruffly commanded, "Now drop that nasty weapon of yours."

Derian hesitated, but he couldn't take the chance. There was no doubt in his mind Gemdorin would do exactly as he threatened. The gun lowered until his fingers reluctantly let it slip to the floor.

"That's a good boy. Nicely done."

Derian tried to convince his enemy, "She's worth more alive, and you know it."

But Gemdorin continued to toy with him, play-acting like it was an original thought. "You know you might be right! Just this morning I was wondering how I could heighten my command. Interesting that you brought together this powerful necklace and its bearer—for me. I suppose I could be persuaded to let her live, if she agrees to share her secrets. And then, when I'm through using her, I'll slit her throat and keep the treasure for myself! Besides, she'll have far more fun in my company than yours, considering how much she *hates* you." An evil grin flashed wide.

"How long have you been here?" Derian asked, realizing his previous conversation had been overheard.

"Oh, a *very loooong* time. It's wonderful how these wristbands make you completely undetectable. Remarkable technology actually. Too bad those people didn't want to share it. Oh well, stealing it was much more exciting anyway."

"Where do you intend to take her? What sort of corrupt scheme are you planning now?" Derian was desperate, obviously fishing for any information he could get.

Gemdorin laughed aloud. "Don't worry, I promise to take care of your precious little princess for you. The important thing to remember here is that *wherever* I go, *whatever* I'm up to, Eena and the necklace will be under my control. *Not yours.* And you, once again the unfortunate loser, shall never, ever, ever see her

147

alive again.   Sorry, Derian, but as usual......*I win.*"

Then he disappeared.

"Gemdorin!   Gemdorin!   You'll never make it off this ship! *Gemdorin!*"

Unprepared and unsuspecting, the captain suffered a forceful punch to his gut.   It knocked the wind out of him, and he doubled over.   A low voice hissed in his ear.   "You were never a descent match for me anyway, *little brother.*"

The blow was worse than any ambush.   Derian was entirely unprepared.   How could he fight an invisible enemy?   It took a minute to catch his breath before he staggered over to the control panel and gave the order for every exit to be sealed off. Gemdorin was invisible, but that didn't mean he could walk through walls.

Next, the captain's attention turned to Ian who was still lying on the floor.   After finding a pulse, Derian gave the guy a rough shake.

"Ian!   Ian, wake up!"

No response forced another attempt.   He went for the collar this time, hefting Ian into a sitting position.   Jostling him, he barked, "For criminy's sake, wake up!   Eena's gone!"

When a groggy moan escaped his lips, consciousness was helped along by a sharp slap across the face.

"Hey!   What was that for?"

"Eena's gone!" Derian growled.   "Gemdorin has her.   Come on, we don't have time to sit around."

Once the truth sank in, it took only a moment for Ian to move. "How?   How could he have gotten to her?   I didn't even see him enter the room!"

"No one can see him, he has some kind of invisibility cloak— some advanced technology he apparently stole.   There's no way of knowing how long he's been here watching us.   How the criminy am I supposed to contend with an enemy I can't see?"

Ian had no answer.   He followed the captain, stunned and perplexed, headed for the exit.   Rhoen and Jerin met them just inside the doors.

Derian pointed two accusing fingers at his men and hollered, "How the hell did you get in here?"

They stopped dead in their tracks.

148

"I ordered every exit sealed off! Gemdorin's on the ship and he's taken Eena! We can't let him get away!"

The captain stopped and ran a claw of rigid fingers over his scalp, taking a moment to swallow back a portion of his anger. "Look, Gemdorin has some kind of alien cloaking device, so we're unable to see or detect him."

His men glanced at each other. Derian answered their incredulous expressions.

"Yes, you heard me right. Our enemy is invisible, but I'm guessing he's not capable of passing through solid objects, so all exits are to remain sealed. Understand? We can't allow him a way off this ship."

Jerin's jaw dropped. "If he's really invisible, sir, how are we supposed to find him?"

"I don't know," Derian admitted. "But we can't let that bastard leave with her."

"Yes, sir." They split up to search every corridor on the deck.

Meanwhile, Gemdorin was implementing his escape plan, maneuvering his way through the ventilation system with barely enough room to drag an unconscious body behind him.

"You better be worth this effort," he hissed at the sleeping girl. "It'd be a whole lot easier to end your life and my misery right now."

Having received a layout of the ship from Rhoen, Gemdorin took the most direct route to the docking bay. Once he was certain his position was somewhere above the hangar, he stopped to listen for voices. The muffled echo of conversation carried from a distance, but nothing sounded close by.

He carefully removed a sizable vent cover and then peeked below the opening to take a look around. Directly beneath him stood a pile of hefty cargo barrels stacked three high. It was a four foot drop to reach the top. Gemdorin lowered his hostage through the vent, dumping her body onto the pile. He then jumped down himself, creating a loud thud in the process. The echo carried. He froze for a few seconds and listened. His noisy entrance seemed to go unnoticed. After lowering his unconscious prize clear to the ground, he climbed down the pile himself, keeping an eye out until the girl was tossed over his

149

shoulder, concealed once again by an invisibility cloak.

Gemdorin headed straight for his ship—a sleek glider tucked away in a corner, as invisible as he and his hostage. Earlier that morning, he had managed to enter undetected during the Kemeniroc's regular tactical drills, trailing the small battle cruisers when their flights were completed. He had set down in a secluded space unlikely to be crossed.

He wasn't about to wait for anyone to offer him an open door this time. The bypass code Rhoen had provided would negotiate the bay doors from his ship's controls. All he needed was a large enough gap to slip through. By the time they discovered the breach, he would be outside and long gone.

Blackmailing Rhoen had proven to be one of his most lucrative ventures—a covert collaboration where no one was the wiser. It all worked exactly as planned. Gemdorin was navigating through space with his valuable prize before any rift in their system was detected. He laughed aloud, impressed by his own cleverness.

"Captain!" Marguay's urgent call rang over Derian's PCD. "The docking bay doors have been activated. I'm overriding the commands now."

"*Nooooo!*" Derian screeched. His hands punched at the air, conveying extreme frustration. He knew it was too late. This meant only one thing, Gemdorin had escaped with their queen. But how had he gotten to the docking bay with every exit secured? Did he have access to the ship's controls now too?

"Scan for a vessel!" he commanded Marguay. "Scan the entire area for anything traceable we can follow.....and unseal all these accursed exits!"

"Yes, sir," Marguay replied.

Derian reversed his steps to head for the bridge. Outside the elevator, he waited impatiently while Marguay entered ship commands, restoring crew access to interior passage routes. It took only a few seconds. As the lift sped to the highest deck, his mind rushed just as quickly through options on how to proceed.

Leisha and Marguay were on the bridge scanning for signs of an enemy ship. A handful of additional crewmembers manned other stations: running tactical, navigation, communications, and monitoring reports from all decks.   Every head turned when the captain stormed through the doors demanding to know exactly what in the blazing underworld had gone wrong.

"He used our own codes from the inside," Marguay explained. "We stopped the doors almost as soon as they were initiated, and no vessels were detected leaving the hangar.   We're scanning the area now but have found nothing so far."

Derian wondered if there was still a chance…

"Sir, wait."   It was Leisha.   "There is a faint radiation trail. It's deteriorating rapidly, but I can trace it back to our ship."   She looked up, sour-faced.   "It didn't originate with us."

The captain hung his head, feeling his spirits sink likewise. He smacked the back of a nearby chair, managing to bite his tongue.   Their brief moment of hope was shattered.   Gemdorin had escaped; it was certain.   And to top it off, the bastard had used their own codes.   But how had he obtained access to their database?

"I don't get it.   We saw nothing on the screen," Marguay marveled.

"You wouldn't," Derian told him.   "He has cloaking technology.   He must be using it on his ship too."

"Captain?   Where did he acquire that kind of technology?" Every face in the bridge looked up, concerned.

Derian answered honestly.   "I don't know.   But *I will* find out."   He turned to Leisha and ordered her to follow the radiation trail as far as it would take them.

"Yes, sir."   She was already on that detail.

"Marguay, I want you, Jerin, and Rhoen to meet me in the charting room in one hour."

"Yes, sir."

The captain left the bridge.   There were two people he wanted to see before the scheduled meeting.   Dogged strides took him straight to the medical bay first.

It was reasonable to expect the doctor to be in her office, but when Derian arrived, the room was empty.   He turned to leave just as she walked in.

"Where is she?   Where is Eena?"   Jinatta's big eyes were red and swollen, her face streaked with tearstains—traces of

151

mourning another pointless death.

The captain frowned. His head shook as he admitted, "We couldn't stop him."

Jinatta stumbled backwards over the news. She looked ready to fall apart. "No! No, no, no! Don't you know what this means? We're finished! Our world is doomed! He's murdered them all!"

Derian took the doctor by both arms, forcing her to settle down. "Jinatta, no. Listen. Gemdorin didn't harm her. I don't think he's planning to either. He wants to know how the necklace works. He told me so, and he'll never know how it works with her dead. She's valuable to him alive." A gentle hand moved to the doctor's chin. The touch made her weepy eyes look up.

"I'll get her back, Jinatta. I will."

"Then you better do it quickly, before he changes his mind."

Derian nodded. "Agreed. Tell me, did you plant that tracking chip on her? Can we follow it?" He had ordered the insertion to be done during Eena's medical examination, in case something like this happened.

"Yes, yes I did. It's imbedded behind her right ear. I doubt anyone will discover it."

"Good," he sighed, a small sound of relief. Here was some hope at least. He forced a smile, and with a gentle voice said, "I need to know you're alright. Do you think you can get some rest?"

She attempted a feeble smile in return, but her sorrows were too deep-seated. "I don't know if I can sleep right now, but I'll be fine. Just please, Derian, please get her back."

As soon as the captain finished his business with the doctor, he left the medical bay in search of Eena's protector.

He tapped the communicator attached to his vest and spoke. "Ian, where are you?"

A dismal voice replied. "In the docking bay."

"Why? What are you doing there? You're not leaving this ship."

Ian's tone was too distraught to argue. "I just don't get it. How? How did he get in and out so easily? How did this happen?"

"Gemdorin had our codes and access to the ship's computer. He was able to open the doors from inside the hangar."

"How did he get our codes? Where did he acquire his technology? Derian, how are we ever going to find her?"

"I was about to ask you the same thing, Ian. Stay where you are. I want to talk to you."

The captain made his way down to the docking bay, entering from the back elevator. He immediately scanned the massive room, catching sight of a tall frame slouched before the bay doors. Ian was staring at the massive barrier as though it held a secret it refused to reveal. Derian stepped up beside the man.

"We failed her," Ian uttered, sounding entirely defeated. "We failed everyone."

"No we haven't. It's not over yet." Derian wasn't willing to give up. "As long as she's alive, we can get her back."

Ian looked sideways at his captain. "How? We can't even see them! We can't fight the unseen!"

"Ian, I need to know something. The truth. Can you tell me for sure if she's alive?" He was entirely serious about the question. Derian had been amazed at how Ian knew all along Eena was well and fine on Earth. When everyone else had given her up for dead, he had insisted otherwise. His gut told him this man had a secret he wasn't sharing.

Ian studied the floor. He didn't utter a word.

"You knew she was alive on Earth, Ian. How did you know that?" Derian waited for an answer that took a while in coming.

"I just knew, that's all."

"I need to hear the truth, Ian. Don't lie to me. Do you have some way of sensing her existence?"

Ian looked up and stared at the captain, scrutinizing his face as if deciding whether or not the man was trustworthy. When he spoke, it was one word.

"Yes."

"How?"

"I can't say." Ian rubbed his hand across his forehead and down the side of his face as if he had a serious headache.

Derian exhaled a sharp sigh of impatience. The more time they wasted, the harder it would be to find and retrieve Eena. He grabbed Ian by one arm and held on firmly, speaking to the man in

153

a low, stern voice. "Ian, this is no game. You need to tell me how you know. I'm ordering you!"

Ian hesitated. He felt torn—reluctant to choose between a direct order and a vow of secrecy.

"Okay! Okay." He pulled his arm free from Derian's grasp. "But you have to promise to keep this to yourself. I'm forbidden to tell anyone." He hesitated again, hoping he was doing the right thing, realizing the retrieval of their queen was more important than any other consideration. Finally, he confessed.

"I can see her dreams. When she sleeps, I can see her dreams. That's how I know she's alive. If she's dreaming, she's alive."

"Are you serious?" It was a crazy admission.

"Yes," Ian nodded. "All her life I've been able to do so. While she was on Earth I could see into her dreams every night. I never stopped watching over her. My father witnessed Sha Tashi's dreams. We're their protectors; it's part of how we look after them. It's always been that way, only it's not common knowledge."

"Your family has kept this a secret for ages?" Derian was shocked. "Why?"

"Because people wouldn't like it if they knew we were observing their Sha's dreams every night. How do you think the council would react? They might accuse us of thought manipulation. But that's not the case. Eena doesn't even know I'm there; I don't interfere. And don't ask me how it works, because I'm not sure—it just does."

"Do you realize that if you had disclosed this information a long time ago, a few individuals might still be alive?"

"I know, but it's forbidden! And I had no idea you were going to put the necklace on someone else until it was too late to do anything about it! If everybody would've listened to me in the first place…"

The captain spoke over him. "You didn't give them a good reason to listen! Now *this* would've been a good reason!"

"My father would never have forgiven me!"

"Can she see your dreams too?" Derian asked, now highly curious. "I mean if you were to let her, could she see into your dreams?"

Ian grumbled, shaking his head back and forth. "I shouldn't have told you anything."

"But you *did*. Now tell me the truth, can she see your dreams?"

"What does it matter?"

"She can, can't she? That's great!"

"What?" That wasn't exactly the reaction Ian had anticipated.

"If she can see your dreams, you can communicate with her!" Derian explained. "We have to find her, Ian. She needs to know we're looking for her. You find out everything you can. Try to let her know we're coming. And you report directly to me, understood?"

Ian agreed, though he felt a knot forming in the pit of his stomach for having shared his secret. "Don't tell anyone, please, Derian. People won't like it."

"I won't tell." The captain's word was good. "Now go get some sleep. You find her. Find her and we'll get her back."

Ian left the docking bay at once. In the gloomy quiet of his quarters, he drifted off to dream.

CHAPTER NINE
Deceived

Eena was trapped in a deep slumber brought about by tranquilizing chemicals the necklace had released into her body. It was actually a kinder way for the joining to take place; unconsciousness meant no pain. But until the union was complete, she wouldn't wake up. While unaware of the events transpiring around her, this symbiotic entity was filling her head with a wealth of information.

Images of past Shas of Harrowbeth swept through her mind— great, great, great, great grandmothers from centuries ago. These former queens had each left one selected memory to be passed down to future Shas, accruing gems of wisdom to benefit successors. Now this accumulation of memoirs was being shared with Eena. Most of the information would help her interact successfully with the diverse species that shared their world. It would also help her understand her relationship with the necklace, how its powers were at her disposal if she learned to use them and wished to use them. Even an understanding of their native language was revealed in her mind. She would be able to address and comprehend her people when she awoke.

After numerous visions of former Shas, one final image—the last reigning queen—lingered in Eena's mind. A troubled mother spoke to her only child in a dream….

Sha Tashi's arms beckoned, open and inviting. She was beautiful. Mother and daughter resembled one another remarkably—long, straight, red-brown hair, bright green eyes, and fair skin. Sha Tashi stood a few inches taller than her daughter. She was elegantly dressed in a full gown that shimmered an evergreen color in Eena's imagination. Long, flowing sleeves hung open from her reaching arms. The image of Harrowbeth's last queen still donned the necklace she had worn for many years in life.

"Eena, my sweet, darling girl," she cooed tenderly.

"Mother?" The young Sha stared with wide eyes at the

likeness of her birth mother.   It was shocking to recognize how many physical traits they shared.   A smile spread across Eena's face as understanding sank in that she was seeing her real mother for the first time since three years of age.

"Mother, is it really you?"

"My darling, I am but a memory, stored here for you and your posterity.   There is so much to tell you.   I know this experience must be overwhelming.   The entity placed around your neck is a part of you now and will not remove itself until the day you pass away.   To try and remove it would prove foolish and fatal."

Sha Tashi approached her daughter in the dream, placing a hand gingerly on each shoulder.   Eena could see her own face mirrored in her mother's eyes.

"Stored within the necklace are brief memories, one from each past Sha.   They are to prepare and assist you in your calling; however, much remains to be learned independently.   These memories are merely a guide, they cannot teach you everything there is to know.   The necklace will act as a protection from most harmful threats and will keep you well all the days of your life.   These are two significant benefits of this union, my child.

"As you learn to work with the necklace, you will sense remarkable powers available to you, such that others are not aware of.   Stories exist alluding to these hidden powers.   They circulate across our world and throughout the galaxy, but most are accepted as mere myth.   You will note that many past Shas have warned against abusing any powers the necklace affords us.   It is said that doing so will bring about unspeakable consequences. I'll admit, I've been tempted to test this greater potential myself, especially with the unrest in our nation at this present time, but I fear what would come of it."   Sha Tashi's face bore heavy concern as she stressed the necklace's main function.   "Care for our world and its inhabitants.   This you must do.   But to risk anything beyond that is to chance bringing on these unspeakable consequences."

"Mother, I don't think I'm ready for this.   I'm not sure what to do."

The image of Sha Tashi smiled tenderly, but a wealth of worry remained in her eyes.

"Your strength will increase as you and the entity continue to bond. Your abilities will blossom as you make use of the necklace for its purpose. It will do nothing you do not wish to be done."

It was all so confusing. "I don't understand, Mother. What exactly am I supposed to do?"

"My time is up. I must go." Sha Tashi placed a caring hand on her daughter's cheek, and they exchanged a weepy gaze. "Oh, my darling child, how I love you. You are Sha Eena of Harrowbeth now. You must rise to your calling. If my suspicions are correct, as I sadly fear, our people will have long awaited the aid of their new queen."

The image vanished abruptly, well before Eena was ready to say goodbye.

"No, wait! Mother, come back! Tell me what to do! What consequences are you talking about?"

In her dreams, Eena searched for her mother but never found the desired image again.

The necklace continued sharing information with its new host. Eena was astonished and troubled by the unfamiliarity of each scene. She saw her world, healthy and swarming with lush, vibrant plant life so different from Earth. Moccobatra was a smaller planet, but still colorful and similar in natural landscapes. She was aware of the various nations occupying the planet and the relationships past Shas had developed and maintained with them. The inhabitants of this world had originated from all over the galaxy, settling on Moccobatra centuries ago and making it their home.

She could see the mighty, stout giants that populated the northern continent. They were called the Grotts—an intelligent, talented, and sociable people. Being easy going and cooperative by nature, they worked well with the Harrowbethians.

Up in the high Blue Mountains lived a race of Icromians—lanky and lofty characters with legs nearly as long as Eena was tall. When they walked, their strides were great but their steps slow. Walking wasn't the Icromians' preferred means of travel. They flew most often by means of translucent, thin wings that buzzed on their backs, carrying them swiftly from place to place. History bragged they were one of the first races to inhabit the planet, a fact their people considered significant, allotting them an arrogant right. They looked down on most of Moccobatra from their location and stature.

Then there were the Boarattas and the Mishmorats, both dynamic and friendly tribes normally found encamped in warmer climates. They were nomads really, sometimes making camp in an area for years, but eventually moving on to new surroundings. These two races had similar athletic features with comparably simple and practical cultures. The Mishmorats were only distinguishable from the Boarattas by their spotted skin—small cheetah-like specks that ran down each arm, leg, and both sides of the face and neck. Other than that, they were mutually beautiful, bronzed people.

Eena could picture these varied groups in her mind and so many more.

She recognized a common language, one shared across Moccobatra. It seemed strange that numerous and unique races would share one tongue, despite most nations making use of indigenous languages within their own borders. But their planet was small, and as often as the Shas of Harrowbeth visited outside lands, it was reasonable that over time a need to communicate prompted one accepted universal language.

The only issue that remained vague was how to utilize the powers of the necklace. No clear procedure existed in her memories. Sha Tashi had said certain things would require personal discovery, and this was one of them. Learning to activate the necklace was a feat realized through trial and error. It wasn't a knowledge to be passed down, but more of a talent and strength requiring intimate cooperation between host and symbiont.

"Eena! Eena!" Her name was repeated again and again, sounding distant at first. She glanced around, wondering if it might be a returning Sha.

"Eena! Eena, can you hear me?" The voice grew nearer and louder, unmistakably male. When an image appeared, she instantly recognized the personage. Her lips thinned automatically, forming a happy smile.

"Ian, what are you doing here? Am I still dreaming?"

"Yes, you are dreaming. I've come to warn you."

Her expression wilted at once; Ian wasn't smiling. "You've come to warn me? About what?"

"Eena, you're in danger. Gemdorin has taken you, and we don't know where he's headed. You need to try and find out where you are—where he's going."

"What? Gemdorin? Are you serious?" This was the man she had been told killed the other girls like her.

"Eena, when you wake up be observant and cautious. We're coming for you, but we need your help."

"What if he tries to kill me? Ian, what should I do?"

"We're coming, Eena, we're on our way. We'll find you."

He tried to console her but failed with words of comfort.

"Just be observant. And please be careful." His image disappeared, leaving her alone to wrestle with an abundance of frightful thoughts.

Gemdorin traveled toward the center of the galaxy, cloaked by stolen technology. It didn't take long to arrive at his destination. The glider he piloted met up with a monstrous Ghengat mother ship waiting to rendezvous amid a cluster of meteoroids. The black ship was nearly impossible to see if not for silver wings protruding from either side. It was a wide, flat vessel resembling a manta ray slicing through space, the central portion being considerably thicker than the thin, rigid wings. Displayed in sharp, silver characters on the ship's hull was its designation, the *Mahgshreem*. In the Hrenngen language it meant *"death wish."*

This colossal ship was a replacement vessel, one Gemdorin had acquired from the Ghengats after a devastating battle two years prior. Derian had managed to destroy the greater part of his previous fleet, including a stolen Harrowbethian carrier along with a large number of mercenary Ghengat soldiers. That skirmish had been a terrible blow for Gemdorin, nearly shattering the confidence of the Ghengats whom he had convinced would benefit from joining his crusade. It had taken some fancy talking to persuade them to continue on as allies. If there was one thing he was good at, it was handling people. He had a knack for reading personalities, knowing what folks hungered after. All he had to do was convince the fools they were on the right road to attaining their desires so long as they followed the master.

Gemdorin's glider emerged from out of the blackness, swallowed whole by its eerie mother ship. The glider landed gently in a hangar among extended rows of identical aircraft. Slung over one shoulder, he carried his limp prize aboard.

Back on the Kemeniroc, Derian met with his head strategic officers, Jerin and Rhoen, and his senior officer in engineering, Marguay. These were the men he had entrusted with the critical task of freeing Eena from the restricted military facility on Earth. These soldiers had fought side by side with Derian for years; they were expert in their areas of training. Presently, the group was brainstorming for a viable way to find and rescue Sha Eena, despite Gemdorin's obvious advantages. Leisha kept them on course following the faint trail left by their enemy's ship. It was her job to calculate a probable destination based on the direction and distance they had already traveled.

After two hours of deliberation, Derian gave his men their orders.

"Jerin, form a small team to infiltrate the ship. I need your best men, alert and stealthy."

"Rhoen, you will lead the air strike. Make sure your men understand we may have very limited visibility."

"And Marguay, any ideas you can come up with to help detect them, invisible or not, would be extremely helpful."

"I'll see what I can do, sir, but without access to the technology, I have no idea what kind of shielding we're trying to disrupt. Sharp instincts may prove to be your best weapon I'm afraid."

"Then we better all pray for sharp instincts. This mission will not fail. We won't be returning without Sha Eena. Understood?"

Accord was chimed in unison. "Yes, sir!"

"I'll inform each of you when Leisha locates their ship. Dismissed."

Jerin and Marguay left the room immediately. Rhoen dragged his feet in the direction of the exit. He turned around near the door, looking troubled as if he had something he wanted to say.

161

Derian finally acknowledged the man, sensing his reservation to leave. "Rhoen, did you need something?"

"Yes, Captain," he started, "but I don't know exactly where to start, sir." His eyes refused to meet his superior's scrutiny.

Derian realized his officer had a significant announcement to make. He set down the plans he was evaluating and approached Rhoen, stopping to lean against the edge of their oval meeting table across from him.

"If you have something important to tell me, spit it out."

Rhoen wavered in his resolve and considered leaving without admitting anything. But his conscience wouldn't allow it—not this time. He started with a justification for what he was about to confess.

"I have a family, sir. A wife and two young boys. They mean everything to me."

"What are you talking about?" Derian was unaware that his entrusted officer had been anything but a lone soul the past six years serving under his command.

"They're not here, sir. Gemdorin has them. He's threatened to kill them if...." Rhoen couldn't quite confess. The captain urged him along.

"If what, Rhoen? What have you done?"

"I didn't want to. I mean......I...I didn't have a choice. I certainly couldn't allow him to kill my family."

"Rhoen?" Derian's voice hardened as he began to sense this man was implicating himself.

"Gemdorin is merciless, sir. He murdered my father—shot him right in front of me! My mother died shortly after. She couldn't live with what Gemdorin had done." Rhoen begged with pained eyes for understanding. "If I don't report to him every two weeks he claims he'll murder my wife and sons. That was his promise. He told me that my only chance of saving them was to agree to board the Kemeniroc as a spy. I never meant to harm Sha Eena, I swear! I feel I've made a horrible mistake, but I know I can help you get her back, sir, only—my family's lives are at stake!"

Derian was in shock. Every muscle in his body tensed at the confession. He could feel his blood boiling, not only from being deceived by one of his closest men but more so from learning that

162

this fool had willingly handed over their world's last hope for survival.

He rose to his full height and growled at the traitor through gritted teeth. "Give me one good reason not to break your neck right here and now."

Rhoen stepped backward out of fear. "Wait, wait! I have something useful; it will help you."

Derian stayed his anger. He watched the coward pull a flexible, gold wristband from his pocket. It was offered with an extended arm. The captain recognized the contraption at once.

"Where did you get this?" he demanded, swiping the band.

"Gemdorin. He gave it to me so I could gather information undetected." Rhoen's features cringed, a mix of remorse and guilt. "I can help you get her back, sir. I can talk to Gemdorin and find out where he's headed, and I can…"

Derian exploded. *"Shut up! You've done enough already!"* It took every ounce of effort to check his temper. "You will tell me where Gemdorin got this technology."

"Yes, sir. It came from a planet in the Radrak System. A place called….I think he called it Primas Quar. The people there are far superior to us—to anyone I've ever heard of—in their sciences. Gemdorin told me he stole the device when their king refused to share his secrets. He didn't seem worried about retaliation either. He called them docile, claiming they were more interested in chasing after treasure than engaging in battle."

"So, Gemdorin has boarded my ship more than once?"

Rhoen hesitated with his answer. "Yes, sir."

Derian couldn't believe what he was hearing. He had put complete trust in this man for years, and now everything Rhoen was confessing made him wonder if he could trust anyone. His head moved from side to side, highly distraught.

"You, Rhoen, are a loathsome, conniving traitor. You are the lowest of cowards and through your selfish actions you have possibly sentenced your own queen to death!"

"No, sir…"

"Shut up!" the captain hollered. He was through listening. "You will be confined to the brig. If….or *when* we get Eena back, you will be tried for your crimes and sentenced accordingly!"

163

A security team entered the room just then—summoned by the push of a button.

Rhoen hung his head in shame. He knew the captain was right, but there had been so much at stake for him.

"My wife and my boys will be killed if I don't contact Gemdorin..." He hoped for at least some understanding as to why he had done what he had.

"You may have secured a death sentence for all our families."

Rhoen's gaze flickered up for a moment. "No, sir, I don't think he'll hurt her. I convinced him to keep her alive, to use the powers of the necklace for himself. He said he wouldn't harm her."

"He's murdered all the others in pursuit of her! You know darn well he'll grow tired eventually and her fate will be the same!"

Rhoen looked away, harshly reproved. Tears stung his cheeks, but he held them back. "I know," he uttered remorsefully, "and that's why I'm putting everything I care about on the line right now to tell you these things. I want to help you get her back—to make amends for what I've done."

"You were wrong for following Gemdorin in the first place."

Rhoen looked straight at the captain, finally able to meet him eye to eye. "I didn't choose to follow that awful man! My father did! He joined with Gemdorin twelve years ago, and I had no choice but to go with him, as did my mother and my brothers! Now the only ones left alive are my wife, my young children, and myself. *You* more than anyone should understand what it's like to be condemned by your father's choices!"

"Get out of my sight," Derian hissed, having heard more than enough. "Take him to the brig."

The security team cuffed the traitor, hands behind his back. They hauled him off, leaving the captain alone to contemplate how this unsettling news would alter their plans. Having access to a cloaking device changed everything. Now they had an advantage—a small one, but better than none.

"Marguay, Leisha," he called over his PCD, "meet me in the charting room now."

"Yes, sir. We're on our way."

It was dark except for a faint yellow light that shone from a lamp on the night stand. The air felt comfortably warm. Heavy crimson covers draped the bed where Eena sleepily opened her eyes. At first, she believed herself to be in Derian's quarters. She reached for Yaka but found him missing. Then her eyes caught sight of the area beyond the bed. Though lighting was minimal, it was impossible to miss the vastness of the room and its elegant décor. Eena roused immediately, realizing she wasn't at all where she belonged.

Scooting to the edge of the mattress, she climbed down from a lofty bed, endeavoring to recognize unfamiliar shapes in the dimness. The extravagance made her head spin. The room was easily four times the size of Derian's quarters and ten times as lavish. On the side nearest her, five long curtains hung equally-spaced apart. Delicate, gold embroidery decorated the crimson fabric. Approaching the nearest drapery, she pulled it aside unveiling millions of stars streaking across black space.

I'm still on a ship, she observed.

Her stomach rumbled, and she pressed on it, stifling the hunger pains. It felt as if her last meal had been a while ago.

She turned to survey the room again. Darkness proved too concealing to make out details, other than the enormous bed. Both the headboard and footboard appeared to be formed from solid wood with designs carved deep in the grain. Strange sculpted creatures were perched on all four bedposts. Oversized pillows in gold and crimson were piled against the headboard. Eena reached for the lamp on the nightstand and turned it up. The room seemed to expand under a soft yellow glow.

Just past the bed, a stunning divan matched the length of the footboard—sleek and cream-colored with rolled arms on either end. Beyond that, seats were arranged in intimate social clusters. It made her think of a royal English sitting room from Earth's Victorian era.

Crystals dangled from fancy chandeliers up above. Even the minimal light managed to disperse through these shards, forming beautiful rainbows on the walls. The arms and legs of every piece of furniture were curved and twisted into swirls, either dark-stained or painted gold. Cushions matched the crimson and marigold color scheme, enhanced by occasional green and rose

165

accents.   Each patch of upholstery was congested with motif detail, and beneath it all a blonde carpet pulled everything together.

Eena wondered, Where in the world am I?

As she wandered across the room, closer to a set of gold doors, the sound of footsteps made her halt.   She waited with a lifted ear, straining to hear.   A slight hiss signaled the parting of doors, and she found herself facing another stranger.   A striking man.   His most noticeable traits were a pair of brilliant blue eyes and a scar that topped his left eyebrow.   Dressed just about as richly as the room, he stepped up to her and smiled.

"Why, Eena, how delightful!   You're finally awake."

He spoke with such liveliness in his tone, she naturally smiled in return.

"Do you realize this marks four days you've been slumbering, my dear?   I thought I might have to come stand you up myself. Apparently, you read my mind.   So, now I suppose a 'good morning' and 'welcome aboard' are due."

Eena stared at him, bemused.   His greeting was pleasant enough.

"Who are you?" she asked, "and where am I?"

"You are safely aboard the Mahgshreem, the ship on which you belong."   He introduced himself with an outstretched arm, accompanied by an exaggerated bow.   "I am your humble captain, Kahm Gemdorin."

Eena's smile vanished as her eyes grew big.   She recalled Ian's warning from her dream.   Feeling suddenly vulnerable, she turned and ran to the other end of the room.   There was really nowhere to go, but putting distance between herself and this dangerous man seemed critical.

"Stay away from me!" she warned.   The necklace gave off a faint glow as she pressed her back against the wall.   Gemdorin caught site of this and spoke up immediately.

"Calm down, my dear, you're alright.   No one's going to hurt you here."   He motioned for her to relax, and he took a seat near the doors.   "I won't go anywhere near you, I promise."

The necklace dimmed.

She accused him straight away of brutal deeds.   "I know who you are, and I know that you killed those other girls from Earth."

His expression made it appear as if a light of understanding

166

had been switched on for him. "Ohhhh, so that's what has you so upset. Well, I'm afraid you're mistaken about the facts. I didn't kill any one of those unfortunate women. My brother, Derian, was responsible for their deaths."

Of course she didn't believe him, but her brow creased at the word *"brother."*

"Derian.....is your brother?"

"He didn't tell you?" Gemdorin shook his head slowly, a clear gesture of disappointment. "I'm sure there's a lot of truth he's hidden from you, my dear. Yes, regrettably, Derian is my little brother. Did he mention our father?"

"Your father—Vaughndorin?"

"*Our* father," he corrected.

She was unconvinced, but curious. "Derian said the man was *your* father—that he killed my mother and that you've followed in his footsteps. Are you planning to kill me too?" Eena couldn't help but ask the question. She was afraid Ian's dreamed warning was a portent. Her necklace began to glow again as she pressed her back firmly against the wall.

Gemdorin patted at the air softly. "Eena, please calm down. It's alright. The things you've heard about me are all lies. While it is true our father killed your parents, I was the one to convince the council that Derian and I were in no way connected to our father's actions. I kept him from being locked up and imprisoned as an accomplice. Did he tell you that?"

She didn't answer.

"Well, apparently my little brother never appreciated all the hard work I went through defending him. Instead, he rose up against the council and tried to declare himself King of Harrowbeth. Can you imagine? He's always had this crazy idea that our freedoms should be tossed aside, that a society must be told exactly what to do and when to do it. He does have a control issue, I'm sure you noticed. He gets rather nasty when people don't follow his silly orders."

Eena considered Gemdorin's words. What he said seemed......well, accurate. Derian had given her a rather unpleasant lecture about following orders. And Ian had reacted adversely to his difficult nature as well. She recalled what her best friend had said about the man: *"He's an unreasonable, demanding brute! He expects too much from everyone.*"

"Derian told me you were the one who wanted to declare yourself King of Harrowbeth."

Gemdorin laughed aloud as if greatly amused by the idea. "That is absolutely not true, my dear! I have wanted nothing more than to protect the rightful freedoms of our people. Ask anyone."

"There's no one to ask," she pointed out.

"Yes, well, there are plenty of people aboard this ship, and you have full access to all decks here. That is, all but those pertinent to our security. You do understand."

"You mean, I can go anywhere? Really?" She liked the sound of that.

"Roam the ship. Speak to anyone. There are many people here excited to have you back, Eena. We were afraid Derian had stolen you away for good. I'm just so relieved he didn't harm you."

"He was fine," Eena said, feeling unsure about the picture being painted. Why would Ian warn her about a man who was so kind? She trusted her best friend and chose to stick with her gut feelings.

She pointed an accusing finger at the smiling stranger. "*You* stole me away from *him*. *You're* the one to be wary of!"

Gemdorin lowered his head and remained silent for a long time. It made Eena nervous. Perhaps she should have kept quiet. When he finally spoke, his voice was soft and compassionate.

"Eena, I can see this is going to take some time. I assure you, though—you are where you belong. Our people…*your* people…were in the process of coming to retrieve you from Earth when Derian and his allies, the hideous Ghengats, attacked us and nearly destroyed our fleet. Derian captured you and all the other young women we meant to return to Harrowbeth. When he wasn't sure who the real Sha Eena was, he proceeded to place the necklace on each girl, one by one. That's how they died. Only a true Sha can survive the joining with the necklace. You know that. You're just lucky you were the honest heir to the necklace, or I'm afraid you would have been another victim of Derian's lust for power. He only planned to use you, my dear. He's not the

168

noble man he would have you believe."

Eena's head shook intuitively, refusing to accept his story even though it was making a lot of sense. Derian had admitted to putting the necklace on one girl. Maybe he had done so on all the others as well. And he had insisted she put the necklace on too, only he had made it sound as if it were for her protection. Still, she kept going back to what Ian had told her. Or had that been a dream? But she trusted Ian. He was her best friend—wasn't he? He wouldn't lie to her—would he? Well, he *had* spent the last year deceiving her under Derian's orders....

"But....but, Ian said..." she started.

Gemdorin could tell she was beginning to question things. "Ian is a victim as well, Eena. He's been brainwashed by Derian. I believe he's reluctantly followed my brother in order to be there for you. It could be that Derian has threatened him, perhaps blackmailed him. Such a nasty act would not delve below the unscrupulous nature of my brother. I do know it's a regrettable and sad situation. I only wish, for your sake, we could have saved poor Ian as well."

"Just leave me alone," Eena demanded. She'd had enough. "I don't want to hear any more. If you really mean me no harm, then go." She pointed to the door and waited to see how Gemdorin would react.

"Alright, I will leave you. But I don't wish for you to be alone." He touched a device worn on his collar and spoke into it. "Angelle, you may enter."

The doors parted, allowing a young woman to step inside. She was modestly dressed, radiating an obviously sweet nature. She had long, wavy brown locks, friendly green eyes, and delicate mannerisms. With fingers locked at her waist, she stood by and waited for instructions.

"Angelle, you will assist Sha Eena with anything she needs. Make sure she is comfortable."

"Yes, captain," the woman nodded. She then curtsied for her queen, respectfully uttering, "Sha Eena."

"I will speak with you again when you feel up to it. Until then." Gemdorin offered his own cordial bow before leaving the room.

Eena was left unsettled and confused. She wondered if it

was possible she had been so terribly deceived.

Angelle remained motionless on the opposite end of the room, appearing to await orders.   Eena wanted to run away, but the only place she saw to escape to was a bathroom.   She ducked inside and locked the door behind her.

This adjoining room turned out to be as impressive as the other.   For an evil villain, Gemdorin wasn't lacking in providing his captive with more than comfortable accommodations.   An odd thing to do if you planned to murder someone.   She stood against the door, contemplating her new captain's claims.   Could it be that his version of events was the actual truth?   Or was he just a good storyteller?   How was she supposed to know whom to believe?

Eena glanced at an extra-long counter that took up one side of the room.   It cradled an exquisite stone basin cut from pale marble.   The countertop was constructed from heavy red clay, bordered by detailed embossing painted over in gold.   It was really much too fancy for a restroom.   On the counter's edge sat the item that drew her forward—a small hologramming device similar to the one Ian had previously demonstrated for her.   She turned it on and attached the gadget to the same white gown she had worn for the past few days.   Her mirror image materialized, staring back in hologram form.

"You look awful," she said, scowling at herself.   "What I wouldn't do for an old pair of jeans."   She pulled her hair up into a ponytail to take a better look at her neck, turning her head side to side.   This was her first view of the necklace on.   She touched it and swallowed hard, realizing it was perfectly formed to her upper chest like a leech that wouldn't let go.

"Oh my," she whispered, letting her hair fall.

She stepped into a nervous pacing—back and forth and then back again.   Her hologram copied her.   Now and then she looked sideways to speak to herself.

"What am I supposed to do?   You know I'm stuck here until Derian comes to rescue me.   Or, if Gemdorin's telling the truth, then Derian would be coming to abduct me.   So, what am I supposed to do?"   She stopped and looked at her mirror image as if expecting it to answer.

"You're a lot of help," she finally grumbled, returning to her

170

pacing. It was somehow calming.

"Okay, you would think if Gemdorin were planning to kill me he'd have done it, you know, while I was sleeping. But he didn't. Soooo....maybe it's safe to presume he's not planning to kill me?" She looked at herself again. "At least not yet."

She tightened her brow and thought hard, adding the habit of twisting strands of hair around a finger. After a few moments of unproductive deliberation, she sighed with a note of frustration.

"Do you remember when this entire nightmare started back on Earth and I told you that you weren't crazy? Well, I lied! It wasn't everyone else, it was you. You are absolutely, one-hundred-percent, certifiably crazy! Are you listening to me?" Her hologram's eyes tilted pitifully. "Because if you're not listening to me, it means I really am talking to myself, which only goes to prove that I *am* crazy!"

Eena stepped up to the counter and rested against it, folding her arms over her chest. Her hologram appeared to lean against nothing but air.

"What are you going to do?" she asked her double, sounding utterly desperate this time. After a deep, shaky exhale, she managed a weak laugh and told herself again, "You really do look awful."

Her finger went back to coiling strands of hair into a tight ringlet.

"Okay.....who do you believe? I believe Ian, right? He's my best friend; he'd never lie to me. Would he? If it's true he's been brainwashed or blackmailed, well.....then he *might* lie to me. Or worse, maybe he doesn't *know* he's lying to me!"

Eena pulled her finger from her hair and shook it at her hologram. "I dreamt last night that Ian warned me about Gemdorin. But that was a dream. I mean, dreams aren't real, yet here I am on Gemdorin's ship. So how could that be? My subconscious maybe? Yes! I was consciously unaware of what was happening, but subconsciously I must've known. So I *imagined* Ian warning me because he's my friend and all and......oh crud, I really am crazy."

It seemed easier to think while pacing, so she returned to walking back and forth beside the counter. Gemdorin hadn't given her any reason to feel threatened. In fact, his conduct had

171

been rather nice.   Patient and charming even.   He purposefully had kept his distance to not frighten her, and he had provided ridiculously beautiful quarters for her to stay in, *and* he hadn't murdered her in her sleep.   All good things.

What was it he had said?   *"Ask anyone."*

Of course!   That was the answer!   That's what she needed to do, to talk to those on board the ship!   If she spoke to others besides Derian and Gemdorin, she might stand a decent chance of figuring out who was telling the truth.   Gemdorin had granted her access to any area not prohibited for security reasons—whatever that meant.   So, why not accept his invitation and find people to talk to, starting with Angelle?

That was something else that bothered her about Derian.   He had kept her confined to his quarters and the medical bay, never offering her opportunity to roam the Kemeniroc freely.   He would probably say it was for her own protection.   But here she had been granted private quarters and free access to the ship right off the bat.

"Just be cautious," she reminded herself.

Eena turned off the hologram and unlocked the bathroom door.   She stuck her head out just enough to peer around the corner.   Angelle stood up from a nearby chair, waiting to be of assistance.

"Hi," Eena said.   "Um…..just, uh….do whatever you want."

She closed the door and locked it again, figuring she might as well make good use of the facilities.

It was hard to relax, soaking in a hot tub, even though she wanted to.   Her fingers kept rubbing over the strange texture of the necklace.   It had lost its supple feel, and now adhered to her skin like a tight crust.   It was eerie how the necklace conformed to her shape precisely.   She stretched her neck and grinned, realizing none of her natural movements were hindered by this new addition.   It would take some getting used to, but at least it didn't hurt anymore.

When she finished bathing, Eena stepped out to find that Angelle had been busy preparing for her.   The bed was perfectly made, and on the outside of an armoire were arranged three lovely gowns: one a pale rose, the second red, and the third a light green.   On a low table, a delectable arrangement of food had been laid out, including a steaming ceramic kettle.   Angelle motioned for the young queen to come sit.

"Would you like a drink?" Angelle asked, holding up the kettle.

"What is it?" Eena asked.

"Meersh."   Angelle poured the hot drink into a dainty cup. "It's very sweet.   You'll like it."

Eena held the drink under her nose and breathed in a pleasant aroma.   It smelled of intense citrus and honey.   She tasted a sip. It was delightful.

"I do like it."

Angelle seemed pleased.   "I knew you would.   You must be hungry.   Please, help yourself."   She gestured at several plates of food that all looked delicious.   Eena tried a bite.

"This is very good, thank you."   She was eager to get something into her stomach and quickly downed a handful of hors d' oeuvres before easing up on the gorging.   Angelle ignored the momentary lack of manners.

"I took the liberty of preparing a choice of gowns for you. Which do you prefer?"

Eena examined the three dresses more closely.   They were full-skirted, each one richly decorated.   Not at all what she would select for herself.

"They're really fancy, aren't they," she commented.

Angelle's smile faded.   "You don't like them?"

"No, no, they're beautiful.   I'm just not use to fancy things." Eena tried to explain, "I'm more of a simple girl.   Down to earth, you know?"

Angelle appeared highly concerned.

"You wouldn't happen to have a pair of jeans, would you?" This question—made mostly in jest—elicited an even deeper look of distress.

"Never mind," Eena said.   "I like the green one."   It reminded her of Sha Tashi's image, the one she had seen in her dreams.

Angelle helped her queen step into the gown.   It was a perfect fit.   The bodice contoured her waist snugly while the long skirt hung an inch off the ground.   A low, V-neck outlined the necklace, emphasizing its presence.   The velvety material felt

173

good against her skin.   Angelle wrapped a thin matching belt twice around her waist and let it drape in the back.   Long sleeves fit snugly at the top and flared open around her wrists.   A delicate, white lace lined the inside of the open sleeves.   She felt like Cinderella.

"How do I look?" she asked, after Angelle finished fastening the many ornate buttons following her spine.

"You look beautiful."

"Thank you.   Well now," Eena began, clasping her hands together, "can we go see the rest of the ship?   Maybe I could meet some of your friends."

"Oh, no, no, not yet." Angelle ushered her to a seat.   "We must do your hair."

"Right," Eena groaned.   She wasn't really interested in taking time for such unnecessary grooming.

It actually felt good when soft bristles were combed through her long locks, almost like a finger massage on her scalp. Angelle made use of an assortment of beauty supplies neatly arranged on a tray.   She lifted the hairs away from Eena's face, securing each swag with an emerald hair comb.   The rest was left cascading down her back, heat-set into long ringlets.   When the hairdo was perfectly in place, Angelle began applying makeup, adding color to her queen's cheeks and lips before outlining her hazel eyes with strokes of brown and apricot.   During all of this, Eena took the opportunity to ask questions.

"I appreciate all you're doing for me, Angelle.   Honestly, I'm not use to this kind of treatment.   You really don't need to make such a fuss."

"It's my pleasure.   I'm honored to assist you in any way I can."

There was silence for a while as Eena considered what to ask first.   She wanted to know everything, but wasn't sure where to begin.

"Angelle, do you enjoy being here on this ship?"

There was no immediate answer.   An uneasy inhale preceded Angelle's reply.

"Things have been difficult.   But now that you're with us, I know everything will improve."

"Why do you say that?"

174

"Because you are Sha Eena.   You can heal our world and our people."   The statement was made with such confidence, Eena felt the tremendous weight of expectations dumped on her shoulders.   She wondered if she could honestly live up to everyone's hopes.

"And what about Gemdorin?   What do you think of him?"

"Kahm Gemdorin has been our leader since I can remember. He has told us stories of our world, how wonderful a place it once was before his brother, Kahm Derian, rose up to challenge him and the council."

"How much of that do you remember?"   Eena asked.

"I was very young when Kahm Derian forced my family to leave Harrowbeth.   Six or seven years old, I believe.   My parents have since passed away.   They died in battle, fighting against Kahm Derian and his soldiers.   My sister, Nischeen, and I are the only members of our family remaining."

"I'm so sorry to hear that, Angelle."   It was saddening to know such hard sacrifices had been made throughout the war. Still, Eena wasn't convinced it was Derian who had put these events into motion.

"Angelle, do you really know much about Derian?"

"I know he forced my family to leave Harrowbeth.   I know his militia has killed many of our people in numerous bloody battles.   My parents are dead because of him.   He tried to steal you away from us too, didn't he?"

Eena considered the sufferings and struggles endured by these people while she was living a simple, comfortable life on Earth, oblivious to it all.   Yet, in the couple days she had spent with Derian, he hadn't struck her as the monster Gemdorin would have her believe.   He was intimidating and bossy perhaps, but....

"Are you sure it wasn't Gemdorin who attacked the council twelve years ago in Harrowbeth?   I mean, what if Derian is the one trying to save our world and me along with it?"

Angelle stopped what she was doing to stoop down and meet her queen eye to eye.

"Sha Eena, I realize I was young when this war commenced, but if you had lived through what I have lived through, if you knew the horrible stories told about our enemy, you would never doubt that Kahm Derian is an awful, evil man."

The words were bothersome, but the conviction in Angelle's eyes troubled Eena most.   What if this woman was right?   What if Derian was the deceiver—and Ian, one of the deceived?

No more questions came to mind.   She sat silently, waiting for her assistant to finish.   As soon as she was done, Angelle handed over a small hologramming device.

"Take a look."

Eena attached the gadget to her dress.   She was stunned by the mirror image that appeared.   Staring back wasn't the young, simple, high school girl she expected to see, but a mature and elegant princess.   Make that a *queen*.   She was speechless.

Angelle took a step toward the doors.   "Are you ready to go?"

Eena glanced at her image once more.   She certainly looked the part, but could she fill the shoes she was destined to fill?

"I think so," she answered, and with a deep breath added, "as ready as I'm ever going to be."

CHAPTER TEN
Discovering Secrets

It was a mix of excitement and anxiety that churned in Eena's stomach as she set out to meet the people on the Mahgshreem. Stepping past Angelle, she was startled to discover two soldiers positioned outside her door. She instinctively shied away from them.

"It's alright," Angelle assured her. "These are your guard, Sha Eena. They'll be escorting you around the ship.

The men, dressed in drab uniform, turned to her with readable awe on their faces. Both soldiers bent at the waist, reverently murmuring her name in the process.

Eena leaned in to whisper to her assistant. "Is this really necessary?" She wasn't fond of the idea of armed chaperones.

"Yes. Gemdorin insists, for your protection."

"From whom?"

Angelle flashed a momentary look of bemusement and then voiced the obvious answer. "Kahm Derian, of course." She turned to lead the way without another word. Eena followed, shadowed by her guard.

The ship's environment was in stark contrast to her luxurious quarters—each passageway gloomy and bare. It was unlike the warm, colorful hallways on the Kemeniroc. No moving pictures animated the walls, nothing but endless stretches of striated gray. She shivered, reminded of the cold, empty hallways at the military facility she had recently escaped. What a miserable memory.

Her escorts kept at her back until Angelle paused at a set of double doors that automatically opened upon approach. Eena noticed how no authorization was needed to gain entry—no scanning handprints—as was the case on Derian's ship. One guard quickly sidestepped both women to be first inside a spacious elevator while the other man ushered the women in.

No words were exchanged as they stood waiting. Eena wondered if it was against protocol for soldiers to distract themselves with conversation. The quiet felt uncomfortable, and she found herself longing for the consolation of trivial dialogue. Someone else's dialogue. She was too nervous to open her own mouth.

A few decks down, Angelle led them further on through another gray passageway. She finally stopped and turned to her queen just strides from a wide pair of doors.

"Sha Eena, would you mind if I entered alone in order to prepare everyone for the wonderful surprise of finally meeting you?"

"If you think that's best." Eena stepped rearward and then halted, sensing the guard at her back. "I guess I'll just wait right here."

It was five minutes at least that she lingered in the hallway. Had it not been for her escorts, she might have quietly stolen off. Her stomach fluttered with imaginary butterflies as she questioned whether or not this was a wise idea after all. Meeting strangers would be hard enough, but being presented to wartime refugees whose expectations were no doubt great after years of awaiting their queen's return.......this now seemed a foolish undertaking. It occurred to her, as ordinary as she knew herself to be, that they might see her as a huge disappointment. She had worried herself into a pacing fit by the time Angelle returned.

"Sha Eena, we're ready for you."

The young queen froze. She wanted to move, but her feet were unwilling. Pale and panicked, she looked to her assistant.

Angelle encouraged her with reassurances. "Don't worry, I'll stay nearby. Everyone's eager to meet you."

Eena forced one foot forward and miraculously the other followed. When she reached the open entryway her eyes took in a vast dining hall. Hundreds of individuals stood in a semicircle, waiting, watching. A sweeping glance revealed mainly women and children present, a few elderly men interspersed among the numbers.

The crowd appeared like statues—utterly silent and posed as still as death. Every eye in a sea of faces seemed to widen at the sight of her. She had expected a staggered reaction to her entrance. It was unnerving nonetheless. Then in one collective act, young and old bowed their heads and reverently chimed her name. The gesture was overwhelming.

A sick feeling washed through her, and she identified it as shame. Such revered recognition was undeserved. It seemed a certainty that this calling was far beyond her ability. As she stood there frozen, her palms broke out in a sweat. Her mind blanked, unable to think of anything intelligent or sensitive or even witty to say to a waiting crowd. It was the innocence of a child that saved her, breaking the silence with a straightforward question.

"Are you really Queen of Harrowbeth?"

A young boy separated from the group, maybe six or seven years of age. He approached with confidence, a look of skepticism on his face. Eena bent down to his level to speak to him. His big brown eyes melted her heart.

She answered his question. "Yes, I think so."

He didn't appear convinced. "My mom says you are."

Eena grinned crookedly. "Well, that settles it then. I must be Queen of Harrowbeth because mothers are always right, you know."

The boy brightened up instantly. His stubby fingers reached out to take her by the hand. "Do you want to see my tree then?" Eena heard a single voice of concern, probably from his mother, but ignored it. She was too grateful for this brave child's friendliness at the moment.

"I would love to see your tree," she answered with a smile.

"Come on then!" He tugged on her hand and she followed. The crowd parted as he twisted his head back to introduce himself.

"My name's Willum."

"I'm pleased to meet you, Willum. I'm Sha Eena."

"I already know that."

He led her clear to a lonely back corner where the saddest collection of dwarfed trees was accumulated. The poor plants had been more than neglected. Frankly, she wouldn't have been surprised to discover them all dead.

Willum pulled her over to one that was his and declared, "My mom gave it to me when I was born. She says it's a pahna tree. Mom told me you can fix it. Will you fix it for me?"

The young Sha didn't know what to say. Apparently, this was her job, only she was clueless as to how to proceed. Her eyebrows bunched together as she looked down at the eager and expectant child. Maybe she wasn't so terribly grateful for his greeting after all.   Looking back to the tree, she groaned internally.   Oh crud.   Now what?

As if the boy could read her mind, he tossed out an order. "Touch it."

There seemed no harm in trying.

As her hand rose, reaching for a fragile branch, the necklace glimmered beneath her chin.   At the same time, a miserable sensation settled in her chest.   It was a disturbing mix of pain and despair.   Fearfully, she recoiled from the branch.   Then it hit her from where the emotions had stemmed.   It was the tree!   She was actually feeling the suffering of this neglected tree!

"Oh my gosh," she breathed in disbelief, "the poor thing's dying."

"Go on, touch it," the boy pressed again, wondering why she had stopped.

"Willum!"

Eena turned her head to find his mother at the forefront of the crowd, reprimanding him for speaking rudely to their queen.   The look on the woman's face was apologetic for herself as well as for her son.

Eena managed a kind smile.   "It's fine, really."   Then she drew in a deep, preparatory breath and focused on the tree again.

A soft light emanated from her chest, and the miserable feelings returned.   Despite the pain, she forced herself to continue.   Grasping tightly onto a thin, dry limb, she marveled at a sudden warm surge that traveled down her arm, melting through her fingertips where it absorbed like sunlight into the hungry tree. An instant color-change occurred along the limb in her grasp, painting it a deep umber.   The color seemed to bleed from her fingers, creeping downward the length of the bark until it saturated the entire trunk.   This was accompanied by a physical growth that made the tree swell to fill its pot.   From there, umber shot up through the remaining branches, making bare twigs extend and expand, forming strong arms that straightened and reached toward an artificial sky.   Tiny, white sprouts soon appeared, unfolding into pretty flowers on nearly every bare spot of branch.   Rich greens surrounded these puffs of white.

Eena felt the pain recede, replaced by tranquility.   She perceived gratitude coming from the tree, and she wondered how a

180

plant could feel.   Never before had such a notion occurred to her. She knew flora was technically alive, but harboring genuine emotion?

As the miracle progressed, Eena's other hand reached for a higher limb.   Beneath her touch, new leaves and buds formed, expanding and blossoming in fast motion.   It was like watching the changing of spring and summer occur in a matter of moments. When the white buds had enlarged with layers, they suddenly withered away, their crumpled petals raining to the floor below. Tiny, round fruits formed in their place, inflating like water balloons.   They were black at their smallest, turning a dark purple as they swelled, and finally tightening into a firm reddish-lavender. The fruit matured at the size of a fist—round, plump and pleasantly scented.

The necklace ceased glowing when Eena's hands dropped to her sides.   Weak and light-headed, she reached for Willum's shoulder to stabilize herself.   It was clear the process had physically drained the young Sha.   Her attentive guards responded quickly, helping her to a chair.   Willum plucked two round pahna fruit from his tree before following.

"I'm okay," Eena told the guards, waving off further assistance.   They stood close on either side of her anyway, and eyed the little boy holding up a ripe fruit in offer.

"You *really are* the queen!" Willum exclaimed, wide-eyed. Her demonstration had convinced him and every other witness. He placed one pahna in her hand, keeping the other for himself. "Eat it," he ordered.   She could see he wanted to bite into his own but was waiting for her to go first.

She took a small bite.   The flesh was comparable to an Earth plum casing the soft texture of an Asian pear.   It was extra sweet with a sugary-lilac scent.   "Mmmm," she hummed.   "It's delicious."

The little boy smiled and bit into his own with great enthusiasm.

"Maybe you should share one with your mother," Eena suggested.   Willum promptly acted on the idea.

That was all it took.   The room was instantly abuzz.

Willum and his mother began plucking ripe fruit from the tree, handing out pahnas to everyone wanting a taste of their home world.   Eena smiled at the collective excitement.

There were no shy onlookers anymore as people approached their queen, introducing themselves and presenting more plants to be touched and healed.   Eena learned that this little garden had fed their families years ago when the fruit had grown abundantly. But over time, the plants had slowly withered and dried, many crumbling into kindling.   Those remaining were kept in the hope their Sha would return as healer someday.   It was a hope finally realized.

Eena wanted to help everyone, but the renewing process was draining.   After restoring two additional plants to good health—a neum bush with burgundy berries and a tall ongrea tree weighed down with orange, bottom-heavy fruit—she had to quit, feeling completely exhausted.   Angelle finally stepped in and asked the crowd to wait for another day.

"Sha Eena needs to rest now, but she'll be back."

Angelle helped the young Sha up from her chair while the guards positioned themselves on either side to assist in escorting her out.   But before she had taken a step, Willum and his mother were back.

"Thank you, Sha Eena," the woman said.   "Thank you so very much.   You've no idea how happy you've made us all today."

Eena smiled for mother and son.   "I only wish I were strong enough to do more."

"Eventually, you will be," Angelle assured them all.

It was disappointing having to leave before questioning anyone about their captain, but the miracle she had accomplished was worth her time and depleted energy.   She insisted on walking out of the commissary herself.   One misstep in the corridor, however, had the guards supporting her the rest of the way.   As soon as Eena returned to her quarters, she dropped onto the big crimson bed and fell fast asleep.   Her dreams started off in a recurring manner....

She was walking through a forest, lush and dark, gazing up at tall surrounding trees.   Twisted branches jostled in the air, shaken by wind that threatened colder days ahead.   From these boughs, autumn leaves rained down in spirals, not pliable but unnaturally brittle. Her footsteps crunched on a thickening carpet of dead leaves. She cringed at the sound, afflicted by it as if stepping on the backs of black beetles. The uneasiness escalated, mounting into a state of distress, until fear wound its tendrils around her heart. She perceived that the woods had eyes, hundreds of them watching her every move. Though unseen, the danger felt real.

Her pace quickened in an attempt to flee, weaving through a maze of standing timbers. But the forest seemed to thicken as if purposefully hindering her advance. The wind picked up and slapped against her body, whipping her with dry leaves and debris. She froze at an imagined whisper, faint at first, growing progressively louder. Her eyes darted every which way in search of a presence. She was certain it wasn't the wind; it was a definite murmur hissing in her ears. She could hear them. All of them. They were calling to her. She gasped at the realization the trees were calling her name.

"Come to us! Eena, come to us!"

She covered her ears, frightened. "No! Stop it!"

There was no escape—no way out of the enclosing forest or its chorus of despairing. Again her name carried in the air, but this time pronounced by a lone voice. Her heart leapt at the familiarity of it.

"Eena? Eena?"

"Ian, is that you?"

"Eena, can you hear me?"

She glanced around in her dreams. The hungry timbers vanished, and she found her best friend standing alone in the center of a meadow. He had returned.

"Ian, you're here!" she cried, running to hug him. "How is this possible? I'm still dreaming, aren't I?"

"Yes, you are dreaming," he assured her. "Are you alright?"

She nodded that she was fine, feeling safe in his arms. He moved her away to ask what he had come to find out.

"Eena, do you know where you are?"

"I'm on Kahm Gemdorin's ship, which is really weird because I dreamt you told me I'd been abducted by him, and when I awoke it was actually true. How could that be, Ian?"

"I did tell you. And I warned you to be careful because your life may be in serious danger."

"This isn't possible; you can't be in my dreams." She was still convinced her mind was playing tricks on her.

Ian hesitated before sharing the guarded secret his family had kept for generations.

"Listen, Eena, I have to tell you something. It may sound impossible, but the truth is……I've always been able to visit your dreams. That's the real reason I knew you were alive on Earth. That's how I found you, by watching your dreams and observing what you were imagining at night."

"You've always been able to do this?" She was stunned. "I don't recall seeing you in my dreams before."

"That's because I never spoke to you before. I'm only supposed to observe, not interfere. But right now I don't know how else to help you."

She was upset by his news. Having someone watch her dreams unbeknownst to her—that didn't settle well. She felt exposed by his invasion of her privacy; all her personal thoughts no longer personal. Her next words came out crossly.

"When are these surprises going to end, Ian? Every time I turn around, there's something else I don't know, more craziness you failed to tell me."

"I'm sorry, but honestly I wasn't supposed to tell anyone—including you."

"And why not?"

"Because it's a protector's secret. My father watched over your mother in her dreams too. He'd be furious if he knew I'd divulged this to you, not to mention the lecture I would have to endure if he found out I actually showed myself in your dreams. Eena, I simply observe, and only for the sole purpose of protecting our queen. But with you in enemy hands…" He shook his head, signaling he had no choice.

"Derian suspected I might have some way of finding you because of what happened on Earth. So I told him the truth, which I'm not sure I won't live to regret."

His excuses weren't good enough to snuff out her irritation. She was still angry.

"Why is it you all feel the need to keep secrets from me? I

184

end up finding out anyway.   Like the fact that I'm not human but was living dangerously among them.   Then all the 'hush hush' about this strange necklace.   And now you say you've been watching my dreams?   Oh, and let's not forget this little pearl that Gemdorin slipped to me—Derian and Gemdorin are brothers? No one bothered to share that major news!   Or is the fact they're related some big conspiracy?"

"People are only trying to protect you."

"Protect me.....or themselves?"

"Derian would've told you eventually, but he's not exactly proud of his family.   He's fought hard in this war to compensate for the crimes of his father and brother.   I don't know that I'd brag about being related to them either."

Eena breathed a sigh through her nose, growing more sympathetic as she thought about it.   "But it's true they're actually brothers?"

"Yes."

She frowned.

"Gemdorin hasn't hurt you, has he?"   Ian was more concerned for her physical safety than her sore feelings.

"No, no, I'm fine.   Actually, he's been very nice to me."

Ian's face twisted up with incredulity.   "Gemdorin?   Nice?"

"Yes.   He was a real gentleman when I met him.   He even gave me my own amazing quarters.   The room is huge!   I have full access to his ship, the Mushroom or something like that.   And I have my own assistant.   I was able to meet some of the people on the ship too—and, Ian, you won't believe it!   I made a tree grow!"   She was getting excited remembering her earlier accomplishments.

"Really?"   He was stunned.   He had expected a fearful or anxious reaction to her situation, not enthusiasm.   And who in their right mind would ever call that monster a gentleman?

"Really!" she repeated.   "Actually, I made three plants grow, but then I could hardly stand up.   Do you know how exhausting it is to do that?"

He shook his head in honest answer.   "No, I don't.   But I know you'll get stronger over time, don't worry about that."

"Good, because I can't imagine making much progress only three plants at a time."   Her lips spread wide with the next announcement. "Ian, I ate a pahna fruit today.   Willum gave me a bite from his tree."

"Willum?"

"He's a little boy, maybe five or six years old.   He wanted me to heal his pahna tree, so I did.   It was mind-blowing!   I still can't believe how the necklace works!"   She was delighted to have her best friend to talk to.   She wanted to express her feelings to someone who would understand.

"What did Gemdorin do?"

"He wasn't there.   Angelle went with me."

"Ang...Angelle?   She's there?"   Ian's voice faltered as he nearly choked on the question.   Eena wondered at his reaction.

"Do you know her?"

"I did know her—once.   Her family, I mean.   I didn't think they were still alive."

"Her parents aren't, I'm afraid.   Angelle told me that her sister, Nischeen, is the only family she has left.   I feel sad for her. Actually, I feel sad for all these people.   They look like they've been living a nightmare."

"I'm sure they have," Ian agreed.   Curiously, he asked, "How is Angelle?"

"She's great.   She's the one Gemdorin asked to assist me."

"Oh.   Oh, that's good."

"Ian?"   She pulled him out of a deep thought.

"Yeah?"

"Angelle talked to me about Derian.   She doesn't think very highly of him.   She blames Derian for running her family out of Harrowbeth and for the death of her parents.   Is it true?   Did he really do those things?"

Eena watched carefully for a telling reaction, which turned out to be an immediate display of defensiveness.

"Of course not!   It might be true her parents died in battle, but Derian never set out to harm anyone.   He only fights to defend Harrowbeth from Gemdorin.   And he didn't run her family off; they followed Gemdorin willingly when he left.   Her father chose to leave.   No one forced him to go.   Angelle was too young to clearly remember these things, and I'm sure Gemdorin has filled her mind with lies about everything that really happened."

Eena dared to ask another hard question.   "Ian, how old

186

were you when the war started? Do you remember things clearly?"

He was surprised she would probe him like this. "Yes, I remember! If you must know, I was ten years old and I remember it vividly!" His eyes scanned her with disbelief. "Do you doubt my knowledge of the truth? Eena, I hope you're not actually listening to Gemdorin. He's a liar! He'll twist everything around to make himself look like the hero, but he's not! I know, because I was there when he attacked the council, and when he tried to chase you down and kill you as a child!"

She backed off. "Okay, okay, but I don't think he's going to kill me now. If that was his plan, wouldn't he have done it already? And why treat me so nicely and give me all these things? I just don't understand……I mean, it doesn't make any sense."

Ian looked her squarely in the eyes, adamant that she hear his warning. "Eena, you can't trust him. He killed the other girl we were protecting before he stole you away. I don't know why he's feigning kindness towards you, but I assure you it's a devious and dangerous ruse."

Her stomach rolled, sickened. "He really killed her?" She couldn't believe it. "But why? If he knew I was Sha Eena, why kill her?"

"That's what I'm trying to tell you. He is as far from nice as you can get! He's the enemy! A horrible, evil monster! Beware of him, Eena, and his self-serving motives."

Fear gripped at her heart again. She repeated her previous thought, one that seemed to deliver some comfort. "He could've killed me already if he wanted to, you know."

"I know," Ian admitted. "I think he's interested in that necklace you wear. That may be what's saved your life."

She touched the item clinging to her neck, remembering just a few days ago when Ian had placed it there.

"I saw my mom. When you put the necklace on me, it was full of memories. All sorts of images from every Sha who's ever lived. My mom, she was there. She talked to me, Ian."

"What did she tell you?"

"She told me the necklace is very powerful."

"It is," he agreed.

187

"No, I mean more powerful than anyone knows. She warned me not to abuse those powers or there would be unspeakable consequences. What do you think she meant by that?" Eena studied Ian's face, hoping he knew more.

"I'm not sure. I don't remember your mother using the necklace for anything other than keeping our world alive. I know it gave her perfect health, and it will for you too. I know it can heal your injuries. That's about all I'm aware of."

"Do you think my mother could've defended herself against Vaughndorin if she had used those other powers?"

"I don't know." Ian pointed out the obvious, "You're the one wearing the necklace."

"Yes, but that doesn't mean I have any clue what to do with it. Until today I didn't even know I could make a tree grow. I just wonder what she meant by 'unspeakable consequences.' Do you think she meant it could hurt me?"

"I doubt it. The necklace protects you. It would have no host if it were to harm you," he reasoned. "That wouldn't make any sense."

"I guess you're right," she decided. "Ian, do you know if there's anything written about the necklace? Any historical documents or journals?"

"You mean like an instruction book?" Ian grinned. "Sorry, there's nothing like that. However, there are a number of folktales about the necklace, but they're all just creative legends. You know—ghost stories to scare young people."

She wondered if some hidden truths were buried in those folktales. "Will you tell me one?"

"Okay. Well, let's see," Ian began. He started to amble across the meadow that extended endlessly in Eena's dream. She stepped along beside him through knee-high grasses, waiting to hear a story.

"No one's really sure where the necklace originally came from, so there's a handful of folklore about it. Some say it was a gift to our people from a group of highly advanced alien visitors who came to Moccobatra as friendly explorers. The story tells of how they wiped out most of the vegetation on our planet. In a gesture of apology, they gave us the necklace as a tool to revitalize all the plant life. They granted one special woman the ability to

188

wear and use the powerful necklace. This ability she could pass down to her female children. The necklace has been handed down ever since."

The young queen wrinkled her nose at the likelihood of that tale.

"Well, another story depicts the necklace as a magical piece of armor created by the Gods. In order to keep its powers and secrets hidden from mortals, it was buried in a chest guarded by two ghastly grembloines."

"What on earth is a grembloine?" Eena interrupted.

"No," Ian corrected, "you mean, what on Moccobatra is a grembloine?"

She grinned crookedly.

"A grembloine is the absolutely worst possible creature you could ever come across—next to Gemdorin that is."

"Okay, okay," she groaned.

"I'm not finished. Grembloines are the ugliest, smelliest, most hideous giants. They're strong enough to crush a man with one huge claw. They're as fast on four legs as the wind—you can't outrun one; it's impossible. The only hope of escaping a grembloine is to outwit him. Lack of brains is his only weakness. Still, if you ever get a whiff of a grembloine, your best bet is to keep hidden."

"This is, of course, all make believe, right?" A tilt of her eyebrow conveyed a bit of concern.

Ian shrugged. "Well, I've never actually come across one, but..." Struggling not to crack a smile, he went on with his tale.

"As I was saying.....one day a brave warrior dared to search for this armor of the Gods. His hope was to find the perfect gift for his true love—one that would protect her when he was off at war—and thus win her hand in marriage. The story tells of how he discovered a secret lair in which he defeated a ring of grembloine guards and then victoriously claimed his prize."

Ian added actions to his words as he went along, placing a hand over his heart while brandishing a pretended sword. Eena giggled at his antics.

"When the warrior brought his gift home, he placed the charmed necklace on his true love. She became the very first Sha, while he became the very first Shen."

189

Eena grinned. "That was much better."

Ian held up a finger, prepared with another story.

"I've also heard rumor of an ancient dragon who watched over Moccobatra long ago. According to this tale, our world was once home to thousands of dragons, centuries before men ever settled on the surface. But the dragons were discovered by galactic hunters who traveled throughout space searching for challenging prey. Thousands of the beasts were slain by these ruthless hunters. To save their own lives, the dragons were forced to leave Moccobatra and search for a new world to hide on. No one knows where they went, nor have they been spotted since.

"The supreme, guardian dragon, however, would not leave, because it was his duty to care for Moccobatra. He tried to hide from the hunters, but eventually they found and slew him, not realizing his life-force sustained the planet. It's said the spirit of this brave dragon entered that necklace—" Ian pointed to Eena's neck. "—so that the wearer would have supernatural power to continue caring for our world. Some believe it's his life-force that enables every new Sha to keep the planet thriving."

Ian stopped walking and waved off the likelihood of any truth to these tales. "You see, they're all just silly ghost stories."

"I suppose," Eena shrugged, "but the necklace does seem alive in a way. It behaves like it has a will of its own sometimes."

"Hmm." Ian gestured for Eena to take a seat in the grass and get comfortable. He sat beside her, ready to share one final story.

"My favorite tale of all is one your father, Shen Laynn, loved to recite to me when I was little. He was a master storyteller. Totally dramatic. He lived to scare you to death! His story goes like this...

"In a dark and fearsome time thousands of years ago there existed two immortal sisters. They were the most beautiful, bewitching creatures you could ever set eyes on, possessing the ability to lure any unsuspecting, love-sick fool into their treacherous schemes. For you see, as undeniably attractive as these sisters were on the outside, they were just as ugly and evil on the inside, to the point they lacked any remorse whatsoever for the terrible things they did. Now, not only were these two sisters immortal, but they had the incredible powers that come with

190

immortality.   The more they used their powers, the more formidable they became.   The more they schemed, the worse their plots deepened."

"They sound absolutely awful," Eena broke in.   She was really enjoying Ian's storytelling.

"Oh, they were," Ian agreed, "but, these evil sisters made one grave mistake.   For you see, they were not the only immortal beings in existence.   And immortals all live by one very strict rule."

"What is it?" Eena asked, eager to know.

"I'm getting to that."   Ian cleared his throat, purposefully stalling to heighten the suspense.   "The number one rule of immortality is—you never, ever, ever interfere with mortal societies.   In other words, you aren't allowed to get involved with mortal politics or wars or advancements in science, because doing so might disrupt the natural evolution of a world.   The undying are very particular about not causing any major changes in the universe."

"Huh."   Eena wondered what it would be like to have powers incredible enough to alter the fate of an entire world.   She imagined strict rules would be necessary.

"Well, believe it or not, in one of their most appalling schemes, the two sisters crossed the line and broke that crucial rule.   Their interference was the cause of a near world annihilation!   This brought down the wrath of the other immortals.   But the undying are exactly that—never dying.   However, they're not irrepressible.   These evil sisters were sentenced to an eternity separated from their natural bodies.   Their immortal shells are said to be preserved in stone deep inside the mystical cave of Wanyaka, while their spirits are trapped in a red crystal prison, chained by a powerful spell that holds them there forever.   They say the crystal beats a deep, steady rhythm next to their bodies inside the same cave.   They're stuck this way, tortured by the constant presence of their beautiful, unchanging corpses, longing for their souls to be reunited so they can once again wreak havoc on all mortals across the universe."

Eena groaned, shaking her head suspiciously.   "Wanyaka is the name of Derian's pet."

"I know.   He was named after the cave.   It's a popular

ghost story in Harrowbeth. Now, will you let me continue?"

Eena leaned forward, eager for more.

"It's said that the necklace you're wearing right now actually belonged to one of those awful sisters. Before her spirit was separated from her body, all her powers were recalled and placed within that necklace. It was buried for centuries in Wanyaka cave until the day a young princess happened upon it completely by accident and claimed the charmed necklace as her own. When it clung to her neck, she received those great powers to use at her beckon call. Since that time, the necklace has been passed down from Sha to Sha, but instead of being used for ill purposes it works for the good of our world—to keep things alive and thriving. For you see, the powers themselves aren't evil. It's all dependent upon the person wielding them."

"What happened to the two sisters?" Eena asked.

"I imagine they're still stuck in the crystal somewhere inside a mystical cave back on Moccobatra—probably awaiting some unsuspecting fool to discover and release their spirits. One can only imagine how dark and dreadful the universe would become if that happened."

"Oh, wow," she breathed.

Ian released a hearty chuckle, and Eena shoved at him.

"Are you laughing at me?"

He couldn't seem to stop. "You should see your face; you look like you believe every word!"

She tried to justify her wide-eyed reaction. "Well, with all I've been through lately, it's hard to tell what's true and what's make-believe anymore. It sounds about as likely as anything else. Except for the whole 'immortal' thing; that's a little far-fetched. I mean, do you really think there are people out there who will never, ever, ever die?"

"I don't know," Ian shrugged, still chuckling, "and I don't really care."

Eena shoved at him again.

"What if..." she began, eyes tapering, "what if when a Sha uses all the hidden powers of the necklace, those 'unspeakable consequences' turn her into a horrible, evil immortal creature just like those two sisters!" Eena raised her arms high over her head, curling her fingers like claws. She made a scary, growling noise

192

as she loomed over her unsuspecting victim.

In her best witch's voice she hissed, "You can't resist my powers, you poor mortal boy! You will do exactly as I say!"

Ian broke into a fit of laughter, chortling even harder when Eena lost her balance and tumbled on top of him, sending them both backwards onto the soft grass. She rolled off to his side, giggling. When their amusement subsided, they smiled up at a dreamy blue sky.

Ian turned his head to look at her. "It's just a story," he repeated.

"I know," she said, smiling back at him. She was having fun, like old times. This all reminded her of the numerous lazy afternoons they had spent together as best friends on Earth. She missed that. Being with Ian in this way was precious, even if it was merely a dream.

For a long time they lay still, watching a string of wispy clouds cross overhead. Eventually, Ian broke the silence.

"Eena, the reason I'm here is to find out your location so we can organize a rescue." He sat up from the bed of grass and crossed his legs.

"I know," she said, sitting up as well, "but I have no idea where Gemdorin's ship is or where it's headed."

"Then I need to go." He pushed himself up off the ground. She was up right behind him.

"Why?" She pulled a disappointed face. "I don't want you to go."

"It's not proper, Eena. I'm not supposed to..." He started with a reason, but was sharply interrupted.

"So what? I don't care if it's proper or not. You're my best friend and I want to visit with you, and I can't visit with you when I'm awake now, can I?" Sad eyes begged him to linger. "Stay with me. Please."

He was teetering on a fence between desire and duty. Truth be told, he didn't want to go. "Eena, I'm interfering in your dreams."

"No you're not. I would've imagined you here anyway." She offered the possibility. "Besides, it's just a dream."

Ian considered her argument. He missed the friendship they shared back on Earth as much as she did, although he had known

193

it would come to an end someday.   But here in her dreams it didn't have to end.   And besides, he had already broken the rules by telling his secret.

"You're right," he shrugged, "it's just a dream."

Eena smiled wide.   She was clearly pleased he chose to stay. "Watch the sunset with me then."

As quickly as she voiced the request, their surroundings transformed into a familiar hillside with a grand weeping willow planted directly atop the highest point.   Cornfields covered acres of surrounding farmland, while a beautiful red-orange sun sank way off on the horizon.   Eena's appearance altered as well.   She stood before Ian in her favorite attire—a pink t-shirt and faded blue jeans.

Stealing a head start up the hill, she shouted over her shoulder, "Race you to the top!"

Ian glanced up at their tree where Paka, Eena's horse, nibbled on the grassy slope.   It only took him a second to chase after her.

"Hey, that's cheating!"

She beat him to the top, largely because gentlemen let ladies finish first.   Eena planted herself against the tree and scanned the view.   The sunset was as beautiful as she remembered it.   Ian plopped down beside her.

"I'll stay and watch the sunset for old time's sake.   But then I really should go."

"Fine.   It's a deal," she agreed.

They talked, mostly of Earth.   They reminisced about things done together in the rural town of Royal City.   They discussed everything—from the time Eena had set Ian up on a disastrous blind date with her friend, Jackie, to the time he had "accidentally" broken Erik's nose to prevent the boy from asking her to Homecoming.   That whole incident made a lot more sense now, understanding that Ian was her protector.   They laughed and smiled for hours until Ian realized the night was nearly over and the sun still hadn't completely set.

"I swear this is the longest sunset I've ever seen, Eena."   He arched an eyebrow, looking sideways at her.

She shrugged like she hadn't noticed.

"It's morning," he announced.   "I really do have to go."

She sighed at the truth.   "I know.   Thanks for staying.   This was the best dream I've ever had.   I'm glad I discovered your secret, Ian."

She smiled sweetly at him.

He smiled back, although her words caused him concern.   He knew he couldn't keep visiting her dreams, but for now it was a means of helping her.   This was all just to help save his queen.

CHAPTER ELEVEN
How Strange

When Ian awoke, the first person he saw was his captain, Kahm Derian. He reported that Eena was fine but not certain of her location. He told Derian about Gemdorin's kindness toward her. The news was troubling, although they both agreed it was better to hear she was being treated well and not poorly.

"Have you detected her tracking device yet?" Ian asked.

Derian shook his head. "Which means she's either well beyond this system, or Gemdorin has found and removed it already. Ian, anything you can learn from Eena will be of great value."

"I know. I'll keep after her."

When Eena awoke, the first person she saw was her captain, Kahm Gemdorin. He was lounging in a chair a few feet beyond her bed when she sat up and noticed him. He was the last person she cared to awaken to.

"Good morning!" he greeted cheerfully. "It's about time you chose to join the living." He was dressed as impressively as the day before, showing a flair for the dramatic in both style and behavior. Eena quickly scrambled out of bed, keeping a wary eye on him.

"What are you doing in my room?"

"Don't be alarmed, my dear, I mean you no harm. I've brought breakfast. Come. Sit." He gestured for her to take a seat across from him. She didn't budge.

"Really now," he sighed, 'tsk'ing disappointedly. "Would you feel better if I were to move to the far side of the room again?"

"Maybe."

"Oh, very well, if it makes you comfortable." Gemdorin grabbed a mug of hot meersh and a purple fruit from off the table at his knees. He then changed seats, settling into a chair near the exit. "Is this far enough for your liking?"

"What do you want?" Eena asked, annoyed that he hadn't

continued walking right out the door.

"What do I want?   Well, let's see……..at the moment an ounce of trust would be nice."   He winked over a grin that appeared mildly humored.

"I have no reason to trust you," she reminded him.

Gemdorin took a big bite from the pahna in his hand.   He chewed it slowly, savoring the sweet flavor.   After swallowing, he gestured to the young Sha with the remainder of the fruit.

"These are absolutely delicious!   You've done some excellent work here, my dear.   You really should have one."

"Did Willum give those to you?" she asked.

"Of course he did.   Willum was very impressed with your performance.   In fact, you're all that boy's jabbering about."

This news made her smile.   "He's an impressive child himself," she said, daring to approach the abandoned table for a pahna of her own.   "What exactly did Willum say about me?"

"Oh, that he's hoping to see you again today."

She beamed, pleased.

"I told him not to count on it since he's spending the afternoon with me, and you seem to have a problem being anywhere near me at the moment."   Gemdorin watched for a sour reaction.   He got one.

Eena screwed up her face and dug a fist into her hip.   "And why would a child be spending the day with you?"

"It's, oh…uh……get-to-know-your-captain day!"   Gemdorin grinned cleverly.

Eena rolled her eyes.   "Right.   Nice try."   In her mind she was considering Ian's warnings, but this man wasn't anything like the horrible individual her best friend had described.   His personality was charismatic and pleasant.   Even charming.   How could *he* be Gemdorin?

"If Willum and his family agree to have lunch with me, will you accompany us?"

Her first inclination was to refuse, but she took a moment to think about it.   A visit with Willum and his mother sounded nice.   And she wouldn't be alone with Gemdorin.   Besides, if the man's intentions were to harm her, opportunity existed at any time.

With slight reservations, she accepted his invitation.   "Okay, but just lunch—and *only* if Willum is there."

197

"It's a date! Until then, my dear." Gemdorin rose swiftly. With a grand bow he slipped out of the room.

Eena was relieved to have him gone, and yet the discrepancy between his cordial conduct and nasty reputation left her feeling puzzled. "How strange," she sighed. "How very strange."

After a quick bath, Eena wound herself in a wrap and returned to the bedroom where her waiting assistant offered a morning greeting. Angelle presented another selection of fancy wardrobe on the front of the armoire. Eena chose the least glamorous of three gowns—a violet dress with velvet sleeves and a high bodice. Angelle once again groomed her queen before the pair set out under escort.

The morning passed by pleasantly. A larger audience had gathered in the commissary, excited to finally see their young queen in person. In an effort to preserve her strength, Eena healed only two plants, allowing recuperating time in between. Surprisingly, she found her energy not nearly as drained as the evening before.

It seemed like the day had barely begun when Angelle announced the noon hour.

"We should be going, Sha Eena. It would be rude to keep the captain waiting."

A nervous stomach suppressed the young queen's appetite, and she regretted ever agreeing to the lunch date. Reluctantly, she allowed herself to be escorted out of the commissary.

They climbed five levels before stepping into a gray corridor as bare and dismal as all previous passageways. Angelle dismissed herself outside a wide set of unfamiliar doors, leaving Eena to face Gemdorin with just her guard. Drawing in a deep breath, the young queen recalled why she had agreed to this—for Willum's sake. The boy's company was worth a few raw nerves. Just when she was about to tap on the door, it slid open. Kahm Gemdorin stood before her, smiling brightly.

"I'm so glad you could make it, my dear." He welcomed her into a small dining area, leaving her escorts outside.

Eena scanned the room, painted marigold, adorned with a selection of realism works of art. They were sizeable prints set in thick, elaborate frames. Additional artwork rested on a cinnamon floor, leaning lazily aside. Hanging over a long, rectangular table was a crystal chandelier with far-reaching arms of gold. The low lighting made the room feel both comfortable and cozy.

Eena promptly realized she and Gemdorin were the only two individuals in the room. Willum's family was not in attendance as promised. She backed away from the captain, ill at ease.

"Where is everyone? Where is Willum?"

Gemdorin pretended not to notice her nervousness. "They'll be here shortly. Have a seat."

He positioned himself at the head of the table, a heavy piece of furniture upholstered in ivory. Four broad legs peeked from beneath the scalloped edges of a lacy table cloth. Five place settings suggested more guests were expected. Eena chose to sit opposite Gemdorin, leaving the middle chairs for Willum's family.

"Tell me, how was your morning, my dear?"

"Fine." She paused before asking out of politeness, "And yours?"

"Excellent as always."

The pleasantries ceased and the room fell perfectly silent. For an awkward period of time they faced each other across the table, neither uttering a word. More unsettling than the silence was the captain's fixed gaze. Eena wanted to disappear. And she would've gladly done so had the necklace granted her such power. Instead, she did her best to look cool and composed until Gemdorin vocalized a reason for staring.

"I'm trying to figure out how my brother was able to turn you against me in such a short period of time."

Eena fidgeted. "It wasn't Derian's doing. Though he did warn me you were not to be trusted."

"Who was it then? Tell me who clouded your judgment." Gemdorin sat up taller in his chair, appearing both curious and defensive. It was hard to believe he could come across as more intimidating than Derian.

"Ian warned me about you," she admitted, sitting up taller herself. It was an attempt to hide her own shaky confidence.

"Ian. Ah-hah, of course. And I gather you put full faith in Ian's opinion?" His scarred eyebrow climbed, waiting for an answer.

"He's my best friend. He would never lie to me."

199

Gemdorin glanced down at the table, thinking. "No. No, I'm sure he wouldn't. But consider the possibility his opinion is based on hearsay and not fact. I told you yesterday, Ian has been deceived by my brother."

Accusations were blurted out by the young queen—provided by Ian. "He knows everything because he was there! He witnessed your attack on Harrowbeth, and he saw Derian chase both you and your followers from Moccobatra! He was old enough to comprehend your treachery!"

Gemdorin grinned unfittingly at the charges. "Oh, my dear, is that what you've been told?"

"Ian would never lie to me," she insisted. "Never."

"Unless misleading you is a lie." Gemdorin didn't wait for a comment, but went right on with his point. "Your protector may have been living in Harrowbeth, yes, but he was not *there*. He was not in the room when Derian and I fought. He was never a participant in our private conversations. If he had been, he would realize I wasn't the one planning to subjugate Harrowbeth. Or have you not noticed how everyone, including the council, follows Derian's advice. He maneuvered himself into the powerful position of chief of their armed forces, and now he leads our government by the ear, directing the moves of weathered dignitaries who see him as some sort of charmed prince! The council may pretend to run things, but I guarantee it is Derian who guides their actions. It's only a matter of time before he finds a way to declare himself king."

"But you were the one trying to…"

"No, my dear…" Gemdorin interrupted. He pointed a rigid finger across the table. "You nor Ian know what I was trying to do, because neither of you were there with me. You've both chosen to believe Derian's stories, just like so many other misguided fools. What I was truly trying to do was keep my power-hungry brother from exploiting a crippled kingdom! I already explained this once. Only a year after your parents' deaths, I overheard my brother pompously bragging about what he planned to do when he was king. I knew then he had to be stopped. He had gained too much influence over the council, taking advantage of the sympathy they felt for him because *your* mother had catered to him so openly." Gemdorin's voice lowered

200

momentarily—a distinctly jealous grumble. "The poor, little, baby victim of circumstances."

"He was no baby."

"Regardless! There my brother was, bragging as if he were already King of Harrowbeth!" Gemdorin scoffed, "Shen Derian! Can you imagine it? And you, the rightful heir and queen, too young and helpless to do anything about it. I tried talking some reason into the council, but the fools wouldn't listen! So I stepped forward in an attempt to save our people from the shady actions of Vaughndorin's youngest, spoiled son. What I was trying to do was defend our only living Sha's rightful position as ruler."

Eena stared at the man who was painting himself as her would-be hero. She said nothing.

"Ian was nowhere around when my men were being slaughtered by Derian's followers. Despite his youth, my brother had already established himself as a dominant presence. People followed him blindly! Realizing it was too late to convince anyone of his true intentions, I took my men and their families and we stole a ship in order to escape Harrowbeth with our lives. If we had stayed, Derian would have had us imprisoned or executed for our actions and effectively rid himself of all remaining opposition. We had no choice but to commandeer a ship and leave! That's what *really* happened."

Eena found it difficult to refute his story. Perhaps both brothers were trying to defend Harrowbeth in their own way, but that didn't excuse blatant acts of violence.

"What about all those girls you murdered. Ian told me you killed them."

"And have you asked Ian *where he was* when these crimes supposedly happened? Because I'll guarantee you, he wasn't anywhere near the unhappy events. He was back in Harrowbeth."

"How do you know where he was?" she asked.

"I have spies, Eena. I keep my eye on Derian's every move."

"You have spies on his ship?"

"Yes."

"Who?"

Gemdorin released a riveted chuckle. "You would love for me to tell you, wouldn't you? So you could betray me and put my men in danger? I don't think so, dear." A grin spread askew when Eena's gaze dropped to the table. He could see the wheels turning in her mind.

"Eena, I played no part in the murder of those girls, I assure you. Derian has always been the one intent on hunting you down. *He* killed them. He murdered each and every one by forcing the necklace on them. Ian wasn't there to witness any of it. Ian showed up much later when only two of you remained—against my brother's wishes, I might add. Derian made up the whole ridiculous story of how I put to death those poor, innocent young women, but it's just another of his many lies. All lies, Eena. Awful, cunning lies. Derian wants you alive so he can use you and become King of Harrowbeth. As far as Ian goes, he's been deluded like so many other members of Derian's crew."

"But….no….Ian said….." she sounded as if she might cry.

"Eena, dear, I'm sure Ian's intentions are honorable, but everything he thinks is based on Derian's deceptions. Ian has been absent for the majority of our battles. I'm not sure he's observed *anything* firsthand. Do you really believe it's fair to base your opinion of me and my moral objectives on hearsay and rumors?"

Eena's face tangled up miserably as her picture of the truth was challenged. Their discussion was cut short when a light knock sounded at the door. She wiped at a wayward tear, realizing Willum and his family had arrived.

"Our guests are here," Gemdorin announced, rising from the table. Starting toward the door, he paused for a second beside her. "Are you ready?"

"Yes, of course." She rose from her seat as well.

When the doors parted, six-year-old Willum stepped inside wearing a collared shirt with brown slacks and matching vest. He was accompanied by his nine-year-old brother, Xander, and their mother, Sarii. It was obvious they were dressed in their best clothing, not nearly as impressive as the captain's or Eena's attire. Xander's outfit appeared similar to his brother's excepting pants that were two inches too short. Sarii wore a plain, pink dress. Her chestnut hair fell past her shoulders, pulled back on one side by a pearled clip that matched a simple single-pearl necklace. These were the finest accessories she owned.

"Eena!" Willum shouted, hustling to greet his new favorite person. He hugged her hips as tightly as he could manage before looking up and extending his lower lip. "All my pahna fruit is gone."

She couldn't help but smile at the pitiful look on his face. "For goodness sakes, we can't have that now, can we? I guess I'll just have to come touch your tree again."

Willum smiled wide.

Sarii and Xander gave their queen a more formal greeting, bowing their heads while chiming "Sha Eena."

"Come in and take a seat," Gemdorin instructed the family.

They separated around the dining room table finding their places. Gemdorin courteously helped each lady with her chair.

"Thank you," Sarii uttered. Eena saw that the woman was pale with anxiousness.

A side door opened up from where a three-course lunch was served by attendants in uniform. The meal began with an interesting herb salad—a mix of colored leaves Eena didn't recognize. The salad was followed by a creamy soup served with crispy grain wafers. Dessert consisted of sliced fruit smothered in a sweet, dark syrup.

The boys were quick to clear their plates. Either they were good eaters or exceptionally hungry. Given their slender frames and the hardships everyone had faced over the years, Eena bet the later to be true.

Conversation moved nonstop throughout the meal, mainly due to Willum's exuberance. He never failed with things to say while shoveling spoonfuls of food into his mouth. His mother reminded him a number of times not to speak with his mouth full, but without much success. Eena finally gestured that it was perfectly okay. What he lacked in table manners he made up for in sociability.

Willum's brother, Xander, on the other hand, proved to be a timid sort, making only quiet comments here and there. He would answer any question asked of him but with one or two word responses.

Gemdorin did more listening than talking which surprised Eena. She assumed he would dominate the conversation.

Eena's ears perked up when Willum mentioned his father—or

lack thereof.

"I don't have a father," he told her when the topic arose.

His mother quickly corrected him. "Yes you *do* have a father, Willum, he's just not here with us."

That's when Gemdorin stepped in, talking directly to Eena while stealing a glance at Sarii. "Unfortunately, Sarii's husband was captured by Derian's forces six years ago. We haven't heard from him since that time. It's probably correct to assume he's no longer alive."

"I'm so sorry, Sarii." Eena felt horrible for the small family but wasn't sure what more to say.

"He was a good husband and a good father," the woman declared, looking proudly at her queen. "If Rhoen is dead, then I was blessed to have known him. But if by God's grace he still lives, then I hope to see him again someday. Either way, my boys *do* have a wonderful father."

"Rhoen?" Eena repeated.

"Yes," Sarii nodded. "That is my husband's name."

"An unusual name," Eena commented, trying not to show her surprise. She *knew* Rhoen. He was one of Derian's men. He had helped free her from the military facility on Earth. Without Rhoen's help, she might never have escaped the clutches of Dr. Braxton.

Part of her wanted to blurt out that Rhoen was definitely alive and well, but something held her back. It didn't sit right, Rhoen and his wife being separated on enemy ships.

"Well," Gemdorin announced, "lunch was delightful. Thank you Sarii and boys for the pleasant company." He rose, suggesting it was time for them to leave. Eena didn't mind. She was eager to get on her way. She wanted to question Sarii about her husband, but privately.

At the exit, Gemdorin took Sarii's hand and ushered her outside with her sons, but not before Willum gave Eena another big hug, making sure she promised to come fix his pahna tree soon. Goodbyes were quickly said while Gemdorin put himself between their guests and the young queen, blocking her easy exit. He closed the doors before she could make her way around to leave. Her eyes scrunched accusatorily when he turned to face her. He stepped on past without a glance.

"Come," he ordered.   "There's something I want to show you."

Eena hesitated, but when he stood waiting by an open back door, she decided to follow.

"What's in there?" she asked, attempting to peer through the opening.

"Come along, you'll see."   A strong hand pressed against the small of her back, essentially pushing her through the doorway.

She found herself in a room twice as large as the adjacent dining hall, filled from wall to wall with a multitude of treasures. It was a staggering sight.   Eena glanced over piles of unique artifacts: lifelike statues, impressive displays of armory, antique chests, bejeweled boxes, hand-painted vases, and more remarkable artwork arranged haphazardly on the walls.

"What *is* all this?" she asked, scanning the wealth of items in amazement.

"A few things I've collected during my travels.   Some discoveries, some gifts from friends and allies.   A portion are treasures from Harrowbeth."

He walked over to where a small wooden box sat flat on a counter's edge.   Its appearance was strikingly similar to the jewelry case Derian had presented her with back on the Kemeniroc.   Gemdorin unlocked the box and lifted out a fat green gemstone.   It was approximately three inches long and oval in shape, coming to a sharp point on either end.

"This," he said, holding up the gem for her to see, "belonged to your mother, Sha Tashi."   He placed the jewel in her hands to examine, watching her reaction with interest.

The second Eena touched the stone, the necklace came to life. She felt an overpowering desire to keep it, as if the necklace recognized and craved the gem.   Unsure of Gemdorin's intentions, she forced herself to keep calm.   With effort, she made the glow dim.

"What was that all about?" Gemdorin asked.   "Do you recognize the stone?   Do you know what it's for?"

She flickered a glance at him and then looked back on the emerald jewel in her hands, turning it over.

"I...I'm not sure..." she shrugged.   It was the truth.

"But your necklace, it glowed."

"I know. I...I was trying to detect something from the stone," she lied. It was a mystery to her why the necklace had reacted as it had.

Eena concentrated on the item in question, sensing an incredible store of energy trapped within its structure. It felt like a bolt of lightning rolled up and locked inside a sealed container.

Desiring to know more, she attempted to release the power trapped within the gem. The necklace once again shone, even more brilliantly. But the feat proved impossible. Something was missing—a catalyst needed to free the energy inside. And there was still the question, what was it meant for?

"Well?" Gemdorin asked, seeking answers.

Her head shook unknowingly. "Are you sure it's supposed to do something?"

"I was hoping you could tell me," he admitted, sounding disappointed. He reached for the stone, but Eena pulled it closer to her.

"May I have it?" she asked. "I mean, it did belong to my mother; it's rightfully mine."

Gemdorin held out a firm hand. "No. I'm afraid until I understand its purpose, it must remain under lock and key."

There was a strong urge to defy him, an impulse that wasn't her own. It was clear, however, that Gemdorin would never allow her to keep the gem. She surrendered it with a great deal of disappointment. "I suppose you're right."

The curious stone was returned to its wooden box and locked away. Eena watched as Gemdorin deposited the key inside a tiny container which was then buried inside a drawer. Lastly, he pulled a circular disk from a glass bowl. The thin, plastic circle looked like a miniature coaster.

"This you may have. It was also your mother's. I believe it's a lullaby she must have sung to you when you were very young."

Eena took the disk. "Thank you." She placed it in her pocket to examine at another time.

"Come," Gemdorin ordered, heading for the back of this second room.

She didn't follow. "I'm ready to go now."

"In a minute. I have one more thing to show you. It'll be

worth your time, I promise."

Sensing she had no choice in the matter, she huffed irritably and stepped after him.

The next door was unique. Round and heavy, it rolled sideways to allow open access. Gemdorin motioned for Eena to step through, but when she peered into nothing but blackness, she refused.

"You go first," she insisted.

"Very well," he agreed, grinning at her distrust.

Cautiously, Eena followed him through the circular entryway. It closed behind her, leaving her blind. Her breath caught for a moment as she realized she was trapped in the dark with a potentially dangerous man.

The passing of seconds adjusted her eyes to the lack of light, and she noticed white streaks developing in the blackness above. She recognized the peculiarity as stars. Upon further examination she discovered herself to be within a clear, tube-shaped enclosure—something like a skywalk. Gemdorin stepped aside to engage a control bar, causing a set of handrails to rise from each edge of the walkway.

"You might want to hold on," he cautioned.

Eena grabbed onto a handrail, clutching it firmly, unsure of what to expect. She observed how the skywalk was crystal clear all the way around. The entire structure jolted, drawing her attention downward. Below her feet, the ship appeared to push away. Her eyes flickered up to a vision of space that grew steadily encompassing. The skywalk rose maybe fifty yards from the ship's hull and remained there.

Gemdorin spoke into his PCD and the next thing they knew, every streak of light collapsed, leaving only glowing dots sprinkled throughout an eternity of space. The stars formed no recognizable constellations.

From the corner of her eye Eena caught sight of a smear of color—a bluish haze—and turned to marvel at a rising sphere. A gigantic, beryl-blue planet seemed to ascend from below like a sunrise in space. Its great size made it seem like it would bump right into them. Eena reached without thinking, tempted to touch the surface. Her head turned at the shadow of two moons orbiting the planet. The Mahgshreem drifted directly between both.

"This is so cool," she breathed, overcome with awe.

"I thought you would like it." Gemdorin stepped up to the rail beside her. "This planetary group is referred to as the Millan System. That blue planet is called Pegisar. There are twelve planets that orbit its sun, all uninhabitable."

Eena gawked at the immensity of the world before her. It was colossal compared to the view of Earth she had witnessed only days before.

"There's more to see," Gemdorin told her. "Keep an eye out there to your left." He pointed up above her head. They watched as the ship crept past the blue planet, a black sky again taking over.

After a few uneventful minutes she grew anxious. "What exactly am I supposed to be looking for?"

"Just wait." Gemdorin's grip slipped over the handrail. Eena pulled away when the warmth of his hand fell too close to her own.

"There it is!" he announced. His fingers moved to lift her chin toward the left sky. She didn't appreciate his touch, but was quickly sidetracked by the emergence of a hazy stripe that extended from behind another orb in the system. It flashed past, its fuzzy tail headed toward the central sun.

"Oh my gosh, is that a…?"

"Dergan's Comet," Gemdorin finished. It comes through this way once every thousand years. And you, my dear, were lucky enough to see it. Astounding, isn't it?"

"Yes," she agreed. "Astounding."

They watched as the tail grew smaller, disappearing behind a distant jade world.

"Well, are you ready to go?"

For the first time that afternoon she felt saddened by the idea of leaving. Traveling through space this way, observing incredible sights, it was far too exciting.

"I guess so."

When the skywalk was secured against the ship's hull once again, Gemdorin opened the circular door and allowed Eena to exit. He walked her through his room of treasures where he stopped to enter a security code that allowed them to reenter the cozy dining room.

"It's been a real pleasure, my dear," he said, standing beside the final exit. He took hold of her hand and tenderly kissed the palm.

Eena felt confused. She didn't know what to say, but managed to stammer a goodbye.

Gemdorin opened the door, and she turned away, heading down the corridor with two guards trailing. Earlier, she had wanted to find Sarii and talk more about Rhoen. But now she felt a stronger desire to spend time alone. Her fingers played with the disk in her pocket, wondering what kind of lullaby her mother had recorded. She retained no memory of childhood serenades. A fact that wasn't surprising.

Safely inside her quarters, Eena pulled aside a handful of crimson curtains and gazed out at the immensity of space. The ship still traveled at impulse, allowing individual stars to twinkle from every direction. They were slowly skirting the jade planet that had seemed as small as a softball from a distance.

Eena removed the disk from her pocket and examined it. The entire plate was about a quarter inch in thickness, light brown, with tiny grooves forming an intricate design around a central button. She held it in the palm of her hand and pressed lightly.

A miniature hologram appeared atop the disk, maybe six or seven inches high. It was her mother's likeness dressed in a white nightgown, rocking a baby in her arms. Eena understood the infant was herself. She watched and listened as Sha Tashi sang a beautiful yet distressing lullaby.

"Eena, Eena, my daughter dear.
Hush my child you've nothing to fear.
I'll be with you, though you won't see.
You are our future, Sha Eena to be."

It was sung in minor tones, a somewhat haunting melody. She listened to it over and over again. It occurred to her that her mother was singing a farewell to the baby, like she knew the future rested in this child's hands. Eena wondered how that could be. Did her mother know her life was in danger? Had Vaughndorin threatened her?

"Why didn't you stop him?" she asked her mother's singing

image. "Why didn't you use the necklace, Mother? Then you would be here now when I need you. Why didn't you stop him?" she asked again, knowing she would receive no answer.

That night Eena fell asleep to a strange, new dream.

She was walking along a dirt trail, passing through an all-too-familiar forest, one that often haunted her nightly visions. The same crooked branches swayed in the wind above, but when her eyes looked up she caught a glimpse of a dragon's head peering from behind the treetops. At first he appeared like a spirit—opaque and ghostly. But after a few sightings his image changed to a solid, physical form. She caught him in this state, his scaled face looking down at her from behind branches. A snort blew smoke from his nostrils as he disappeared into thin air. The gray puffs rose, thinning and twisting in the wind's currents.

"What do you want with me?" she finally asked out loud, growing tired of the dragon's peek-a-boo game.

She turned clear around looking for a sign of him, only to find herself standing face to face with the colossal dragon. His eyes were wide, observing her closely. His warm, smoky breath blew stray hairs away from her face. For some unfathomable reason she felt no fear—no sense of threat from this monstrous creature. In fact, his presence seemed strangely familiar. When she peered into his large eyes, a clear image stared back of the same green, oval gemstone Gemdorin had shown her. In the dragon's other eye glistened a similarly shaped stone, only it was translucent gold.

"What is this?" she asked the dragon. "Are there two gems? What are they for?"

But the beast never answered.

With a puff of smoke, his wings fully extended, spanning the open clearing. One flap lifted him into the air where he soared out of sight. Eena watched him fly away.

"I don't understand," she said to the sky.

"What don't you understand?"

Ian's voice was a pleasant whisper in her ear. She quickly turned to face her best friend. He was staring up at the sky too, trying to see what she was seeing.

"Ian," she breathed, delighted he was back again.

"What are you looking at?" he asked, still squinting at the clouds.

"Nothing. I don't know. It was just a silly dream." She shrugged the whole thing off.

"So," Ian started, giving her a warm smile, "you look pretty. I assume Gemdorin is still being....nice?"

Eena glanced down at her dress, only to find she was wearing the same gown in her dreams she had worn that day. It was overly fancy for her taste.

She tried to explain. "I don't have a lot of choice here; it's one icky ball gown after another." Her cheeks flushed, embarrassed, and she quickly changed the subject. "I had lunch today with Gemdorin and with Rhoen's wife, Sarii, and her two boys."

"You did?" Ian lost his smile.

"Yes. You remember Willum from yesterday? It turns out that he's Rhoen's son. Imagine that!"

"Wow, imagine that." Ian thought about telling her what had happened to Rhoen, but he decided against it. If she were to let it slip that Rhoen's spying had been discovered, it might jeopardize people's safety, not to mention ruining Derian's plans too. Ian bit his lip, prepared to feign ignorance, but Eena was already onto a subject of higher priority.

"Oh!" she exclaimed, remembering her star walk after dinner. "I found out where we are! At least at the present moment. Gemdorin told me we were passing by the Millan System. I saw a gigantic blue planet close up, Pegisar, with its two moons! It was so cool! And then there was this comet……the Dragon's…..no, no, that's not it. Draken? No, that's not it either…"

"You mean Dergan's Comet?"

"Yes, that's the one! I saw Dergan's Comet today. 'Once every thousand years,' Gemdorin told me."

"How can that be?" Ian asked, stunned. "That's nearly three weeks travel at top speed from where we are now. How could he possibly be that far ahead of us?"

"You mean the Mahgshreem can travel that much faster than the Kemeniroc?"

"Apparently." Ian shook his head in disbelief. "Are you sure he said the Millan System?"

211

"Absolutely sure."

"I have to tell Derian right away. We're going to need help." *Ian swiveled on his feet like he meant to leave.*

"You're not going now, are you? Can't this wait until morning?"

He turned back to face her. "Eena, I know things seem fine to you at the moment, but it won't stay that way. We have to catch up to Gemdorin. We have to get you back. Derian needs this information right now so he can find some way to close the gap." Ian's hand squeezed her shoulder as he assured her, "I'll see you again soon, I promise." Then he vanished, leaving her alone and disappointed.

For the rest of the evening her dreams were fragmented and disturbing. Dragons with gemstone eyes along with faceless snakes haunted her. Smelly grembloines in white lab coats chased her through darkened woods. In her worst nightmare, she could hear young Willum calling out from somewhere on the ship. She ran down one passageway after another trying to follow the sound of his voice, but every time she thought she was near to his hiding place, he was nowhere to be found. It wasn't the best night's sleep.

The week to follow was repetitive and uneventful on the Mahgshreem—a fine regular routine as far as Eena was concerned. Her assistant greeted her each morning with a warm breakfast and another choice of elegant dresses. Eena always chose the simplest design. Angelle performed her magic on the young queen's hair and applied cosmetics before they set off for the commissary, escorted by loyal guards. The majority of each day was spent mingling with friendly people and healing numerous withered plants.

Eena especially enjoyed pleasing the children. These youngsters were always eager to ask for their favorite fruits to be grown, offering their queen a sample when the job was completed. She was happy to taste a variety of fruits and herbs, many of which had similar flavors to foods from Earth. Some, however, were an entirely new experience. The oddest was a gittahna fruit from a gitta tree, its taste an unusual twist of tang. The best way she could think to describe it was to imagine sucking on a mint leaf while simultaneously biting into a lemon-soaked watermelon—strangely sour and sweet and minty at the same time. When finished with the flesh of the gittahna fruit, she had to spit out the seeds before they turned bitter.

Eena's strength seemed to increase daily. She was able to heal more and more flora without exhausting herself. This was significant, since she found it difficult to send anyone away without touching the plants they so patiently waited for her to tend to. And, of course, she helped Willum with his pahna tree again. It would have produced fruit on its own eventually, but the necklace replenished its branches without delay, much to the boy's delight.

The young Sha was able to spend an afternoon with Sarii where they talked about her husband, Rhoen. Sarii told her how he had left soon after Willum's birth, piloting an attack glider in one of many battles against Derian's cruisers. On this particular occasion Rhoen's ship failed to return. Since then Sarii had learned nothing of his fate. His ship was never found and no one seemed to know whether he was taken prisoner or killed in battle. As a caring mother, she did her best to recount pleasant stories to Xander and Willum about their father, hoping to at least keep his memory alive. At times she considered burying the past and moving on with her life. But a nagging ache deep inside just wouldn't allow it.

"It's like I can sense he's still out there. I know that sounds crazy, but I can't shed this hope I might see him again," Sarii told Eena. "Sometimes I dream I can hear his voice."

"It doesn't sound crazy to me. I believe in miracles, Sarii, and I don't think you should give up on him." Eena's gut insisted she not say anything more. If Sarii or Gemdorin knew that Rhoen was on the Kemeniroc working as one of Derian's trusted crewmen, she wasn't sure what would come of it. The whole situation didn't make sense.

Every now and then Eena noticed Gemdorin standing in the background watching her, usually propped against the door of the commissary. When her eyes found him, he simply smiled and nodded. That was it. And that was fine with her. She still wasn't sure what to make of him, so the less they interacted, the better. When she asked people about their captain they would

213

never speak ill of him, but they didn't seem eager to talk either. When she brought up Derian's name, there were a few unpleasant scowls and grumbles, especially from younger folk, but not enough viable information to condemn him. Her opinion on the brothers wasn't helped along much.

If there was one thing she was truly grateful for within all of this, it was the fact that she could still see her best friend, Ian, every night. Sleep quickly grew to be her fondest desire, bedtime her favorite time of day. Ian was always there in her dreams: first, checking to be sure she was alright; secondly, finding out if she knew where Gemdorin's ship was headed; and thirdly, making her smile. Since witnessing Dergan's Comet she had learned nothing new of her whereabouts. Seeking information from those aboard the ship had produced no useful news either. She got the impression the weary crew had given up on tracking their travels, leaving it all up to their captain.

Eena somehow talked Ian into watching the sunset with her six evenings in a row. The practice was becoming habit, much like old times. They sat together on the hillside beneath her favorite willow tree overlooking her earthly father's cornfields. Behind distant sagebrush-covered hills, a scarlet sun slowly sank and darkened—a performance that never entirely concluded in Eena's dreams. One hour they would talk non-stop, their conversations revolving around memories of Earth, while the next hour passed in sweet silence. When the evening came to its end, Ian would remind Eena to be observant and careful. Then they would part ways to live out another day on separate ships.

If life had continued in this manner, Sha Eena might have remained content on Gemdorin's ship forever. But, inevitably, things changed.

The morning began much like previous ones. Eena chose an evergreen dress to wear with a matching lace overlay. The sleeves were long, widening substantially like lilies from elbow to wrist. Angelle decorated her queen's hair with two emerald clips to match.

Before they took off for the commissary as usual, Eena drew back a curtain to steal a glance out the window. She expected the typical picture—lines of stars smeared over a black canvas. It was a real surprise to find a large, yellow planet blocking her view.

214

The globe was encircled by particle rings—five separate, glittering loops. It was a beautiful image, but what caught Eena's attention were the numerous battleships outside the Mahgshreem. She wasn't sure if the round, gold ships belonged to Gemdorin or if they had originated from the surface. Either way, it didn't look good.

Eena motioned for Angelle to come see. "What do you make of this?"

Angelle hurried over to the window. "Those aren't our ships," she said. "I'm not sure what they're doing."

"Do you think we're in any danger?"

As if the Mahgshreem meant to answer the question itself, the whole room trembled. Both women stumbled and fell against the wall.

"Oh crud, they're shooting at us! Why are they shooting at us?"

"I don't know!" Angelle grabbed the bedpost, using it as an anchor. "I think it's best if we stay here."

Another blast jostled the lights above, causing dangling crystals to clang like chimes. The doors suddenly parted. Gemdorin marched in, crossing the room with swift, dogged strides. His approach was as heated as the look on his face. He walked directly up to Eena and seized her by the arm.

"Come on!" he ordered, pulling her along in haste. She had to run to keep up with him. His grip remained secure as he led her out and up to the bridge.

"What's going on?" she asked while riding a lift to a higher deck. He gave no answer, not even acknowledging she had spoken.

When the final set of doors parted, Gemdorin dragged his hostage onto the bridge and positioned her before of a large viewing screen. She found herself face to face with an elderly gentleman. The man's attire was elaborate and regal, but it was his big blue eyes she found most captivating. They widened with recognition the moment he saw her.

"Here she is!" Gemdorin growled at the screen. "Are you sure you want to keep firing on us?"

The white-haired gentleman stared in astonishment at the young woman on his view screen. His face paled as if he were

215

eyeing a real ghost.   Eena glanced at Gemdorin for an explanation but received none.   The old man ordered his ships to stand down immediately.   The intermittent jarring on the Mahgshreem halted.

"My sincere apologies, your highness," the man said, bending respectfully at the waist.   His big eyes never left her.

Eena had no time to respond.   Gemdorin ordered her escorted off the bridge and back to her room.   Angelle was there waiting when she arrived.

"Sha Eena, what happened?"

"I'm not really sure, but I don't think we're in danger anymore."   She sat across from her assistant and went over the whole bewildering ordeal.

"How strange," Angelle uttered at the end of her queen's account.

"Yes, I agree.   How very strange."

CHAPTER TWELVE
A Reason to Celebrate

Curiosity ate away at the young Sha as she stared out her bedroom window, pondering the possibilities transpiring between Gemdorin and the people of this yellow, ringed planet. Angelle listened intently to her queen's retelling of how a distinguished, older gentleman had ordered his fleet to stop their attack once he realized she was a passenger on the Mahgshreem. But why? She had no clue.

"Let's go," Eena finally decided. Rehashing the peculiar incident wasn't proving productive. "We can check on Sarii and the others. Maybe they'll know more."

"Good idea," Angelle agreed.

They made their way to the doors only to find four dutiful soldiers blocking the exit. One guard informed the young queen she was not permitted to leave by order of Kahm Gemdorin.

The women exchanged curious looks. "What about Angelle?" Eena asked, "May she leave?"

"I have no orders keeping her here."

Eena told her assistant to go check on Sarii and her boys. "Find out what you can about what's going on."

"Yes, ma'am. I'll return soon with news."

Being stuck alone in her room didn't prove fortunate. Without anyone to act as a positive distraction, the solitude allowed Eena plenty of time to think, thus allowing her overactive imagination a chance to get carried away. Having a multitude of unanswered questions churning about in her mind, she began to answer them with ample possibilities.

Why had they fired on the Mahgshreem? Why halt their attack because of her? What was Gemdorin's interest in this planet? Who was that elderly man, and how could he possibly have recognized her?

She assumed Gemdorin was seeking something. Something located on this alien planet. Maybe it was treasure he wanted to add to his already impressive collection. The item would have to be of great worth to risk a fight—a prize of immeasurable value. The gentleman…..the stranger…..he had looked at her with shock and recognition, acting as if her face was familiar. Or, more likely, it was the necklace he recognized.

"Oh no," she breathed, reasoning things out.

How far would Gemdorin go to get what he wanted? Would he trade the necklace? Would he promise it to these people? Would he abandon her on some alien world, leaving her subject to the whims of complete strangers?

Eena pressed her palms against her temples, attempting to stop the downward spiral of disturbing thoughts. "This is ridiculous; I need to stop speculating. But what in the world is that man up to?"

Convincing herself that the only reasonable option was to wait for real answers, she spent the next few hours with her nose pressed against the window, watching. The majority of gold ships had retreated after their earlier attack, leaving only a sparse frontline positioned between the Mahgshreem and the yellow planet. Eena paid close attention when a black glider headed for the surface. Two identical gliders followed close on its tail.

"Gemdorin's going down there," she told herself, positive her guess was correct.

Eena waited for hours for the three gliders to reappear but never spied them. Angelle was first to return.

"I've brought lunch, Sha Eena." A tray of food was set on a table. "I'm sorry it took so long."

Eena was hesitant to abandon her lookout post, not wanting to miss anything. But hunger pains won out over curiosity. She went to sit across from her assistant.

"Thank you, Angelle, I'm starving. Did you gather any news?"

"Not much," the girl admitted. "Rumor has it Kahm Gemdorin is on the surface negotiating a treaty of some sort. The men are talking about an alliance with the people from this planet."

"Who are they?" Eena asked, desirous for more information. She snatched a piece of flatbread from off the food tray.

"I don't know, but I hear they have very sophisticated technology, far ahead of our own. That's probably why the captain is seeking an alliance with them."

218

"And what is he offering in return?" Eena asked. Concern for herself was mounting. She nibbled on the piece of bread, anxious for an answer.

"Our aid and friendship?" Angelle guessed.

Eena chuckled. "From how things started out here, I'd say they have little interest in our friendship."

"They don't know us yet."

"Or maybe they do, and that's why they attacked."

Both women paused to think, picking at their food while pondering the situation. Eventually the young queen voiced her main concern.

"Is it possible Gemdorin is desperate enough for their technology that he would trade my necklace?"

Angelle gasped, "Sha Eena!"

"I'm serious. Would he leave me behind?"

"Absolutely not! Our people need you! He would never do such a thing!"

"I only ask because I can't think of anything comparable to superior technology they would want in exchange."

Angelle bit her lip, now appearing as stumped as her queen. "Maybe that's not why we're here," she suggested. "All I've heard are rumors. I can't say for certain any of them are true. Perhaps it would be best if we stopped speculating about the captain's intent. Most likely this visit has absolutely nothing to do with you."

Eena smiled knowingly. "Then why drag me to the bridge?"

Neither could come up with an answer.

Lunch continued in contemplative silence. When the tray was emptied, Eena went back to watching the ships outside her window. Angelle quickly tidied things up and left.

For a long while there was little activity to observe. The entire day passed sluggishly with Eena staring out at a bright planet, hoping for some visible clue as to what was happening. Angelle remained absent the majority of the time, searching for reassuring answers to her queen's questions. Eena noticed that none of the gold ships ever docked on the Mahgshreem. All the negotiating was apparently being conducted on the planet. It was early evening when Eena spotted three gliders returning home.

"Gemdorin's back," she whispered to herself.

Bored by the lack of activity, her mind continued to entertain itself with far-fetched stories of conspiracy in the works. She was deep in thought when the gold ships turned toward home. Concentrating on the alien retreat, she didn't sense a lone figure enter her room. She nearly hit the ceiling when a deep voice breathed in her ear.

"Interesting view?"

Eena whirled around to face the culprit; her back pressed against the window.

"Gemdorin!" She covered her pattering heart. "Don't do that."

He leaned in, peering out over her shoulder. "Do what?" His words sounded much too innocent to be so.

Eena slid sideways into the curtains, away from him. "What is all this about?" she asked, gesturing to the world outside.

A smug grin crept across Gemdorin's face as he made a big announcement with his usual dramatic flair. "This, my dear, is a day to celebrate! Today, you and I have accomplished a wonderful thing indeed!"

"We have?"

"Yes, absolutely! And it would not have come about so perfectly without your beautiful assistance." With that, he folded his arms and nodded once in her direction.

Eena turned back to the window. "I didn't do anything." She had to glance over a shoulder when Gemdorin laughed aloud.

"Ohhhh, oh, oh! You've accomplished more simply with your presence than I ever dreamt possible on my own. I had no idea how much admiration that silly old man has for you and your renowned necklace. He probably knows more about it than all past Shas put together. If ever I've met a master treasure hunter, that gentleman is by far the best!"

Eena watched Gemdorin's reflection prance about in the window. He was as animated as she had ever seen him. "Did you promise him the necklace?" she asked, convinced the old treasure hunter wanted it.

"What?" Gemdorin stopped to cast the girl an incredulous look which Eena caught in his reflection. "Of course not! I wouldn't even let the babbling fool come see it. And believe me he wanted to!"

Eena twisted her neck to look at Gemdorin. "Then what did you do?"

"My dear, we simply came to a mutual understanding. We agreed that being united as allies for a common cause would prove much more lucrative than continuing on as enemies."

Eena turned completely around, wondering, "And what common cause would that be?"

The answer was voiced like it should be obvious. "Well, of course, to protect Harrowbeth's precious queen from those who might attempt something dastardly."

"Why would he care..." she began.

"Because! Like I said, the old codger holds deep admiration for your priceless heirloom and its unique history. He's visited Moccobatra and met your mother, Sha Tashi. He even met your grandmother once. He was so excited to see you alive and well today. Didn't you catch the look on his face when he saw you standing on our bridge? He thought I was kidding when I told him this was your ship. After that magical appearance, you were all he wanted to talk about. Sha Eena this! Sha Eena that! I promised him a meeting with you sometime in the future, but for now we'll keep him wanting and waiting. We'll get what we want—and eventually he'll get what he wants."

"The necklace?"

"*No, I'm not giving him the necklace!*" Gemdorin tensed up with frustration. "Why would you even think that?"

"Because you said he's a master treasure hunter and he's smitten with it." To her it made perfect sense.

A second bout of laughter hit the air. "Ohhh, oh, oh, dear! Are you so worried I would give you away? Believe me, you're not going anywhere. The necklace will stay here with me....with you," he corrected himself. "Now, my lady, quit fretting because I feel like celebrating our new alliance!"

"One more question," she dared.

He sighed impatiently. "What is it?"

"Why did they fire on us in the first place?"

"Because, my dear, they've come across our people once before, and it was not a pleasant meeting."

"When did they come across our people before?"

His scar spiked over a perked eyebrow. "When they

encountered my brother, Derian."

Shock altered her expression, but she didn't utter a word. Gemdorin swiftly closed the gap between them, his large hand taking hold of her delicate fingers. She tried to pull away, but he wouldn't allow it.

"I would be honored to have your presence at dinner this evening where we can properly celebrate our achievement." He kissed the back of her hand before letting her reclaim it. "I won't take no for an answer, my lady." He then started for the exit.

When the doors opened, he twisted back around with final instructions. "Your guards will escort you to dinner in two hours. Wear something red. I like red." Then he left, the essence of triumph trailing him.

"Oh crud," Eena groaned, plopping down onto the bed. Her eyes fell closed as she wondered what in the world she was getting into.

About an hour before the scheduled dinner date, Angelle returned to help her queen change into a crimson gown. Eena's hair and makeup were freshened up as well, darkened for an evening environment. When the young Sha was beautifully put together, she stood before her mirrored hologram, frowning. A dismal sigh slipped from her lips.

"What's wrong?" Angelle asked.

"Nothing." Eena didn't want to bother anyone with her concerns.

"You've been quiet and melancholy this whole time. What's wrong?"

Managing a bleak grin, she confessed. "I really don't want to go."

"Did you tell the captain this?"

"He said he wouldn't take no for an answer." Eena looked at her friend and forced another feeble smile. "I'm sure it'll be fine."

"Yes, I'm sure it will be."

The young queen left with her guard, escorted to an area of the ship she had never set foot in before. It was far from the captain's dining room where she had assumed dinner would take place. A soldier knocked for her as they stood outside a new set of dark doors.

Gemdorin's towering figure stepped forward when the entry opened. He quickly dismissed Eena's escorts and turned his eyes on her.

"Ah, my lady. You look lovelier than an ember moon. Please come in."

She moved inside, stiffening at the warmth of his hand on her lower back. Gemdorin guided her a few feet in where the sound of closing doors whooshed like a swift breeze behind them. Her eyes swept over the room, examining the impressive layout. The first thing to draw her notice was a flicker of orange flames inside a large, rock-wall fireplace. It was only a replica of the real thing, but naturally softened the atmosphere. Two intricate chandeliers hung from the ceiling, one positioned above a sturdy, square dining table, the other over an intimate sitting area. The floor was divided into two sections as well, with area rugs beneath each arrangement. A thick, fur carpet stretched out invitingly before the fire.

The furniture was elegant. Bronze, gold, and crimson were woven into every inch of canvassed cushion. An abundance of heavy throw pillows and fresh flower arrangements embellished the room. On the dinner table stood a tall vase of long-petal lilies surrounded by three beige candles of differing heights. Two place settings sat side by side on one end. Eena could smell a mouthwatering dinner waiting beneath a silver serving tray.

After appraising the room, she turned to Gemdorin, unsure of what to expect.

"Come. Have a seat," he said, chivalrously pulling out a chair.

Accepting the seat, she could feel her shoulders climb and had to conscientiously force them down.

Gemdorin uncovered the silver tray where the smell of stew and homemade bread escaped in a steamy swirl. Included were two warm jars of preserves. Eena couldn't help but smile. Dinner smelled and looked wonderful. And she *was* hungry.

The captain dished out the food, making conversation in the process. "I'm so glad you chose to come here tonight, Eena."

"You told me I had no choice."

"No, that's not what I said," he corrected, twitching his

scarred eyebrow.   "What I said was, I wouldn't take no for an answer.   You had a choice.   However, it did get you here, and for that I'm glad."   He grinned, flashing smugness in the expression.

After the stew was served, Gemdorin grabbed a couple of rounded goblets.   He poured two drinks from a slender bottle, passing one to Eena.   Then he offered a toast.

"To present great accomplishments and future successes!" They tapped the tips of their glasses and drank.   Eena discovered with one gulp that the beverage was exceptionally strong.   It burned her throat, sending her into an immediate coughing fit.

Gemdorin slapped her gently on the back.   "Are you alright?"

"What is that stuff?" she rasped in between coughs.

"Why an indulgence, my dear!   The stuff celebrations are made of!"

"I don't want any more of it," she said, rubbing at her warm neck.

Gemdorin's lips pursed into a clearly disappointed line. "Very well."   He set her glass aside.   "Will water do?"

"Yes, please."

A new glass was filled from a different pitcher.

"Thank you."   She took a sip, making sure it was drinkable.

Dinner began with light conversation.   Gemdorin asked about Eena's activities on the ship.   She asked him questions about the day's events in return, most of which he sidestepped.   Eventually, she dug for better information concerning his visit to the yellow planet.

"I did learn one very interesting thing about your necklace today," he informed her.   His eyes seemed intent on her reaction. "The old gent told me it's capable of more than what the Shas use it for.   Is this true?"

She shrugged, communicating ignorance.   "I don't know. It's not like it comes with instructions."

"Have you tried to do anything else with it besides reviving those plants?"

"No, Gemdorin, I haven't.   And I don't think I want to," she frowned.

"Why not?"

"Because it takes a lot out of me for one thing."

224

"And?" he asked, sensing there was more.

"And because there's been no need to try anything more."

"And?" he urged again, hunting for the real excuse.

She was growing uncomfortable with his persistence. "And—and because my mother left behind a warning that there could be very bad consequences if I were to abuse the necklace."

"Really? What kind of consequences?"

"Well, uh, honestly......I don't know," she admitted. "My mother didn't specify."

"She didn't?" Gemdorin chuckled. "Did she know for certain there were any? Or is her threat of mysterious consequences some sort of superstitious rumor?"

Eena snapped, offended at how his laughter seemed to insult her mother's memory. "I don't know, okay? Why do you even care?"

He ignored her hostility, leaning in to ask a crucial question. "Doesn't it bother you knowing your mother had access to greater powers within that necklace, and yet she never called upon them to prevent herself from being murdered?"

"Stop it." The necklace smoldered—a sudden soft swell of light. A warning.

Gemdorin observed it, but didn't back down, choosing to press the issue. "Well, doesn't it bother you? Your mother could have saved herself but chose not to. Is that what you would do too? Would you allow yourself to be slaughtered for fear of some unknown, perhaps even nonexistent, consequence?"

Eena stood up abruptly. "I'm done here."

"No you're not." Gemdorin grabbed her by the arm and forced her to sit back down. "I will know how you feel about this."

She was furious, and refused to look at him, staring at the flickering candles on the table instead. The glow beneath her chin pulsated.

"Eena, listen to me. You may have access to powers that could protect you and your people from being harmed by dangerous enemies. Yet because of some ridiculous fear, fear of the unknown no less, you would choose not to defend yourself? What are you going to do if Derian finds you? What if he tries to kill you?"

She turned her angry eyes on him, not believing for one second that Derian would ever do such a thing. Nonetheless, she answered the question.

"I have thought about it. I've thought about how my mother might be here now if she *had* used the necklace's full powers. I wish she had. But I don't know if she even knew how." Her cheeks stung as tears welled up inside. "I'm not sure what I would do. I don't know how much worse it would make things."

Gemdorin dared to move closer, a grave expression on his face. "Your mother had an heir. She knew that when she died there was someone to take her place. You, Eena, have no heir. If you die, no one will take your place. If that isn't a serious enough consequence, I don't know what is."

She stared at him, honestly considering his words. What he said was true. If she were to be killed, no one alive could wear the necklace. Moccobatra would literally wither and die.

"Eena, in order to protect yourself you may need to call upon the buried powers in that necklace. I suggest you try and see if you *can* use them."

"But what if something bad happens?"

"What if nothing happens?" Gemdorin retorted. "No one said you had to abuse those powers, just see if you can summon them."

She looked uncertain as to where to begin. "How?"

Gemdorin thought for a second. He rose and blew out the three candles sitting centerpiece on the table. Then he pushed Eena's plate aside and positioned the candles in front of her. Thin lines of smoke trailed from the hot wicks.

"Light the candles," he ordered. "Use the necklace to light the candles."

Eena looked at him as if he were crazy. "Why?"

"To see if you can," he explained. "I'm sure there won't be any horrible consequences if you simply light these candles."

Her shoulders shrugged involuntarily. "I'm not sure how to do it."

"How did you make the plants grow?"

"I touched them."

"Then touch the candles," he suggested, gesturing at the still-smoking wicks.

Eena reached out and touched one candle.   It was warm from use.   She waited for a few seconds, but nothing happened.   No sensations.   No spark.   Nothing.   Her eyes turned to Gemdorin.

"Your necklace wasn't glowing.   Concentrate."

With a deep exhale she tried again, focusing on her objective: to create a growing flame on just one candle.   A soft glimmer radiated from beneath her chin as she reached out and touched the wick.   Still nothing happened.   Her hand dropped to the table and the necklace dimmed.

"I don't know how to do it," she grumbled.

"You're not trying," Gemdorin accused.

"I am so trying."

"Then try harder," he hissed.

Once again she concentrated.   Closing her eyes, she envisioned the candle lighting voluntarily.   She imagined it happening in her mind's eye.   *I must light the candle*, she thought to the necklace.   As a brighter glow lighted her face, she reached out and touched the wick again.   A warmth of energy rushed down her arm, soaking into her fingers.   Her hands tingled but still no flame appeared.

"I can't do it," she announced, groaning as if giving up.

"You *can* do it," Gemdorin insisted.   "You and I both know you can do this."   His eyes tapered into slits—an ill-tempered look to accompany his impatience.   He was thinking, working on a way to motivate her.   His steady stare made her nervous.   She attempted to stand but was forced once again to sit.

At length, he made an announcement.   "If you don't light at least one of those candles, I'm going to kiss you.   A long, hard, passionate kiss.   If you do light a candle, I won't."

"How dare you!"   She tried to leave, but he grabbed her arm and yanked her back into the chair.

"You can't make me do this!" she protested.

"No, I can't.   But I won't let you leave without your kiss."
His stare, intense and earnest, communicated a firm resolve.

She was furious.   He had no right to treat her this way!   He and his overbearing brother were exactly alike—demanding, controlling, and just plain mean!   She curled her lips under, biting down on them stubbornly.   There was no way in the boundless universe she was ever going to let him kiss her.

As her anger increased, so did the necklace's brilliance. She could feel a buildup of energy flush through her like a hot flash. Determined to keep Gemdorin from carrying out his threat, she waved both hands over the candles, utilizing an enormous amount of power. All three wicks caught fire, balancing high flames that eventually settled into a gentle orange glow. The display was like a magic show that surprised even the magician herself. Eena found her energy drained.

"Well done, my dear, well done!" Gemdorin crooned, a satisfied grin painted across his face. "Very well done, indeed."

She caught the pride in his eyes before his features blurred. Then everything went black.

She was facing a smoldering fire when her eyes reopened. A pillow supported her head. Beneath her body, silken fibers of carpeting made a comfortable bed. She tried lifting up to her elbows only to suffer a wave of dizziness. Her mind was disoriented, her body weak. Looking up, she noticed Gemdorin in a chair above her, thumbing through a leather-bound book. His blue eyes peered over the pages before the book puffed closed. Gemdorin set it down on a side table.

"Ahh, my lady, you're awake. How are you feeling?"

"Not great," she admitted, managing to sit up all the way. "What happened?" She faltered, attempting to rise to her knees. Gemdorin quickly grabbed her arm and helped her into the chair beside him.

"Are you alright?"

"I will be."

"Do you want something to drink?"

"Yes, just water, please." Then she remembered, "I did it, didn't I? I lit the candles."

Gemdorin handed her a goblet of water. "Yes, you did. And nothing terrible happened."

"I passed out."

"That wasn't so terrible. Besides, you'll grow stronger." His hand went to cover a chesty cough, and he grabbed a second goblet. In one swallow, he finished the remainder of his drink.

"What's that you were reading?" Eena asked, purposefully changing the subject. She didn't want to talk about the necklace

228

anymore.

"This?" He held up the book by its spine. It looked both antique and worn. "It's a collection of historical folklore that tells of an ancient, magical gem hidden away centuries ago. That old codger I was visiting with today gave me this book. I was thumbing through the pages to see what kind of information it contains."

"Is the gem for real?" Eena asked, genuinely curious.

"Oh, absolutely! Most of the entries in here are useless— nothing but ancient mythology and rumors. The trick is learning to decipher truth from fiction." He looked over, perceiving her interest. "Do you like treasure hunts?" he asked.

"I've never been on a real treasure hunt," she admitted. "The idea does seem fascinating though."

"Very!" he assured her. "If I can locate this gem, I'll have found a great treasure indeed, Eena." His eyes sparkled with excitement at the thought.

"Do you have any idea where it might be? Have you tried to look for it?"

"Yes, but with no success. I was hoping to find more information in these pages, perhaps a clue to solve the mystery. I'm positive I've got the right planet, but exactly where the treasure is buried, I can't seem to figure out." He offered the book to her. "Would you like to look at it?"

"Thank you." She grabbed the cover with both hands. It was cracked and faded, bound by a strong chord. Her nose wrinkled at its musty smell.

The discolored pages held numerous illustrations: old shields of armor, dragons, a rounded red gemstone that looked about the size of a fist. She paused on a detailed black-and-white depiction of two armies engaged in battle. What appeared to be two beautiful goddesses hovered on either side of the battlefield. The next page had a large map of a solar system with eight planets orbiting a red sun. Continuing on, she noticed a section of missing pages ripped out in a collective bunch. There were notes jotted throughout the book in a script she didn't recognize.

"Can you read any of this?" she asked.

"Portions of it—not all," Gemdorin said. "The text is an obsolete script. I was told this book is over three thousand years old. The pictures are what interest me. I'm trying to learn whatever I can from them."

She pointed to a detailed sketch of a red, round jewel. "Is this the magical gem?"

"Yes. That's the dragon's eye. That's what I'm going to find." A deep cough made him stand to refill his drink.

"What happened to the missing pages?" she asked, following him to the table with her eyes. She watched him pour and guzzle another glass of water.

"I don't know." Gemdorin winked playfully at her. "Perhaps another treasure hunter got ahold of them. Someone we might need to beware of."

She looked over the drawing again. "What does this dragon's eye do? Why do you want to find it so badly?"

"It does something very wonderful."

"You're not going to tell me?"

"No, I'm not." He returned to his seat with a fresh goblet of water.

Eena continued sifting through the book, studying every intricate picture. She wondered if this dragon's eye had anything to do with the green and yellow gems from her dreams—gems set inside a dragon's eyes. It was too coincidental not to be connected. But what was their purpose?

The pair continued talking well into the night. Gemdorin recounted more treasure-hunting adventures, bragging of how he had unraveled one challenging mystery after another that led to the discovery of valuable prizes. Eena found herself perfectly entertained by his engaging accounts. So much so, she completely forgot Ian's caution to be wary of this man. As a dramatic narrator, Gemdorin appeared to enjoy his solo audience. He seemed to find pleasure in relating his adventures to a captive and interested listener.

After a while, Eena noticed the room had dimmed substantially. The candles had burned down to almost nothing.

"How late is it, Gemdorin?"

The captain pulled a small timepiece out of his pocket. "It's just past zero-three-hundred hours."

She gasped, "It's morning!" Ian would be wondering why she wasn't dreaming. He was probably worried sick by now.

230

She stood up at once to leave.

"What's the rush? You've nowhere you need to be."

"But it's late. Very late," she said. "And I am tired. I want to go."

He appeared disappointed, even irritated that their evening had come to such an abrupt end, but he didn't argue with her. "If you insist."

"I'm sure I can find my way back," Eena said, following him to the doors. But he insisted on walking her to her room.

She wanted to move faster than the leisurely pace he set. It was difficult to force herself to keep in step with him, but she did so to avoid questions about a desire to rush. When they finally arrived outside her quarters, she said a quick goodnight and slipped through the doors. Inside, she noticed a figure lying on the divan at the foot of her bed. Eena recognized her sleeping assistant right off.

"Angelle," she whispered, administering a gentle jostle. It took a minute for the girl to wake up. She seemed both happy and concerned at the sight of her queen.

"Sha Eena, you're back! Did everything go okay? Are you alright?"

"I'm fine. Were you worried about me?"

"You said you didn't wish to go tonight. I wanted to be sure you returned safely. It's so late."

Eena gave her a reassuring smile. "We were telling stories. I lost track of the time, that's all."

Relief settled over Angelle's sleepy features. "I'm glad you're alright. I'll go now."

"Can I walk you to your room?"

"No, Sha Eena, I'll be fine. Thank you and goodnight."

Eena accompanied her assistant to the exit where they were surprised to find Gemdorin lingering in the hallway.

"What's going on here?" he asked, narrowly eyeing Angelle.

"Nothing," Eena said.

Angelle tried to explain, "I was waiting up for Sha Eena, and I must have fallen asleep, that's all."

The captain frowned. "Did you have reason to be worried about her?"

"No, no, of course not, I just wanted to…..to say goodnight."

Angelle swallowed nervously.   It was a lame excuse.

"How very thoughtful."   He reached for the timid girl, taking her by the wrist.   "Come with me.   I'll walk you to your quarters."

"Yes, sir."

Eena watched them head for the elevator.   Then she hurried to bed.   It took no time at all to doze off.

Looking uphill at her favorite willow tree, she scanned the area for her best friend.   Ian was nowhere to be seen.   Now in jeans and a t-shirt, she hustled up the hillside without delay. Finding herself alone, she called out his name.

"Ian!   Ian, are you here?"

"Where have you been?"   The words were barked in her ear in an exasperated way.   Ian materialized out of nowhere.   She jumped at his close, sudden appearance.

"For goodness sakes, Ian, don't scare me like that."

"Don't scare you?" he scolded.   "I've been worried sick! Do you realize it's morning?   I was starting to think something terrible happened to you!"

"I'm really sorry.   I lost track of time."

"Where have you been?" he asked again.

"Um....well, I was at dinner.....with Gemdorin," she admitted sheepishly.

Her news served to upset him further.   "Dinner, huh?   So you were with him all night long?"

"Nothing happened.   We....I mean....he was telling me stories about his treasure hunting.   It was interesting, and time just flew by, that's all."

"Treasure hunting," Ian groaned.

Eena thought about Derian's star charts and weaponry collection.   "It must run in the family."

Ian exhaled irritably.   "Are you sure you're alright?"

"Yes.   Honest." she insisted.   The way he stared at her—as if she were on trial—made her feel guilty.

"Stop looking at me like that.   I haven't done anything wrong."   She dropped to the ground beneath the willow tree.

"You're fraternizing with the enemy," he accused, standing over her.   "Are you letting him get to you?"

"I'm stuck on his ship, Ian. What am I supposed to do? He asked me to come to dinner and said he wouldn't take no for an answer. I had no choice but to go."

"And he forced you to stay up all night?"

"No—I told you, his stories were interesting. I lost track of time, okay? I didn't mean to worry you; I'm sorry." She looked up at him, her face earnestly apologetic.

He couldn't stay mad at her.

"Fine," he grumbled, "I'm just glad you're okay." Taking a seat beside his best friend, he forfeited a smile. The gesture made Eena feel better.

"Do you have any new information about where you're headed?"

She shook her head. "No, sorry. To tell you the truth, I think we're jumping from place to place. I think Gemdorin's hunting for something. Some treasure."

"What makes you think that?"

"He told me he's looking for a gem called the dragon's eye. He showed me an old book about it. Have you heard of it?"

"No, but why does he want it?" Ian was intrigued.

"I don't know; he wouldn't tell me. I just know Gemdorin's determined to find it. Perhaps Derian knows more about it. If he does, maybe it will give him a clue as to where we're headed."

Ian nodded. "I'll be sure to ask him."

They spent the last couple hours of the morning together, watching the sunset while talking about folktales and treasures. It was a nice but short visit. When Ian had to leave, Eena wished him a good day and stayed to catch up on her sleep. It didn't take long to slip into another dream……

She was in the same dark forest again, wind blowing, branches swaying as if reaching for her. She felt the usual apprehension that accompanied this place but chose not to run.

"I don't have to be afraid," she told herself.

Her footsteps kept to a trail slightly overgrown with underbrush. Glancing up at crooked branches, she saw the dragon from her previous dream. He was watching her, looking down from behind the treetops. His eyes were aglow—one green, one yellow.

233

She called to him. "Who are you?" But he disappeared like a ghost in the mist.

Her walk continued on until again the dragon showed himself, this time blocking her path. She felt no fear, no threat from the beast. In fact, it was like they were old friends.

When he lowered his head to her level, she gazed at the green gem in his eye, clear and brilliant. Then her attention focused on the gold gem. It didn't have the same brilliance, appearing translucent and hazy. Yellowish.

"They're different," she uttered, voicing her observation.

The dragon reared his head, letting out a wild cry. Eena covered her ears to shield them from the shrillness of his call. He flapped his wings and—with a puff of smoke—rose into the evening sky.

"I don't understand," she whispered.

The dream didn't end there. Eena cast her eyes about for something more, but she spotted nothing of significance. Her feet continued down their chosen trail. Soon, the same fretful feeling swept over her that seemed partnered with this gloomy forest.

"I don't have to be afraid," she repeated, but the words held no comfort.

Her pace automatically hastened until she was hurrying faster and faster, trying to escape something as yet unknown. Now and then her eyes shot up to scan the treetops for a threat.

Then she saw him. A second dragon.

He appeared similar to the first but smaller, possibly younger. And he was swift on his feet. This one she instinctively feared. The beast glared in her direction from behind a line of trees. Then he disappeared, only to emerge again shielded by another tree. His moves were alarmingly fast. She tried altering her path to avoid him, but he followed.

"Stop it!" she finally yelled aloud.

She stepped into a run to escape him, moving deeper into the forest. The trees crowded in clusters the further in she traveled. She could hear their desperate cries.

"Come to us! Come to us, Eena!" But she was afraid.

"No! No! Go away!"

Without warning the sky seemed to fall, and the young dragon dropped to the ground. He landed with a loud thud directly in

*her path.   She fell backwards to keep from running into him.
While scrambling to her feet, the scaly beast shoved his face in
hers.   She was shocked by the image in his eye—a round, red gem
exactly like the sketches of the dragon's eye.   The gem pulsed
with a heartbeat, glowing and fading in brilliant scarlet.*

*The beast reared his head in a swift and hostile manner.   His
neck swelled as he prepared to spew a breath of deadly fire, but
from out of nowhere the first dragon swooped down in time to
protect the girl from a torch of flames.   The red-eyed dragon
screamed aloud, a shrill complaint that pierced the air.   He flew
off into the night with the larger dragon trailing him.*

*"Oh my gosh, that was the dragon's eye," Eena told herself.
"It's not a good thing.   Not good at all."*

CHAPTER THIRTEEN
Healing Jase

It was past noon when the young Sha awoke. She stretched out in bed, feeling refreshed and rested, having already forgotten any disturbing dreams. Her toes inched from beneath the covers before she climbed down to prepare for a late start. Angelle wasn't anywhere to be found, understandable considering the time.

Hungry and finding nothing set aside for breakfast, Eena headed out. As usual, two guards met her outside the door. Luckily, no orders kept her confined to quarters.

Just inside a busy commissary Eena greeted the woman who had become a dear friend.

"Hello, Sarii! And hello to you too, Willum," she added. "Where's your brother?" A quick glance over the crowd didn't find the timid boy anywhere in sight.

Sarii greeted her queen in turn, bowing respectfully. "Good afternoon, Sha Eena. I'm afraid Xander's not feeling well, he's developed a persistent cough and fever. They thought it best for him to remain in the medical bay today. I'm a little worried. His symptoms seem to have worsened overnight. I'd be with him now, but Willum was restless and hungry."

"Oh, Sarii, I'm so sorry to hear that Xander's sick. Maybe I should go sit with him for a while."

"Would you?" Sarii's furrowed brow seemed to relax a little. "It might be just the thing to cheer him up."

"I'd be happy to. You haven't seen Angelle anywhere around, have you?" Eena scanned the busy room once more.

"No, I'm sorry, I haven't."

Eena gave up the search and turned her attention to the six-year-old. "And how about you, Willum, how are you?"

"I'm great! I shot a grembloine today and buried him in ice! Now he's frozen forever!" The energetic child poised like a superhero, announcing his victory.

"Wow! That sounds very....... creepy." Eena's nose wrinkled at the thought. "But I suppose you should keep up the good work. We don't want those nasty grembloines chasing us down." She smiled at how their folktales were kept alive by young minds. It was delightful to see Willum's imagination at work.

Eena made her way to the rear of the commissary to pick fruit from one of several trees revived days earlier. This was breakfast. After replenishing the yield and then visiting with a few friendly persons in passing, she left the commissary. Sarii had shared directions to the medical bay—her next destination.

"Hello? Doctor?"

Eena called out for any member of the medical staff, but no one in the infirmary responded. It was obvious at first glance that their facility was inferior to Jinatta's immaculate sickroom on the Kemeniroc. The room felt cramped and depressing, permeated by a malodorous smell that stung the nose. Ailing patients took up every available bed, including extra cots meant to accommodate the overflow of sick. This left very little aisle space to maneuver through. Most figures were balled up beneath blankets, shivering and coughing, their despondent whimpers coming from multiple directions. Every health monitor appeared to be in use, some flashing silent warnings that seemed to go ignored.

"My goodness," Eena breathed. "What's happening here?"

The lighting was exceptionally dim, perhaps to accommodate sleeping patients, but such darkness created a dispiriting mood. It was worsened by the reek of sickness—a vomit and sweat stench. The shadow of death practically loomed over the place.

Eena started down the main aisle, surveying the situation. She glimpsed a mix of ages but noticed far too many young people occupying most beds. A number of worried mothers sat wearily beside their children, petting their foreheads. The scene was disheartening.

"And what in tarnation do you want? Can't you see we're full up here?" The words were grumbled by a loud and cranky female.

Eena twisted her neck to find an older woman blocking the aisle, her fists digging into heavy hips. Around her thick neck hung medical instruments, more peeking out from pockets on a soiled apron. A deep-seated frown conveyed displeasure at

237

having another body to deal with.   Her dark hair was worn in a tight bun, accentuating a scornful expression.   She reminded Eena of a strict, old nanny.

When the young queen turned fully around, the woman's eyes dropped, landing on the distinguishing necklace.   Her demeanor transformed in an instant.

"Sha Eena!" she exclaimed, "I…I didn't realize!   My apologies, ma'am."   Her head lowered in a show of respect, her face red and mortified.

"Why are there so many people here?" Eena asked, disregarding the woman's initial impoliteness.   She was more concerned with the surplus of patients in the room.

"You ought not be here, ma'am.   There's a fierce fever goin'round right now.   And there ain't much I can do about it. You'd be better off headin' back to where you came from."   The stout figure attempted to walk Eena to the exit, taking a firm grip on her arm.

Eena planted her feet before the door.   "I'm not leaving."

"Ma'am, this ain't no place you oughta be."

"I assume you're the doctor?"

The woman grimaced.   "I s'pose you could say that.   I'm the closest thing you're gonna get to one."

"Aren't there medicines for them?"

"It's a nasty virus, ma'am, and we ain't had much in the way of decent medicines for some time.   There's no cure as far as I can tell."

"Will they get well on their own?"   She hoped perhaps it was a contagion similar to a flu or cold that would eventually pass.

There was no optimism in the woman's response.   "Some will—the lucky ones."

Eena glanced around the room again, noting a lack of help. "Where are your assistants?   Where are the nurses?"

The big woman chuckled aloud, an unfitting sound for the circumstances.   She pointed to the sullen visitors leaning against many bedsides.

"I'm afraid you're lookin' at 'em.   People gotta fend for themselves 'round here.   I nurse 'em as best I can, and now and then I get a helpin' hand at it.   Our battles have been many, ma'am, and our medical force just ain't here no more."   She

238

turned to a boy who had gone into a coughing fit and slapped him roughly on the back. "You oughta get goin'. Ain't nothin' you can do."

The stout woman shook her head, communicating the bleakness of their situation. She then turned her back on the young queen to attend to numerous sick patients.

Eena wasn't about to heed the nurse's advice. She continued further into the bay, stopping at a rear wall only to realize that around a corner existed additional beds with more ailing. One patient in particular caught her eye. Most of his body, including his face, was wrapped in bandages. Eena approached his bedside and looked down on the long lashes outlining his closed eyelids. He was asleep. She wondered about this poor boy's story. The answer came in a whisper from behind.

"He was burned badly—all over. Magg keeps him asleep so he won't hurt. She says he's going to die soon."

Eena turned toward the quiet voice. Xander lay on the bed behind her, balled up beneath a single blanket. Her sympathetic eyes took in his pallid complexion.

"Are you feeling alright?" she asked.

He covered a chesty cough. "I'm okay."

She turned back to the burn victim, unwilling to believe nothing could be done to save him. She thought of Jinatta's cellular regeneration tools. Such medical technology was far superior to anything found on Earth. Wouldn't the Mahgshreem have similar instruments? Couldn't something like that be used to heal him? She lifted a loose bandage to peek at the boy's face. Every visible inch was blistered or scabbed. She assumed from his size he couldn't be more than thirteen or fourteen years of age.

"Xander, do you know this boy's name?"

"He's called Jase." The nine-year-old slipped into a fit of congested hacking. Eena went to pat his back.

"How could this have happened to him?" she wondered aloud.

Magg was the one to answer, stepping out from behind the barricading wall. "It was an unlucky accident's all it was. The lad was in the back o' the kitchen in the commissary when our ship was attacked yesterday. The hits we took caused a couple big pots o' boilin' water to fall right over on the poor dear. Nothin' anyone coulda seen comin'. Just plain ol' bad luck."

Eena's face twisted up with compassion. "Is there no way to help him?"

"Sorry, ma'am. Ain't nothin' I can do but keep him comfortably sleepin'."

Moisture pooled in her eyes as she looked on the boy. Why was it that no one stood at his side?

"Where are his parents? His family?"

"Ain't got none," Magg sighed dismally. "They disappeared when them murderin' Ghengats raided our ship over a year back."

Eena's gaze shot up, wide and alarmed. "What? The Ghengats? I never heard about this."

"People don't talk much about 'em. They've raided our ship twice now. Take whatever and whomever they want with 'em. Those that've been taken ain't never come back. You'll wanna be careful; they'd prob'ly go for the likes of you."

"Be quiet, Magg," Xander broke in. "Don't scare her. The captain won't let anyone hurt Sha Eena."

The young queen smiled at her little hero, touched by his voice of protectiveness. He started into another coughing fit which the heavy nurse responded to by administering a few strong slaps between his shoulder blades.

Eena turned again to the burn victim, watching his chest rise and fall in his sleep. She felt additional sorrow for how he had lost his parents in such a horrible way.

"Do you have an extra chair?" she asked the nurse.

"For you, ma'am, I do."

Magg left, but quickly returned with a wooden stool wiped clean with the edge of her sleeve. She plopped the seat down between both boys. Eena was sure the stool had been heisted from another owner but accepted it anyway, certain it would be needed.

Scooting up to Xander's bedside, she gently brushed the sweaty bangs from his forehead.

"You're warm."

"I feel cold."

"It's because of the fever." She pulled the blanket up around his neck and tucked him in tight. "Better?"

"Yes, thanks." His eyes closed. Soon after, a faint snore sounded from his open mouth.

240

Eena sat in silence, contemplating the awful situation in the medical bay. She couldn't bear leaving these boys alone. Her fingers combed repeatedly through Xander's damp bangs as she mused over his condition. A wild question kept haunting her. Could it be that the same power she used to heal suffering plants had the capacity to heal people as well? She had a strong feeling it was possible, that the process was merely a matter of knowing how—figuring out what the necklace needed from her to do the job. The previous night's experience suggested the task might prove difficult and ultimately draining, but if those were the only consequences, she could certainly live with them.

The real worry hung on her mother's warning. What exactly constituted abusing the powers of the necklace? What would it take to bring on those unspeakable consequences? She didn't have to think much about it to decide none of those concerns would stop her from trying to save a life. It would be far worse to let Jase die if she could honestly heal him. And Xander—he too needed her help. She chose to concentrate on Sarii's son first. His ailment seemed less complicated somehow.

Eena scooted herself as close to Xander's bedside as possible. She glanced around the room to be sure no eyes were watching. Magg was gone, and everyone else appeared to be asleep or preoccupied with the sick. Her hand moved to hover above Xander's chest in preparation. Meanwhile, the necklace kindled. Her eyes fell closed, focusing on what she hoped to accomplish.

"Heal him," she whispered, lowering her hand onto the boy. Maybe, somehow, the necklace would understand her wishes and respond accordingly.

An uneasiness crept in as she fixed her mind on the task. It quickly worsened into an achy discomfort. Her lungs hurt like they had taken on liquid and swollen. With effort, she resisted the urge to remove her hand, understanding what was happening. It was not unlike her first experience with the pahna tree when she had felt its pain. But now the suffering she shared was Xander's.

Eena worked to focus over the distracting malaise. She repeated the same pleading words in her mind. Heal him, heal him, heal him...

Then something remarkable happened. An instant understanding of his ailment came to her in the form of a vision.

241

She could picture the virus invading his lungs, see the infection constricting his airways, hindering his ability to breathe. The coughing and heaving felt like her own as his youthful body attempted to combat the spread of germs. Strangely, it seemed like a simple thing to remedy.

As the necklace increased in brilliance, Eena felt a wave of energy disperse, traveling down her arm, through her fingers, and finally into Xander's body. She focused on his immune system, sending antibodies to swallow up the virus. It was as if she were directing his internal functions—teaching his body how to combat the disease while providing it the power to do so. Within a few short moments she felt the pain lift and his ailment recede, the fever completely erased. The boy coughed lightly, his lungs attempting to expel any lingering congestion. Then he relaxed and breathed normally.

Eena opened her eyes.

She had done it! She had actually healed a person!

Brushing his bangs away from his forehead, she smiled at the comforting touch of a normal body temperature. Xander stirred in his sleep. His legs straightened out, no longer feeling the instinct to ball up for warmth. The young Sha whispered sweet assurances in his ear. "Rest now, Xander. All is well."

The experience was emotionally exhilarating but also exhausting. Her pulse raced as she realized the power to heal people—not just plants—existed in her touch. The only drawback was the incredible energy drain. Her body slouched over Xander's bed, craving rest, but at least she hadn't blacked out.

Two hours passed with Eena propped on her elbows, watching her young friend sleep. Magg came by a few times, insisting the young queen depart, but Eena made it clear she wasn't going anywhere. The nurse eventually quit harassing her.

With Xander still slumbering and Magg occupied with duties, Eena felt it safe to turn her attention to Jase. Her concern was over the degree of his burns. She worried that his flesh might be too damaged to repair, and that his pain might be unbearable to experience. But the suffering would only be temporary. She couldn't allow him to die for lack of courage.

Positioning her stool at Jase's bedside, Eena leaned over the bandaged boy. Her gaze darted about once more to make sure no curious eyes were watching. With an uneasy inhale she moved her hands to hover over his chest. It was unnecessary to communicate her desires to the necklace; it was aglow with expectation.

Ready, her hands lowered and made physical contact. Pain tore through her entire body.

She gasped, recoiling like a snake as her eyes shot wide open. The agony had been more intense than anticipated. It took a few moments to regain a steady breath, and even longer to find the nerve to touch him again.

"I have to do this. I have to heal him," she breathed, working hard to convince herself.

Calling on natural stubbornness, Eena determinedly grabbed at his chest, clasping onto the bandages in order to keep from letting go. She smothered a yelp in her throat but was unable to keep from whimpering altogether.

Her eyes sealed tightly shut as she worked to focus on the task and not the pain. The burned skin needed to regenerate. With more force than before, she sent a surge of energy through her fingers, cramming healing power into the boy. Her mind oversaw everything—sending impulses through his body, directing the immune system to regenerates tissues quickly and thoroughly. Infection had already developed beneath his skin, but she summoned antibodies to eradicate it. As the seconds passed, his suffering eased. Jase's strength returned by increments while hers waned.

All she needed was a little more time.....another minute. But her energy was nearly spent. Utter willpower forced her to give every last ounce of herself.

Eena barely heard Magg call her name behind an amplifying ringing in her head.

"Sha Eena! What in the blazes are you doin'?"

Then everything went black.

Flames of blue and orange flickered behind a familiar hearth. Eena awoke to the sight. She didn't recall dreaming, nor did she remember seeing Ian while asleep. In fact, there was no clear recollection of anything. Carefully, she lifted onto her elbows, still weak and shaky. Her eyes glanced up. Gemdorin was sitting in the chair above, clearly upset.

"What exactly did you think you were doing in the medical bay?" he asked. If the hardness of his expression wasn't enough to convey irritation, his tone of voice certainly did the trick.

Eena fell back onto a waiting pillow, her arms too weak to hold her up. Gemdorin's question jogged her memory just enough to recollect what she had accomplished before blacking out.

"How did I get here?" she asked, evading his question.

"Magg called me when you passed out. She explained how you refused to leave sickbay, even when she insisted. Now that's hard to believe." His cross tone rubbed in the sarcasm. "But the biggest news she had to report on was how two boys, whom apparently you spent the afternoon with, miraculously recovered from their ailments. Imagine that!"

He paused to purse his lips into a deeper frown. "Now, Xander I could explain. Realistically, the boy could've overcome the virus on his own. But Jase?" Gemdorin huffed with frustration. "That one's going to be difficult to account for."

Wary of his foul mood, she tried skirting the blame. "You're the one who suggested I test the necklace's powers. I thought this would make you happy."

"Happy? Did you even stop for one second to consider how dangerous it would be if word of these new powers got out? Have you any clue what sort of expectations people would have if your enhanced abilities became common knowledge? Use your brain, Eena!"

Gemdorin's volume rose along with his level of irritability. "If people had discovered your capabilities, the entire medical bay would have swarmed for your attention! What you did was dangerous and foolish! You hardly possess the strength to heal two individuals without completely exhausting yourself, how were you planning to handle a desperate mob? You're lucky Magg sent for me first. The woman nearly had a tizzy over what she had witnessed! Jase, completely rid of his burns—burns that should've killed him! It's all I could do to silence the woman, and believe me she isn't an easy mouth to silence!"

Eena considered his argument. Perhaps this was what her mother's warning referred to. People might overreact if they

244

learned of her extraordinary powers.   She could see the potential for problems.

"I couldn't just let him die," she muttered, defending her actions.

Gemdorin growled deep in his throat.   He loomed over her from his seat, silent and stiff, considering his next move.   It was unsettling for the young queen to endure his angry glare.   She did her best to return it, unable to keep from glancing away.   Regardless of the captain's feelings, if it meant keeping that boy alive, she would heal him all over again—whatever the consequences.

At long last Gemdorin decided on a sentence for her crime. "For now, you are confined to these quarters.   You are not free to roam the ship until I'm positive that some semblance of wisdom exists in that foolhardy head of yours sensible enough to out rule your emotions."

"What?"   She struggled to rise to her elbows.   "What on earth is that supposed to mean?   You can't force me to stay here!"

Gemdorin leaned far forward to respond.   The severity of his expression made her sink back into the pillow.

"You are not on Earth anymore, *Sevenah!*   If you haven't noticed, things work much differently out here.   There is more at stake than some silly, young schoolgirl's immaterial wishes!   It's time for you to grow up!   You're supposed to be a queen! You've been handed a position of significant authority that requires a greater deal of wisdom and common sense than you seem to possess!   I can *and I will* keep you here until I feel you've matured enough to utilize your powers without putting yourself or others at risk!   Have I made myself clear?"   The lecture was worse than the one Derian had delivered back on the Kemeniroc.

In a near whisper she dared ask a question.   "What about the others in the medical bay?   I can heal them."

"I know you can, but you won't.   Exposing your abilities will cause significant problems, Eena.   And anyway, it would take weeks for you to heal them all given your lack of strength and...."

She cut him off, pleading.   "I'll grow stronger, you know I will.   Please, let me help them."

"No!" he snapped.   "You will not expose these powers!

Eena, it's not just our people who would take advantage of you, but desperate souls from all over Moccobatra and from worlds within our galaxy where there is awareness of the necklace. As of this moment the buried powers of the necklace are exactly that…..buried and forgotten. Only rumors exist—rumors that have never been substantiated by any Sha in history. That is except for one. And do you know what happened to that foolish *one*?"

Eena's brow scrunched, puzzled. "What are you talking about?"

"A story. A true story, regardless of those who call it myth, about a Sha who lived over a thousand years ago. It's said that a Harrowbethian queen, Sha Ruhnar, discovered how to use the necklace for more than traditional purposes. With these uncovered powers she was able to do magical things, even so far as to change the weather at will. Word of her remarkable abilities spread quickly, reaching well into our galaxy. Some people feared the queen because of her powers. Others took advantage, calling upon her for favors. But ultimately, do you know what became of Sha Ruhnar?"

"No, I don't know." Eena shook her head, mystified. Not because the ending to the story eluded her, but because she had no recollection of a Sha Ruhnar. If this queen had ever truly existed, a memory should have been stored in the necklace, but there was none.

"That reckless Sha was murdered!"

Eena swallowed hard. Perhaps this was a tall tale meant to scare her.

"The necklace was found discarded in the brush, deep inside Lacsar Forest. Her body was never recovered. No trace of her ill fate remained. Luckily, she had an heir who was old enough to take her place—Sha Krishta—a woman wise enough to comprehend the problems the necklace had caused for her mother. When Krishta took over as queen, she made sure everyone knew her abilities were far less impressive. She convinced people it was a rare talent her mother had possessed. Rumors were started then and there, but as time passed, this story became accepted as nothing more than myth. There's not one recorded account in our history about Sha Ruhnar's extraordinary powers."

"Then it must be a lie," Eena decided.

Gemdorin's eyebrow raised in contradiction. "Some say it was Sha Krishta who erased all proof that her mother ever possessed such abilities. I imagine that could be where the warnings started regarding consequences for abusing the necklace. No one since has unlocked its potential—that is until you."

He grinned, and Eena tensed at the deviltry in his expression.

"I'll admit I wasn't sure about the reality of those powers myself until you showed me. And here you go displaying them openly in only two days of attempting to use them. Not a wise move, Eena."

She dropped her eyes. Sha Krishta had left a memory behind—a firm warning against abusing the necklace's powers— but the memory didn't include any mention of a Sha Ruhnar.

Eena glanced up when Gemdorin rose from his chair and headed for the exit.

"I have duties to attend to. If you're hungry, there's bread and water. Make yourself comfortable because you're not going anywhere."

She yearned to discuss the fate of those in the infirmary, but didn't dare say more with him so upset. Her eyes kept at the captain's back until the doors shut him out. Then she relaxed. She was still tired and drained from healing Jase.

A smile crept across her face as it sunk in what sort of miracle she had actually performed. Her actions had healed a dying boy and erased all evidence of severe burns that would otherwise have claimed his life.

"It was so worth it," she breathed. Worth any stupid, lying lecture.

It took no effort at all to drift off.....

"It's about time you showed up," Eena grumbled, leaning against the weeping willow tree. "Where have you been, Ian?"

Her protector froze, shocked by the reproachful tone of her voice. "I know I'm late, but not that late." His eyes widened as her mood reminded him of his own the previous night. "Ah-ha! So now you know what it feels like to sit here and wait and wait and wait and worry."

She made a face. "I wasn't worried."

247

Ian plopped down beside her and glanced at the familiar sunset. "How long have you been here?"

"Since this afternoon."

"What?" He gawked at her. "Why?"

"It's a long story. You go first."

"Okay, well, I'm late because we had a meeting with Derian this evening. He's really worried about you, Eena, and it's starting to take its toll on him."

"I'm alright," she assured her best friend.

"I told him that, even though we both know it's not the truth. So long as you're in enemy hands you're in danger, Eena."

She nodded, letting him know she was aware of his concern.

"Derian's main worry is that we can't seem to track you. And now, knowing the Mahgshreem can travel faster than the Kemeniroc, he's stressing over what to do about it. What makes things worse is that the trail Leisha was following suggests Gemdorin went a different direction than toward the Millan System."

"I told you, I think Gemdorin's jumping from place to place. He's hunting for something. In fact, we recently stopped at a large, yellow planet. For all I know, we may still be nearby."

"Do you know the name of the planet or its system?" Ian was eager, hopeful for another clue.

"No, I don't," she admitted. "Sorry, Ian. We can't be too far away from the Millan System, though. How long has it been since we were there?" She began counting the days on her fingers. When she counted beyond her first hand, her eyes bulged with disbelief. "Oh my gosh—that was more than a week ago!"

"Eight days," Ian agreed. "Sixteen days ago you were stolen from us."

"Over two weeks," she muttered to herself, honestly surprised by how time had flown by.

"When you were observing Dergan's Comet, our traveling distance from the same location was an estimated three weeks. So it appears a week of travel for Gemdorin equates to twenty-one days for us. That right there is why Derian is so worried."

She finally understood their dilemma. "Does he have any idea what he's going to do?"

"Actually, yes. Leisha and Marguay have been working on a

way to accelerate one of our battleships. This evening they informed Derian their current modifications will potentially allow travel at twice the rate of our normal top speeds. That's not as fast as Gemdorin, but better than anything else we've got. And if you're right about him making frequent stops, we may stand a chance of catching up to you. The only problem with this modified ship is its considerably smaller size. Derian has decided to go alone."

"By himself?" Eena was surprised.

"I know," Ian shook his head contrarily. "We told him it was foolish to go unaided, but he insists. He seems to think he can ration his resources better this way while keeping any risk to the crew minimal. He made the decision an official order. No one dares argue with him."

"Because he's a bully who's now bullheaded. And what exactly is he going to do if he does find me? Will he take on Gemdorin's entire fleet all by himself?"

"He has a plan, Eena, and besides, we'll be following in the Kemeniroc. Eventually, we'll catch up to assist."

"Eventually?" Her upper lip curled, conveying serious doubt. "Where does he plan to start looking?"

"He'll head for the Millan System first and then go from there. He's called on a couple of friends to help track you down. Shanks and Agus have agreed to commit a portion of their interstellar fleet to the task of looking for the Mahgshreem. They'll let us know if they find you."

"Who are Shanks and Agus?" She thought the names sounded unusual.

"Oh—Shanks and Agus are brothers, Viiduns from the planet, Rapador, in the Paegus System They're basically crazy if you ask me. They own a trading ship called the Triac 38. Shanks is also Rapador's Commander of Defense, overseeing their deep-space battalion. Derian happened across him once while searching to replenish our food supply. Shanks and Derian hit it off right away. These brothers travel with two partners—Heth and Efren. Shanks and his lot are exceptional traders, mostly because they're incredibly large and beyond intimidating. More than anything, they're just big, bulky, mean warriors with some serious attitude."

"And Derian is friends with them. Why doesn't that surprise me?"

Ian smirked. "Now, now, Eena, these are the guys you definitely want on your side. They live for a good fight! If I didn't know better I'd swear it was impossible to do any one of them in. From what I've been told, Shanks has saved Derian's tail a handful of times. Derian didn't want to call on the Viiduns because he's already indebted to them, but we desperately need the help. These guys will find you, Eena. Not only are they great warriors, but they're avid treasure hunters as well. They can track down anything. They're the ones who got Derian into collecting all those antique weapons."

Eena laughed. "Is that what all you men do, search the galaxy for hidden treasures?"

"No, not all of us. Some of us are too busy trying to keep track of impossible women."

Eena pulled her mouth to one side, showing her lack of amusement at his remark.

"So, what's your story anyway?" Ian asked, ignoring the sour face. "Why have you been hanging out here since this afternoon?"

"Do you want the long version?" she asked, "or the longer version?"

"I have all night." Ian stretched out his legs and crossed them, making himself comfortable.

"Alright then," she began. "Last night when I had dinner with Gemdorin, he told me about a rumor claiming the necklace possesses buried powers. He then insisted I try using these powers in case a need arose for me to defend myself against an enemy. He seems to think that since I have no heir there's more urgency for me to learn to protect myself."

"You mean protect yourself from him," Ian grumbled.

"Actually, he suggested I might need to protect myself from Derian."

Ian rolled his eyes.

"Anyway, he pressed me to try and unlock these powers."

"How?"

"He placed three candles in front of me and insisted I try to light them using the necklace."

250

"Oh, how romantic," Ian groaned, conveying his disapproval of her dining with the enemy.

"Would you please stop it," she scolded. "It's my turn to talk now."

Ian pretended to zip his lip and throw away the key.

"Alright, where was I?" She paused to gather her thoughts. "Oh yes. I tried touching the candles to light them, but it didn't work. Gemdorin wouldn't allow me to leave, however, until I successfully completed the task. He told me…um…" She glanced warily at Ian before finishing her sentence. "He threatened to kiss me if I didn't do it."

Ian's eyes bulged and his eyebrows climbed, but he didn't say a word.

"Well of course I didn't want him to kiss me!" she exclaimed.

Ian pretended to wipe his forehead—a sign of relief. This made Eena laugh.

"The whole thing just made me mad," she continued. "And the angrier I got, the more I could feel this energy building up inside. The next thing I knew, I waved my hand at the candles and they all ignited. I couldn't believe it! The only drawback was it completely exhausted me."

"But he never kissed you?" Ian couldn't keep from asking the question.

"No! I wouldn't allow it!"

"Good." He pretended to zip his lip again.

"Well, today I visited the medical bay for the first time, which was a horrible experience. I've never seen so many sick people in one place. And most of them are children—poor things. I went there to visit Xander because he wasn't feeling well."

Ian made a silent gesture by raising his shoulders and turning up his palms.

"You don't know who Xander is? Didn't I mention him before?"

Ian shook his head.

"He's Willum's brother—Rhoen's oldest son. He's nine years old."

She got the OK sign and continued with her story.

"I found Xander resting in the back of the medical bay. The boy was suffering from a high fever and a bad cough. His bed was next to another boy, Jase, who had burns covering his entire body. It was an awful thing to see. Jase had been in an accident the day before. The nurse attending to him told me it was just a matter of time before he died from his injuries. She was keeping him sedated so he wouldn't suffer any pain. I knew I couldn't just stand there and watch him die."

Eena's eyes moistened recalling Jase's dire state. Her protector showed sympathy by mirroring the same agony.

"I wondered if perhaps I could use the necklace to heal him, especially after what I had done the night before. So I gave it a try. And, Ian—" She paused to hold his attention. "—it worked. It actually worked! I used the powers of the necklace to heal Jase's burns, and I cured Xander's illness too!"

"Seriously? You actually healed a person?" Disbelief shaped his features, and he stared incredulously for a moment.

"Yes, Ian, I did! The only thing is, well……I passed out afterwards. Gemdorin was called in. He discovered what I'd done and yelled at me for it. He said I was irresponsible and foolish for advertising my abilities in public." Her voice mocked Gemdorin's deep tone as she repeated his reprimanding words. "If people were to discover your abilities, everyone would swarm for your attention! What you did was dangerous and foolish!"

Eena rolled her eyes when she finished, huffing with annoyance.

"He's right about that," Ian said, "not that I want to agree with the jerk or anything. But I can see potential problems if word spread that you could do these things."

Eena twisted her neck so her best friend wouldn't miss how she wrinkled her nose at him. "Whose side are you on anyway?"

"Yours, of course. I'm totally, absolutely, entirely, one-hundred-percent on your side. Completely. Really." He smiled a crooked smile for her.

She pursed her lips in an unimpressed manner. "Well, the whole thing got me confined to quarters. I can't go anywhere. So I'm probably not going to be much use to you when it comes to finding out where I am. Not that I've been much use up to now."

"Oh, Eena, I'm sorry." His arm fell across her shoulders and squeezed, remaining there afterward. She leaned on him and whined about the situation.

252

"What I hate the most is that he won't even consider letting me heal the other patients in the medical bay. And I can heal them. I know I can."

Ian was pondering the whole incident. Wondering. He made a sound of suspicion as he thought.

"You know, it's strange that our people were so much healthier before your mother died. Since then we've suffered increasing illness. More and more die from contagions every year. It's never been this bad before. We all presumed it was the native fruits and herbs that kept us healthy, and I'm sure there's some truth to that, but I'm wondering if..."

He dropped his arm from her shoulders to tap a contemplative finger on his chin.

"What if all this time the Shas have healed our illnesses without anyone knowing? I mean, when your mother was alive she visited people constantly, traveling all over Moccobatra. And she was always hugging people or placing a gentle hand on them. And the necklace continually glowed and dimmed. You just got use to that. I wonder if she used the necklace to keep people healthy without anyone realizing it."

"You think maybe my mother healed people secretly?" Eena considered the idea. "She did tell me to use it to care for our world and our people. That constitutes caring for people, I'd say."

"Yes, but since no one understood her actions, no one sought her out or took advantage of her power."

Eena's mouth dropped open, hit by a sudden idea. "Ian! You're a genius! I've got it! I've got it!"

"Great! Uh....what exactly have you got?"

"I can do the same thing here without anyone knowing! Oh, it's so obvious; I can't believe I didn't think of this before!" She gave him a big hug. "Thank you, Ian."

"No problem," he shrugged, wondering how she was going to do anything while confined to quarters.

Just then, Eena's dream form flickered transparent. She was rousing from sleep.

Ian took her by the arm, attempting to hold onto her. "Eena? Why are you leaving?"

"Gemdorin's here," she explained. "I can sense him

kneeling beside me."

Her image blurred and then refocused.

She looked at Ian.   "He's touching the necklace.   I need to go."

"He wants those powers, Eena.   He wants your necklace. Promise me you'll be cautious."

The young queen vanished from sight, trailed by two words. "I promise."

Gemdorin's fingers ran across the necklace, softly outlining two oval grooves.   He repeated the pattern over and over again. Eena kept still, feigning sleep, but his caressing touch bothered her so much she rolled away from him, continuing a pretended slumber.   A moment later she was gently jostled.

"Eena, wake up.   Eena, you've been asleep long enough, wake up."

She turned her head to face him.   "I'm awake.   What do you want?"

"I have dinner.   Come."

He offered a hand up and she accepted, following him to the table where he pulled out a chair for her.

"Thanks."

Two plates were set, each topped with a sandwich and a serving of sliced fruit.   The same goblets from the night before were half filled with a sweet-smelling drink.   Feeling extra hungry, she started in on the sandwich.   Gemdorin sat by quietly, watching her eat.

"I was thinking," he said after a few silent moments, "that I may have been a bit harsh with you this afternoon.   I still believe what you did was careless, and you will continue to be confined to these quarters for now, but I….I apologize for shouting."

Eena glanced up but didn't say a word.

Gemdorin covered a cough with his fist and then reached for his goblet.   The young Sha picked up her drink also, sipping at it as she watched the captain sooth his irritated throat.   She recalled how he had struggled with a cough the night before.

"You're getting sick," she said, "just like the others."

"I'm fine."

"No you're not, but I can help you."   She held out her hand, offering a simple cure. "Take it," she urged.

Gemdorin inclined his head, considering the offer. He knew he was ill, having grown fatigued the past few days. Recently, he had suffered bouts of chills and an aggravated cough. As fit and hardy as he was, he figured he could kick the virus on his own. After all, many others were recovering. The strong ones anyway. However, the idea of suffering through a prolonged illness wasn't appealing. Ending out in that dreadful sickbay would be unthinkable. Hesitantly, he reached for Eena's hand.

She stood and approached him, placing her other hand on his chest. Her eyes fell closed as she concentrated. The necklace shimmered to life. She communicated her desires by thought, telling the necklace exactly what she wanted. A minute later it was done.

"Do you feel better?"

"Actually, I do," he said, drawing in a deep breath and exhaling without the slightest tickle. "Are you sure I'm well? I hardly felt a thing."

She smiled. "All is well now."

Eena finished her dinner feeling much, much better herself.

CHAPTER FOURTEEN
Antivirus

"Would you like to take a walk?"

Gemdorin was already waiting by the doors. Having just finished eating, Eena downed the last of her drink and stood up to leave.

"Where are we going?" she asked, not that it mattered. It was a relief to be leaving her place of confinement, even if only for a short time. She was shocked he was allowing it. Then again, maybe he felt guiltier for his earlier display of anger than he let on.

"Let's take a stroll on the star walk. There's bound to be something interesting in the heavens tonight."

Eena smiled at the suggestion, hoping to spot a galactic landmark she could report back to Ian.

It was a short jaunt down the corridor before Gemdorin slipped inside another room. Eena looked in, finding a private sleeping area decorated with nautical materials. She hesitated entering at first, seeing how the majority of the space was a stack of mattresses buried under a generous pile of plump pillows. She watched the captain cross a carpeted floor and stop. He stood beside a small, round door—an exact replica of the one in his treasure room.

"This is the other end of the walkway," he explained, activating the control that allowed them access. When the door rolled sideways, Gemdorin ducked through and waited for Eena to follow.

"Was that your room?" she asked, stepping past him into the dark.

"Yes. My sleeping quarters."

The exit sealed shut behind them, stealing Eena's eyesight. She didn't panic as she had the first time. Her ears recognized the metallic groan of lifting handrails, and she imagined them rising to just above waist level until her eyes adjusted enough to actually see the bars lock into place. Her fingers curled around a rail, using it as an anchor for balance as the walkway detached from the ship.   Her gaze followed a swarm of vivid streaks resembling chalk lines on a blackboard.   Gemdorin ordered the Mahgshreem to slow, causing every white streak to fall into itself, leaving nothing but splatters of dots in the night—millions of shining stars.

There were no planets or celestial moons to be seen, only the awesome immensity of the universe.   Eena tried to imagine no end to the abyss when an object caught her eye, barely a shade lighter than the background of space.   She squinted to focus on it, noticing how it blocked the light of distant stars.   A second form crossed her view, nearly imperceptible with its muddy color.   All at once her eyes focused on an entire field of irregular shapes, suspended and drifting in the middle of nowhere.   Her eyes widened, recognizing the anomaly as a meteoroid belt.   Giant chunks of craggy boulders hovered everywhere.

"Where did all these come from?" she asked, staggered by the number.

"Remnants from a comet probably," Gemdorin guessed. "Worthless rock."

"That's a lot of worthless rock."

"Speaking of comets, you might earn the opportunity to see Dergan's Comet again......*if* you mind your manners," he added with patronizing emphasis.

"You mean we're going back?"

"Yes, right past the Millan System.   The comet should still be in the vicinity."

"Why the backtracking?" she asked.   "I thought you were taking me home?"

He placed a strong hand on her shoulder and squeezed. "Don't worry, my dear.   After I'm done with business, I'll make sure you wind up where you belong."

She thought about his "business" and then voiced what she already knew.   "You're searching for the dragon's eye."

"If I'm lucky enough to find it, then by all means, yes."

His hand remained on her shoulder.   Eena moved along the walkway, forcing him to remove it.   He followed her to the middle of the ramp where they both looked up at the darkness. The ship was maneuvering through the meteoroid field.   One giant boulder came so near, its rugged texture was plain as day.

"I never imagined seeing things like this," she marveled.

"Eena." The captain spoke her name as if requesting her full attention. It drew her eyes to him. "Your eighteenth birthday is coming up shortly isn't it?"

She had to think for a moment and add up the lost time on Earth with the weeks since. "I believe it is in a few months."

"Has anyone discussed with you Harrowbethian tradition?"

Her forehead creased with uncertainty. "What do you mean?"

"In our culture, a young girl is 'promised' by at least eight years of age." He kept an earnest eye on her, interested in her reaction.

"Promised what?" she asked innocently.

"No, no. Not what......*whom*," he corrected.

"Whom?" she repeated, still confused. "What are you talking about?"

Gemdorin turned to lean backwards on the handrail in order to face her more directly. He began to explain. "Harrowbeth honors a longstanding tradition. When a couple has a baby girl, they must make an arrangement referred to as a 'promise' before her eighth birthday. It's an agreement between the girl's parents and the parents of a male child. The two children are promised to marry when the girl turns eighteen. Both children wear matching pendants throughout their growing years to show commitment to one another."

"Are you talking about arranged marriages?" She was shocked and troubled. "No one told me about this. Are you serious?"

"Perhaps they never intended to tell you," Gemdorin suggested, "but yes, it's true. It's been our custom forever. Of course, your parents died when you were only three years old; they still had five years to promise you to someone."

"Are you saying I'll never marry?"

Gemdorin laughed at her naïve assumption. "No, no, of course you'll marry. You *must* marry to produce an heir. How else will the Sha legacy continue?"

Eena's eyebrows knit together. She stared at Gemdorin, wary of where this was going.

"I imagine you'll have to choose a suitable husband for yourself, given the fact that your parents are no longer able to do so for you."

She was actually relieved by this news. The last thing she wanted was to be told she had to marry some guy she didn't even know.

"It's expected for a young woman to wed somewhere within her eighteenth year. That's not too far away for you now, is it, Eena?"

"It's far enough," she grumbled, meaning to end the conversation.

"I just thought you should know." Gemdorin turned to the handrail again and rested on his forearms. His gaze traveled, connecting the stars. "There's a lot of emptiness in the galaxy, isn't there?"

Eena didn't reply. Her thoughts were preoccupied.

"Are you ready to go?"

"Yes," she nodded. "I'm tired."

"From healing me?" he asked.

She hadn't thought about that. "Perhaps." Honestly, she was hoping it wasn't too late to talk to Ian again.

Gemdorin led her back to the room with the warm fireplace. He left her for the night and retired to his own quarters. Eena snatched a pillow and blanket and curled up on the sofa, snuggling up in one corner. Warmed by a flickering fire, she fell asleep fast.

"Ian? Ian, are you here? Ian, please still be here."

"I'm here, Eena." His dream image appeared out of nowhere. There was no willow tree or farmland or colorful sunset to witness. She dreamt of nothing but open space.

"Is something wrong?"

"We've turned around. We're headed back to the Millan System. Gemdorin told me we would see Dergan's Comet again soon. We'll probably pass right by you."

"That's great news! The break we've been looking for!" Ian was beaming, eager to leave. *"I'll tell Derian right away."*

"Wait. Just one question." Her face tightened up. It was obvious something was bothering her.

"What's wrong, Eena?"

"Is it true that in Harrowbeth girls are promised to a future

husband by eight years of age?" She was anxious, hoping he would call Gemdorin on another lie. But he didn't. Her best friend dropped his eyes, his all-too-familiar way of refusing a response.

"Arranged marriages, Ian? Another huge thing you didn't tell me? Why?" There was hurt in the way her voice trembled.

"Eena, did Gemdorin say anything else about that?"

"Like what? Like how I'm almost eighteen years old and apparently I'm expected to marry by then? That's a big deal, Ian! I'm not ready to get married!"

Ian asked his next question carefully. "Eena, did he suggest you were promised to him?"

"No!" Her eyes grew big. "He said my parents died before I was promised to anyone. Ian?" She looked to him for an explanation. For reassurance.

"You're not promised to that monster, but I'm sure he's up to something or he wouldn't have mentioned this."

Ian tried to justify his silence on the subject.

"There are traditions in Harrowbeth we haven't discussed, Eena, but not because I meant to keep them hidden from you. Believe it or not, Derian was planning to bring up all of this as soon as he had the opportunity. He told me so when we were looking after you in the medical bay. But he never got the chance because Gemdorin snuck in and stole you away."

"Why can't you explain these things to me?" Her eyes begged for him to do so.

"Because it's Derian's place. Just be patient and he'll talk to you. He'll answer all your questions when you get back."

"Gemdorin may answer them for me first," she said bitingly.

"And how will you know he's not lying?"

"How do I know you're not lying?" she retorted bitterly.

"Eena?" He was visibly hurt by her remark.

She dropped her head, calming herself before apologizing. "I'm sorry, I didn't mean that. I just feel like I'm the only one stuck in the dark. I hate it."

"I know, but Derian will explain everything. He will. Honest."

"He has to find me first," she reminded her friend.

"And now that we know you'll be in the Millan System soon,

260

we'll be ready." Ian sounded hopeful, even optimistic. "It won't be much longer."

"Ian?"

"Yes?"

"One more question."

"Okay." He braced himself.

She breathed in deeply before asking. "Are you promised to someone?"

His green eyes did nothing but stare at her. It took a moment for him to reply.

"Yes."

The answer hit her harder than she had anticipated. Eena struggled to show no emotion. "Who is she?"

"To tell you the truth, I wasn't even sure she was alive," Ian started. "Eena, please understand that in peaceful times, promises were a natural and beautiful thing. A boy and girl understood from an early age they were promised to marry someday, and they grew up knowing this, learning about one another while developing a friendship years before marriage. Their families did things together to make the bond stronger. By the time they reached adulthood, a sound foundation had already been built, uniting them as a couple."

Ian went on, growing more despondent. Eena couldn't continue to look at him.

"This war has spoiled everything. Families and couples have been separated—too many killed. Jinatta was promised to a soldier who died in battle six years ago. Jerin was married on the Kemeniroc, only to have his young bride pass away five years later from some cruel disease. The woman I was promised to......well......her family followed Gemdorin when she was a child. I haven't seen her since. I assumed she was dead, and if not, the probability that I'd ever see her again was small. You were the one who told me she still lives."

Eena couldn't help but lift her eyes, questioning Ian with a look. The wheels turned in her mind. Whom had she talked about to Ian?

The name fell softly from her lips, the only person it could be. "Angelle."

Ian nodded.

261

"You don't even know each other."

"That wouldn't be the case had we grown up together in Harrowbeth."

"She's a nice girl.   Very nice."

Ian tried to smile.   "I need to go talk to Derian.   Okay?"

"Of course," Eena mumbled.   "Go on."

"I will see you tonight."

"Yes."   She forced a smile.   "You're still my best friend, right?"

"Always," he said, taking her hand.   He pulled her in for a reassuring hug, and softly repeated the promise in her ear. "Always."

Sleep was restless after Ian left, beset with fragmented and unsettling dreams.   Eena woke up three hours later.   At the foot of the sofa, a change of clothes had been laid out.   The sweet smell of breakfast drifted from the table.   She wondered if Gemdorin ever slept.

Back on the Kemeniroc, Ian hurried to Derian's quarters to share what he had learned.

"Is she absolutely sure Gemdorin's reversed course?"

"She's sure.   He told her they might see Dergan's Comet again.   They have to be turning around."

"Then we'll be ready for him."   The captain turned to move out, eager to assemble his crew to review plans for a rescue mission.

"Wait, Derian, there's one more thing you should know."

He paused and turned back.   "Yes?"

"Gemdorin told her about our marriage custom.   He told her she would need to choose a husband by her eighteenth birthday. She was very upset about the whole thing."

Derian's eyes shot up at the ceiling.   He shook his head, huffing irritably.   "That bastard's trying to win her over.   He wants to be king.   If she were convinced to marry him of her own free will there'd be nothing I or the council or anyone could do about it."   His gaze dropped to Ian, sharp with determination. "We're going to stop him."

"Yes," Ian agreed.   "Yes, we are."

262

They left with renewed purpose and a deadline.   The Kemeniroc was already on a course for the Millan System, but the sooner they reached their destination the better.   Leisha and Marguay had completed successful tests on modifications made to a small battle cruiser.   Derian would have taken off in the Abbos One already had it not been for one thing.   Gemdorin's ships had cloaking capabilities.   His did not.   He would be a sitting duck out there, alone and visible.

Leisha, Marguay, and their staff were studying the design of Rhoen's wristband in detail.   They had been testing its unique properties ever since Derian handed the item over.   It worked like magic on any person.   A demonstration by the captain had shown that with a single touch he could make another person or a minor item disappear right along with him.   Erasing an entire starship, however, was proving to be more complicated.   The engineering team had attempted to integrate the wristband into the ship's systems with the hopes of cloaking the Abbos One.   But no matter what theory they tested, the results were always the same.

"It requires too much energy," Marguay kept saying.

They had discovered a liquid metal flowing through the wristlet's core and had determined it to be a power source. Unfortunately, it was an alloy they had never encountered before. When Leisha tested a miniscule fraction of the metal, it released all its energy in one swift surge—not a steady flow as expected—and created a minor explosion.   The entire engineering team was baffled.

Within closed conditions like what the wristband offered, the flow of power remained constant but hampered, not amplified enough to cloak something as massive as a ship.   Leisha was convinced that a greater flow of the alloy would produce enough power to easily cloak a small ship for an indefinite period of time. But the best they had managed so far was to overload the engines and cause the Abbos One to flicker in and out of visibility for a few seconds.   They were close to a solution, but time was running out.   Now that Derian knew Eena's location, he wasn't going to miss the chance at a rescue mission—cloaked or not.

On another level of the Kemeniroc, doors to the brig parted to expose a lone prisoner tended by a single guard.   Derian motioned with his head for the guard to leave the room.   He then

263

approached the criminal behind bars.

Rhoen stood up from a single bench in a sealed cage, his face long with weariness. He grasped at the metal rods between them and began to plead.

"Kahm Derian, please. It's been over two weeks since I've reported to Gemdorin. I know your upset with what I've done, but my family, sir—their lives are in serious danger. If I don't report something soon, he'll kill them! You know your brother; you know he'll do it!"

The captain's reply conveyed no sympathy. "You chose your own fate."

"Fine, yes, I accept that. You can punish me all you want. Beat me senseless for all I care, but please, sir, please! My family doesn't deserve to die for my mistakes! All I have to do is contact him, even with no news. It would be for a minute. There's a small communicator in the Stellar Six, tucked in beside the furthest seat. I need that device to call him. I'll tell Gemdorin whatever you want. I'll set him up for you if you want, just please, please allow me to talk to him. Otherwise.....my children....my wife......Derian, he'll kill them!"

The captain spoke to the prisoner as if he hadn't heard a word. "I want to know exactly how that wristband works. Tell me how to modify it to cloak a small ship."

Rhoen's forehead fell against the bars. His family was in danger of being murdered, and this man wouldn't even listen. "You can't possibly be this heartless," he breathed. "The only reason I came forward with the truth was to save Sha Eena."

"Then help me now or we may never get her back." Derian repeated the command, "Tell me how to modify the wristband to cloak a small ship."

"I don't know. I only used it on myself; I have no idea how it works."

The captain spoke louder, desperate for answers. "Don't lie to me, traitor!"

"I really don't know!" Rhoen insisted, lifting his head to stare earnestly at the man.

"Then you're of no use to me." Derian turned on his heels, moving swiftly toward the exit. He paused when Rhoen shouted at his back.

"Wait! Please, please wait! Let me talk to Gemdorin and I'll ask him how the strap works! I'll ask him where he's taking Eena!"

The captain swiveled around to growl at his prisoner. "I already know where Eena is! What I need to know is how to get to her undetected!"

Rhoen was an anxious wreck, beseeching the captain, his knuckles ghostly white gripping at the cell bars. "Then let me talk to your brother. Please, Kahm Derian, please! I'll find out everything you want to know, just let me talk to him."

"Right. You expect me to give you an opportunity to communicate with your conspirator? To divulge more secrets to the enemy? To fill him in on my plans like you have *for the past six years!*"

Derian stormed out of the brig leaving behind a frantic man crying out for mercy. In the depths of utter hopelessness Rhoen fell to the floor and wept, regretting his decision to come clean.

An hour later, the doors to the brig parted again. Derian paused in the doorframe, a small transmission device held at his waist. The prisoner uncurled from off a hard bench, his pulse thundering in hopeful anticipation.

When they stood face to face, Rhoen breathed with expectancy. "Thank you, Derian. Thank you."

The captain's jaw locked taut. For a moment he looked as if he might change his mind. He spelled out the ground rules.

"If you mention anything that even hints at our location or our plans, I will talk to Gemdorin myself and spoil your secret and your family's security. Do you understand me?"

A simple nod communicated a perfect grasp of the warning.

"I want to know how to use that technology to cloak a ship."

"Yes, sir. I'll find out." Rhoen took the offered communicator, the one retrieved from the Stellar Six exactly where he had explained it would be.

Derian stood silently by while an attempt was made to contact Gemdorin.

"Setta Nii keeahma."

It was dead quiet as they waited for a reply. When none came, Rhoen tried again.

"This is Private One. Do you read me?"

265

Still silence.

"Private One reporting, Kahm Gemdorin, please respond."

No one answered.   Rhoen glanced at Derian who stood as cold and fixed as a cell bar.   Then came the anticipated voice.

"It's about time I heard from you, Rhoen.   You're cutting it awfully close, aren't you?"

"Yes, sir."   There was a tremor in the answer.   "Derian's been keeping a close eye on the crew since Sha Eena was taken.   He suspects someone aboard may have helped.   It's been difficult to find an opportunity to contact you."

"So, how is my little brother handling his defeat?   Has he given up yet?"

Rhoen's eyes flickered at the stoic figure standing quietly by.   "No sir.   He's still hunting for her."

Gemdorin snickered in wicked amusement.   "He'll never find her.   Where is he anyway?"

Rhoen looked to Derian for an answer.   He was unsure of their present location and less sure what the captain would have him say.   Derian grabbed a computer pad from off a nearby desk and typed out the words, "**between Meagra System and Devil's Mist.**"

"Rhoen?" Gemdorin grumbled impatiently.

"Yes, sir."   He read from the screen held up for his view.   "We're between the Meagra System and Devil's Mist."

They heard Gemdorin's derisive laugh again.   "Poor lost soul!   I almost feel sorry for the buffoon, trying to compete with his far superior older brother.   He's light years away!   I needn't worry about running into him even reversing course.   Ah, Rhoen, we make a fine team, don't we?   Six years on his ship and the fool's none the wiser."

Ashamed, the prisoner didn't dare look up.

"Sir, I was wondering if you could tell me how to modify the cloaking band to accommodate a small ship.   With Kahm Derian searching for a spy among his crew, I'm nervous of being found out.   I might need a way to escape.   A cloaked vessel would make it much easier for me."

"Rhoen, if you're ever found out, you can say goodbye to your pathetic little family.   You *will not* fail me, do you understand?"

"Yes, sir.   I...I was just wondering if it was possible to cloak a ship with the band."

"Of course it is.   A boost of initial power would need to run through the band first before reaching the engines.   You'd have to link it to the reactor to create a complete circuit through the power drive.   It'll sustain a cloak for as long as needed."

"How could you possibly do that when the band is closed?" Rhoen wondered aloud.

"Slit it open at the juncture point, idiot!   And make sure your power flow remains steady unless you care to set off one hell of an explosion.   But considering that a botch in your duties would result in the loss of your entire family—well….you'd be better off blowing yourself to pieces, and Derian's ship in the process."

"R...right, of course."

"Now, anything more to report?"

"N...no, sir.   Everyone's concerned about the welfare of their queen most of all."   Rhoen hesitated, squeaking out the next question.   "How is Sha Eena?"

"You needn't worry.   She's having one grand adventure here—a far better time than she would have had with my dull brother.   And I must say, the girl's not terrible company.   You were right, Rhoen, she has her assets."

Rhoen was relieved to hear their queen was alive.

"Yes, sir.   I'd better go before I'm missed.   Please, sir, be aware that I may have difficulty contacting you under the circumstances.   With Kahm Derian searching for a leak among his crew, I must be extra cautious."   Rhoen hoped this news would protect his loved ones if he couldn't report again soon enough.

"Lucky for you, Rhoen, Eena has taken a liking to your family.   I haven't a clue as to why.   It amazes me she isn't bored to tears, listening to those ridiculous stories your boys are always dreaming up.   She spends hours with them, though.   She and Sarii are constantly chattering about all sorts of pointless nonsense."

"Really, sir?"   He was elated to hear such news, but Gemdorin squelched his moment of joy with a threat.

"It won't stop their ill fate if you fail me, Rhoen.   Mark my words."

"Yes, sir.   Private One out."

With trembling hands, the prisoner handed back his communications device.

"Thank you, Derian. Thank you." His heart was comforted. For the next two weeks, if not longer, his family would be safe. Furthermore, they were spending time with their queen.

Derian took this new information directly to Leisha and Marguay, hoping it would be what they needed. No one had thought to risk severing the wrist band completely. It was worth a calculated try.

The next three days confined to quarters were excruciating for Eena. There were no windows to peer through and no one to visit with except for Gemdorin who came by every afternoon and evening for meals. Each night she begged him to let her roam the ship again, but he flatly refused, reminding her of the need to exhibit more maturity by demonstrating some intelligence in her decision-making. He was never cruel, just strict. Even so, his inflexibility was upsetting.

Eena finally resorted to making the most of what was available to her and spent hours sorting through a short pile of historical books Gemdorin had left behind. Each one contained illustrations, maps, and stories about the dragon's eye. Plagued with boredom, she attempted to decipher the ancient script. It was an impossible task, but what else was there to do?

On her fourth morning confined to the same limited quarters, Eena woke on the sofa, warmed by a flickering fire. The night had passed pleasantly, dreaming with Ian. She had managed to put the whole "promise" custom behind her, choosing not to worry about it for the time being. After all, who knew what the future held given the separation of Derian's and Gemdorin's crews?

This particular morning Eena noticed that no change of clothing had been set out, nor was the sweet smell of breakfast awaiting her as usual. She wondered what was keeping Gemdorin away.

To pass the time, she flipped through the pages of a favorite book, one she had been trying to decipher for three days' time. Little progress had been made with the script, but she had put together some ideas about the dragon's eye—assumptions made from studying drawings included in the pages.   A great many were sketches of the red gem.   In some, the stone was centered on a circular object.   One picture had a warrior holding the circle above him, his eyes widely focused on the gem.   She wondered what he was seeing.   Did the stone have some sort of mesmerizing effect on his mind?

The most recent book collected by Gemdorin included an illustration uniquely different from the others.   It was a black-and-white sketch of a busy battlefield.   Over each side of the skirmish appeared a powerful goddess.   Eena assumed opposing armies had their own deity to call on for help and protection.   It wasn't uncommon for a group of people to believe in higher powers.   What didn't make sense was a minor item she had noticed only after a thorough examination of the scene.

On one side of the field, a warrior stood grasping a round object with a gem attached to its center.   In this picture, the circle appeared to be a shield.   The gem was drawn with lines encircling it, suggesting it glowed.   It looked like the dragon's eye.   But on the other side was a rival warrior positioned in the back lines, directly below his goddess.   He had a helmet in his hands with what appeared to be a second gem.   It too was drawn as though it glowed.   It was inconspicuous among the mass of detail included in the drawing.   Exhaustive scrutiny had brought it to Eena's attention, and she wondered if this was another magical gem. Maybe there were *two* dragon's eyes.

At the sound of doors parting behind her, Eena closed the book.   The captain entered the room without breakfast or a change of clothing.   More worrisome was the hardness in his face.

"Eena."   He addressed her tersely, finding her awake.   His arms crossed over his chest as he chose to stop and lean against the edge of the table.

"I'll give you one guess where I've been this morning.   I was summoned first thing to a place unexpected, uninviting, and certainly not part of my normal routine.   Where do you think that was?"   The question sounded like a riddle.

"I don't know," she said, grateful he remained at the table.

He answered the riddle immediately.   "Your recent hangout—the infirmary."   With tight eyes, he watched for a reaction. She did her best not to show any.

"Eena? Do you have anything you wish to tell me?"

Her head shook in quick, tiny moves.

Gemdorin frowned. He drew in a deep breath and then released it in one steady stream. It was apparent he was trying not to lose his temper. "It appears that everyone who had a case of that nasty virus has miraculously recovered, and rapidly I might add. Magg is puzzled. She wants to know why. More importantly—*I want to know why.*"

Eena responded immediately to the demand. "I haven't left this room. You haven't let me out. I've been nowhere near the medical bay, just ask Magg."

Gemdorin's arms came unfolded. "What. Did. You. Do!"

"I didn't do anything," she insisted, before admitting in a near whisper, "you did."

The captain's face contorted in a perplexed manner. He straightened up and approached her. She rose to meet him, trying her best to act unafraid.

"Don't play games with me," he warned.

"I'm not. It was you who delivered the antivirus that healed them. I, uh…" she swallowed before mumbling, "I just sort of created it."

"You did what?"

She decided it was best to come out with a good and quick explanation. "When I healed you the other day, I realized the virus was airborne. That's why everyone was getting sick, because they were passing it on to one another through the air. That meant it was only a matter of time before everyone eventually fell ill."

She had his attention. "Go on," he said.

"Well, when I went to heal you, it occurred to me that I could kill the virus, or I could alter it and create an antivirus. It too would be airborne. There's no way anyone can trace this back to me. I haven't been near the medical bay in days. I knew that all you had to do was breathe and the cure would be passed on to others. It did no harm to you. And I didn't want anyone else to die if they didn't have to. So you see.....you healed them." She sucked in a breath of air and held it, hoping he wouldn't be too

270

upset.

The captain remained impassive at first, examining her face for the longest time.   Eena stood her ground, not budging, not breathing.   Regardless of his opinion, she would not regret her actions.

The first sign of reaction to her story was a deep, low chuckle. Gemdorin's lips turned up at each corner and then parted into a growing smile.   As the laughter developed into a full expression of amusement, his head shook from side to side.   Eena wasn't sure whether to smile or shy away.

"How terribly, terribly sneaky of you, my dear.   Now *this* is what I call using your head!"

She released a sigh of relief, understanding he approved.

The laughter endured as Gemdorin contemplated exactly what she had done.   "You actually created an antivirus simply by touching me—and without my awareness.   That's phenomenal, Eena!   Do you have any idea how powerful this is?"   He reached out, taking her by the shoulders.   "You could wipe out your enemies with a virus, and they'd never be the wiser.   Who needs weapons?"

His avenue of thought concerned her.   "I heal people, Gemdorin, I don't harm them."

"Of course, of course," he agreed, "but if it came down to having to defeat a nasty enemy in order to save innocent lives, well......look at what you *could* do."

Her brow creased uneasily.   "I can't imagine ever choosing to."

"Right," he nodded, backing off.   "Well, Eena.   People are recovering as we speak and no one can trace this miracle back to you.   Well done.   I think perhaps you've learned a lesson. You're free to go."

"I am?"   Her eyes grew big.   "Honestly?"

"Honestly," he grinned.   "Just remember, I can reverse my decision at any time.   Don't give me a reason to."

She said nothing further but followed him to the doors.

"How about lunch today?" he asked before letting her slip out.

"If you don't mind, I'd prefer to go to the commissary.   It's been so long."   Eena noticed a hint of disappointment in his face, although he agreed to her choice.

"As you wish, my dear."

As soon as he gestured her onward, she scurried down the corridor, headed for her own room.

Meanwhile, Gemdorin made his way to a far distant area of the ship—a guarded haunt of which others were unaware.   In the company of some gruesome guests, he held an informal meeting.

Five Ghengats surrounded a conference table with Gemdorin seated at the head.   These creatures were encrusted in gray-blue scales as tough as reptilian skin.   Bald and hairless, their tiny ears were easy to see, pressed flat against each side of the head.   For the most part their facial features resembled any person, but with solid black eyes and notched nose bumps lacking nostrils. Muscular strength combined with larger hands and feet made them a strong force for physical combat.   Sparse clothing included heavy pants and thick belts.   Each carried a weapon at his side. Only one, the lead Ghengat, wore a dark sash across his chest with alien script that bore his title.   Gemdorin addressed them as comrades.

"She's making excellent progress.   I can only imagine what she'll be capable of in time.   It appears her strongest emotions are what really encourage her success with the necklace.   When she's upset, stressed, anxious, the necklace glows brighter and triggers her powers.   So….I propose we push her along.   Let's see what happens when she's afraid.   Genuinely terrified."   For anyone listening, they would have thought him eager to cause the girl misery.

"What if we're the ones that get hurt in the process?" one Ghengat asked.   "If that necklace is as powerful as you say, she could kill us!"

Gemdorin dismissed the soldier's concern.   "Quit stewing over phantoms, you spineless coward.   The girl doesn't have it in her to kill anyone.   I doubt she'll have the guts to do anything at all—in which case the person you'll need to worry about is *me*. After I rush to her rescue, I'll win her complete trust.   She'll be entirely enamored with me."   He smiled cleverly at his own plan.

"When do we get our chance at the necklace?" the lead Ghengat asked.   "You promised us use of its powers."

"Patience, Raugh, patience.   In due time the necklace's potential will be fully realized and it will be for us to command, one way or another.   Now, prepare yourselves.   Tomorrow afternoon you strike."

In the commissary once again, Eena was thrilled to be surrounded by her friends.   Angelle was still nowhere to be found.   The guards normally stationed outside her quarters had been missing as well—a fact the young queen didn't mind.   Perhaps it was an oversight.   They would probably all show up soon enough.

Eena ended out seated by Sarii and her sons who were delighted to see their royal friend after her extended absence.

"Xander told me you visited him in the medical bay four days ago.   I haven't had a chance to thank you for keeping him company."

"I was, uh—"   *Busy* wasn't the right word.   "—detained," Eena explained.   "I'm truly sorry."

"Well, I want you to know I appreciate the time you took with Xander.   Luckily, he recovered shortly after you left.   It seems most of those with the same cough are recovering as well.   Magg believes it's because you're back with us."

Eena gulped down a lump in her throat.   "Oh?   Why would she think that?"

"The fruits and herbs.   They're strengthening our immune systems again.   We've suffered so much illness with no Sha to provide the healthy foods from our world.   But now that you're here, things are already improving."

Eena nodded her agreement.   "That makes sense."

Xander left the two women talking at the table.   He returned a few minutes later with an older boy at his side.

"Sha Eena?" the boy squeaked, timidly requesting her attention.

She turned to face the lad.   "Yes?"

He smiled—a wide and handsome grin.   "You don't recognize me, do you?"

Eena glanced at Xander and then back at the boy in front of her.   "I'm sorry, I don't remember meeting you."

"I'm Jase."   He held out his hand to shake.

Her initial shock quickly turned to joy.   She sandwiched his hand between her own.   "Oh my goodness!   Hello, Jase."

"I wanted to thank you for what you did to heal me," he said.

Eena's smile disappeared with those words. The last thing she needed was to have this information passed around the ship. No doubt she would end up confined to a small room again.

"Jase, I really didn't do anything, but I'm very happy to see you well."

The boy looked confused. "But Kahm Gemdorin and Magg, they both told me it was you."

Now she was the one to look confused. Why would Gemdorin tell him that?

Jase went on. "They said you were trying out a new medical tool—a piece of technology you acquired from that planet we were orbiting. Kahm Gemdorin said it was you who used the instrument to heal my burns. Magg told me if it hadn't been for what you did, I'd have died."

"That's what they told you?" She was both surprised and amazed at Gemdorin's ability to come up with a very convincing cover story.

She grinned feebly. "Well then, Jase, um……I'm glad it worked."

"Thank you, Sha Eena." The boy bowed at the waist, a respectful gesture.

"Sure, sure."

Eena spent the entire day in the commissary, visiting with people and healing their neglected plants. Mostly, she basked in the pleasure of company, grateful to be free from solitary confinement. She listened in when Jase entertained a group of children with an oral delivery of clever pirate tales. Xander and Willum were among the young audience, soaking up a good adventure as much as the other children.

Each time she inquired about Angelle, no one admitted to seeing the young lady. Eena made a mental note to question Gemdorin about it the next time they were in each other's company.

Evening hours seemed to rush by too quickly, and Sarii declared it bedtime when her boys began to talk with whiny voices. The day had been enjoyable yet tiring. After bidding her friends goodnight, Eena headed to her own quarters, anxious as always to spend treasured time with Ian.

CHAPTER FIFTEEN
True Story

The aromatic scent of dinner carried through the corridor where Eena caught a savory whiff and followed it to her door. The smell intensified inside the room where Gemdorin's unexpected presence drew her eye immediately. He appeared quite comfortable lounging on the furniture, enjoying the soft, soothing sound of music descending from somewhere above. The melody was a classical arrangement that incorporated a variety of stringed and fluted instruments.

Eena leaned against the closest wall, her lips shaped in disapproval. "What are you doing here?"

The captain remained seated, one foot swaying in time to a lazy tempo. "I missed you. I haven't had to suffer through dinner alone the past few days, and I didn't care to do so tonight."

"I'm awfully tired, Gemdorin. It's late."

"Nonsense." He straightened up in his seat, motioning for her to come forward. "Sit with me."

She didn't budge.

Unhindered by her show of obstinacy, Gemdorin rose and walked the length of the room to retrieve her. Reluctantly, she allowed herself to be towed to the divan where the captain sat her directly in front of himself.

"Close your eyes and relax," he ordered. His fingers went to work kneading her shoulders.

Eena moved to stand, uncomfortable with the personal attention, but he wouldn't let her get away.

"Relax, I'm not going to hurt you."

Her muscles tensed up despite his word; however, a few moments of massaging seemed to melt away all concern. The young queen closed her heavy eyelids and succumbed to the tranquil effects of soft music and a therapeutic touch.

As soon as her shoulders went slack, Gemdorin gathered every long strand of hair and moved the handful to one side, exposing the back of her neck. Working his fingers along her spine, he continued kneading across the area of bare skin until he reached the rim of the necklace. It was impossible to distinguish where it latched together, forming no apparent beginning or end.

Curiously, he brushed his fingers over the border, feeling at its tight, solid texture. He marveled at how the width of bronze was secured at every point like a second layer of skin, contouring even the slightest curve. His inquisitive touch pressed against dainty, gold details that trimmed the upper edge. He then examined a line of tiny, green gems slightly jutted along the bottom.

These intrusive actions disrupted Eena's state of tranquility. The massage had been pleasant enough, but this prodding made her feel uneasy. The jewelry glimmered to life, glowing like a night light.

Eena rose to her feet before the captain could stop her. "Why are you touching it?"

"Because it's fascinating; I can't help myself." He grinned goofily. "You would be curious too if it were adorning someone else."

"Perhaps," she admitted, "but I don't care for you poking at it. It makes me uncomfortable." She took a seat across from him, letting her hair fall down her back again.

Gemdorin remained curious. "I can't imagine how it must have felt to have that thing grab on and attach itself to you."

"It hurt," Eena told him truthfully, "very badly."

"But it doesn't now?"

"No. I hardly know it's there unless I see my own image.......or someone reminds me of its presence." She shifted her eyes to look at a covered basket centered on the table between them.

Gemdorin followed her gaze, sensing she didn't care to discuss the necklace any longer. He snagged the basket; it smelled of dinner.

"Hungry?"

She shrugged. "Maybe a little."

Pulling out a pair of slender candles, he instructed her to light both while he set out the food.

"Do you have a match?" She was perfectly aware he wanted her to utilize the necklace, but she feared draining her remaining energy.

"Oh, I'm so sorry, my lady, I must have forgotten to pack one." Eena noted the insincere rise and dip to his apology. "No worries since *you* don't require such things."

She hesitated, afraid of passing out again.

"Go on," he urged.

Leaning forward, she closed her eyes and imagined the candles alighting with the smallest spark. Calm and focused, her hand waved over the wicks—gently this time. Both candles flickered, each with a tiny flame that grew as it burned. She had managed to expend little energy.

Gemdorin praised her. "Nicely done. You're definitely improving. I suppose this means I can't kiss you tonight either?"

"No, you can't," she quickly agreed.

He flashed a crooked grin, handing her an empty plate.

Three platters of food were laid out: one of sliced cheese and fruit, a second piled with thin slices of fresh bread, and a third warmed by stewed meat responsible for the rich, savory scent that saturated the room. The captain started up conversation as they served themselves.

"So, my dear, how did you choose to spend your freedom today?"

"With my friends in the commissary."

"Are Sarii and her boys well?"

Eena smiled. "Yes, they're fine. I saw Jase too. He told me about a wonderful, new piece of medical technology that healed him." Her eyebrow arched accusatorily as she looked to Gemdorin. His grin came across as both guilty and smug.

"It was a viable explanation," he said.

Eena remembered who she hadn't seen. "Do you know where Angelle is? I miss her. She wasn't around today."

"I'm sure she's fine."

Eena pushed for a better answer. "Where is she, Gemdorin?"

"She's not feeling well, but I'm sure she'll be on her feet again soon."

"Why didn't you tell me she was sick?"

"You couldn't have seen her anyway, being confined to quarters."

"You could have allowed it. She is my friend you know."

Gemdorin straightened up in his seat, his expression stern.

"The reason you were restricted to one room was to keep you away from the ill and thus eliminate any association between you and those miraculous healings. This was all done for your safety and security, Eena."

She rolled her eyes, groaning.

"It was a precaution for your protection."

"Whatever. Can I go see her now?"

"Absolutely not." The answer was swift, given without a moment of consideration. "You will stay away from the infirmary henceforth. In fact, you will avoid that entire deck so as not to be tempted to heal anyone else in public view."

She huffed an exhale, obviously upset with his orders. When the captain's scar spiked above a look that forbid her to argue, she grumbled consent under her breath.

"Fine."

They ate in silence until Gemdorin brought up a topic he knew she couldn't resist.

"What did Willum have to say? Did he pass along any more fascinating stories?"

Eena's mood lifted just thinking about her young friend. "Willum never got a chance to tell any stories. He was too busy following Jase around like a shadow, listening to *his* spooky tales."

"Jase is a storyteller too? Big surprise." Gemdorin's tone was unimpressed.

"He's a very good one," she defended. "Believe it or not, he had all the children in the commissary glued to his every word for a very long time. He shared one story in particular that I liked."

"About witches, grembloines, pirates, meerlots, or dragons?" Gemdorin asked, knowing how the young people loved to tell ghost stories.

"None of the above," she said. "It was about a Sha."

"Oh?" He looked interested. "Go on; tell me."

"Well, Jase said that once upon a time there was a queen named Sha Tappen who lived in Harrowbeth during one of their more troublesome periods. The council was having difficulty dealing harmoniously with some nearby neighbors, the Icromians."

"That's hard to believe," Gemdorin cut in, his tone thick with sarcasm.

"Anyway, Sha Tappen was doing her best to strengthen

diplomatic ties between the two nations, but it wasn't going well. The Icromians insisted the necklace rightfully belonged to their people. They argued that their race was first to inhabit Moccobatra and that the necklace had originally been discovered by them. Thus, they reasoned, it should be kept in their possession. Apparently, the fact that none of their people could successfully wear it didn't matter. They seem like a stubborn race."

"An accurate description," Gemdorin attested.

"Well, having grown frustrated with the Harrowbethian council and their Sha, the Icromians contrived a plan to kidnap Sha Tappen and hold her captive in their city high up in the mountains. They justified their actions by this reasoning: as original keepers of the necklace, they ought to be in charge of all decision making regarding its use. Somehow, they successfully pulled it off."

"And did she destroy them by summoning the necklace's buried powers?"

"Of course not!" Eena exclaimed, casting her listener a look of appall. "The Shas are women of good character. She did no such thing."

"Then what *did* she do?"

"Nothing. She stayed with them, confined to her quarters." Eena raised an eyebrow at the captain. "Sound familiar?"

He pursed his lips, yielding no reply, so she continued retelling Jase's story.

"It didn't take long for word to spread all over Moccobatra that Sha Tappen was being held prisoner in the mountains of Icromeia. Nations worldwide wondered what it would mean for their own people. They worried the Icromians might horde the necklace for their own uses, keeping the power all to themselves. The possibility of it becoming a force of leverage caused many groups to take action."

"And you don't think the Harrowbethians ever did the same thing? Used their Sha's power as leverage in diplomatic relations?" Gemdorin asked.

Her reply was certain. "No, sir. I know the Shas wouldn't do that. It's against their very nature."

Gemdorin's eyes tightened with skepticism, but he didn't argue.

She went on. "Armies from all over the world assembled,

devising strategic rescue plans. The first attempt came swiftly from their giant neighbors, the Grotts. The Grotts assumed sheer strength and stature would guarantee their success.
Unfortunately, they were quick to fail. The steep, wooded terrain proved a natural fortress for Icromeia. The Grotts expended most of their energy trying to scale the mountain. They were attacked halfway up and forced back to their own land.

"Next, the Monturians tried their hand. This army was wise enough to know that only a surprise attack stood any chance of devastating the Icromian guard. Being undersized and quick on their feet, they chose an elite group to steal through the mountain forest. Unfortunately, they too were stopped by the continual watch of the guard who flew by day and night, keeping a lookout for trespassers. One by one the Monturian soldiers were discovered and weeded out. Their rescue attempt also failed.

"Still others sought to free Sha Tappen, but no one was successful against the watchful Icromians. It seemed Sha Tappen's powers would be at the command of the Icromian leaders for good."

"How fortunate for them," Gemdorin smirked.

"No, not really," Eena said. "You haven't heard what happened next."

"I'm all ears." The captain shifted edgily in his seat. "Go on."

"Eventually, the Prime Director of Icromeia allowed Sha Tappen a reprieve from her secured chambers so she could use her powers to nurture the plant life around their great city. Naturally, she was under guard the entire time."

"Naturally," Gemdorin repeated dryly.

"Despite the annoying escorts, she was highly productive— moving from plant to plant and tree to tree, touching the branches, causing them to grow beautiful and robust, drooping with abundant fruit. The Icromians were proud as peacocks!"

"Peacocks?"

"Birds," Eena explained, "with fancy tails."

Gemdorin didn't appear to understand or care, gesturing for her to go on.

"They were pleased with the great quantity of fruit they gathered…"

281

"Because those self-seeking, high-and-mighty Icromians are nothing but greedy hoarders."

"Would you quit interrupting my story?"

"Would you finish it already?"

"I'd very much like to, if you could keep quiet."   She daringly widened her eyes in response to his tapered stare.   He held his tongue.

"Alright, where was I?"

"The Icromians were pleased as peacocks."

Eena frowned at his apparent need to interject, but started up from there.   "*Proud* as peacocks……until they harvested the bounty.   A sample of the newly-formed fruits and herbs revealed what Sha Tappen had done."

"What had she done?"

"Gemdorin!"

"Get on with it and tell me."

"Fine.   She had spoiled their entire food supply.   Happy?"

"Ha-hah!"   He seemed to approve.

"Anyway, it turned out that every bite of food was bitter and sour to the taste.   Their leader demanded she repair the damage, but she refused until he agreed to take her home.   She was certain they wouldn't harm her because her powers were necessary to the survival of Moccobatra.   It took little time for the Icromians to realize they could never really control the powers of the necklace. They finally understood that Icromeia was better off as an ally of Harrowbeth than an enemy.

"In the end, they relinquished their hold on Sha Tappen, offering an acceptable apology.   Before returning to Harrowbeth she made the rounds a second time, touching every plant in the area and healing the vegetation.   Sweet, delicious produce sprang forth once again.   One tree, however, she purposefully ignored, leaving its branches teeming with sour fruit in the very heart of Icromeia.   This tree still stands as a memorial to all people—a symbol of the consequences of selfishness."

"And what would that be?"

Eena smirked.   "Well, obviously, the moral of the story is that selfishness reaps only bitter fruit."

"Of course!" Gemdorin groaned, tossing his hands into the air.

"It's a true story."

282

"Oh? And how do you know this?"

She thought of Sha Tappen's memory stored in the necklace, one meant to teach future Shas to deal patiently with their neighbors, even under difficult circumstances. Eena had recognized the tale as soon as Jase had begun rehearsing it in the commissary. She knew it to be true. That's why she liked it. However, she didn't want to explain all of this to Gemdorin.

"Someone told me," she decided. It wasn't a lie.

"Ah, I see."

Gemdorin rose and moved over to the chair beside Eena where he made himself comfortable. "Now it's my turn," he announced. "I have a true story too. Have you heard of a race called the Ghengats?"

Eena screwed up her face. "Yes. I've heard they're horrible."

"They do have a nasty reputation, and most people would describe their appearance as…"

"Monstrous," she finished.

Gemdorin chuckled. "If I didn't know better I would think you already met one."

"I haven't, and I hope I never do."

His gaze fixed on her as he voiced a word of warning. "If Derian tracks you down, you may be forced to deal with the monsters."

She returned his strong stare. "I don't believe you."

"I'm telling the truth. My brother has sent those Ghengat allies of his to attack my ship more than once. They raided our supplies and abducted a large number of crew members before we were able to fight them off."

Eena's shoulders leveled in a defensive manner. "Derian told me it was *you* who allied with the Ghengats."

"Of course he did!" Gemdorin laughed. With a tilt of his head he posed one question. "But answer this—why would my allies raid my very own ship?"

The smugness on his face was annoying, yet she didn't have an answer for him. It honestly didn't make sense to attack your own ship.

"Anyway," he continued, not waiting for a real reply, "I still have a story to tell you."

283

She was eager to hear it, charmed by his animated words and actions; they brought his adventures to life.

"This true story occurred centuries ago on a world called Hrenngen—a large, red planet in the Elrah Gyan System. At the time, it was home to a thriving race of Ghengats. They're a fierce people, mostly warriors, with skin protected by bluish armor-like scales. Their hands are large and powerful, capable of clutching onto a person and leaving little chance of escape. Being extraordinarily strong, they are formidable foes in hand-to-hand combat."

Eena was mesmerized by Gemdorin's description. She had already mentally painted the most fearsome likeness of what a Ghengat must look like.

"As a race, the Ghengats were once consumed with the idea of world domination. Their nations fought continually, each hoping to claim the title of Supreme Ruler of Hrenngen. Wars were constant on their world. As technologies developed, weapons became more severe and effectual. Chemical weaponry grew in popularity. With it, they managed to wipe out entire armies. With the invention of devastating warheads, eventually the inevitable occurred. The deployment of massive vaporizing explosives caused catastrophic global destruction. Hrenngen's planetary life was virtually obliterated."

Eena voiced the irony of their actions. "The Ghengats managed to destroy the one thing they were fighting to control. How depressing."

"They nearly did so. The majority of their population had been wiped out, either by missiles or the devastating aftermath. Those who managed to survive soon discovered their world was uninhabitable. With all the caustic chemicals in the air and poisonous debris spread over the land, everything was fast dying. About this time, one of the wiser Ghengats came forward with a plan for survival. As the others accepted his proposal, he naturally became their leader, overseeing a difficult and risky venture to ensure the continuation of their species. His name was Raugh. They began to call him Grah Raugh, or Commander Raugh. He became highly respected for his leadership efforts in saving their lives. Every commander since has been called Grah Raugh regardless of his real name."

"So what was his idea?" Eena asked.

"Well, at that time in their history, along with the development of more sophisticated weaponry, the Ghengats had acquired the means for space travel and related progresses. Raugh had been instrumental in these advancements. He proposed escaping their poisonous atmosphere by taking a small collection of ready starships to the moon. Once there, they could live on the spacious ships while constructing an enclosed city to sustain life. They would have access to new soil and sunlight within transparent walls. Raugh convinced the survivors that remaining on Hrenngen amounted to nothing more than a slow suicide. It would take thousands of years for the atmosphere to clear up enough to let through any decent amount of sunlight, and longer for the poisoned air and soil to neutralize."

"Did they really build a city on the moon?"

"As a matter of fact, they built many. To this day, the majority of Ghengats live on their moon. Over the years their world has slowly become inhabitable again. The air still carries traces of gas, but in bearable amounts. The Ghengats who returned to the planet are there for one reason only. To mine quarrin."

"Quarrin?" Eena repeated. "I've never heard of it."

"No one had until the Ghengats discovered it in their soil. It's a unique liquid-metallic substance that contains a great deal of chemical potential energy within its structure. Given the right catalyst, it can release explosive amounts of energy."

"That sounds dangerous."

"Not if used in a controlled manner. It can power a ship for years. Properly manipulated, it can release greater or lesser measures of energy so long as there's an uninterrupted way to sustain the flow. The Ghengats discovered this quarrin when they returned to their planet to evaluate its recovery and potential habitability. They found the deposits near a semi-active trio of volcanoes. The really interesting story is how they say this quarrin came to be."

Eena leaned forward, eager to hear the next story.

"During the centuries in which Hrenngen was shrouded by a poisonous cloud, a very powerful being came to visit their world. The Ghengats say he chose their planet because he believed it to be abandoned. This visitor brought with him a young dragon—a terrible and fierce beast. The being sought to put away the dragon in a place from which he could never escape or be released."

"Oh my," Eena breathed. She could picture a violent contest between a mighty warrior and a vicious, fire-breathing dragon like the one from her dreams.

"After an arduous struggle, the creature was finally overcome and sent to an underground prison deep beneath one of the volcanoes. The Ghengats say this trio of volcanoes grows hotter and more massive every year because of the dragon trapped below, thrashing about, fighting to escape confinement. They believe the quarrin is a magical liquid-metal created from a combination of the ores beneath the volcanoes, the intense heat that exists there, and the magical powers the dragon expels in his attempts to break free."

Eena fell back in her chair. "For crying out loud, you said this was a *true* story. It sounds like one of Willum's fairytales."

"It *is* a true story," Gemdorin insisted. "Don't you believe in dragons?"

Eena thought about the two from her dreams. That didn't mean they were real. Of course it didn't mean they weren't.

"I don't know," she shrugged. "But there's no way a real dragon could be kept alive underneath a volcano. At the very least he would run out of air and die."

"Not if magic were involved," Gemdorin suggested.

"There is no such thing as magic." Her statement was a matter of fact.

"Oh?" he questioned. "This from the girl who lights candles with the wave of her hand?"

"That's not magic. It's just a manipulation of energy."

"It looks like magic to me."

"Well it's not. The necklace uses energy in all its different forms. It simply changes it into whatever form is needed to accomplish what I want to accomplish. It may be heat or light or electricity or any source of potential energy—but the process is not magic."

"And you understand how to do this?" he asked her.

"Not really," she admitted, "but the necklace does. The more

286

I work with it, the more I'm beginning to understand. Like when I lit the candles, I knew I needed to produce enough heat to create fire."

"Where does the heat come from?"

"From me. The necklace uses my energy, altering and concentrating it enough to spark a fire. The first time I did it, I exhausted my available energy and the result was a huge flame. Remember? That's why I passed out. This time I knew I only needed a fraction of that power, just enough for a spark. And it worked."

She sat back against her chair, seeming pleased with herself.

"So you see, Gemdorin, it's not magic. It's simply an understanding of what energy is and how it works."

"Maybe. But perhaps the mighty being who buried a dragon beneath a volcano understands more than you do about manipulating energy. And if that's the case, *it is* a true story."

"Ugh," Eena groaned, "whatever."

Gemdorin laughed out loud, letting his head fall back against the seat. Eena ignored his amusement and went to peek inside the picnic basket.

"What are you looking for?" he asked with an enduring grin.

"A drink. I'm thirsty."

"I put two bottles in there."

She pulled out a pair of clear, glass bottles from the bottom of the basket. They were filled with a clear bubbly liquid, corked on top.

"What is this?" she asked, remembering the strong beverage he had served her once before. She hoped this wasn't the same stuff.

"It's seltzer nectar. Hand me one."

Eena gave him a bottle and watched him pop the cork. Liquid fizzed up and over the top. He took a long swig and set it down, motioning for her to hand over the other. He easily removed the second cork. Once the liquid settled, he handed it back to her.

"Try it."

She took a sip. It was fruity and highly carbonated. "I like it," she said, thankful it was something she could drink.

Returning to her seat, she announced it was her turn again.

287

"I have a *real* true story."

Eena started into another adventure involving a long-past Sha of Harrowbeth.   The two continued swapping tales well into the night which effortlessly crossed over into early morning hours. Eena was enjoying herself so much that an awareness of time completely betrayed her.   She searched among her memories of past Shas for the best accounts she could find, and then related them to Gemdorin who seemed interested, although annoyed with her inclusion of proper morale endings.   When he asked her how she knew these things, she simple shrugged and said, "Someone told me."

Gemdorin came back with his own adventures concerning mystical planets and eerie, magical beings.   Eena didn't believe for a second that his stories were anything but fables, but he insisted they were absolutely true.

"You prove to me it's *not* true," he would say.

The final tale was delivered by Gemdorin.   It told of two powerful immortal beings who wreaked havoc across the galaxy. They were sisters who eventually ended up having their souls imprisoned for all eternity to stop their brutality.

"I've heard this one before," she told him, "and I don't believe for one second it's a true story either."

Gemdorin laughed aloud.   "Well, I believe it is!"

"You're talking about two immortals.   The undead.   The everlasting.   Do you honestly believe anyone can live forever and ever and ever and ever and ever?"

"Yes.   I staunchly believe it."

She heaved a sigh of surrender and had to cover her mouth to hide a sizable yawn.   It was then she noticed the candles had burned completely down to nothing.   They had been sitting in the dim light of a yellow lamp and hadn't even noticed.

"Oh no," she worried.   "What time is it?"

"What does it matter?   You're in your quarters, you have nowhere to go."

"But you're messing up my sleeping hours.   I'll be sleeping all day now."

The captain looked at his pocket device and informed her it was just past zero-four-hundred hours.

Eena was panic-stricken.   Ian would be beside himself.   It

288

was morning, and if she didn't hurry she would miss him altogether. He would worry all day long about her.

She stood up from her chair. "You have to go. Now, please."

Gemdorin appeared reluctant, but he eventually rose as well. "As you wish."

He placed his empty bottle on the table and moved directly in front of her. His hand slipped beneath her hair, landing against the side of her face.

"This was fun. I enjoy spending time with you."

Eena's pulse hastened at his touch, but she didn't shy away from him. She had enjoyed his company as well, yet Ian's critical voice in the back of her head made her hesitate. This man was supposedly no good.

When it was obvious what Gemdorin wanted, Eena stopped him. She could hardly breathe to whisper. "You can't kiss me."

His lips paused close to hers. "Why not?"

"I lit the candles, remember?"

"They're not lit now."

"You promised." Her heart beat so thunderously, she was certain he could hear every knock against her ribs. Truthfully, part of her wanted him to kiss her anyway. Just once.

He backed off. "Very well."

For a moment he stood still, holding her in a longing gaze. Then he turned away and started for the doors.

"Very well," he repeated in a louder voice, "I will go and consider your punishment for telling me such outlandish lies." He glanced over his shoulder to catch her reaction.

She followed him to the doors. "Oh please! My stories were absolutely true. Yours were obvious fairytales!"

"Prove it," he said, turning around to face her.

They stood by the exit, Eena waiting for him to leave. Gemdorin stole her hand and planted a kiss on her palm. Bowing in a grand manner, he declared, "Parting is such sweet sorrow." Then he winked. "Now that was a true story!"

He disappeared around the corner. Eena poked her head into the corridor and called out after him. "No way; that's from William Shakespeare's *Romeo and Juliet!*" She stood there stunned for a second, wondering where he had heard that line.

289

Then her thoughts returned to Ian, and she hurried off to bed. Beneath the crimson covers, her knees climbed toward her chest, curling her into a ball.   As soon as her head hit the pillow, reality faded into a dream.…

She was dressed in her favorite jeans and pink t-shirt again. Glancing in every direction, she searched for Ian, desperate to find him.   She worried he might react badly to her extremely late arrival.   He did.

"Criminy, Eena!" he barked, appearing out of nowhere. "Have you been wasting your time with Gemdorin again?"

Her stomach muscles tightened at his harsh tone, and her shoulders climbed toward her ears, suggesting guiltiness.   "Well, sort of."

Ian's hands flailed in the air.   "What do you think you're doing?   Did he force you to stay with him all night?"

"It hasn't been all night…" she started.

He hollered over her, "It's already morning!"

"I know, I know," she admitted, "but we just lost track of time."

"We?   Eena?   Do you hear yourself?   Don't you understand how dangerous that man is?   Haven't you listened to a word I've said?   He's a murderer!"

She understood Ian's reaction was protective, but he was behaving more crossly than she had ever seen him before.

"Criminy, Eena, don't you get it?   The man has killed people, and believe me, he won't hesitate to kill you too when he's good and ready!"

She cringed at his words.   "Stop it, Ian.   You don't have to yell at me."

"Apparently someone has to, because you're not listening!"

His criticism made her jump to her own defense.   "I didn't do anything wrong!   Gemdorin was in my room; he brought dinner. We sat, we ate, and then we started telling stories.   That's all that happened.   We just kept swapping stories and I truly lost track of time."

"More treasure hunting stories," Ian groaned with disgust.

"No, they were true stories about…"

"It doesn't matter!" he snapped.

She snapped back at him. "I was having fun, alright? So shoot me!"

"Eena, can't you see what he's doing? Can't you see what you're doing?"

"I'm not doing anything. I'm just trying to survive here on this ship."

"No. Gemdorin is trying to seduce you so he can be the lawful king of Harrowbeth—and you're leading him on!"

"I am not!"

Both had resorted to shouting, upset and defensive.

"You're letting him control you! He's using you!"

"I am not and he is not!"

"You are so gullible!"

"Oh, you're one to talk! Derian orders you around all the time! You do everything he says; you won't even speak unless he gives you permission!"

"That is totally different. Derian's not a mass murderer!"

"Gemdorin hasn't laid one hand on me, and he allows me more freedom than Derian ever did!"

"Is that why he locked you in a room for four days?"

"That's no different than Derian forcing me stay in his room!"

"Derian was trying to protect you!"

"Funny, that's the same thing Gemdorin tells me, but at least he's nice to me!"

Ian stood there speechless. He was shocked by how completely she had been deluded.

Eena stopped yelling, but stood her ground, ready to defend herself. When Ian spoke up again it was with a lowered voice.

"Eena, Derian has left the Kemeniroc. He's on his way to find you. He'll be in the Millan System about the same time you are. When he brings you back here, we'll show you how wrong you are about Gemdorin. He's not nice, Eena, he's horrible. He's a liar and he's using you."

"Like everyone else is using me?" she growled.

"It's not the same thing and you know it."

"I didn't do anything wrong, Ian."

"Did he kiss you this time?"

"No!" She hid the fact that part of her had wanted him to.

A pang of guilt twisted up the pit of her stomach for ever having had those feelings. *"I wouldn't let him."*

"But he tried?"

"I said no."

"Don't lead him on, Eena. It will end out in nothing but trouble."

She bit her lip and refused to comment.

"I have to go. Believe it or not, it's morning already."

"Go then," she muttered.

"Derian will be with you shortly. Just hold on until then. Please, Eena."

She turned away from him. Ian disappeared, leaving her alone in her dreams. She looked up at the sky and tried hard to hold back the tears. If Ian was right, she really was being foolish. But if Ian was wrong....

He could be wrong.

Upset and exhausted, she let go of her dreams. They transformed on their own until she found herself suffering through the same old childhood nightmare.

She was five again, her red-brown hair long and braided, tied back with a pink ribbon. She was scared but not alone. The young, faithful Ian was with her. He had brought her inside the darkening forest.

Ian took her by the hand when they heard voices—urgent, adult talk that carried through the trees. They ran as fast as her little legs could manage, so hard and long that she tugged on his hand, begging a minute's rest. He stopped and allowed her a break. She fell on her knees, panting from the sprint. Her eyes wandered up to look at twisted limbs that seemed to lean downward from every encircling tree. It felt as if the woods were closing in.

Eena realized at this moment that her perception of events had changed. She was standing outside the action now, observing the scene as if it were being acted out for her. She watched as a five-year-old Eena shivered through a chilled gust of wind. That's when the faceless snakes appeared. They burrowed up from the ground, the same as in every rerun of this nightmare. Eena suffered a wave of dread.

She hollered at the girl. *"Run, Eena! Get up and run!"*

But the child didn't move.   The snakes slithered across the soil, closing in on their mark.

"Mommy!   Mommy!"

Eena started toward the frightened girl, calling to herself. "Hold on, I'm coming!"   Before she could reach the child, however, her path was blocked by the arrival of a dragon.   He fell from the sky like a shooting star and immediately wrapped her up in his wing, trapping her.

She protested and struggled against him.   "No!   I have to help!   Let me go!"

But the dragon kept her securely within his hold.   She grabbed at the boney frame of his wing, tugging down enough to peer overtop.   Wide-eyed, she watched her nightmare unfold. With a helpless and sick feeling, both Eenas waited for the enclosing snakes to do something horrible.   The child continued to cry out incessantly for her mother, but it was a futile wish.   Her mother was dead.   Tears moistened Eena's eyes for them both.

Then she spotted the boy returning to the child in his care. "Ian!" she called out.   He had been there to help her so many years ago, just like he was trying to help her now.

"Eena, I'm here!   Take my hand!"

The little girl reached without any hesitation, but the snakes had grown in numbers and were continuing to rise from the soil. At the same time, the trees seemed to crowd around both children, their limbs intertwining like a thicketed dome.

From an outer perspective Eena examined the scene more closely.   The slithering life forms were long, skinny, and faceless. They wrapped around the arms and legs of both children, tightening their hold like entwining rope.   That's when she suspected they weren't snakes at all.   She recalled what Jinatta had told her.

"There are no snakes on Moccobatra."

"They're not snakes," she realized, speaking to the dragon who kept her hostage.   "They're roots.   The roots of the trees! It was always the trees!"

She watched in amazement as the coiled roots lifted both children into the air, placing them gently in the sturdiest, highest branches.   Once the youngsters were safely set in the treetops, the long roots withdrew, shrinking back beneath the soil.   The hovering woods straightened up as if a powerful wind forced their trunks upright.

"The trees were helping us!" Eena turned to the dragon, meeting his green-and-yellow stare with a look of incredulity.

She screamed with her next breath, startled by the crash landing of another dragon. His colossal body hit the ground with thundering force. He skidded across the dirt, pushing up a cloud of dust in his path. Behind him another dragon jarred the ground. This creature growled at the downed beast before him. Both jumped up on clawed feet and circled one another with arched wings.

The first dragon made a swift strike at the second, attempting to sink his daggered teeth into his opponent's neck. The targeted dragon jumped backwards, hissing. Both raised their wings and screeched aloud—a high-pitched, ear-piercing cry. Their heads dropped in sync, levelled in a glowering stare-down.

Eena recognized the first dragon by the red gem glistening in his eye.

"It's the dragon's eye," she whispered to her protective beast, fearing the combatants might overhear and turn their attention on her.

Curiously, she leaned forward, trying to glimpse the eyes of the newest dragon. She gasped at the sight of another gem. It was a brilliant blue stone gleaming in his right eye.

"What is this?" she inquired in a whisper. Her questioning gaze shifted to the old dragon. "How many gemstones are there?"

He offered no answer. His attention was focused on the others. His wing tightened its hold, and Eena turned back to the combatants. Terror struck when she found them staring directly at her. They had torn away from each other, now focused on a new target. With pounding steps they marched forward.

Her protective dragon stood up taller, screaming out a warning that halted their approach. The red-eyed beast strained his neck, cautiously moving his head forward enough for Eena to clearly see into his eye. The red gem gleamed before hazing over. Deep inside the stone, a parting mist revealed a vision.

A group of hideous, gray-blue creatures had corralled someone into a corner. They had weapons pointed at the form *trapped against a wall. It was a woman, cowering, afraid for her life. Eena identified the monsters as Ghengats; they matched Gemdorin's description of them perfectly. She recognized the young woman as herself.*

Horrified, Eena watched as the Ghengats surrounded her. One of them attempted to grab her arm, but as he did so the necklace shone with blinding brilliance. The woman pushed at the air, utilizing an invisible force that sent her attackers flying backwards.

"I'm okay," she gasped.

Then the scene blurred and changed.

She witnessed the violence of two men engaged in a barehanded brawl. Each struggled mightily to overcome the other. Both suffered severe blows, dodging vicious near-misses. But in the end, Gemdorin stood triumphant while a defeated Derian stole off into the shadows. She watched as Gemdorin took her by the arm, the two walking off together.

"Why are you showing me this?" she asked the dragon. "What does this mean?"

The visionary beast reared his head. His chest and neck expanded, filling up with a breath of fire. Eena ducked beneath the protective cover of her dragon's wing and felt the heat of the blaze blow overhead. The next thing she knew, both hostile dragons were rising in the air, disappearing from sight. The remaining dragon released her from his hold.

"I don't understand any of this," she told him. "Are you real? What do these things mean?"

But the old dragon provided no answers. With a quick stretch and flap of his wings, his great body lifted into the air. Soon, he too vanished.

Eena woke with a start. It took a minute to convince herself that the troubling vision had been nothing more than a dream. It's not real, she thought to herself. It was all those crazy stories. I've got to quit listening to ghost stories.

When her head hit the pillow, she was out again.

CHAPTER SIXTEEN
Ghengat Raid

It was noon when Eena finally opened her eyes. She felt awful. Partly due to sleeping half the day away, but mostly because she and Ian had fought. Never had they quarreled like that before. Not in the harsh way each had yelled at the other last night. Her stomach knotted up just thinking about it.

She dragged herself out of bed, partly wanting to lie there like a log for the rest of the afternoon, or at least until her mood improved. Luckily, she glimpsed something naturally cheering. In the center of the table on which Gemdorin had set out dinner the night before stood a sizeable bouquet of flowers. A note rested against it. Eena couldn't help but smile at the sweet gesture until the thought of Ian's accusations dampened her joy.

She went to sit in the chair that had cradled her the night before. Taking the note from the table, she read it aloud:

Eena,

Good morning, or afternoon as the case may be. I apologize for interfering with your sleeping hours, and yet I'd do it again if it meant spending another lovely evening with you.

Until tonight,
Gemdorin

This couldn't be the man Ian kept cautioning her about.

She touched the flowers, pressing a petal between her fingertips. It was soft and silky, coated with a light dusting of powder. She rubbed the dust between her fingers, enjoying the velvety feel. It made her skin glisten. The blossoms resembled hydrangeas from Earth but with broader petals blended in shades of pink and cream. She leaned in for a sniff and found it sweetly intense, as pleasing as jasmine.

It was impossible not to be touched by the gesture, despite Ian's warnings. This attention from Gemdorin was.........well, it was nice. Besides, what did they expect her to do? It wasn't her fault she was stuck on his ship. She was simply trying to cope with the situation in a positive manner—sensible advice in anyone's book. As her father from Earth use to say, *"You have to make the best out of what life throws at you."*

It didn't take long to dress and ready herself for the afternoon. She looked pretty with her hair pulled back in a ponytail, tied with a pink ribbon borrowed from the flower arrangement. Her final look wasn't as elegant as what Angelle would have masterfully fashioned, but it was satisfactory.

While applying last-minute touches of color to her face, she was distracted by the sound of commotion. The closeness of it drew her into the next room. Garbled voices carried from outside her quarters, growing progressively louder by the moment. She quickly made her way to the exit to find out what was going on.

As soon as the doors parted, her young friend Jase looked up, his eyes wide with panic. Two guards had the boy detained between them. He was arguing with the men—something about an emergency.

"Let him go," she ordered. The men released their hold, and Jase tumbled to the floor. He seemed both anxious and rushed as he scrambled to his feet.

"Sha Eena! The Ghengats are back and they've taken Xander!"

"W...what?" She worried she had heard him correctly. "The Ghengats? They've boarded our ship?"

"Come on!" Jase grabbed her by the hand, attempting to pull her along with him, but he was prevented by a vigilant guard.

"Halt, young man! She's not going anywhere."

"You're safer here, Sha Eena," added the other guard.

297

"But….but someone has to save Xander!"

Concerned and frightened, Eena wondered what Jase expected her to do. "I'm not sure how I can help."

The boy turned to the men in uniform. "You two, call the captain and tell him we're in trouble! Tell him the Ghengats are taking prisoners again!"

Rather than listen, they attempted to reassure the young man. "Kahm Gemdorin is already aware of the situation. Our orders are to keep Sha Eena here. It's better for both of you to stay out of harm's way."

Jase scrunched up his face disgustedly. "Cowards," he breathed. He backed away from the company and then tore down the corridor, hollering, "Somebody has to do something or Sarii will lose her son forever!"

That was enough to motivate the young queen. Eena dodged her watchmen and took off after Jase. The runaways barely managed to escape in an elevator, leaving disgruntled soldiers behind to pound their fists on closed doors.

Eena's stomach churned as they headed down to the Mahgshreem's docking bay. She visualized a host of dangers awaiting, doubting that a fourteen-year-old boy and a novice queen could do much in the face of an army of Ghengats. When the elevator came to a stop, she stepped in front of Jase.

"Stay behind me. Keep at my back no matter what happens, understand?"

He nodded his head in short quick moves, looking as scared as a rabbit among wolves. Eena wondered if he was reconsidering his earlier vow of valor.

When the way cleared, both queen and child breathed sighs of relief. The docking bay was empty. Unoccupied ships lined the floor as far as the eye could see, but not one grisly Ghengat stood in sight.

Jase stepped up next to his queen; his relief turned to concern. "They were here earlier……and they had Xander!"

"What were you two doing down here in the first place?" Eena asked with a hint of parental frustration.

"We wanted to look at the ships, that's all. We didn't touch anything." His eyes continued to dart about the open area, searching for a sign of his friend. "When we heard voices, we hid.   Then Xander saw it was the Ghengats.   We tried to sneak out to warn people, but Xander tripped over a box of equipment and they heard us.   Those monsters caught him and......and that's when I ran to get you.   We have to find him, Sha Eena!   He didn't do anything wrong!"

"I understand, Jase, but I'm not sure where to look."   She shrugged helplessly.   "Where would they go?"

The young man turned back to the elevator.   "The commissary," he guessed.   "That's where everyone is.   If they've come to take more prisoners, they'll go there."

Eena groaned and followed.

They traveled up again, to the commissary.   Everything looked normal when they arrived—no sign of any trouble.   Eena pulled Jase aside, not wanting to needlessly alarm people.

"Are you absolutely sure you saw Ghengats?"

"Yes!   I did!   I'm not lying, Sha Eena, they really did take Xander!"

"Alright, alright," she sighed, "we'll just have to keep looking.   Come on."

The pair left the commissary and hurried back to the elevator.   As Eena tried to imagine where the Ghengats had gone, one scary thought crossed her mind.   She decided to retrace their steps, hoping her suspicions were wrong.

Back at her floor, she stepped off the lift hesitantly.   Not a soul was present, not even the guards who were most likely searching for her.

Jase followed as Eena crept along the passageway.   Gemdorin's words echoed in her mind the entire time—"*If Derian tracks you down, you may be forced to deal with the monsters.*"   She refused to believe it, and yet the possibility wasn't entirely inconceivable.

They reached her room without any incident.   A peek inside her quarters found it empty.   Eena exhaled deeply—relieved once again.

"If they're not in the docking bay or in the commissary or here, where else do you think they would go?"

Jase stood there shaking his head.   He had fully expected to find the ship overrun with Ghengats, exactly as he had the day his parents were abducted.   It didn't make any sense.   Where was the enemy?   Where was Xander?

"Maybe we should find Sarii and see if Xander's not with her," Eena suggested.   "It's possible he made it back on his own."

"Okay," Jase agreed, puzzled about the whole thing.

Eena's nerves were calmer on the way out, happy to have run into no monsters during their search.   She blamed the whole scare on a hyper imagination, understanding firsthand what that was like. Perhaps Jase and Xander had been telling stories when they stumbled across a group of men in the hangar.   Ducking to avoid detection, they may have mistaken uniformed soldiers for enemy Ghengats.   A creative mind could play strange tricks on young boys.

The elevator was humming as they drew near, rising to a stop. It was uncommon to hear the lift in motion; almost no one came to this area of the ship.   Eena slowed her approach, hesitant for no certain reason.   When instinct gave her a shove, urging the young queen to run, she obeyed without question.

"Run!" she ordered Jase, "Go, go, run now!"

The young man seemed confused, but did as he was told, racing at her side down the corridor.   They could see the elevator behind, and glanced frequently, watching it open up for a group of scaly life forms.

The monsters had arrived.

One Ghengat caught a glimpse of the retreating Sha and growled at his comrades to give chase.

Eena tore down an unfamiliar passageway, not knowing where it headed.   When shots were fired, she screamed and checked to be sure Jase was unharmed.   She pushed him in front of her, shielding him from the rear, aware that the necklace would heal any injury she sustained.

Around a bend, a second elevator came into sight.   "Hurry, hurry!   Go in there!"

Jase ran right up to the doors expecting them to open.   When nothing happened he pressed on the manual control, jabbing at it a number of times.

"Come on….come on!" he begged.   "It's not working!"

Eena reached to pound on the button herself with no results.

When she realized their pursuers had nearly caught up, she rotated her body, keeping in front of the boy.   The aliens slowed their approach, seeing their prey successfully cornered. One Ghengat smiled fiendishly before speaking.

"So, here stands the great Sha Eena. Kahm Derian will be pleased to have you back."

"Get away from us!" she commanded, growling in the fiercest tone she could manage. It was irritating to hear her own voice tremble.

"We're not going anywhere until we have what we came for," a creature snarled.

Eena took a brave step forward. "Is it me you want?"

"Oh yesss," the Ghengat hissed. "We'll be paid handsomely for your return."

"Then let the boy go. He's of no consequence." Her hands curled into fists, waiting for them to decide.

The Ghengat jerked his head to one side suggesting the young man could leave.

Eena whispered over her shoulder, her eyes fixed on the enemy. "Run, Jase. Go to Sarii. Tell her what's happened."

"Not without you! They'll take you away like my mom and dad!"

"I'll be alright. Just go."

The boy peeked out from behind and started past, slow and wary in his walk. The Ghengats ignored him, concentrating on the real prize.

Eena saw Jase look back repeatedly, his eyes wilting as if he couldn't bear the thought of leaving her behind. But somehow he made himself continue, past the enemy and down an empty hallway. As soon as he was out of sight, two Ghengats reached for Sha Eena. They stopped short at the pounding of footsteps. Jase was headed back, full-steam, prepared to attack the first challenger he came upon. He never got the chance. Hearing his return, one Ghengat twisted at the waist and fired a shot at him.

The boy collapsed.

Eena screamed. *"Noooooooo!"*

She shoved past the others to run to her friend, falling on her knees beside his motionless body. Her fingers pressed at the side of his neck. No pulse. She put her ear to his mouth. He wasn't breathing.

"No, no, no," she cried. Her hand slipped beneath his head,

301

cradling it, hoping his eyelids would flicker open.   But the child was dead.

"You killed him," she whispered before shouting out the truth. "You killed him!   You murderers!   He was just a boy!"

The Ghengats froze momentarily, stunned by her hysteria.

"He was an idiot to turn back," one of them hissed callously. The Ghengat stepped forward as if he meant to drag her off the corpse.   "Get up!   You're coming with us."

Before he could grab her, the necklace came alive, glaring without warning.   Eena shoved her hands in front of her as if signaling an urgent stop.   It was a quick, self-protective reaction. By use of the necklace she created a thrusting force that hit every standing Ghengat.   They sailed through the air, crashing into a far wall before slipping unconscious to the floor.

Eena's attention returned to Jase.   She wasn't prepared to let him die.

"You can do this," she told herself.   "Bring him back."

Her hands fell on his chest the same way they had in the medical bay.   Only emptiness could be sensed from him.   It felt awful.   Concentrating, she focused on reviving the boy.   Steady pulses of energy were directed to his two hearts in order to start them beating again.   She sent electrical impulses to the brain, instructing his body to breathe.   His chest rose and fell beneath her hands.

"It's working, it's working."

His muscles twitched and the boy coughed.

"Jase!" she squealed, "Jase, are you okay?"

He nodded.   His eyes glanced around, suffering disorientation.

"Eena!"   Her name carried down the corridor, shouted by a familiar voice.   The young queen looked up, and her fears diminished at once.

"Gemdorin!"

An attempt to stand failed; the necklace had left her weak. Affected by a wave of dizziness, Eena fell over onto an elbow.

Gemdorin knelt down and slipped his arm around her back for support.   "Are you okay?   What happened here?"

She started in with a frantic explanation.   "The Ghengats! Those terrible creatures were after me and they shot Jase......he

302

wasn't breathing!   They said they were here to......they said they came because...."   She couldn't quite spit out the words.

"Because Derian sent them," Gemdorin finished.   "I headed for your quarters as soon as I realized they were aboard."   He turned to the dazed boy.   "Jase appears to be alright."

"I healed him, but I had to; he wasn't breathing.   I had to!" Tears streamed down her face as her lips began to tremble. Gemdorin pulled her close where she bawled into his chest.   "I can't believe they shot him!"

"It's okay, my dear, it's okay."   He caressed her hair and held her close.   "Jase is fine, and you will be too."

"But, Xander!"   Eena pushed away from the captain remembering why they had started hunting for the Ghengats in the first place.   "They have Xander!"

Gemdorin brought his eyes down to meet hers, demanding her focus.   "I know, Eena, I know.   We have him.   Don't worry, he's fine."

She nodded her understanding and collapsed in his arms, exhausted.   Her body shook, overwhelmed by the terrifying ordeal.   She sobbed within the solace of Gemdorin's embrace, not just for fear's sake but because it was clear now that Derian had betrayed her and all of Harrowbeth.   The Ghengats had admitted to working for the traitor.   She had heard their condemning words with her own ears.   There was no denying it.

"Eena, can you walk?"

She tried to stand at Gemdorin's request, but couldn't.   The energy sacrificed to protect herself and heal Jase had all but taken her last bit of strength.   The captain scooped her up easily and carried her to her quarters.   He laid her on the divan at the foot of the bed.

"You rest.   I'll take Jase to the medical bay so Magg can check him over."

"Thank you," she sniveled between softening sobs.

Sleep claimed her effortlessly after he left.

Four hours later, Eena woke to a gentle nudging.   Her eyes blinked open to find Gemdorin's kind face gazing down on her.

"Feel better?" he asked softly.

She was curled up on the divan where he had placed her

earlier, her mind foggy, having no recollection of dreams. A few seconds brought back the scary incident with the Ghengats. She wanted to know only one thing.

"The boys—are they alright?"

Gemdorin took a seat beside her. "Xander is fine and back with his mom. She and I had a good long talk with him about steering clear of restricted areas."

Eena sighed with relief. "Boys are naturally curious."

He patted her knee and let her know, "Those bothersome Ghengats have been eliminated. There's no need to worry about them sneaking up on you."

"For now," she said, unsettled. "They're awfully creepy."

Gemdorin laughed. "You did a fine job of thwarting their plans, you know. Maybe next time you can rush to *my* rescue."

His witty remark made her smile a tiny bit. "I warned them to leave Jase alone. Really, it was just an automatic reaction. I didn't want them to touch me."

"And they certainly didn't." He seemed impressed by how well she had handled the situation.

"How's Jase doing?"

Gemdorin didn't answer right away. His lips pursed and his jaw clenched.

Her stomach reacted anxiously to his reluctance to respond. She asked again. "Gemdorin, how is Jase?"

"Eena..." he started, "I'm very sorry."

"No." Her head began to shake, refusing any bad news.

"There must have been internal bleeding. Magg didn't detect it, but he.....well...there's no easy way to say this. Jase is dead."

She went rigid at his words. Her hands pressed against a stomach that couldn't bear any more pain. She couldn't have heard correctly.

"No, no, no, that can't be. I healed him; he was fine; I know it. I know I healed him," she insisted.

Gemdorin took her by the shoulders. "Yes, you did. He was fine at first. Magg checked him over and he appeared to be in perfectly good health. He was tired, however, so she kept him in the medical bay to rest and recuperate. We all assumed he was sleeping. But when Magg went to check on him a couple hours later, he had passed away. There was nothing anyone could do."

"Why didn't you come get me?" she cried.

"Eena, it was too late. There was nothing you could have done."

"No......no, no, no, no, no!" She kept repeating the word, shaking her head in denial. "I healed him; I know I did; he was fine! I healed him!"

"You must have missed something, maybe a slight internal bleeding or head trauma. It's not your fault."

The captain moved in closer, offering his arms as comfort. She slumped against him and surrendered everything. The tears started up again, spilling a flood of remorse as Gemdorin stroked her hair consolingly.

Eena thought of her Harrowbethian parents—the only other people whose deaths she had experienced. But that loss had occurred in her toddler years, and there was no memory of the tragedy. Jase's death was the first connected to real feelings of bereavement. It hurt horrendously—the loss, the regret, the guilt. It was unbearable. No wonder she had suppressed her memories from childhood. She never wanted to recall the pain of losing her parents. Not ever.

Her mind kept replaying the moment she had connected with Jase, sensing every ailment in his body. Certainly, she had detected everything. Had there been further damage, she was positive the necklace would have revealed it. The necklace was thorough; it wouldn't have missed a scratch.

"I healed him. I know it; I felt it." She racked her brain for another explanation.

Gemdorin disrupted her murmuring. "Eena, you've barely begun to use your powers. In time you'll see a huge improvement in your abilities."

She cried even harder.

He continued with attempts at consolation. "You did your best. It's not your fault."

"It's Derian's fault!" she sobbed. "If he hadn't sent those horrible creatures after me, Jase would still be alive!"

"That's true," Gemdorin agreed. "Yes, my sad, sweet lady, that is very true."

Eena felt grateful for the strong and caring arms that pulled her in. It was a safe harbor from the devastating storms abroad.

Gemdorin had come to her rescue; he had rushed to save her from Derian's Ghengats. He freed Xander from their grasp and tried to help Jase. Poor, ill-fated Jase. Gemdorin had proven to be her true protector and comforter.

She sank into the arms of her hero, eyelids closed and heavy with sorrow. In no time at all she cried herself back to sleep.

Things were just as miserable in her dreams as in the waking world. From atop a seaside boulder, Eena stared out blankly over rough ocean waves that battered against a beachfront of massive rocks. Her body slumped as if it possessed no strength to hold up her frame any more than her spirits. The sky above appeared unusually low, weighed down with black storm clouds. Now and then, jagged flashes of lightning burned across the horizon while thunder screamed in accompanying agony. This was exactly how she felt.

Her mourning form sat motionless and alone for a very long time as the nightmare played over and over in her mind. It shouldn't have happened like that. Things weren't supposed to go like that—to heal Jase of his burns so he could turn around and be murdered by Derian's ghoulish thugs! No! Life wasn't supposed to go like that!

It was late in the evening when Ian showed, unprepared for the disturbing scene he entered into. He remembered how they had fought the night before. He had regretted his behavior and had resolved to apologize for yelling at her. But when he saw how she wilted beneath this stormy sky, he approached with caution and concern.

"Eena? Are you alright?"

"No, Ian, I'm not." She lifted her drooping head to look out over troubled waters.

Ian stepped up beside her rocky perch. His concern escalated when he observed the evidence of excessive weeping on her face. "Eena, what's happened?"

She turned her red, swollen eyes on him, and his heart sank.

"Jase is dead," she said. "Derian killed him."

"What? What are you talking about?"

She raised her voice. "You heard me, Derian killed him! He killed my friend!"

306

"Eena, there's no way that can be true," Ian argued. "Derian hasn't even reached you yet." His face tangled up, worried and disbelieving.

"He's lying to you," she growled. She slipped down from the rock and stood inches from Ian's face, her red eyes burning with anger. "He sent those horrible Ghengats here to steal me away today and they shot Jase. They killed him for trying to protect me. He was just a boy, Ian! He was only a boy!"

"No, no, Eena, the Ghengats don't work for Derian..."

"Yes they do!" she snapped. "They told me he sent them! They told me Kahm Derian promised to pay them handsomely for my return! They admitted it, Ian!"

"They're lying!" Ian's eyes widened. How could she believe them? How could she believe the lies of vicious monsters over the words of her best friend?

Eena's eyelids fell closed and her neck rolled back. A disturbing laugh escaped her throat directed up at the black sky.

"Ian, why do you insist on defending Derian? He left the Kemeniroc alone so he could do what he wanted without witnesses. You have no idea what he's up to, do you? Do you!" She was angry—frustrated with her friend's proven ignorance.

"I know he doesn't work with the Ghengats, Eena, Gemdorin does."

She laughed again, almost hysterically. "If that were so, why would the Ghengats raid Gemdorin's ship? What kind of allies would that make them?"

"It's an act, Eena. He's trying to turn you against Derian."

"No! Derian's done a fine job of that on his own! I don't want the Ghengats or him around me, do you understand? You tell him to back off and leave me alone. I won't go with him. Give him that message, and you tell him I will never forgive him for what he's done to Jase! Never!" Her finger jabbed in Ian's face, shaking.

"He didn't do it, Eena."

"Yes he did! I was there!" She sucked in a deep breath to gain some control over her trembling body, but her fuse wasn't yet extinguished. "Those Ghengats came after me with weapons. As soon as I was cornered, they talked about how Kahm Derian had sent them, how he meant to pay them for my return.

*Gemdorin came to my rescue, Ian.   He's the one who stopped
them.   He saved Xander too—and thank goodness for that, or I
would've lost two friends today!"*

*"Eena, please—you've got to listen to me.   I know how it
must appear to you, but it isn't what it seems.   Gemdorin's setting
you up.   It's a trick!"*

*"It doesn't matter.   I've already decided; I'm not leaving
here.   It's more than what happened today.   I have friends here.
People need me here.   I don't want to leave."*

*"No, Eena, you can't…"   Ian was desperate to get her to see
his side, but she wasn't about to listen.   She cut him off.*

*"You tell Derian to stay away from me.   I won't go anywhere
with him."*

"He'll reach your ship in two days, Eena."

"No!   You tell him to go away!   Tell him NO!"

*She didn't want to hear any more.   Ian attempted to talk to
her, to plead with her, but her dream image vanished and he was
left alone not knowing what to do.*

"Wake up, Eena, wake up."

Gemdorin's voice registered in her head.   She opened her
eyes to find herself on the divan, lying on Gemdorin's chest where
she must have fallen asleep.

"You were yelling in your sleep," he told her.   "Is everything
okay?"

"Oh, uh….yes.   It was just a bad dream.   I…I'm alright
now."

She pushed away from him to sit, and he followed her up.
Slumped forward in the same somber fashion as in her dreams, she
stared at her feet.

"Do you want me to put you to bed?"

"No.   Thanks, but I can't sleep anymore; I've slept too
much."   Truthfully, she didn't want to see Ian.   He probably
hated her.

"How about something to eat?" Gemdorin suggested.   "You
never did have dinner."

"I'm not hungry."

"A walk?"

"I think I want to be alone."   She glanced up at the captain.

He took in her sad eyes and reached for her cheek, caressing it tenderly.

"Okay, if that's what you really want." He stood to leave, then hesitated and removed the small communications device from his collar. Handing it over, he told her, "If you need me, call. I'll answer."

She took the device, uttering a quiet thank you.

As soon as Gemdorin left the room, Eena escaped into the bathroom and locked the door. With her back pressed against the wall, she sank to the floor and pulled both knees to her chest. Curled up, she let go and wept again, releasing the anguish her broken heart lacked the capacity to contain.

This emotional hurt was far worse than any physical pain she had ever experienced. It was the agony of losing someone who never should've died, the agony of a deceived friendship, and the agony of tremendous guilt all wrapped up in one miserable package. Tears poured for over an hour without an end in sight, spilling like a waterfall until her body grew so exhausted and sick that the source necessarily dried up. Instead of succumbing to sleep, she leaned her head against the wall and contemplated her existence.

Reality had changed so drastically in the last three months. What she wouldn't give to return to Earth and have this madness amount to nothing more than an awful nightmare. She longed for home with a ferocity that made breathing itself seem nonessential by comparison. She needed to go home—back to her *real* home. Not some alien world she couldn't even recall in one lousy memory. But no. There was no going back now.

Everything was complicated now. All the secrets kept, revealed to her in only bits and pieces of what she needed to know—keys to her purpose and destiny. It didn't seem fair that she was the only one floundering in the dark, and yet *she* was the one they all desperately needed. This calling exceeded anything she had ever wanted; it was too heavy and costly a burden to bear. To be responsible for countless lives and the survival of an entire world!

It was too much to ask of one person.

How could they do this to her—to someone they called queen? How could they tear her away from a life she had loved? A place where she had fit in as one of many young women—all normal, equal, regular. To be the same as everyone else. To not be sought after. To profess nothing extraordinary. She would give anything to be plain old Sevenah Ruth Williams again.

And now—on top of all this unwanted responsibility, this loss and tremendous fear—it was impossible to know for certain who was trustworthy. That included Ian. Yes, he had been a good friend, but could she trust his judgment? His intentions? Not to mention those two pushy brothers, Derian and Gemdorin. She wondered how one small family could cause such chaos in the universe. Maybe Harrowbeth was better off without either of those domineering characters.

Eena lifted her head from the wall, feeling it throb and spin. With everything blurring together into one big impossible mess it was hard to reason. She picked herself up off the floor, unwilling to think anymore. Unwilling to feel.

Taking a seat on the edge of the tub, she let the water run for a hot bath. She would wash it all away—the pain, anger, and frustration, including the evidence of her mourning. Today was a new day, a new beginning. She would start over, trusting in herself, believing in her own instincts. She didn't need the others as much as they presumed. The necklace was turning out to be her greatest and most reliable protection.

A long, hot soak in the tub helped clear her mind of all unpleasantness. She dressed and loitered in her quarters, circling the room, brushing her hands along the backs of chairs while gawking with unfocused attention at the elegant items in front of her. There was a great deal of time to kill before the ship would be awake again. She ended up staring out of a window, the curtains pulled aside to expose a universe of overbearing blackness.

Time crawled by.

It was nearly zero-three-hundred hours, much too early to go visit anyone. Yet she didn't want to sleep and risk an unpleasant encounter with Ian. There was nothing left to say to him.

As she stood there, staring out at the vastness of space, a whisper caught her ear. The voice sounded like a frail version of the captain. A moment later she heard it again, distant and weak as though the utterance were coming from a tiny, sealed box.

That's when she recalled Gemdorin giving her his PCD.   She rushed to the divan where she was certain it had been left.

"Eena are you there?"   It was his voice, a little louder.

"Yes, I'm here," she responded, holding the device up to her lips.

"Eena, answer if you can hear me."   She realized the thing wasn't activated.

"Crud, how do you work this?"   She quickly eyed the device and tried pressing on the front.   Then she spoke again.

"Gemdorin?"

"There you are."   He sounded relieved.   "I wondered if maybe you went back to sleep."

"No, no, I'm here."

"Are you feeling any better?"

She shrugged, even though he couldn't see.   "A little, I suppose."

"Well, I can't sleep either and was wondering if you might be up for an early breakfast.   You're going to have to eat sooner or later."

"I know," she agreed.   "I guess I am getting hungry."

There was distinct pleasure in his voice as he instructed her to wait for him.   "I'll be right over.   Gemdorin out."

"Okay.......bye."   She tapped on the device, hoping a touch turned it off.

The captain arrived at her room in no time, and the pair made their way to his personal dining hall for breakfast.   Matching place settings were already laid out on a corner end of the table. Gemdorin sat at the head, Eena by his side.   They were served a warm breakfast consisting of fried bread topped with sautéed herbs and vegetables.   A drizzle of thick sauce sweetened the dish. Eena liked the food, but suspected those preparing it weren't thrilled about the early request.

They ate in silence for most of the meal.   Eena slipped back into mourning without realizing it.   Her face fell dismal as she sank deeper into gloomy thoughts.   When she started picking at her food, Gemdorin spoke up.

"At the risk of sounding callous, my dear, I think you need to get over this."

She flickered a glance up at him.   "I'm sorry.   I know; I just can't seem to get it off my mind."

"Does dwelling on it make you feel better?" he asked.

She shook her head.

"Will dwelling on it make the boy come back?"

"Of course not," she murmured.

"Do you think Jase would want you to make yourself miserable like this?"

She sighed and closed her eyes for a second. "I'm sure he wouldn't."

"Then you need to stop agonizing over his misfortune. It doesn't mean you don't care, Eena, it just means you realize life goes on."

She shook her head, staring down at her leftover breakfast. "It's not that easy. I lost a good friend last night." In all honesty, she feared two friends may have been lost. "I don't know how to let him go."

"I'm not asking you to let him go. I'm asking you to stop making yourself miserable over it." Gemdorin dropped his fork onto his plate and stood up. "Come with me. We'll find something to take your mind off things."

She followed him into his treasure room. It was the same as she remembered from the previous time with valuable articles haphazardly stacked all over the place. Gemdorin went straight for a table centered against the rear wall. He picked up what appeared to be a decorated metal headdress. It looked like something uncovered from an Egyptian tomb—a golden helmet, elaborately etched, filled in with colorful stains.

He handed the gear to her. "Here you go. Try this on."

She turned the heavy item over in her hands. "What is it?"

"Just put it on." He grinned, watching her lift the thing over her head. "Go on," he encouraged when she hesitated.

Eena lowered the hood, letting the base fall clear to her shoulders. It felt too large; the crown came down just above her eyes. She giggled at the thought of how silly she must look in the oversized headgear. Before she had a chance to say anything, the contraption underwent a swift alteration. Like some robotic transformer, the metallic sides swiftly extended all the way around, meeting in the front. It covered her face. Then a solid collar secured itself below her chin, encircling her neck and making it impossible to take the thing off. Worse still, there was no way to see out.

"Hey! What is this?" she exclaimed. "Get it off! Get it off me!"

She gripped both sides of the helmet attempting to pull it off, knowing full well there was no way it would budge with the neck secured. She panicked until Gemdorin's laughter hit her ears.

"This isn't funny! How does it come off?"

"Can you see anything?" he asked, taunting her between chuckles.

"You know I can't!" she growled. "This is so *not* funny!"

Certain he would be of no assistance until he had acquired his fill of amusement, Eena decided to call on the necklace for help. She stopped struggling and concentrated on communicating her intentions, imagining the head piece recoiling back to its original form. An image of its design appeared in her mind. She could see a simple control switch within the front cover. Using her energy to engage the control, she caused the metal extensions to fold up and retreat back into the headdress. Free of its hold, she pulled the thing off her head and gave the stunned captain a nasty look.

"How did you do that?" he asked. He wasn't laughing anymore.

"I used the necklace to turn it off. That wasn't funny. Why would you even design such a thing?"

Gemdorin smiled, chuckling again. "It was *very* amusing," he disagreed, "and I didn't design it. It came from Deramptium. It was created as a snare for thieves who might attempt to steal from their royal treasury. Anyone rummaging through royal goods might find this crown tempting, given its extravagant and rich appearance. All they would have to do is set it upon their heads and be blindly trapped inside. There's no way out without this remote device." He presented what looked like a small round rock. She watched him slide the top of the device sideways and then back into place again. "It controls the headdress."

"How terribly clever," she groaned with bitter sarcasm.

Gemdorin moved on, still wearing his devilish grin. He placed the item back in its original spot and in exchange grabbed a pair of golden gloves. They were as colorful and decorated as the headdress.   The material sparkled, reflecting the room's dim lighting.   He handed these to Eena, but she refused them.

"No way.   I don't trust you."

"Come now, my dear, I was merely having fun.   You know I would have removed the head piece if you hadn't lost patience and done so yourself."

She still refused and cast him an over-my-dead-body glare.

"They're harmless," he insisted.

She shook her head, communicating an adamant no.

"Alright, I'll put them on myself."

Gemdorin slipped his fingers into the gloves.   They were tight on his large hands.   Turning his palms up and then down, he examined the detailed stitching.

"These are quite valuable, you know, and even richer in history.   They belonged to the Princess Tribiat from Deramptium. She was known as one of the wisest and wealthiest women in their royal lineage.   She was also known for her extravagant taste in clothing and accessories.   He slipped off the fancy gloves and offered them again.

"See, no harm done.   Try them on," he urged.   "The material is rather unique."

Feeling relatively safe since he had worn the gloves with no adverse effects, she took one and slipped it over her right hand. The material was interesting—warm and yet tissue thin.   She studied the fine design with admiration.   The next thing she knew, her fingers were tingling.   When she went to remove the glove, her hand lifted on its own, rising and reaching outward, compelled by some invisible force.   Pulling her hand down proved impossible; the force only grew stronger until there was no other choice but to follow her fully-extended arm wherever it led.

"Gemdorin!" she cried, knowing full well this had to be his doing.

Her tingling fingers ended up grasping at a tall cylindrical pole—stuck there, much like a powerful magnet holds onto a metal object.   She tried yanking her hand away but to no avail.   And, of course, the glove wouldn't come off either.   Once again, she could hear Gemdorin's amusement.

Between chortles he seemed to pout.   "Now why didn't you put them both on?   That would've been much more fun."

314

"Turn it off!" she ordered, frowning her disapproval.

"You turn it off," he said.

"Gemdorin!"

He conceded, and pressed on the small remote in his possession. Eena's hand fell away from the pole. She ripped off the glove and threw the golden pair back at him.

"Another way to catch a thief," he grinned. "Princess Tribiat wasn't too terribly trusting."

"Obviously!"

Eena decided to take a look around the room herself, choosing to stay away from any items on what appeared to be the Deramptium table. She wasn't interested in falling for any more booby traps. While glancing over a few articles strewn about the floor, her eyes landed on a clear chest filled with a variety of sizeable jewels. Lifting back a creaky lid, she picked up a red gemstone from the top of the pile. It was about the size of a golf ball but more oval in shape.

"This must be worth a fortune," she breathed, rolling the red gem around in her palm. It reminded her of the dragon's eye from Gemdorin's books. Then her dream from the other night came to the forefront of her mind. It hit her all at once that the vision she had seen in the gem—the images beheld in the dragon's eye—had actually come true. The Ghengats attacking, her pushing them back—it had all come to pass as predicted!

"Oh my gosh," she gasped.

"What?" Gemdorin stepped up beside her.

"The dragon's eye…" she started.

"No, no," he interrupted, taking the ruby jewel from her open hand, "that's not the dragon's eye. It's substantially larger."

"I know," she said, gawking at him. "And it tells you the future."

Gemdorin's form stiffened. His expression turned serious.

"And what makes you think that?" he asked. The scar above his eyebrow twitched as he focused on her, awaiting an answer.

"I just realized it. I had a dream the other night about the dragon's eye. It showed me a vision where I was being pursued by Ghengats. I saw the entire incident before it happened. They cornered me and I pushed them away using the necklace, only Jase wasn't in the dream. The dragon's eye showed me what was going to happen. And then......oh my gosh, it actually happened!"

She looked wide-eyed at Gemdorin who maintained his sober face.

"The dragon's eye shows you the future, doesn't it?" She pressed him to tell her the truth. "That's why you want to find it so badly. You want to know the future, don't you?"

"Have you had any other dreams like this?" he asked, stalling for answers.

"No, none. This is the first time anything like this has happened."

"Have you told anyone else about your dream?"

"No. I'd forgotten about it until right now when I saw that red gem. Besides, who else would I tell?"

He must have believed her, because he came forward with the truth. "Okay....yes. Yes, the dragon's eye shows images of the future. Not only your own, but the future of others as well. With it I plan to put an end to our civil war once and for all."

"It's too dangerous." She remembered the vicious behavior of the dragon in her dream. "It's not a good thing, Gemdorin. It's evil."

He laughed at her admonition. "Anything can be used for evil purposes, Eena." He pointed at the entity adorning her chest. "That necklace you wear could be a terrible tool in the hands of the wrong person."

She touched the necklace, realizing its powers could be used for ill purposes if the bearer chose to abuse them. But that wasn't the point. This dragon's eye from her dreams was mean, ferocious, and a threat to her. She was certain of it.

"I think you should leave it buried."

He ignored her advice. "If you have another dream about the dragon's eye, you must tell me."

"I did see something else," she confessed. "I saw a vision of you and your brother in hand-to-hand combat."

"Oh?" A curious eyebrow arched high, tickling his scar again.

"Yes, and you won."

"Hmm. I like your dream." His lips thinned, grinning. "I *will* beat Derian someday. You'll see."

Eena dropped her eyes on the chest of jewels. They were stunning. She picked up an azure crystal that reminded her of the other young dragon in her dreams. She decided not to mention him, sure that neither gem was good. Sending Gemdorin off after two would certainly be a mistake, although curiosity as to the blue gem's purpose ate at her.

"Come here, Eena." Gemdorin called her over to the same drawer he had opened on their previous visit to this room. "I'll show you something else interesting."

He reached into the drawer and pulled out a little square box that held a collection of keys. With the lid removed, Eena could see what looked like a big black beetle inside. It was made of stone but appeared extremely lifelike.

"What is that?" she asked.

"Wave your hand over it," he instructed.

She moved her hand over the box and watched the beetle come to life. Four wings fluttered on its back, and the head lifted up. Gemdorin pulled her hand away when she got too close.

"Be careful; it will sting you."

"It's not really alive is it?"

"No. It's a mechanical invention like a safe. I keep important keys inside here. This little guy would fatally sting anyone who tried to remove them without my knowledge." Gemdorin then proceeded to grab the beetle. He did so without any adverse consequences.

"Why didn't it sting you?" she asked, her eyebrows knit with intrigue.

"It recognizes me; my DNA is encoded in the device."

"Amazing."

She imagined his whole treasure room was filled with dangers and surprises. No one would want to disturb a thing without knowing what to beware of.

They both heard the call when a crewman from the bridge attempted to contact the captain. Gemdorin spoke briefly into a tiny communicator before turning to Eena.

"I'm sorry, but I must leave for a moment."

"It's alright," she said. "May I stay here and look around?"

"Be my guest, but be careful what you touch." He left in a hurry, pausing just long enough to input an exit code at the door.

Meanwhile, Eena scanned the room, glancing over a number of interesting treasures.   A larger item caught her eye, situated beside the entrance to the skywalk.   The object was tall and rectangular, reaching up to her waist.   It had a flat, square surface. Stepping up to it reminded her of standing at a conference podium. She ran her fingers over etchings on the face—a circle within a circle within another and so on.   They were positioned so close together it was hard to guess the number of rings.

Eena waved her hand casually over the podium when something astounding happened.   A thin beam of light shone straight up from the central sphere.   Her gaze shot up to the ceiling where the light expanded and took shape.   She gawked at a translucent, three-dimensional replica of the galaxy hovering above her head.   Her eyes danced across spiraling arms nesting millions of sparkling star systems.

"I wonder where Earth is?" she uttered aloud.   The device responded to her request, producing a hologram of the planet Earth, moon and all.

"Oh wow!   Show me…."   She paused, aware that her knowledge of planetary names was limited.   Gemdorin's story of the Ghengat home world came to mind.   "Show me Hrenngen."

Orbs shrank and flashed by until a big red planet with one circling moon grew in magnification overhead.

"Show me the Elrah Gyan System."

The red planet minimized at the expansion of an enormous red sun orbited by eight planets.   Hrenngen was the fourth world from the sun.

"Show me the Millan System."

The hologram changed again, displaying a large yellow sun encircled by twelve planets.   She recognized the beryl-blue planet, having seen it up close with Gemdorin.   There were two moons circling it exactly as she remembered.

Acting on a different idea, she reached over the podium's top and touched the next ring from the center.   Above her head, two galaxies appeared side by side.   Her finger tapped the third ring, and the images transformed into six galaxies.   They moved in slow motion around each other.

"It's a giant map of the universe," she realized, intrigued by this discovery.

When her ears picked up a disturbance in the next room, she waved her hand over the top of the device and shut it down.   All the glittering galaxies vanished.   A moment later, Gemdorin entered the room.

"That was fast," she remarked.

"Yes," he agreed.   "It was only a minor emergency."   There was mischief in his grin as he noted, "I see you've managed not to trap yourself in anything."

"No, I've been careful."   She pointed to the skinny podium. "What's this here?"

"I'm not sure," he admitted.   "It was supposed to be some kind of navigational device, but I've never been able to make the thing work.   Rumors have given me only stray bits of information.   I was told the device functioned for select individuals.   Apparently, I'm not one of them.   Most likely it's damaged."   He inclined his head slightly, giving the young queen a curious look.   "Why don't you try your hand at it?   Maybe it will work for you."

She immediately stepped away from the platform.   "No, sir— no, thank you, I'd probably end out stuck again."

Gemdorin laughed good-humoredly.   He had a gold band in his grip he was toying with.   He slipped it over his hand.

"Eena, look here.   You'll enjoy this."

He held up his wrist so she could observe the armband.   With a single finger he pressed on it, vanishing from sight.

Eena's jaw hit the ground.   "How in the world?   Where did you go?"   She turned every which way to find him.   When the weight of his hand fell on her shoulder he instantly reappeared.

"Now you're invisible too," he told her.   "It's a cloaking device.   If you hold onto someone or something while you wear it, they vanish right along with you."

"That is too cool!" she exclaimed.   "Can I have one of those?"

He took no time to think it over.   "Absolutely not.   The last thing I need is to have you haunting the ship with an invisibility cloak."

Her exuberance promptly wilted.

Another call from the bridge interrupted them—the same officer as before.   After a quick conversation, Gemdorin

319

announced they would have to leave.

"It's okay," Eena said, "I have other things to do."

The captain walked her out of his treasure room, stopping at the door again to enter the correct combination in the security system that kept them locked inside.

Before they parted, he asked her, "Did you forget about your sorrows for a while?"

She nodded. "Yes, I guess I did. Thank you."

She honestly had put them out of her mind, entranced by the incredible treasures he had been thoughtful enough to share with her. Perhaps the day wouldn't be as dismal as expected, so long as she could turn to Gemdorin.

CHAPTER SEVENTEEN
Memorial

The exact time was hard to guess, but it felt short of normal waking hours—definitely too early to hope Sarii and her boys were up.   Wandering the ship took Eena to their quarters nonetheless where she eventually found herself standing outside their front door, staring at the drab paneling, wishing the barrier would move aside and invite her in.   It wasn't that she wanted to bother her friend at an unreasonable hour, but being alone meant succumbing to dismal thoughts, something she hoped to avoid.

Hesitant to rouse their household too early, Eena began pacing the empty corridor, purposefully killing time.   Just when she had convinced herself to leave, she glanced a figure standing in the open doorway, beaming.

"Were you planning to loiter out here all morning, or did you want to come in?"

"Sarii!"   Eena's cheeks flushed, embarrassed to have been caught walking circles.   "How did you know I was out here?"

"I have my ways.   Actually, Xander helped me fix a camera in the vent.   Years ago, Rhoen did the same thing on our previous ship so we could monitor the corridor.   He was a bit paranoid, my husband.   Always reminding me *'you can never be too careful.'* I'll admit he was right, it does come in handy."

Eena attempted a smile.   She yearned to blurt out that Rhoen was alive, but feared uncertain consequences.

"Forgive my manners, Sha Eena, please do come in."   The woman stepped aside, allowing room for her notable guest to enter.

"Thank you."

Sarii's quarters weren't new to the young queen who had visited on prior occasions.   It wasn't a fancy or roomy space, but it was comfortable.   Eena loved the inviting atmosphere and the cozy feel.   The feature most endearing, however, was a wall in the living room plastered with family pictures spanning end to end. The heart of the wall was claimed by a stunning photograph of Rhoen and Sarii on their wedding day.   This large portrait was surrounded by smaller photos of Xander and Willum. And just below the family collage hung a row of original artwork created by the boys.

Eena glanced over a number of illustrations, admiring the doodling done by young hands. She especially liked a drawing of Willum's family where he had portrayed each member as an animal rather than a person. On a previous visit, she had asked him to describe the animals, being unfamiliar with forms of wildlife on Moccobatra. He had explained the entire picture to her.

"Mom is this tall, furry one here. She's a kruah because she's pretty like they are, and she has long, soft hair." Willum had pointed to a slender animal with a lengthy mane and whiskers to match. Next, he pointed out a tiny, round creature that looked ready to burrow a hole in the ground.

"This is Xander. He's a lennguina because he's sneaky and quiet and always scaring me. I'm this one, a wrev." He put his finger on a rodent with large, beady eyes. "They're smart and small and I'm really smart and small too. And my dad—he's a cheekta roh because they're strong and they run fast. Mom told me my dad was like that. They're smart like him too."

Eena focused on the giant head of a tall cheekta roh flashing a set of sharp, white teeth. The whole idea behind Willum's picture was absolutely wonderful to her. Eena had asked Willum what kind of animal she might be. His response had been sure after only a moment of thought.

"You'd be a crioness."

"Oh? Why is that?"

"Because they can fly."

"Why would that remind you of me?" she had asked, unable to guess his reasoning.

"Because few animals can fly. You can do things others can't do. Like flying. It's magic."

The comparison had left her both impressed and flattered.

Eena found a seat in the living room on the end of a long, puffy couch. She turned her shoulder to the back and rested her head against the overstuffed cushion. There were two sofas in the room alongside a pair of wooden chairs, all neutral in color. The only source of light shone dimly from a standing lamp. In the center of the floor sat a squat table, its surface scuffed from abuse. Xander and Willum had left their toys strewn on the tabletop which Sarii quickly gathered and tossed down a dark hallway. She observed the way her queen sank into the sofa.

"Are you alright, Sha Eena?"

The young lady nodded while her mouth pursed into a conflicting frown. "I'm okay, it's just..." A heavy sigh bared her sorrow. "I keep thinking about Jase. It's just not fair."

Sarii took a seat beside her friend and patted her knee—a gesture of sympathy. "I know, I know. Xander's pretty torn up about that too. What I'm really asking, though, is if *you* are alright after what happened to you yesterday."

Eena lifted her head to meet Sarii's look of concern. "Who told you what happened to me?"

The woman shuddered at an unpleasant memory. "The captain. You can imagine my surprise when he showed up *here* with Xander in tow. He was very upset. He said a handful of Ghengats had boarded the ship in search of you. Jase and Xander happened to be in the wrong place at the wrong time when they came across the horrid creatures. Kahm Gemdorin was irate, to put it mildly, and scolded Xander for sneaking around the docking bay without permission."

Sarii's slim eyebrows pinched and tilted in a pitiable way as she recalled the occurrence.

"Xander explained to me that he'd simply wanted to show Jase the gliders, like the ones his father once piloted. He didn't mean any harm, but I don't think he'll be sneaking into restricted areas anytime soon. Not after the lecture he got from the captain. Kahm Gemdorin assured me you were alright, but then he told us what happened to poor Jase."

Both ladies turned their heads at the sound of approaching footsteps. Willum stepped out of the dark hallway, his eyes drooping with sleep until he saw their guest sitting on the couch.

"Sha Eena!" he exclaimed, hustling over to greet her with a big, warm hug. It was exactly what she needed.

"Good morning, Willum," she cooed, holding onto him extra-long. "How was your night?"

The little boy scowled and told the truth. "It was bad. The captain came here and yelled at us. He said Jase was gone and

323

never coming back. He told Xander to stay out of trouble or he might not come back too."

"Oh dear, that does sound bad," Eena agreed. She ran her fingers through his mess of hair, feeling sorry for the child. How intimidating the captain's lecture must have been to such a small boy.

"It wasn't exactly like that," Sarii corrected, "but close enough."

"Where's Xander now?" Eena asked.

The young man in question peeked out from around the corner, half hidden by a wall. "I'm here," he announced timidly. His tone sounded dismal.

Eena forced a cheerful mood greeting him. "Good morning, Xander! Come over and join us."

He entered the living room and took a seat between his mother and Sha Eena, looking both sad and uneasy.

"Are you here to yell at me too?" he asked with legitimate concern.

"Oh, no, no, I'm sure you've endured enough of that. To tell you the truth, I'm not feeling very happy myself. I was hoping to find comfort in your company."

Xander slumped low and stared down at his feet, looking about as miserable as anyone could look. Eena sighed sympathetically.

"You must miss Jase like I do."

His head nodded that it was so.

"I can't stop thinking about him either," she said.

Her words made the poor boy cry. Tears that had been lurking at the surface spilled over as he burst out with a heartfelt apology. "I'm sorry, Sha Eena, I'm so sorry! I didn't mean for him to get hurt! I'm sorry—it was all my fault!"

"What? No, Xander, none of this was your fault!"

"Yes, it was! I took Jase to the docking bay. I made him go with me. If I hadn't done that, he would still be here! It's all my fault!"

"No, no, Xander, no." She took the young man in her arms and held him close. He clung to her, sobbing. Strangely, she could feel the weight of his grief sweep over her. It was immense remorse he harbored. She pushed him back enough to see into his tearful eyes. Her head shook of its own accord as she realized they carried the same heavy burden of guilt.

"Now you listen to me, young man. You shouldn't be feeling this way at all. What happened to Jase was absolutely *not* your fault. The Ghengats snuck onto this ship looking for me. He wasn't harmed because he was with you. He was harmed because he was with me. I'm the one to blame, Xander. Jase was killed in my company; he would've been fine otherwise."

"It's no one's fault," Sarii broke in, speaking as if her word was final. "Things just happen. We are all born into this world and we will all die. It can't be avoided."

Nobody felt any better.

"I know what we need," Eena decided. "I think it would be helpful if we properly said goodbye to our friend." She looked to the boys' mother. "Do you know when the funeral will be?"

The bad news was written all over Sarii's face. "I'm sorry, Sha Eena, but they don't perform ceremonies for the dead anymore. The practice was stopped years ago when battle-related fatalities became too frequent. The numbers were overwhelming and depressing. Now the deceased are cremated. Families and friends mourn the loss of their loved ones alone. It's part of the tragedy of war, I suppose."

"That's horrible." Eena looked at Xander's sad face and wondered what to do. "I propose we have our own memorial for him then—for us. It's the least we can do."

Xander gave his approval in a nod.

"You boys go get dressed. We have work to do."

Xander and Willum disappeared down the hallway, rushing off to ready for the day. Sarii squeezed on Eena's arm as she reminded her friend, "What happened to Jase is not your fault. You do know that."

"I'm not so sure," Eena said sadly. "I wish he had run to you yesterday and not to me. Jase would've been safe with you."

Sarii had her doubts. "Nowadays I don't believe anywhere is really safe."

Eena understood how years of warfare could create such doubts. She thought to ask about others who would miss the boy. "Do you know of anyone we should invite to our memorial for Jase?"

325

Sarii shook her head no.   "Unfortunately, he didn't have family.   And I'm not sure who his friends were.   He and Xander only got together now and then."

The news was disappointing.   "Then I guess it'll just be the four of us."

The boys dressed quickly.   Their mother fed them breakfast—wholegrain toast and sliced ongrea.   She offered a plate to Eena who declined, explaining she had already shared an early meal with the captain.   Seated around the kitchen table, they discussed plans for a memorial service.

"How do we do a memrol service?"

"A mem-*orial* service," Eena corrected.

Willum scrunched his eyebrows.   "That's what I said."

"Right, well, we first need to decide on a place for the *memrol* ceremony.   A nice, peaceful spot.   Often it's a place reminiscent of the person who died.   Once we gather there, we take turns sharing our memories of Jase and saying kind things about him. Then we each say goodbye.   Someone could sing a song at the end.   Songs are customary at memorials."

Xander made a squeamish face.   "I don't sing very well."

"Me neither," Eena admitted.

"But I can draw a picture," he declared.   "I'm good at that. Do you think if I drew a picture of Jase that would be okay?"

"I think that would be wonderful," Eena smiled.   She glanced sideways, noticing how Sarii was focused on her son, clearly adoring him.

The four mourners worked on outlining and preparing a memrol service, as Willum called it.   The plans weren't much, but the work kept them busy and distracted from sorrows, which was its true purpose.   When Xander's picture was drawn to his liking and a simple outline of proceedings was determined, they turned to the chore saved for last—deciding where to hold the service.

"We could do it right here," Sarii suggested.

"We could," Eena agreed.

Xander shook his head.   He wanted it to be someplace special, someplace Jase would have liked.

"How about the commissary?"

"No," Xander said.   "Too many people.   It's not quiet enough.

They made a few more suggestions, but no one could come up with a location Xander approved of.

"Xander," Eena finally asked, "do you have a place in mind?"

He looked reluctant to say.

"Go ahead," she encouraged him. "Where do you want to go?"

He mumbled his answer, knowing it might provoke some negative feedback. "I wish we could go to the docking bay because Jase liked the ships there."

Sarii immediately disapproved of her son's idea. "Absolutely not! I can't believe that after the captain's lecture last night you would even think of returning to that place!"

Xander's head sank between his shoulders. He regretted saying a word.

"What a minute," Eena cut in. "Will you give me a moment?"

She stepped out into the corridor, wanting a private talk away from the boys. Reaching into her pocket, she dug out the PCD Gemdorin had given to her. Pressing once, she spoke into the device.

"Gemdorin? Uh, are you there?"

His answer came surprisingly fast. "Eena, yes. What can I do for you?"

"I want to ask a favor. A really big one," she said, preparing him for her request.

"Go ahead."

"I'm with Sarii and her boys. We're putting together a memorial service for Jase in order to properly say goodbye to him. I know that you talked to Xander about staying away from restricted areas, but……well, I was wondering…….I mean, it seems like it would be appropriate to hold the ceremony in the docking bay. Jase really liked the ships there, and it would only be the four of us. I promise it wouldn't take long. We'd keep to a corner—out of the way. Could we have your permission to go there? Please?"

She waited anxiously for his answer.

He didn't respond right away.

She was prepared to hear him deny her request when he asked a question. "When did you plan to do this?"

"Soon, if it's alright."

"Fine. Wait ten minutes and the bay will be yours for one hour. Is that enough time?"

Her delight came across loud and clear. "Oh yes, plenty! Thank you! Thank you very much, Gemdorin." It made her feel good he considered her wishes important, even though a refusal in this case would have been understandable.

Eena informed Sarii and the boys that Kahm Gemdorin had granted them permission to use the docking bay for one hour. Xander and Willum were excited by the news. Sarii, however, found the whole arrangement unsettling. She voiced her concern at inconveniencing the captain, but Eena put her mind at rest.

"It's a favor to me."

Sarii agreed to go along, and the mourners gathered up their things.

On the bridge, the captain immediately turned to the Ghengat leader and gave him a direct order.

"Raugh, make sure none of your men are in the docking bay or anywhere near it until I say otherwise. Eena's going to be there for a while."

Grah Raugh had overheard the conversation with Sha Eena and was visibly upset by the inconvenience of having his men abandon the hangar. All the Ghengats were growing tired of the increasing amount of time Gemdorin was spending with her rather than concentrating on what they considered pressing matters.

"You're getting soft, Gemdorin," Raugh growled under his breath.

The captain reacted abruptly and in one quick motion grabbed his criticizer by the throat and slammed him against a wall. His fingers tightened around the Ghengat's airway, barely allowing a breath.

"I am not getting soft, you half-brained gat! For your information, it is a delicate operation winning the heart of a woman. It takes a great deal of patience, long-suffering, painstaking attention, and if she asks for something you can easily give her—*you give it to her!*"

Raugh managed to speak while struggling to breathe. "I thought......the plan was......to kill her."

328

Gemdorin released his grip, and the Ghengat dropped to the floor. "I've changed my mind."

"That woman is nothing but a hazardous waste of time," Raugh said, rubbing at his neck. "She's become a hindrance to our progress."

"On the contrary—she may be the key to our success. As badly as you want to locate the dragon's eye, I'd think you'd be itching for use of her necklace."

"It's not worth the risk; we can do this without her, Gemdorin."

The captain made a low sound of disgust. "Pitiful words of cowardice. That necklace of hers may possess greater powers than the gem you're so zealous to find." He leaned over the scaly leader, glaring into his eyes. "I will *not* squander an opportunity to control such a formidable tool."

Raugh climbed to his feet and dared to face his dangerous ally again. "If she's truly that powerful, aren't you afraid of what will happen the day she turns on you?"

"You worry far too much." Gemdorin snickered lowly, thinking of how easily he had manipulated the young Sha so far. "After the brilliant performance your men gave yesterday, she's convinced I'm her hero. She's all mine—heart and will. She'll do anything I ask of her. And that fact alone will torment Derian worse than her untimely death."

He stared off for a moment imagining his brother's certain agony. Then in one swift move, he grabbed the Ghengat leader by the throat again, clutching tight before there was time to react.

"And for the record," he hissed, nose to nose with his suffering victim, "I will *never be soft*." He shoved the Ghengat away. "We need Eena on our side if we're to control that necklace and uncover the dragon's eye. A little tolerance now will pay off handsomely in the end."

Raugh raised a protective hand to his throat, drawing in a vital inhale. He would be careful with his comments about that woman in the future.

"Besides," the captain added, grinning with evil satisfaction, "if I do this for her, she'll feel obligated to repay the favor. And I do like calling on favors."

Eena and her friends hurried down to the docking bay following Xander's lead. She had only seen the hangar once before with Jase, but hadn't paid much attention to it, being more concerned with possible alien intruders. On this occasion she took a moment to observe her surroundings more closely. A slow scan absorbed the enormity of the place while measuring an endless collection of sleek gliders. Just as in the Kemeniroc, there were two floors to the hangar and a large opening in the center that made the second visible and accessible to those below. Every spoken word echoed, whether whispered or hollered, reverberating off high metallic beams.

"Amazing," Eena uttered, awed by the number of starships amassed in one room. "I didn't realize how gigantic the Mahgshreem was."

"It's unreal, huh?" Xander said. He seemed delighted at the chance to be there again.

"Yes—unreal," Eena concurred.

They walked down row after row of impressive aircraft, sliding a hand along polished hulls, imagining the black-and-silver armada in flight. Sarii noticed an area of piled storage bins and suggested they gather there for their memorial service. Eena agreed, and they took their seats on the bins.

At first, an uncomfortable edge hindered the ceremony as they found it difficult to talk about Jase. The boys didn't know what to say. Eena tried her best to preside, attempting to express personal feelings in the hopes that Xander would open up as well. He hung his picture of Jase on a glider's tail so everyone could see it. With encouragement, the young man shared a few stories about his lost friend. Willum began throwing in his thoughts as well, and soon the company was relaxed and voicing fond memories.

Xander expressed how he would miss Jase's adventurous spirit and the times they played spy together. Willum said he would miss Jase's storytelling, and he promised to continue passing down the fables learned from his friend. Sarii shared how she appreciated the young man's good manners and kind deeds. He had been a fine example to Xander. Eena agreed with all of their comments and added how much she admired the selfless way he had acted.

"He honestly cared about doing the right thing, no matter how impossible it seemed," she said. "He was a boy of commendable character."

After bidding Jase farewell in their own way, Sarii whispered that their hour was nearly up.

"Already?" Eena was surprised by how quickly the time had passed. "I suppose we should go then."

"Would you mind if I offered a prayer before we leave?" Sarii asked.

"Oh please do. That would be a perfect ending."

The four bowed heads and listened to Sarii as she prayed for Jase and her family, for their queen, and for the welfare of all their people.

"Amen," they chimed at the finish.

"Amen," a deep voice echoed from behind.

Eyes quickly shifted to catch Gemdorin standing nearby—head high, arms folded.

"Nicely done," he complimented Sarii. "Are you finished?"

"Y...yes, sir," the woman replied, visibly tense.

"Did you enjoy seeing the gliders again, Xander?"

The boy flickered a wary glance at his mother. "Yes, sir. Sha Eena said it was okay for us to be here."

"Correct," Gemdorin assured him. "She had my permission, which is exactly what you need before you go roaming around my ship."

"Yes, sir," Xander agreed. He too appeared tense.

"Well then, I would say it's time for you to go." The captain held out his arm in the direction of the elevator. Sarii and her boys immediately headed for the exit. Eena stepped in line behind them, but was stopped by Gemdorin when he slipped his arm around hers.

"A word," he murmured in her ear.

She looked up at his face, wondering if she had somehow gotten herself into trouble again.

"I'll see you later," Eena called to her friends, waving them on with a forced smile.

Gemdorin waited until the exit closed. Then he started walking, pulling Eena along with locked arms. They strolled silently among the great gliders for a time before he chose to

331

speak.

"That was a kind gesture, what you did for Sarii's family. Do you feel better now?"

"A little," she admitted. "It helped."

"We don't perform ceremonies for the dead anymore," he said flatly. "There would be far too many to arrange."

"So I've heard. That's disappointing."

"On the contrary; it's improved things greatly."

She glanced up sideways at him, perplexed. "Why do you say that?"

"We're at war, Eena, there's no time to be soft. Everyone has learned to accept the realities of war; we've had to toughen up to endure our hardships."

She disagreed. "It's not a matter of being soft, it's being compassionate."

Gemdorin smiled down at her. "Compassion is for more peaceful times, Eena. You haven't been around for the past, what…..twelve years? When you're at war that long, strength is what's required. Physical and emotional strength. There's no room for weaknesses like compassion."

"If you believe compassion is a weakness, then you've been at war far too long."

"I agree. That's why I mean to put an end to it."

"I don't see how a simple memorial service now and then…"

He cut her off. "There will be no more such services after today. If you get started on this, others will want to follow your example. It will become a hindrance to our goals and priorities. The only reason I allowed you to go ahead today was for *your* sake. I realize you haven't had to endure the same hardships we have; consequently, accepting the loss of your young friend may prove more difficult for you."

"It's difficult for everyone," she insisted.

Gemdorin stopped walking and turned to fully face her. "There is too much work to do to dwell on our losses. Jase will not be the last friend you lose. Grieve in your own way, but I will not have unnecessary ceremonies taking up our valuable time and energies. Understood?"

Eena stared up at his hard features, noticing how his scar spiked like a wielded spear when his eyebrow arched high. She felt sorry that this war had made him so unfeeling. She mumbled in response to his firm order, "Yes, sir."

"Good." He patted the hand still draped across his arm.

"Are we done?" she asked.

"Yes."

"May I go back to Sarii and her boys?"

"If that is what you wish." He released her arm.

She turned and started for the elevator but then looked back for a moment.

"Thank you for today."

The captain nodded once.

All the way to Sarii's quarters Eena couldn't stop thinking about Gemdorin's words—about Jase not being the last friend she would lose in this war. She had never considered that possibility. Things had been fairly peaceful since her arrival, other than the Ghengats' brief appearance. The idea of further loss troubled her.

She spent the remainder of the day with Sarii and the boys, grateful to be in their company and treated like part of the family. Sarii wanted to keep a low profile after what had transpired between her son and Kahm Gemdorin; and so, she suggested they eat in their quarters rather than the commissary.

"There's plenty of food here and activities also."

Xander and Willum played well together while the women visited. When lunchtime rolled around, Eena made sandwiches while Sarii diced up a pot of vegetables to start a soup for their evening meal.

After lunch, the boys asked to draw and color, so Eena joined them. She had taken art classes back in school, hoping to improve a talent for sketching. The memory seemed like a lifetime ago. Willum busied himself illustrating a combat scene where a heroic warrior towered over an army of tiny, losing Ghengats. Xander worked on adding color to a picture he had previously drawn—a meticulous blueprint of an original battleship. Eena found herself lost in thought as she penciled out a very good likeness of the friendly dragon from her dreams. It was after two hours of detailed sketching and coloring that Sarii stood behind her queen and commented.

"That's an incredible dragon—such realism in his features. Did you just think this up in your head?"

"Actually, I've had dreams about him." Eena held up the illustration to scrutinize her own work.

"Why one green eye and one yellow?" Sarii asked, noticing how they were painted differently.

"I don't know," Eena admitted. "He's always like that in my dreams. It's strange because he seems so familiar. He protects me from two hostile, younger dragons. I wish I knew what the dreams meant."

Sarii took a seat at the table and examined the artwork more closely. "I'm not sure dreams always mean anything. I think they're often just a way of releasing our fears and concerns in mental images."

"That may be the case," Eena agreed, "but this dream seems different. It's recurring and—" She hesitated, reconsidering whether or not to share how her dream about the Ghengats had come true. "—well, it just feels like they're meant to tell me something."

"Hmm," Sarii hummed.

"That's an awesome dragon," Xander said, stealing a look at Eena's artwork over his mother's shoulder.

Willum skirted the table to take a peek too. He piped right up. "Can I have it?"

"No!" Sarii and Xander answered together.

Eena smiled at the boy. "What would you do with it?"

"Put it on my wall."

Xander warned his little brother, "Then it would scare you every night when you went to bed."

"Nuh-uh!" Willum voiced back, wrinkling his nose.

"He's not a mean dragon at all," Eena told them. "As a matter of fact he's a very nice and gentle dragon. He'll protect you from harm."

"Then *I* want it," Xander announced.

"No! I wanted it first," his brother argued.

"You would ruin it."

"I would not!"

"It doesn't matter because it belongs to Sha Eena," Sarii said, putting an end to the quarrel. "It's her dragon, not ours."

Eena resolved to keep her drawing, knowing better than to undermine a mother's authority.

Dinnertime passed pleasantly.   They sat around the table enjoying Sarii's vegetable soup while talking about the boys' love of drawing.   Willum shared a few creative stories behind some of his sketches, showing off an incredible imagination.   Eena was happy Xander seemed in much better spirits than he had earlier that morning.   They were nearly finished with dinner when the communicator in Eena's pocket called out her name.   They all heard the captain's deep, muffled voice.

"Excuse me."   She stood up from the table and headed for the living room to answer the call privately.

"Gemdorin?"

"My dear, are you ready for dinner?" the captain asked.

"Well, I uh…..actually, I just finished dinner."

"You did?   Are you still with Sarii?"

"Yes.   We're having a very nice time."

"Very well."   He sounded disappointed.   "I'll see you tomorrow then."

"Okay.   Tomorrow."

She was glad he hadn't pressed her to leave.   She wanted to stay with her friends as long as they were happy to have her.

"Is everything alright?" Sarii asked when Eena returned to the table.   All the dishes had been cleared away.   A glance inside the kitchen found both boys busily washing bowls and spoons.

Eena smiled.   "Everything's fine."

Sarii instructed her sons to ready themselves for bed after finishing their chores.

"But, Mom, we're not even tired," they whined.

"I didn't say you had to go to bed," she explained, "just get ready so that you can hop in bed as soon as you're tired.   And don't forget to clean your teeth!" she hollered as her sons ran past, tearing down the hallway.

Eena chuckled at the scene.   "Your boys are great.   You've done such a good job with them."

Sarii blushed proudly.   "Thank you."

The women settled into the living room with mugs of warm meersh.   They visited beneath a soft standing light while the boys played at their feet.   Willum eventually fell asleep on the floor. Sarii carried him off to bed and made Xander retire at the same time.

335

"Goodnight, Sha Eena," he said, giving her a hug. "Thank you for everything today."

"You're welcome." She wished him sweet dreams as she planted a kiss on his cheek.

The women continued to talk late into the evening until Sarii could tell her guest was having trouble keeping her eyes open. She realized her friend didn't want to leave.

"I think you need to get some rest, Sha Eena. Would you like to sleep here tonight?"

"Do you mind?"

"Not at all. You're always welcome in our home." Sarii rose from off the couch and gestured to a darkened hallway. "Come with me; you can have my room."

"No, no, I'll sleep here," Eena said, nuzzling further into the cushions. "I don't want to take your bed from you."

"Nonsense," Sarii came back. "I won't have our Sha sleeping on an old lumpy sofa—not that my bed's much better," she chuckled.

"Really, Sarii, I want to stay right here. Please." She rested her head on the sofa's arm.

Sarii conceded with a sigh. "If you insist."

"I do."

Sarii disappeared from the room but returned shortly with a folded blanket and a pillow. She draped the blanket overtop her queen, who was already sound asleep, and then whispered a soft goodnight.

Meanwhile, Eena slipped into a world of dreams….

Ian was nowhere to be seen, but she assumed he was aware of her. It was disheartening how she ached for his company and yet dreaded facing him. As long as they disagreed on Derian's true character, she couldn't see how they would ever be friends again.

Her eyes lifted up at an overcast sky, searching for the dragons that sometimes haunted her dreams. There was no sign of the beasts—a good thing.

Her gaze dropped, and she envisioned a garden of flowers blooming into the surrounding distance like a pastel ocean. A variety of soft colors—pinks and yellows and lavenders and blues—invaded every inch of the horizon no matter which way she

336

turned.   Nearest her feet were blooms resembling those Gemdorin had left in her room. They grew in thick clusters, leaving only a small patch of grass for her feet.

Two trees pushed through the soil, shooting up tall to act as shade for her little circle of grass.   A comfortable chair appeared beneath the trees, and she took a seat in it.   Eena rested in her dreams.   It was a nice feeling.   Much better than running from vicious Ghengats or ducking mean, ornery dragons.   And more pleasant than arguing with Ian.

CHAPTER EIGHTEEN
I Know What You Want

Eena was awakened by the sweet smell of breakfast, and her eyes opened up to a heartwarming sight. Below her, Willum slept snuggled against the couch. A blanket was wrapped around his shoulders, a pillow held tight between both arms. Xander was curled up in a throw on the opposite end of the cushions, snoring softly.

"I found them there, asleep at your side, when I woke up this morning," Sarii whispered from across the room. She was standing in the entryway holding a small stack of plates. "They apparently can't get enough of you."

Eena sat up, a contented smile on her lips.

"Did you sleep alright?" Sarii asked.

"Yes, I really did."

"Any more dragon dreams?"

"No." Eena was careful to step over Willum as she stood. "I don't remember dreaming about much at all, actually."

"That's not unusual. Are you hungry?"

Eena patted her grumbling stomach. "I certainly am. Can I help you with anything?"

"If you want to, you could take these dishes to the table." Eena gladly accepted the stack of plates.

She set out dishes for four while Sarii prepared a hot tray of fried bread and preserves. Eena snatched a corner sample of the sweetbread, tempted by her favorite food.

"Should we wake the boys?"

Sarii shook her head. "Let them sleep. They can eat when they get up."

The women talked over breakfast, chatting as leisurely as they had the previous day. They mainly discussed the boys, laughing at stories of silly youthful escapades. Eena was happy to have found a good friend in Sarii, in whose company she could be herself. Amazingly, Xander and Willum weren't roused by their periodic bouts of laughter.

When breakfast ended and the conversation lulled, Eena suggested it was time to be on her way. She thanked Sarii for her hospitality, apologizing if she had overstayed her welcome. Sarii assured her otherwise.

"Tell the boys 'good morning' for me," she said before stepping out the door. "I'm sure I'll see you all soon."

In her own quarters, Eena admired the flower arrangement from Gemdorin, still beautiful and fresh-looking. Rereading the attached note inspired the same heartfelt flutter that had touched her initially. She took a moment to breathe in the fragrance of the bouquet, smiling at its intoxicating smell.

Her morning hours were spent soaking in a hot tub. The afternoon found her in the commissary, mingling with crew members. It was surprising that Gemdorin didn't call or make an unannounced appearance. By evening, however, his voice was carrying on the PCD wanting to know if she would join him for dinner.

"Yes," she answered into the small device, "I'd like that."

"Wonderful! I'll be by shortly to get you, my dear."

Eena took time to freshen up, glancing at her hologram image to make sure she looked nice. The gown she chose to wear was pale pink, short-sleeved, trimmed in lace at the hem. She didn't bother with hair accessories, allowing her lengths to fall straight down her back.

"Good enough," she decided, hearing the captain's rap at the door.

His greeting was accompanied by a deep bow. "Good evening, my lady."

She blushed, charmed by his chivalrous gestures.

"Shall we?" Gemdorin offered his arm, and she eagerly took hold.

Dinner was in the captain's dining room. Eena lit a centerpiece of candles without being asked, providing soft illumination to dine by. She had mastered simple feats of manipulating energy such as warming matter, pushing articles aside, and igniting burnable material. Such doings took little effort anymore.

Lighthearted conversation accompanied their meal.

339

Gemdorin made the young queen laugh easily, and he seemed delighted by her show of interest in his stories. He did most of the talking but listened when she spoke about her day.

Eena found the captain's company pleasurable. She ate up his generous attention, blushing now and then at sugary compliments. It seemed natural to be attracted to the man—and why not? He was handsome, attentive, witty, an entertaining storyteller, and he clearly enjoyed her company. But what she treasured most was the sense of security felt in his presence. After her fearful experience with the Ghengats, she appreciated Gemdorin looking out for her.

After dinner, he asked her to join him on the star walk.

"We should be in position to see Dergan's Comet again," he said. "With any luck, we'll steer very close to it."

Talk of Dergan's Comet reminded her that Derian might be near, unless Ian had convinced him to leave well enough alone. Somehow, Eena doubted it. Even so, Kahm Derian and his gruesome Ghengats were no match for Gemdorin and the necklace's increasing powers.

Near the circular opening at the rear of the treasure room, a warm hand landed on the small of her back and guided her through. Not long ago she would have found Gemdorin's touch unsettling, but tonight it felt exactly opposite. His gallantry was nice. His protective manner, comforting.

She continued into the dark to the very center of the walkway, gripping a handrail as it rose into place. The immensity of open space cast a humbling spell, as always. Traveling at impulse made it easy to distinguish individual stars scattered like a swarm of fireflies in the mud. The Mahgshreem coasted on the outskirts of the Millan System where Eena recognized a beryl-blue planet with its two orbiting moons. Previously an ominous image, it seemed a mere juggler's ball from a distance.

She could sense Gemdorin approach from behind, his arms closing her in as he grasped the handrail on either side. He relaxed against her back, taking an intimate stance. She was shocked he would make such a bold move.

"What are you doing?"

"You smell good," he said, sidestepping the question.

A shiver ran down Eena's spine as the captain brushed his

nose against her neck.   He sniffed her floral scent, and her pulse quickened.

"I don't see any comet," she said, hoping to pull his attention to the view.

"Keep watching."

"I am watching."

"You'll see it soon."

Her long hair was gathered up, and Gemdorin draped it over her shoulder.   He pressed his lips against the back of her neck. Eena drew in a ragged breath, mistaken for a sound of consent. Attracted as she was to the man, it felt too intimate too fast.   She shrugged her shoulder to her ear, forcing his lips away.

"Please stop."

He yielded, but continued to keep her securely within his hold. His mouth moved to her ear with a question.

"Do you object to my closeness because of another?"

She made a slight gesture with her head.   "No, that's not it at all."

"Are you sure?" he asked.   "Did you find my brother attractive?   Did Derian kiss you?"

She twisted her neck to gawk at him with a look of disgust. "No!   Never!   I was on Derian's ship for less than two days; why would you even think such a thing?   The man was entirely disagreeable—mean and bossy and uncompromising..."

Gemdorin laughed with satisfaction at her list of faults.   "So he never once tried to kiss you?"

Again she made a sour face.   "No, never!"

"Very good."

Gemdorin turned her head with his hand and looked deep into her eyes.   She wondered at his thoughts until he made an announcement.

"I have something for you.   A gift."

His fingers fished out a small item from his vest pocket.   A gold chain.   He dangled it around the young queen's neck and latched it from behind.   Eena lifted the attached pendant to look at it—a thin, diamond-shaped plate about one-and-a-half inches across.   The embossed image of a woman adorned the front. With windswept hair and a long, flowing gown, she was a lovely vision.   The pendant itself looked antique, every crevice

341

discolored with age.

"It was my mother's," Gemdorin told her.   "I want you to have it."

"It's beautiful; thank you.   Your mother—didn't she die when you were young?"

"Who told you that?"

"Jinatta told me Derian's mother died when he was very young.   I assumed you had the same mother, but that may not be true."

A moment of hesitation preceded a reply.   "We did.   And yes, she died when we were both young.   About the same ages as Sarii's boys.   I was ten.   Derian would've been six."

"What happened to her?"   Eena didn't mean to pry, but she wanted to hear his story.

"It was an accident.   Father took Mother on a test flight—a routine drill that should've been safe enough.   But something went wrong.   They crashed.   Our mother died on impact. Father suffered serious injuries, but survived.   It was a difficult time."

Eena's voice fell soft with sympathy.   "How awful.   I'm so sorry."

"All in the past," he said, icily shrugging it off.   He promptly changed the subject.   "Let me see how it looks on you."

Eena turned, allowing him to observe the pendant.   It sat perfectly framed by the larger heirloom necklace.

"Absolutely perfect," he declared.

She blushed.

He ran the back of his hand along her cheek, causing her to flush a deeper shade of red.   Eena caught her breath—an involuntary reaction—and tried to look away.   But Gemdorin took her by the chin and forced her to meet his gaze.   His blue eyes tapered the slightest bit, filled with serious regard. Cautiously, he leaned in until his lips were a whisker away from hers.

"I made no promises today," he breathed.

"I know."

She inhaled before he kissed her.   It was a gentle kiss that awakened every cell in her body.   Feeling how her lips accepted his own, he repeated the kiss, more eager and lingering.   His hand moved to support her head and keep her close.   His other hand traveled along her curves, stopping at her lower back, urging nearness between them.   A soft moan escaped her throat and Gemdorin responded with more aggressive kisses.   She returned each one, stealing a quick breath at any opportunity.   When the passion slowed to a few simple pecks, her lips thinned into a wide smile.   Gemdorin brushed his nose against hers and then moved back enough to silently gaze at her.

A strange mix of exhilaration and unease filled her bosom. Again, she wondered at his thoughts, studying him in return.   Her eyes were drawn to the battle scar that outlined his left eyebrow. She lifted a hand to touch it.

"I can fix that for you," she offered, "if you want me to."

"No."   He leaned sideways until she dropped her hand. "This scar is a reminder—a souvenir of sorts—to prevent me from underestimating my brother.   It fuels my determination to put an end to Derian's brutality.   The making of this scar nearly cost me my life at one time.   I will never let him get that close to harming me.....or you....again."

He ran his fingers along her cheekbone, and Eena's eyes fell closed.   She melted at the gentleness of his touch.   His attention was sweet.   Potent.   Entrancing.

The captain shifted focus when he noticed movement in the sky.   He whispered in Eena's ear.

"There it is."

"Huh?"   Her mind was all haze.

"The comet," he smiled.   "There it is."

"Oh.   Oh, right!"   She pulled her head from the clouds and turned around.   In the distance, a dazzling tail of light shot across the blackness.   "So there it is."   As she watched the anomaly, Gemdorin moved in and kissed her ear.

"Do you like that?" he asked.

She giggled, "Yes."

"Me or the comet?"

"The comet," she said, glancing playfully over her shoulder.

His arms wrapped around her and squeezed tightly.   She placed her hands on his forearms and let him support her.   For a long while they remained this way, gazing at the universe in one warm embrace.   It was nice to feel secure in his arms, unafraid of

343

Ghengats or Derian or anything else.   Now more than ever she
was certain Ian was wrong.

Gemdorin eventually disrupted the peacefulness.   "Have you
seen enough?"

"I suppose.   It's incredible to watch."   She felt a chill as his
body peeled away and he started for the other end of the star walk.

"Come with me, Eena."

Once the track lowered, secure against the ship's hull, they
stepped through the opposite exit into the captain's quarters.
Eena immediately headed across the room, but was stopped when
Gemdorin snatched her by the arm.   He reeled her in, ready for
another string of kisses.   She responded with pleasant murmurs,
her arms draped loosely around his neck.   Slowly, he began to
walk her rearward until her legs bumped the side of a large master
bed.   As soon as she grasped his intent, Eena ceased with the
heavy kissing.   This was not where she wanted to be.   She
pushed against his chest.

"Gemdorin, no—please, let me go."

"Alright, it's alright," he said, but his strong arms wouldn't let
loose.   He stole another kiss before slackening his hold.
Keeping her hand, his eyes looked her up and down without a
word.

Eena shifted nervously.   She glanced repeatedly at the door.

With a smile, the captain conceded to her wishes and led her
outside.   They headed down the corridor to another familiar room,
the one she had been confined to for four long days.   Her stomach
churned, wanting to call it a night, and yet part of her didn't.
Gemdorin's advances were forward, yes, but on the other hand he
was sweet and attentive.   Still, she feared crossing a line.

She planted her feet outside the next door.   "Maybe I should
go.   It's getting late."

"Nonsense, my dear."   He squeezed her hand tighter.   "The
evening is young.   Come in and have a drink with me.   We can
talk."   She wiggled her fingers, but he wouldn't loosen his grip.

"Gemdorin, please.   I should go."

"I insist you stay.   I'll be lonely without you.   Come in for a
visit; we can talk about whatever interests you."

She regarded him strongly.   "Just talk?"

He smiled kindly.   "Yes, yes, of course."

344

She thought of the many times they had talked late into the night. Those had been enjoyable evenings. Certainly they could just talk. Talking was harmless enough. She breathed in deeply when the anxiety persisted, but agreed to stay.

Gemdorin lit up the mock fireplace before pouring two drinks. He offered Eena a goblet and then rested against the end of the dining room table, sipping on his own beverage.

"So, my dear, what should we talk about?"

"I don't know," she shrugged.

"Hmmm, let's see." His stare seemed to pierce right through her as he thought. "Tell me, have you had any more dreams about the dragon's eye?"

"No, I haven't." She wasn't at all surprised he would pick the dragon's eye as a conversational topic. It was probably on his mind the majority of the time.

"No more foresight into how I defeat Derian in hand-to-hand combat? No further visions where you teach the Ghengats a hard lesson?"

"No, none."

"And you've never before had dreams predicting the future?"

"Never," she maintained, "but I've been thinking about that. I'm not so sure my dream was really a prediction."

"Oh?" His eyebrow climbed with interest.

"Well, we did have a conversation about the Ghengats before I had the dream; you mentioned that Derian might send them after me. I think your suggestion fed my imagination, and so I dreamt about it happening. And since Derian was indeed searching for me, a confrontation with the Ghengats was inevitable. When it happened, I automatically reacted the way I'd seen in my dream. The idea was planted in my head, making it somewhat of a self-fulfilling prophecy."

"Interesting. What about the fact that you saw all of this in the dragon's eye? I never told you how the dragon's eye works."

"No, you didn't," she acknowledged, "but I did spend four long days confined to these very quarters, sifting through those books of yours for hours and hours. They're filled with information about the dragon's eye. I might not be able to read them, but the idea may have been planted in my head subconsciously."

"Ah-hah. What about the vision where I victoriously confront Derian?" Gemdorin grinned.

"Oh please," she laughed. "A dream about you two battling it out would be no surprise to anyone."

"You know what I think?" he asked, taking her drink and placing both goblets on the table behind him. "I think you have a nasty habit of overanalyzing everything."

She inclined her head, showing a touch of defensiveness. "Is that so?"

"Yes. Now, how about you analyze this: What does it mean when a man takes a woman by the hand and pulls her in close to him, resting his other hand on her hip?" As he said the words, he performed them, watching the reaction in her bright eyes the whole time.

She straightened up with a reply. "Well, my initial analysis would suggest he might want to dance with her."

"I'd have to agree with you."

Gemdorin moved her backwards with a gentle nudge to her hip, stepping toward the foot she used to catch herself. He led her in a simple, slow dance. It was easy for Eena to follow as he guided her movements, twirling and drifting over the bare area of floor.

She remarked on the silence of their waltz. "It's too quiet; there's no music."

"On the contrary," he said, "I hear music. Just listen."

He began to sing at that point, an a capella serenade colored by a seductive rasp. It was the same haunting lullaby her mother had recorded on the disk Eena had acquired days earlier. She recognized the melody, but Gemdorin had changed the words.

> *"Eena, Eena, stay with me here.*
> *In my arms there's nothing to fear.*
> *I'll protect you always you see.*
> *Such is the future for you and for me."*

They danced by firelight as Gemdorin repeated his song, softly humming the melody over and over again. Eena fell under his spell until her foot landed awkwardly on an edge of thick carpeting bordering the fireplace. This misstep caused her to trip

346

and plunge backwards.   Gemdorin failed to react quickly enough to catch her, but promptly knelt beside her on the floor.   His hand cupped the back of her head as he asked, "Are you hurt?"

She was stunned.   The fall had been so rapid and unexpected—it took a second to register what had happened.

"I'm okay….I think.   That was scary.   How clumsy of me." She tried to sit up, but Gemdorin pressed on her chest, keeping her flat on the carpet.

"You should stay put for now," he suggested, "in case you have a concussion or something."

"If I do have a concussion, I should get up," she argued.   "I need to stay awake."   Another attempt to rise was prevented.

"Then I'll make sure you do stay awake."   He dropped onto his elbow, extending both legs to lie beside her.

"Gemdorin…" she started.

"We can still talk," he assured her.   "Actually, I've been wanting to ask you something.   I'm curious.   I've known you for only a short time, but what I know about you I like very much."

Eena felt her cheeks warm.

"My lady, I was wondering…….what is it that you want?" He rephrased the question, trying to be clear.   "If you could make a wish and have anything your heart desired, what would you wish for?"

She heard him but found the question surprisingly difficult to answer.   If he had asked her the same thing only months ago, she could have told him right off.   But today?

"I'm not sure," she answered honestly.

"Come now," he frowned.   His finger moved to outline the curvature of her jaw.   His touch was unhurried and gentle. "There has to be something you want—something you desire— something you crave."

Her forehead creased as she contemplated how recent changes had marred her expectations of the future.   Her hand automatically halted Gemdorin's fingers as they traveled slowly down her neckline.   She held onto his hand while attempting to answer his question.

"When I was on Earth I knew exactly what I wanted.   All I dreamt of was going to a prom with Erik.   He was the most handsome guy in the entire school.   I was set to graduate and then head off to college to earn my degree—art or the humanities. After that, I hoped to get married and settle down in Royal City near my parents.   Of course I wanted a family too.   And I always wished for the opportunity to illustrate books; that was a dream of mine.   I do love to draw."

Her eyes flickered up at Gemdorin, wondering if she had answered his question well enough.

His lips pursed, conveying disappointment.   "It all sounds rather boring to me."

She shoved lightly against his shoulder in protest.   "Well, it doesn't to me."

"What about now?" he asked.   "Now that you know you're royalty—a queen born to a higher calling—surely, your ambitions have evolved.   What do you wish for now?"   He pulled his hand free and ran his finger down the crest of her nose, tapping it gingerly on the tip.

She thought for a moment.   "I don't know.   My life has changed so much; it seems like everything is decided for me now, like it doesn't matter what I want.   I do what I'm told to do."

"But you don't have to, Eena.   You're the one with the powers.   You're the one with all the pull."   His eyes grew wide as he spoke.   "Don't you realize you could have absolutely anything you want?"

She grinned crookedly.   "So in other words, I don't really have to listen to you."

"On the contrary," he sternly corrected her thinking.   "I'm your captain, and as long as you're on my ship you will follow my orders."

She cringed at the hauntingly familiar echo in his words.

Gemdorin went on.   "What I'm talking about are all the other people around you.   Their demands are negotiable."

She furrowed her brow.   "You're serious?"

He went back to his original question.   "All I was hoping to learn is what it is you really want."

"I guess……I just want to be happy," she finally decided. "No matter what I'm doing, I just want to be happy doing it."

He seemed disappointed with this answer too, as if he had expected something much grander.   But he managed a bleak smile and dropped the subject.

It fell silent for a while, excepting the sound of a crackling fire. Gemdorin stared at the flames with scrunched, distant eyes, clearly lost in his own thoughts. His finger traced the edges of the necklace, following the same curves and bends repeatedly. Eena wondered what he was thinking.

Finally, she pushed his hand away, breaking his concentration. His gaze shifted to her, staring with an intensity nearly alarming. He then rolled forward, shifting his weight against her body. His hand slid beneath her neck and his lips pressed hard against her mouth. The kiss was more passionate than any previously shared.

Eena responded favorably at first, feeling his whiskers graze her skin like sandpaper. His kisses came so fierce and close together it was difficult to steal a breath in between. When his free hand began to wander, her body tensed.

At first he only brushed along her shoulder, pushing her sleeve down to reveal bare skin.

"Wait…" she muttered, but he wouldn't let her speak.

Then his grip moved to her waist, his fingers feeling progressively up along her torso, lingering alongside her breast.

"Stop…" she breathed, "please…" She turned her lips away from him, pushing against his shoulder without success. He wouldn't budge.

He leaned in to kiss her ear and whispered, "Eena, do you know what I want?"

"No, Gemdorin, please…"

"More than anything, I want *you*."

"No," she declared in a firmer voice. She shoved against him, struggling to move him back even an inch. "Please stop, Gemdorin."

"Eena, it's alright, it's alright." His mellow tone was unsuitably reassuring. "I know what you want and I can make you happy. I *will* make you happy."

His words frightened her. "This is not what I want!" she cried. "Please stop it!"

But he did exactly the opposite. He lifted himself on top of her, pinning her hands to the ground. His eager lips tasted her shoulder, quickly working his way down every inch of exposed skin. She couldn't move, trapped beneath his weight. Her breathing hastened as she felt his lips press warm and moist against her cleavage.   She was terrified where he would go from there.

Gemdorin ignored both her desperate pleas and the increasing glow of the necklace.

"Stop it!   Stop it!   Get off me!"   Tears spilled from the corners of her eyes as she begged him to quit.   The moment his hand found a way beneath her dress, a self-preserving force took over.

The next thing Gemdorin knew, he was sailing through the air, crash-landing at the edge of the dining room table.   A hardwood chair broke his fall.   Out of fear, the necklace had created a force strong enough to shove him away.   Eena was on her feet racing for the exit before he could react.

Gemdorin shook off the blow.   His eyes grew big and wild with outrage.   His temper could be seen fuming through a deepening glower.   When he shouted, the room seemed to vibrate with the same ferocity.

"How dare you turn those powers on me!"

Slowly, he rose to his full height, feeling a painful protest in every muscle.   His finger found her first, rigid in its threatening aim.

"How dare you!   I own you, Eena!"

The trembling girl pressed herself against the doors.   "I told you to stop!   I said no!"

"You will never, NEVER use those powers against me EVER again!   Do you understand!"

When he took a step toward her, she turned her back on him, feeling desperately at the locked doors.   Her palms pressed against the barrier as she begged the necklace to grant her exit. All she wanted was to get away, as far away as possible.   The necklace responded to her wishes in a bright burst of compliant energy.   The doors slid open and she took off down the corridor in a full sprint, lifting her skirts to keep from stumbling. Gemdorin called out after her.

"Eena!   Eena wait!" he hollered.   But she wasn't about to listen.

She raced through the empty halls, unable to outrun her fear. After locking herself in the bathroom, she retreated to the furthest wall.   It seemed not a great enough distance to put between her and what had happened.   But where else was there to go?   Who

350

else was there to turn to? It crossed her mind to seek out Sarii, but she didn't want to bring any more trouble to that family.

Eena cowered in the corner, pulling her knees to her chest. She hugged them tight, feeling every inch of her body shiver. She couldn't calm the shakes. Tears streamed down her face, her lungs heaving with every sob, as her thoughts returned to two nights ago, recalling the nasty argument with Ian. He had warned her. She recalled his words. *"Don't lead him on, Eena. It will end out in nothing but trouble."* She wondered, had she led Gemdorin on? Had she given him the impression she wanted this?

"No!" she cried out loud, "NO!" She regretted not leaving when her better sense had warned her to do so.

It was hard to tell how long she wept in the corner before consciousness naturally surrendered to the dream world....

It didn't make a difference, awake or not. She felt horrible and betrayed and utterly foolish. Huddled against a knarred tree trunk with her head in her hands, her dream took on the shape of a dark, neglected forest—obscured and foreboding. It was a reflection of how she felt. Confused. Dismal. Alone.

"Eena?"

She heard Ian's voice, quiet and close. Without looking she could tell he was crouched down beside her.

"Eena, what happened?"

She hadn't expected him to appear, as unkind as she had recently been to him. Although, why not jump at an opportunity to say "I told you so"? She couldn't stop crying and wouldn't dare turn her eyes on him.

His hand landed gently on her shoulder. "Ecna, please tell me what's wrong." He begged so kindly. Too kind for what she deserved.

When she didn't answer, he carefully placed his arms around her, drawing her near to him. She didn't resist, but cried all the more.

"It's alright, I'm here. It'll be okay."

She wept, long and hard. When the tears ran dry, she finally began to relax in his arms, grateful for his undeserved compassion. At long last, she spoke.

351

"You were right.   Nothing but trouble."

"Eena, what happened?"

"He wouldn't listen to me.   I said no, but he wouldn't listen."
She didn't dare look up.

"Eena…" Ian started but she interrupted him, knowing what
he would ask.

"I pushed him off me using force from the necklace.   I threw
him pretty hard.   He just wouldn't stop; he wouldn't listen!"

"You did the right thing, Eena."   She caught her protector's
sigh of relief before he repeated his own words.   "You did the
right thing."

"He was so angry, Ian.   He screamed at me—told me never
to use my powers against him again.   I didn't stick around to hear
any more.   I ran away.   But it's only a matter of time before he
confronts me.   I'm scared.   I don't want to see him; I don't want
to talk to him.   I'm afraid he'll try to touch me again."

"I'll kill the bastard!" Ian held his queen more tightly,
although they both knew there was nothing he could actually do.

"It started out so…..so nice," she said.   "He was kind and
sweet.   He did listen to me at first."   She shook her head like she
couldn't figure out where things had turned ugly.   "I don't know
what happened."

Ian brushed a hand over her hair in a consolingly manner.
"It's going to be alright.   I promise."

They sat in silence for a long while, both feeling a different
sense of helplessness.   Finally, Ian dared to speak.

"Eena.   Derian has reached the Millan System.   He's
preparing to bring you home."

She shoved away from her comforter.   "No, I don't want to
see him.   I don't want to see either of them.   You can tell they're
brothers because they're exactly the same—both controlling and
devious.   I don't want anything to do with either one of them."

"But, Eena, Derian's not like Gemdorin.   He's not…"

"How can you defend him?   You don't even like him!"

"I don't hate him."

"You two don't get along at all, you said so yourself."

"You're right, I did say that.   And we don't see eye to eye all
the time—okay, most of the time.   But past events haven't helped
our relationship much.   Still…Derian is—"   Ian shook his head,

*searching for the right words which didn't seem to come easily.
"—well, he cares about Harrowbeth, and he cares about you.
He's spent his entire life fighting for you and for our people.
He's honestly nothing like Gemdorin."*

"I don't know if you're right, Ian."

*"Will you please just listen to him? Give him a chance.
He'll bring you back here where I am. I would love to have you
here with me where I can properly protect you."*

*Eena smiled at that. The one person she did seem able to
count on was her best friend.*

"Just give him a chance, please, Eena. For me?"

*She sighed heavily, conceding for his sake. "Okay, I'll listen
to him, but I don't know if I'll believe him."*

*Her weepy eyes looked up, really seeing Ian for the first time
that evening. She wasn't concerned about an impending guilt trip
anymore. He had once again proven to be a true friend. When
she lifted her head, he smiled kindly, until he noticed the gold
pendant dangling from her neck. Concern instantly clouded his
face as he took the pendant in his hand, examining the embossed
figure on the plate.*

"What is this?"

*Her dream image vanished before she could answer. She
woke up to a loud tapping on the bathroom door.*

"Eena, I know you're in there." Gemdorin's voice followed
his knock. Luckily, he was speaking in a considerably calmer
manner.

Fumbling to her feet, she wondered whether or not to respond.
She froze against the wall, waiting to see what he would do.

"Eena? Are you listening? I'm sorry. I'm so sorry for
what happened. I wish you would open up so I could be sure you
hear me."

She took a step toward the door and then stopped.

His rueful voice persisted. "Eena, I have no excuse for my
behavior other than…..I've never felt so strongly for a woman
before. I find you irresistible. I know that's no excuse. I truly
and sincerely apologize for what happened."

There was silence. She sneaked closer, listening for any
indication he was still there. Another gentle knock made her hold

353

her breath.

"Eena, I wish you would open up; I'm so sorry.   Please, please accept my apology.   I swear that will never happen again."

Her hand touched the door, contemplating unlocking it.

"I'll be back tomorrow to see you.   I deeply regret what happened tonight."

His footsteps faded as he left the room.

She went to sit on the edge of the tub, thinking about his apology.   At least he wasn't angry anymore.   Be that as it may, she didn't want to find herself in the same situation ever again. She didn't want to be alone with him.

Her thoughts naturally shifted to his brother.   What if Derian actually showed up?   What should she do?   Ian was convinced he was the better man.   She wondered how Derian would try to explain himself, or if he would send those horrible Ghengats after her a second time.   She decided if he approached her alone, she would listen to him for Ian's sake.   For now, her head hurt too much to think anymore.   All she wanted was sleep.

After washing her face with a cold, wet washcloth, she changed into a pink cotton nightgown.   It was as pretty as a dress, but shorter than the full gowns worn every day.   She climbed into bed and buried herself beneath the covers.   Snuggled up to a pillow, she dozed off quickly.

Back in her dreams Eena discovered Ian had gone.   She imagined him reporting to Derian, passing along false hope, no doubt.   It didn't matter.   All she wanted was rest.

Settling against the trunk of her favorite willow tree, she stared out at the drying field corn below.   A cool breeze picked up as autumn crept in, bringing an end to the vibrant greens and long, sweltering days.   The sunset was as comforting as always with its red and orange hues soaking up the horizon.   She watched alone, the sun never completely setting.

In her heart she wished it was real—the blades of grass between her fingertips, her horse grazing on the hillside, the tree trunk at her back, the white picket fence in the distance, and acres upon acres of fertile farmland.   She longed to shiver from an actual chill in the air while watching her precious sunset—Earth's sun—sink below the hills, stealing genuine warmth and daylight with its departure.   She yearned to go home to her mom and dad, Ruth and Roger Williams, the only people she had ever really known as family.   Tears welled up in her cheeks as she grasped how deeply she missed her old, boring, perfect life.

"I want to go home," she whispered to herself, her head supported by a groove in her faithful willow tree.   "I just want to go home."

CHAPTER NINETEEN
The Painful Truth

Eena was content to watch the sunset alone. She felt at peace in her dreams. After two hours of sleep, she was awakened by the eerie impression of a presence, like a ghost had drifted in imperceptible to normal senses. Imagining eyes watching from the shadows, it wasn't shocking when she was gently nudged awake. Someone whispered her name. It took a moment to fully comprehend who was standing over her.

"Eena. Eena, wake up."

She rolled over and opened her eyes.

Derian stared down, a black form in the darkness. So, he had found her.

She didn't overreact to his presence. As indicated by Ian, it was inevitable the man would show eventually. Sitting up, she propped herself against the headboard and waited for him to speak.

"I know you don't trust me," he started out warily. "Ian has informed me of Gemdorin's effectiveness distorting reality. Please know I'm not here to harm you or to force you to come with me. What I'm here to do is open your eyes to the truth."

"I've already heard the truth."

"What you've heard are lies."

"So you say," she muttered derisively.

"Eena, I'm not going to argue; you wouldn't believe me anyway. What I want is for you to come with me so I can *show* you Gemdorin's deception. If, after what you see and hear, you still chose to stay aboard this ship, I will leave you behind and return to the Kemeniroc alone. You have my word on that."

Eena's brow furrowed with distrust. "You swear you'll let me stay if I chose to?"

Derian held up his hand as if making a solemn oath. "I swear if you decide to stay I will allow it, but only if you first come and see what I have to show you."

"Alright." She stepped down from the bed. "I'll go."

With her standing in front of him, Derian's eyes were drawn

to the gold pendant dangling from her neck; it was more noticeable up close.   His face paled as he took the trinket between his fingers.   His voice fell gruff.

"What is this?   Where did it come from?"

"Why?" she asked.

Again he questioned her with unfitting animosity.   "Who gave this to you, Eena?"

"Your brother did.   He said it belonged to your mother." She wondered about his strong reaction.   Was it a family heirloom the two brothers fought over?

"It was hers," Derian admitted.   With a heavy sigh he let the pendant drop, and the issue as well, but Eena could tell it troubled him.

"Before we go, there's something I have to do."

"What?"

"Gemdorin embedded a tracking chip beneath your skin, much like the humans did back on Earth.   If we don't remove it, he'll know you're wandering the ship."

Eena regarded him skeptically.   "How do you know this?"

"Trust me."   He turned her around and removed a handheld device from his jacket.   With it he scanned her upper back, stopping near the left shoulder.   The device blinked red.

"It's here.   This will sting; I'm sorry,"

Eena braced herself as Derian made a shallow incision where the chip was located.   She winced at a harsh pinch.   "Ouch! You could at least *try* to be gentle."

"Sorry."   He fished out the chip with a pair of tweezers and showed it to her.   "My brother doesn't trust you."

The incision healed itself in a matter of seconds, leaving no scar.

"That's amazing," Derian breathed, witnessing the miracle.

"Now, you can remove the other one," she instructed him.

"What do you mean?   Gemdorin only needed one."

Her tight eyes glimpsed him over a shoulder.   "You don't trust me either.   I bet anything you fixed some kind of locating chip on me too.   How else would you have tracked me to this room?"

Caught like a child with his hand in the cookie jar, Derian bit his lip.   He wouldn't lie to her.   He needed too much to earn her trust.

"You're right," he finally admitted, "but not because I don't trust you.   Jinatta implanted it because we didn't want to lose you."

"A lot of good that did," she groaned wryly.

Pushing her hair aside, Derian prepared to make a small incision behind her right ear.   "I'm sorry, but this will sting again."   He tried to be gentler this time.

After removing the second tracking chip, he placed the one beneath her pillow.   "Gemdorin will think you're still in here sleeping.   We shouldn't have any problems."

"Unless we get caught.   How exactly do you plan to roam the halls without being seen?"

"With this."   A gold wristband was drawn from his pocket. Eena recognized the contraption immediately.

"You stole that from Gemdorin!"   She tried to grab it, but lost to faster reflexes.   Derian's features screwed up defensively at her accusation.

"I did not steal this from Gemdorin.   I got it from Rhoen— the traitor.   He's the reason you were abducted from my ship in the first place."

"Rhoen?"   She was shocked by the news.   How was he involved?

Derian grumbled a quick explanation, still bitter over recent discoveries.   "Rhoen's been secretly assisting Gemdorin, spying on us for the past six years.   I never suspected…..the filthy deceiver."

"So he wasn't working for you," Eena realized, speaking to herself.   "He was working for Gemdorin all this time."   One thing didn't make sense, though.   "If Gemdorin knew this, why would he tell Sarii that Rhoen was most likely dead?"

"Who's Sarii?"

"She's Rhoen's wife and my friend."

Derian nodded.   "He told me he had a wife and kids.   That was his excuse for acting as Gemdorin's double-crossing snitch. He said his family would be killed if he failed.   That's why he betrayed you, his own queen."

Eena tensed up.   She didn't believe Gemdorin would ever harm Sarii or her boys.   He was the one who had saved Xander from the Ghengats, after all.   She frowned, thinking this was probably another lame attempt by Derian to undermine his brother.

"Rhoen gave me this wristband when he confessed his crimes. He used it to cloak himself and roam my ship undetected, collecting information for Gemdorin.   But he claims he's more concerned for your safety now, so he turned himself in, wanting to help rescue you."

"Why would he risk his family and his freedom to help me? I'm fine."

"Because, Eena, even Rhoen understands how unscrupulous my brother is."

She grimaced, refusing to believe him.   "Is Gemdorin aware that you know about Rhoen?"

"No.   Not yet."

Anxious to get on with things, Derian changed the subject. Time was their enemy.   "Eena, in order for this device to cloak us both, I'll need to hold onto your hand.   If we're separated, you'll be visible to everyone around us.   Do you understand?"

"Yes, I know."

"And one more thing.   Just because they can't see us doesn't mean they can't hear us.   You must remain perfectly silent."

"I get it," she snapped.

"Alright.   Let's go then."

He led her to the exit.   Luckily, no guards were posted outside.   The elevator took them up a few decks where they stepped off, continuing down a long, empty corridor.   Near the end, another elevator awaited.   They climbed to the ship's top deck in silence.   Eena scowled when Derian gazed down at her a little too long.   Rather than show offence to her hostility, he smiled in return.   She glanced away, put off by his act of innocence.   There was nothing she could think of that would alter her opinion of him.   And, if this midnight runaround turned out to be some kind of trap, he would be surprised to discover just how effectively the necklace could be used for self-defense.

Eena allowed herself to be guided through areas of the Mahgshreem that she had never roamed before.   Their venture exposed the true enormity of the ship.   She stood silently beside Derian when a third elevator transported them two decks down. Her fingers wiggled at the onset of numbness from his tight grip;

359

he seemed intent on keeping a secure hold on her. No words were exchanged when his hand moved to clasp at her wrist.

They crossed no one roaming the ship up to that point, which was understandable given the late hour. Eena imagined the majority of crew members were asleep in their quarters if not on duty. She glanced up at the man leading her around, wondering how much longer he intended to drag her through empty hallways. A soft *whoosh* announced the lift coming to a stop. The doors cleared. Eena turned her head to look in the same direction her feet planned to move, but a figure made her cringe instinctively into the captain instead—away from a lone Ghengat.

Derian covered her mouth before she could gasp, pulling her against the wall with him. For a second she had forgotten they were invisible.

The scaly creature stepped onto the elevator, behaving like the only occupant. At the same time, Derian shoved Eena out into the hallway. He put a finger to his lips reminding her to keep silent. She nodded her understanding.

As they walked hand in hand down an occupied stretch of gray hallway, Derian concentrated on reading Eena's facial expressions. Three boisterous Ghengats stumbled past, laughing loudly, headed in the opposite direction. Eena's wide gaze followed them, the wheels turning in her mind as to why these foul characters would be wandering the Mahgshreem.

At the end of the corridor Derian pulled her aside near a closed door. He waited, watching for an opportunity to access the room. As soon as another Ghengat stepped through the doorway, the invisible pair stole inside and hurried over to an empty corner. Eena's jaw dropped when she saw Gemdorin sitting at the head of a conference table amidst a group of blue aliens. They were all merry from drinking, carrying on an argumentative dialogue.

Eena rubbed her eyes, refusing to believe what the setting suggested. This was impossible. A lie. A trick! Gemdorin was the *good* brother!

She put a hand to her chest, finding it suddenly hard to breath. Things got worse when her ears honed in on the conversation.

"So you screwed up everything we've been wasting our time on, and for what?" It was an angry accusation made by the only alien wearing a black sash.

Gemdorin replied with apathy.   "This changes nothing, Raugh.   It's a minor setback.   Hardly an inconvenience."

"We'll reach Hrenngen soon, Gemdorin.   Will she or won't she be ready?"

"She's ready now.   Her powers are stronger than even she realizes."

Raugh leaned over the table to snarl his next question.   "And how do you plan to get her to cooperate if she hates you?"   It was clear he was taking the situation more seriously than Gemdorin, concerned for whatever plan they had in store which apparently involved her participation.

"She doesn't hate me, she hates *you*," Gemdorin corrected, seeming amused by his comrade's fury.   He callously brushed off the entire evening.   "Given a couple of days and a first-class apology, maybe a handful of smelly flowers......she'll forget the whole incident.   Besides, the girl's a callow puppet.   She does whatever I say and believes everything I tell her."

"Everything?   She didn't go along with you tonight!"

Eena glanced at Derian with pained eyes.   He looked puzzled, unsure of what the conversation was referring to.   Eena, however, knew exactly what Gemdorin was joking so cruelly about.   How could he?

"She bought the whole story about you thugs working for Derian, and she believes she killed Jase."

A Ghengat snickered aloud.   "Yet you're the one who got rid of the snoop!"   His laughter was joined by others in the room.

Eena stepped forward as if she intended to confront the rabble. Derian pulled her back, warning her again with a silent gesture. She swallowed and nodded, blinking back a rise of tears.

When the amusement died down, Gemdorin made a malicious remark in response to the outspoken Ghengat.   "Now, Gar, I couldn't have the boy running around my ship blabbing to everyone about Eena's healing powers, could I?   The kid knew too much.   He had to go.   Those powers are *mine*, and I'll make sure no one is the wiser until it's too late for anyone to stop me!"

"They're *ours*," Raugh corrected.

"Of course, of course, *our* powers," Gemdorin repeated.   He raised his mug to the Ghengats.   "What benefits me, benefits you all, and vice versa."

"Fine," Raugh grumbled. "Just make sure she's ready and willing when we get to Hrenngen. We've been hunting that dragon's eye for two years now and I *will not* waste more time waiting around."

Gemdorin rose abruptly from his seat, his eyes tight and angry. "Is that a threat?"

"No, no threat," Raugh said, returning the same glare, "It's the truth."

Gar interrupted their stare down. "How are you going to explain being on our home world? Don't you think that'll make her slightly suspicious?"

Gemdorin shifted his focus and appeared to relax. "There's no way around it. That's where the dragon's eye is hidden. I'll tell her we're swiping it right out from under your ugly noses. We'll use the cloaking armbands and sneak right past you."

"And how will you explain the slaves?"

"I might not have to if we can avoid them. If we can't, I'll be just as shocked as she is to discover such terrible treatment of our people." Gemdorin throated a sinister chuckle, exciting a roar of laughter among the other Ghengats as well.

Eena went for Gemdorin, yanking on the fingers clasped around her wrist. She couldn't stand by any longer and watch this wicked display. But Derian's grip held tight. He drew her in close to him and covered her mouth. Her moist eyes cried out for help, but he shook his head. It was regrettable that the truth hurt so much, but he didn't want to leave until he was certain she understood Gemdorin's true character. He also wanted more information about what his brother was up to.

When the laughter died down, Raugh asked one more crucial question. "After she recovers the dragon's eye, what do you plan to do with her?"

Gar voiced his opinion. "I say we kill her and take the necklace for ourselves."

But Gemdorin had other ideas. "Our new allies have informed me it's possible to remove the necklace without harming her. They believe they can devise a way to control it without a host. If that's the case, I'll let the old man remove it. The girl may prove useful to me later."

"For what?" Raugh asked. His scaly features twisted up in

362

disgust. He obviously preferred their original plan of slitting her throat.

"Pleasure?" Gemdorin offered.

His answer produced a roomful of vile laughter.

"Besides, she wears my pendant now which means she's promised to me. When the council sees that pendant around her neck, they'll know that *I* am the rightful king of Harrowbeth. They'll be helpless to do anything about it. I can't wait to see the look on Derian's face when he finds it on her."

Eena now understood why both Ian and Derian had asked about the pendant. Had she known what it represented, she would never have taken it.

Gemdorin wasn't finished. "If nothing else, we may need to keep her alive for her knowledge. That is until I'm sure I can call on the necklace's powers myself."

"She'll never cooperate," Gar grumbled.

"Oh, yes she will. She values the lives of her friends far too much."

Eena couldn't take any more. She couldn't bear another dreadful word. Gemdorin had caused her to forsake both Ian and Derian. Stupidly, she had believed his deceitful lies—that Derian was the villain in line with those awful Ghengats. And he had killed Jase. He was surely responsible for the murders of all those innocent girls from Earth as well. To top it off he had nearly seduced her, manipulating her emotions with false professions of love. Tears flooded her eyes as she hunched over, covering her mouth to prevent audible sobbing.

Derian could see he needed to get her outside. He moved toward the doors, waiting for the next opportunity to sneak out undetected. From there he led her to an abandoned corridor where they entered a dark and empty room.

"Eena, I'm so sorry," he whispered. "Gemdorin is a master of deceit; he's conned countless people with his lies. I'm sorry you had to find out this way, but it was imperative for you to learn the truth."

She couldn't look up, having been proven a fool—the gullible, callow puppet Gemdorin had labeled her. It felt as if a carpet had been yanked out from under her feet, slamming her painfully against the ground. Bent over, she hugged her stomach, pressing

363

at it, unable to take in a decent breath.   One word fell from her lips repeatedly.   "Why?"

As much as he wanted to extend an arm of comfort, Derian hesitated touching her.   She seemed fragile, like she might crumble within his hold, or worse, turn on him for causing her such agony.

"Why?" she cried between ragged breaths.   He answered the question.

"My brother seeks dominion over everything—everyone. Honestly, I'm just relieved you're still alive.   Had Gemdorin not stopped to consider the power you could afford him, he would have killed you too."

Crushed by his words, she whispered grimly to herself, "I wish he had."

"No, don't ever say that!"   Derian's response was almost too loud for their hiding place.   "We need you, Eena.   *I* need you."

She straightened up to accuse him.   "Why?   So *you* can use me too?"

His voice and his countenance immediately softened.   He understood why she might have such thoughts.   "No, Eena."   He stepped up closer, daring to place a hand on her shoulder.   "You have no idea how wrong you are."

But she still didn't trust him.   "Your brother told me about your quest to be king.   That's why you need me."   For a split-second she caught a flicker of something in his eyes.   Was it shock?   Alarm?   Or just concern.   Before she could adequately read it, it was gone.

"Do you still believe what my brother says?"

She lowered her gaze, shaking her head.   "No.   But how do I know you're any better than he is?"

"Because I am.   And because Ian wouldn't lie to you."   His words were spoken as a matter of fact, without any need for explanation, proof, or excuse.

And she believed him.

He held out his hand for her to accept.   "Let me take you home."

She wiped the tears from her face.   "Wait.   I can't go without Sarii."

Derian shook his head, unwilling to alter his rescue plans.

364

"Eena, my priority is to get you safely off this ship."

But she insisted. "I won't leave her behind, Derian. If Gemdorin finds out about Rhoen, Sarii and her boys will be in danger."

The captain dropped his offered hand and sighed with impatience. "Eena, there's no time. If we don't get out of here soon…"

She spoke over him. "You swore you wouldn't make me leave if I didn't want to."

His features twisted up with serious concern. "Are you saying you want to stay here?"

"No, no, I don't want to stay here, but I won't go if Rhoen's family is left behind."

"Criminy, Eena!"

"Derian, you gave me your word. Is your word worth nothing?"

He realized this was a battle he couldn't win. Plainly irritated, he gave in. "Okay, fine. Do you think they'll come with us willingly?"

"Yes, I know they will."

"Where are they?"

She took his hand and tugged. "Come on. Follow me."

They passed no one on the way to Sarii's quarters. As soon as they arrived at her door, Eena tried to shake her hand free from Derian's grasp but he seemed reluctant to have her leave the protection of the cloaking device.

"Let go," she finally demanded. The moment he released her, she was visible. It took a number of tries, but Sarii eventually answered the rapping at her door. She was half asleep.

"Sha Eena?" She noticed the evidence of tears on the young queen standing barefoot in nothing but a nightgown. "Is something wrong?"

Eena quickly stepped inside, not bothering to wait for an invitation.

"Sarii, do you trust me?"

"Well….of course I do. Why do you ask? What's all this about?"

"Sit down." Eena dropped to the couch beside her friend. "Sarii, listen carefully to me." She drew in a deep breath before revealing the secret that had burned on the tip of her tongue for so long. "I know for a fact your husband, Rhoen, is alive. I've seen him. He helped me escape confinement on Earth."

Sarii covered her mouth, gasping. Eena wasn't sure if the woman would scream or cry.

"I'm telling you the truth, I swear. I'm sorry I couldn't tell you earlier." She waited while Sarii grappled with the news.

"Can…can I talk to him?" Her eyes watered at the thought.

"You can do more than that," Eena said. "I want to take you to him, but you have to trust me and do exactly what I say. Understand?"

Sarii nodded eagerly.

"I can't go into detail right now, but I think your life as well as my own may be in danger. You and the boys need to come with me now. Derian's going to take us to the Kemeniroc."

"Kahm Derian?" Sarii reacted immediately to the name. "Sha Eena, no! We can't trust him!"

"Trust *me*, Sarii. Derian is not our enemy; Gemdorin is."

Sarii searched her queen's face for reassurance, and seemed to find it. "Okay," she nodded. "I do trust you."

"Go get the boys and hurry. I'm sorry you won't be able to bring anything with you; we have to move quickly."

When Sarii returned a few moments later with Willum and Xander, Derian was standing in the middle of the living room.

"Those boys have to be kept silent, Eena. And no one can let go of me or our cover will be blown." He seemed both aggravated and anxious about the whole ordeal.

"I know," Eena insisted. "I promise they'll be quiet."

When they noticed Sarii and her sleepy children huddled together off to the side, Eena motioned for them to approach. She delved into a hurried explanation of everything, giving her friends instructions on how to proceed. Derian took Sarii by one hand and the two now-wide-awake boys by the other, reinforcing the importance of their absolute mute cooperation.

"Hold onto my arm," he ordered Eena, but she was already headed off on her own mission.

"Wait, Eena, where are you going?"

"I have to go get something."

"We don't have time for that!" He was well beyond irate

now.

"Just take them, I won't be long.   I'll meet you…"   It hit her that she had no idea where he was headed.   "Where will you be?"

The captain ordered her compliance.   "Eena, come with me now!"   But she refused.

"I can't!   It's important!"

At that moment, he was sure she would someday be the death of him.   "Criminy!   Get over here!"

"No!   You don't understand—it was my mother's.   I have to go get it."

Through gritted teeth he told her where to meet up with him. If his hands hadn't been full…

Derian marched his guests to the hidden Abbos One, making sure they didn't utter one word.   Eena, meanwhile, made her way up to Gemdorin's treasure room, finding every hall vacant along the way.

The door locked at her back when she entered the room, a fact of no concern since she had memorized the combination to get out. She went for a chest of drawers shoved back against the central wall and removed the booby-trapped box.   Opening it brought to life the stone beetle inside.   Layered wings twitched with deadly anticipation, protecting the keys in its belly.   Eena remembered it was Gemdorin's encoded DNA that allowed him to handle the beetle without suffering a fatal sting.   She would need to reprogram it.

It occurred to her that a strand of hair would suffice as a DNA sample.   Aided by unnatural powers, she saw past the stone exterior, visualizing the beetle's internal mechanisms.   She forced the wings open with her mind and dropped a string of hair into the chamber.   It reprogrammed automatically, set to respond to her touch.   She fished out the key without difficulty.

The thought crossed her mind that Gemdorin could now be fatally stung by his own trap.   An ironic notion.   And yet, were it to happen, what a simply fitting end to their enemy.

Eena crossed the room, moving to a second set of drawers— the one that kept her mother's green gemstone.   With both hands she dug out the antique box, placing it flat on a tabletop.   The key slid into a toothed notch and twisted, allowing her to retrieve her treasure.   Eena paused long enough to marvel at the crystal's uniqueness, flipping it over in her fingers.   A soft, pining glow emanated from beneath her chin, and again there was a powerful draw between the gemstone and the necklace.   Knowing time was costly, she set the gem aside and proceeded to remove the pendant Gemdorin had placed around her neck earlier that evening.   She dropped it into the wooden box and slammed the lid shut, dumping it into the drawer.   Then she grabbed her treasure and ran for the exit.

Her fingers quickly entered a secret code into the panel beside the door, a number sequence she had memorized while watching Gemdorin exit the room on two occasions.   All she had to do now was meet up with Derian.

The door slid open, and Eena took a step backwards.   There was nowhere for her to go.   Blocking her escape was Kahm Gemdorin and four Ghengat soldiers with weapons aimed at the most unlikely of intruders.   Gemdorin quickly waved off their firearms.   He appeared as shocked to see the young queen as she was to see him.

"Eena?" he questioned, his gaze incredulous.   "What are you doing here?"

For a second she froze, horrified by his unexpected presence. But quickly enough, she found her voice.   Pointing at the Ghengats, she spit out her own question.   "What are *they* doing here?"

Gemdorin focused on the jewel she held against her chest. "You're stealing from me?"   He seemed genuinely stunned.

She covered the gemstone with both hands, holding it tighter. "It was my mother's.   It rightfully belongs to me."

He grabbed her hands and pried the stone from her fingers. "It's mine!"   That's when he noticed her pendant missing.

"Where's the necklace I gave you?"

In a moment of pained anger, she exposed his charade.   "I know all about that promise pendant, Gemdorin!   I know about Jase and the dragon's eye and I know how the Ghengats serve *you!* *You* sent them after me!   You've lied to me this whole time, and I believed it too!   I honestly thought…"

He grabbed her arm, intolerantly speaking over her.   "How could you possibly know these things?"

She winced at the tightness of his grip but answered the

368

question. "I heard you. I heard every word spoken by your lying tongue." She looked hard at her enemy, daring him to deny his own words.

His mind reeled in overdrive, trying to understand how she could have been privy to his conversation with the Ghengats. His eyes narrowed with concentration, attempting to sort it out. Releasing her arm, he stepped past to pull open the drawer where a container of gold wristlets was stored. He removed the cloaking bands and counted them. None were missing.

"Of course you didn't take one," he mumbled, analyzing every clue. "That would mean you were here once before without setting off the alarm. And obviously, the fact that I caught you here now trying to steal my gem—"

"It's *mine*," she spitefully corrected.

He continued as if she had said nothing. "—that proves you had no idea there was a silent alarm in this room." He thought again, long and hard. When the truth came to him, his face relaxed, painted over with smug confidence. He turned to address the Ghengat soldiers.

"Go search the ship; we have an intruder aboard. And use your wristbands so you can see him. Derian is here and he's cloaked." Gemdorin watched Eena as he delivered his orders, looking for a reaction to his assumption.

She panicked for a split second. Gemdorin caught the momentary widening of her eyes, the rise in her shoulders, and the brief, involuntary gasp.

He knew he was right.

With sure steps he approached her. "You didn't find these things out on your own, did you? To do so would have taken suspicion and foresight—two things you don't possess. You are far too trusting and impetuous. Derian put you up to this, didn't he? But how did he manage to get aboard my ship undetected? Don't tell me; I'll figure it out. You know I will."

She denied his allegation. "That's ridiculous. I have no idea what you're talking about." But the words were unconvincing even to her.

"Nice try," he chuckled. "Your tracking chip is gone. It's still in your room, which is why I had no idea it was you snooping around in here. But you didn't discover the chip on your own,

369

did you? Someone removed it for you. Someone smart enough to know I'd planted it there." A smug grin spread askew as his confidence increased. "Derian's definitely here. And thanks to you, I'm going to find him."

Dread chilled her to the bone. What had she done? What horrible mess had she gotten Derian and Sarii into?

The remaining Ghengats were ordered to take their intruder to the brig.

"No!" Eena hollered. "I've done nothing but reclaim what was mine!"

"Wrong." Gemdorin began to pace a tight line as he listed off her crimes. "You broke into my property and removed a valuable item with the intent of stealing it. You betrayed me by conspiring with the enemy. And clearly you've allied yourself with that rogue, proving yourself a downright traitor—an unwise move considering I'm the one who has provided for you and protected you all this time. Had I not hurried down here tonight and stopped this deceitful act of thievery, you more than likely would have run off with my conniving little brother!"

"You're the conniving brother! You're the deceiver! You weren't protecting me, you were using me! You lied about everything! About Derian! About the Ghengats! About Jase! You're the one who killed Jase and then led me to believe it was my fault!"

The pacing stopped, and Gemdorin thrust his face in hers. She automatically shrunk back. "It *is* your fault! If you had stayed away from the boy in the first place, he would never have come into harm's way!"

"Liar," she snarled.

The far exit slid open, interrupting their argument. Gemdorin turned around to find his brother in the hands of two Ghengat soldiers. They shoved their captive inside—an easy catch roaming nearby. He had been following the signal from Eena's tracking chip, the one discreetly slipped into the pocket of her nightgown earlier. Of course, he hadn't wanted to lose her again.

Gemdorin laughed out loud at the sight. "You both make this far too easy!"

Derian and Eena exchanged furtive glances. This didn't go unnoticed by their enemy who turned to the young queen first.

370

"Are you sure you want to choose Derian over me?"

She stood tall, voicing her own serious charges. "You are a double-crossing liar, a despicable thief, a self-seeking user, and a cold-blooded murderer!"

Gemdorin laughed again. "And still you would find yourself better off with me than with the disappointing failure my brother has turned out to be. You'll never make it to Harrowbeth in his care. You will never see the light of day on Moccobatra as his queen. But at my side, my dear.....you could be queen of many worlds."

He moved in closer until his lips nearly touched her ear. His words were spoken with quiet conviction. "Come with me and you can have whatever your heart desires. Join me, Eena. Stand beside me and we will be the most powerful couple in the galaxy. Worlds will fear and honor your name. Together we can have everything we want."

Eena closed her eyes through his whispered invitation. How could she not have seen what kind of man he was—his true selfish motives? She contemplated her reply, knowing great consequences would follow. When her eyelids lifted, she responded bravely.

"I didn't accept this necklace for power or supremacy. I didn't take it to have people fear me or bow to me. I have never wanted anything like that. I took on this calling, Gemdorin, to help a desperate people recover their homes and their lives and to rebuild what you destroyed. I don't want what you offer, and I certainly don't want it the dreadful way you would go about getting it."

Gemdorin pulled back, scowling disgustedly. "You're both pathetic."

He turned his attention to Derian next. "The only thing I want to know is how you managed your way onto my ship in the first place." Snatching his younger brother's forearm, he pushed back the sleeve. A gold wristband held snug to his tensed muscles.

Gemdorin ripped off the wristlet and turned it around in his fingers. There was a clear fissure line where the device had been altered to separate and reattach as needed. His face brightened instantly, finding the missing piece to the puzzle. There was no doubt in his mind where this cloaking band had come from.

"Rhoen," he grumbled.   Gemdorin recalled his last conversation with the spy where he had explained how to sever the device in order to cloak a ship.

Derian remained statue-still, his eyes glued on Eena who could hardly glance at him.

"How did you get this from Rhoen?" Gemdorin demanded.

Derian kept his silence.   His brother grabbed him by the collar and pulled his face close.

"Did you find him out?   Did you steal it?   Or did the coward give it to you?   Did Rhoen think he could help you retrieve your pitiful little queen?"

Derian's only response was the tightening of hate-filled eyes.

"It doesn't matter anyway.   The traitor's family will pay for his treachery."   Gemdorin turned to his Ghengats.   "Go find Sarii and her boys.   Bring them to me."

"*No!*" Eena reacted on instinct, terrified for her friends. Things had gone awry—all of it her fault—but she couldn't allow anyone to harm Rhoen's family.

The necklace awakened in a sudden burst of light.   She stretched her arms toward Derian's captors and shot a white pulse of energy from her fingertips, hitting her targets straight on.   Two Ghengats fell to the floor.   She repeated the same action without pause, successfully knocking out the remaining guards.

Derian took advantage of the situation and grabbed his severed wristband from Gemdorin.

"Run, Derian!" Eena cried.   "Get out of here!"

But he wasn't about to leave her behind.   His hand balled into a fist before making contact with Gemdorin's gut.   The scoundrel doubled over.

"That's payback," he growled.   "Let's go, Eena!"

She ran past her enemy before he could catch his breath enough to react.   Derian rolled the band onto his arm and activated the device as they took off down the corridor.

"Take my hand," he called, reaching rearward for her.

"They can still see us; they're cloaked too!"

"Not all of them."   He grabbed her outstretched fingers, concealing them both.

The quickest route to the docking bay was straight down by

elevator.   It occurred to Derian that a swarm of Ghengats might be waiting for them, but he would chance it.   He pulled Eena inside the lift, pressing himself against a side wall while shoving her further past him so neither could be seen when the doors reopened.   Then he drew a weapon from his boot.   He counted their descent, one deck after another.

"Come on, come on…" Eena muttered anxiously.

The elevator came to a jerky halt two decks early.

"They've stopped us; we're trapped."

Eena slammed her palm flat against the control panel.   "Not necessarily.   Where do we need to go?"

"Down to the hangar—bottom level."

The necklace glimmered and the elevator started up again, taking them to their destination.   Derian was both shocked and thrilled.

"Impressive."

When the doors cleared, they remained against the wall out of immediate view.   Cautiously, Derian peeked around the corner. Not a soul was in sight.   How lucky could they be?

"Let's go."   He released Eena's hand, gesturing for her to follow him.   While jogging across the hangar, he turned off the cloaking device and prepared it for insertion into the ship's controls; it was necessary for cloaking the Abbos One before taking off.

Eena kept close at his heels.   Derian sensed her right behind him until she squealed.   When he looked back, she was on the ground whimpering, tenting her nose with both hands.

He turned back to help, concerned by how she palmed the air with flat fingers.   It looked like she was pressing against an invisible wall.   Eena rose to her feet and felt along the air in each direction, only to discover she was trapped in on all sides.

Derian felt at the wall himself.   "Can you get past it?" he asked.   He then collapsed, squeezing at his side, moaning in agony.

Eena gasped and dropped to her knees.   "What happened, Derian?   I can't reach you—are you okay?   What happened?"

Out of nowhere, Gemdorin appeared, grinning from ear to ear. He was holding tight to a long metal rod.   Somehow he had managed to reach the docking bay first, anticipating their coming.

"Eena's not going anywhere with you," he hissed at his injured brother. "She's mine now."

Derian looked up from the ground, still hugging his side. "Over my dead body," he breathed.

"I'm nothing if not accommodating."

Gemdorin raised the steel rod above his head and prepared to strike again. But Derian reacted quickly, kicking at his brother's exposed midsection before sweeping his legs right out from under him. The captain of the Kemeniroc then jumped to his feet, prepared to fight.

Gemdorin stood up just as quickly, and the two circled each other, eyes locked in a deadly stare-down. Eena held her breath. The scene paralleled her dreamed confrontation between two dragons.

Derian's firearm had dropped and skidded out of sight when he was first attacked, leaving Gemdorin as the only man with a weapon; he lifted the metal rod high. Derian didn't wait for a swing, but sprang forward and struck his rival in the face with a vicious round kick. Gemdorin recovered quickly and swiped at his brother's head with the steel bar, intent on bashing in his skull had he not ducked. Eena shrieked at the near miss; her cry echoed throughout the open hangar. Without pausing, Gemdorin brought the rod around and jabbed at Derian's ribs only to have the end seized and yanked away. It fell to the floor and rolled off, a loud clanking resounding in every direction. Derian took the opportunity to fully attack his now unarmed enemy. They wrestled with bare hands, landing brutal punches.

Meanwhile, Eena was desperate to find a way out of her prison. She called on the necklace to force the barrier back, but it wouldn't budge. Her energy seemed to transfer directly into the wall with no noticeable impact. She attempted a force field of her own, hoping to make a separation in the wall large enough to escape through, but the very second it appeared to hold, the original force field toppled hers, creating an even stronger barrier. She realized the structure was adjusting, strengthening as it thwarted her attempts at escape. Desperate and frustrated, she brainstormed for a solution, keeping one worried eye on the struggle taking place before her. She could see it was anyone's fight at the moment.

Both men suffered some harsh blows.   Blood trickled down Derian's cheek from a nasty gash inflicted by a hard jab.   But Gemdorin was also bleeding, enduring a torn lip where a ruthless side-kick had landed.   Neither one had any intention of backing down.   Eena gasped when Gemdorin struck at Derian's face again, but the younger brother blocked the punch and struck back, hitting his assailant in the neck.   He then landed a forceful kick to the stomach, sending Gemdorin down, skidding across the floor. The slide sent him beneath the belly of a Ghengat glider.

What happened next was unfortunate.   It was also déjà vu. Eena remembered the scene vividly from her dreams.

While on the ground, Gemdorin spied Derian's weapon beneath the glider.   It had landed in the shadows, dropped at the beginning of their fight.   Gemdorin reached above his head and grabbed hold of the firearm.   He pointed it at Derian who froze.

"You lose again," Gemdorin sneered.   And then he fired a shot.

"*Nooooo!*" Eena screamed, already aware of how things would unfold.   She had witnessed this future in the dragon's eye in a dream.

Derian dodged, but was grazed by a laser blast, enough to cause a nasty burn across his arm.   Realizing he was in serious trouble, he ran from the possibility of being fatally shot.

Eena yelled from behind the force field, "Derian go, just go! I can't get out….you have to go!"

"*Shut up!*" Gemdorin screamed at her.

"You shut up!" she daringly retorted.

She gestured with her hands as if she would use the necklace to attack him, but nothing happened.   The prison kept her from transferring her powers outside its walls.

"Ugh!" she groaned.   There was no way to help.   Derian would have to escape on his own.

Kahm Gemdorin made a string of assumptions: One, his brother's ship was situated somewhere within the docking bay. Two, since Derian possessed the severed wristband, the vessel would be cloaked.   And three, so long as the hangar doors remained sealed, his wounded nemesis was trapped inside the Mahgshreem.   Gemdorin wasted no time organizing a search party to hunt for the cloaked ship.   He called the bridge and made sure all outside access to their main computer was blocked.

"He's shut in," Gemdorin laughed confidently.

But that wasn't the case.

Derian had found no way to fly the Abbos One in or out of the hangar without knowledge of control codes or any insider to offer such information. Instead, he had landed on the hull of the Mahgshreem and secured his vessel to a garbage chute, finding a way to crawl in through the air-tight shaft. He now made his way back to the same chute, climbing out and into his own ship. Sarii and her boys met him, anxious for his return. They were fretful when Eena was missing.

"What happened?" Sarii asked, nearly panicked with worry for her queen. "Where's Sha Eena?"

The captain growled his reply. "Gemdorin has her." He worked frantically to attach the cloaking device to a plug linked to the reactor. "And if we don't get out of here now, he'll have us too."

"But we can't go!" Sarii pleaded. "We can't leave her behind!"

"There's nothing I can do right now. If you weren't with me I might chance staying, but…..I'll have to come back for her later."

Sarii didn't say another word. She felt guilty. It appeared Sha Eena had sacrificed her own safety for theirs.

"Mama?" Willum peeped quietly.

She looked down into her son's troubled eyes, knowing her own held the same anxious questions. "Shhh," she whispered.

Her arms wrapped around her children, drawing them close. They waited for Kahm Derian to pilot the ship. He broke away from the Mahgshreem, and like a ghost they headed off to rendezvous with the Kemeniroc.

Silently, Sarii offered a prayer for Sha Eena's well-being and their safe getaway—hopefully to be reunited with Rhoen.

CHAPTER TWENTY
Dead or Alive

Eena watched in horror as dozens of Ghengats swarmed the docking bay in search of Kahm Derian and his ship. She was helpless to do anything, trapped within a fluctuating force-field prison. Every glance—every passing gaze of interest by the ugly creatures—made her shudder. Their large, black eyes were like something from a child's nightmare where foreboding packs of watchful beasts lurk along a dark perimeter, waiting for the chance to inflict deadly harm.

When Gemdorin felt confident that the hunt for his brother was in hand, overseen by Grah Raugh, he turned his attention to Eena. He stood just beyond the force field, his chest puffed out in a prideful manner.

"Did you really think you would get away so easily? Regardless of how you feel about me, my dear, I own you. And I never allow possessions to be taken from me."

"No one owns me," she murmured.

"Is that so?" His upper lip twitched above a crooked grin. "Then why haven't you left? Go ahead, Eena, walk out of here.....if you can."

She scrunched her eyes at his childish goading. "I have a better idea, Gemdorin. Why don't you turn off this force field and come in." She dared him to comply with a hard look.

He laughed. "Such a silly girl. You must think I'm as foolish as you."

He swiveled on his heels and stepped into a slow pace, casting a glance at his prisoner with every pass. A serious demeanor tightened his features as he quietly concentrated. Eena imagined him internally debating her fate. She tried to act unconcerned, but the ominous silence proved difficult to bear. She was in fact relieved when he spoke up again.

Though his voice sounded cordial, he mocked her with a deliberately malicious offer. "I'll tell you what. I'll send for your dear friend, Sarii. If you cooperate with me, I'll let her live

377

for one more pointless day.   Agreed?"

Eena failed to respond.   She wasn't about to let on that Sarii and her boys were missing.   As long as Derian's ship remained hidden, they were safe.   That truth offered a degree of comfort.

"Gar!" Gemdorin hollered.   "You and your men go fetch Xander and his family.   Bring them directly to me."

The Ghengat grinned irreverently, complying with the order. "Yes, sir."

Turning back to his prisoner, Gemdorin rubbed his hands together, prepared for the next round of taunting.   He was clearly enjoying himself.

"Now then, my dear.   While we wait, I think it pertinent to go over the ground rules.   From this moment on you are considered a criminal.   As such, you will remain in confinement until your services are required.   There will be no visitations, no liberties or kindnesses allotted.   You now live for one purpose only—to follow my command."

Her glowering response only seemed to amuse him all the more.

"Are you impressed by my invisible box, Eena?   It was actually a gift designed just for you.   Good thing one of us thinks far enough ahead to prepare for the worst.   Especially now that you've demonstrated your untrustworthy nature."

"You're the one guilty of betraying everyone's trust, Gemdorin."

"No, no, Eena.   *You* are the guilty one.   In fact, I find you guilty of even worse crimes."

Her face tangled up in disbelief.   "Like what?"

"Betrayal.   Thievery.   Stupidity.   All three for which I have no tolerance."

"I never…"

His voice rose to speak over her verbal protest.   "You are the prisoner here!   I will tolerate no arguments or problems from you! Do you understand me?"

She swallowed, refusing him an answer.

"Any attempt to escape your fate or cause havoc in any way will be dealt with by the immediate execution of a Harrowbethian citizen.   Their lives rest on your head, Eena.   Do you understand *that?*"

"How dare you," she breathed.

"Oh, my dear, I will dare do far worse if you betray me again."

A hint of fear flashed in her eyes. Gemdorin seemed pleased with how his threat affected her. "I'm glad you understand.

"Now, as far as Derian is concerned—you have no chance of saving him. He's been a thorn in my side for far too long. Once he is found, he will be immediately executed, and you will have the privilege of witnessing the long-awaited end of his command. The council in Harrowbeth, even all of Moccobatra, will be at my mercy now."

"You're insane."

"No, not insane, Eena. Passionate, yes. Determined, yes. Extreme, perhaps at times. And ruthless when necessary. But never insane." His eyes flared strongly, daring her to argue any further.

She said nothing.

He went on torturing her with the crushing reality of her situation, observant of her every reaction to his words.

"It's a shame that Derian stuck his nose in where it didn't belong. Ignorance really was bliss for you, Eena, wasn't it? You could've had it all! Queen of Harrowbeth! Queen of Hrenngen! I could have made you queen of the entire galaxy in time! Such a shame. Now you will end up as nothing more than a common, dirty slave to the Ghengats. But don't think I have no compassion. Perhaps, with good behavior, you can earn a place back on the Mahgshreem serving me. That is if you live long enough."

Eena had lowered her eyes, not bothering to look up anymore. It was impossible to hide her bleakness. Gemdorin was trying to frighten her, she knew that. But she also understood that any real chance of escape had left with Derian.

"Kahm Gemdorin." They both heard Gar's voice, but only the captain turned to the approaching Ghengat. "Sir, we can't find Xander or his family. They're not in their quarters or in the commissary. We've searched both decks thoroughly."

Gemdorin's mood instantly wilted. He turned his anger on the prisoner, demanding an explanation. "Tell me where they are!"

Eena said nothing, eyes fixed on the floor.

He demanded more severely, "Where are Sarii and her boys? Tell me!"

Her jaw tightened refusing him an answer.

At last he lost his temper, banging both fists against the invisible barrier. For the first time, Eena was actually glad it stood there. *"You worthless varlet, tell me where they are!"*

A tiny smirk touched her lips, knowing she had gotten one over on him. Silently, smugly, she looked up just enough to meet his ferocity.

"Our agreement is off! When I find her, AND I WILL, Sarii will be executed along with both of her useless boys and my troublesome brother! And you, Eena, will be there to watch them die! When you interfere in the lives of others, this is what happens!"

He stormed off, shouting at the Ghengats who were still searching for Derian. A few moments later, the hangar doors parted and a swarm of gliders left the ship. Eena prayed that her friends now had enough of a lead to safely steal away. There was nothing more she could do to help them.

Gemdorin returned shortly after the fleet dispatched. He was followed by four Ghengat soldiers holding two young girls at knife point. The girls were in tears, terrified by their captors. Gemdorin ignored the timorous weeping.

"We are all here to escort you to the brig," he informed Eena. "If anything goes amiss between here and there, these men have orders to slit the throats of both children. Understood?"

She observed the young faces, so frightened. Their eyes screamed for help. Pained by the sight, her reproving gaze shifted to Gemdorin. "How could you?"

"Understood!" he repeated without the slightest hint of feeling.

She nodded.

Using a handheld control, he shut down the force field and motioned for her to walk ahead of them. The company escorted her up to the brig where she was placed in a cell secured by the same invisible force field.

She was left alone on a cold, bare floor, facing a wooden bench so thin and aged it demanded a great deal of courage to put

380

to use.   A corner latrine sat in open view.   Other than these meager objects, her cell was empty.

Eena paced the floor for a while, but the sluggish passing of time eventually forced her onto her knees, too afraid of the rickety bench to chance supporting her weight.   She wondered if Derian would come back for her, or if the opportunity to be rescued had been ruined completely.   Now that Gemdorin knew his brother had a cloaking device, he would prepare for its use.   And if Derian did manage to return, how would he free her from this invisible prison?

Hours passed before Gemdorin entered the brig again.   Eena stood up to face him, expecting a harsh tongue.

"It seems, Eena, that every soul unlucky enough to have crossed your path has suffered dreadfully from your poor judgment.   I'm here to report that Derian's ship was found and successfully destroyed.   He, Sarii, Xander, Willum, and even Jase are all dead now because of you.   You never should have attempted to save them.   I'm sure Rhoen will soon wish you hadn't interfered in his personal matters.   His entire family would have been better off not knowing you."

Her head shook strongly at the news, unwilling to believe. "No, no, you're lying."

But the satisfaction on his face was resolute.   He stepped up to the cell bars that stood between them and with intimidating authority delivered the rest of his speech.   His eyes gleamed, unwavering in potency.

"On the contrary; you were the best lure I could have asked for.   You effectively managed to bring Derian right to me, making him completely vulnerable in the process.   I still can't believe the fool came alone!   Tracking his ship was easy; his vessel was far primitive compared to my arsenal.   He had no chance of outrunning an entire fleet of cloaked Ghengats!   And now, because of you, he'll no longer be a nuisance always managing to dodge my sword.   I've been trying for years to get rid of him, and finally—*finally*—you provided me the perfect opportunity.   I suppose a 'thank you' is in order."

His words burned like acid as they hit her ears.   It couldn't be true.   Derian always escaped.   Countless times he had eluded his brother's grasp.   He couldn't be gone now, not because of her!

She refused to believe it, shouting at Gemdorin while she backed away.

"Shut up; I know you're lying! It isn't true......I didn't kill him!"

The retort to her outburst was cruel. "You're not fit to be queen, Eena. Harrowbeth may wilt and die—even so, it is far better off without the likes of you."

"You're lying," she repeated, weaker and less sure. She felt a quiver of doubt in her voice.

"I'm afraid not." Gemdorin's malevolence burned clean through her as he squelched all hope. "Derian's ship was obliterated. Blown to shreds. No one could've survived the explosion. Thanks to you, my brother is certainly dead."

She covered her mouth, horrified.

"No, no," she cried. Her retreat was stopped by a confining wall where both legs buckled under, dropping her to the floor. She cowered against the block, her face buried in trembling hands. Tears of guilt and anguish collected in her palms, shed for the loss of her friends. If only she had never been born—not on any planet. Gemdorin taunted her no further, leaving her alone to suffer thoughts of regret.

Eventually, she fell asleep and slipped into another nightmare....

The forest was dark. Heavy, gray clouds stretched out overhead as the wind blew wildly, tossing leaves and twigs into the air. She made her way to a small clearing when a familiar, young dragon fell from the sky. His tail smashed against the ground beside her. He turned to face the young queen, his eye gleaming with the semblance of a round, red gem.

"I'm not afraid of you!" Eena stated boldly.

He made no sudden moves, having no intention of attacking at the moment. His head cocked sideways as he watched her through narrowed eyes.

"They both came true," she said, daring to speak to the beast. "What you showed me would happen in the future, it came true. The Ghengats attacked me. And Derian......he was defeated by his brother, just like in your awful visions."

The dragon cocked his head to the other side, never diverting his gaze.

"Are these images you show me the only possible future? Are the events predestined, or can they be altered? I need to know."

Her fists balled up when he didn't answer. She asked again, demanding a reply.

"Tell me, dragon! Is this future you show me set in stone?" The beast continued his silence.

Frustrated, she paced a few strides in front of him and then made a third attempt.

"When you showed me the Ghengats, Jase wasn't there. But he was with me when it actually happened. Does that mean your visions can change?"

Irritated by his refusal to respond, she shouted at him. "Answer me! I have to know!"

The young dragon reacted by rearing his neck. Eena ducked, afraid of what would come next. It was a deafening scream that rose from the creature's throat to penetrate the forest, forcing Eena to cover her ears. When he snapped his mouth shut, he thrust his head directly in her face. She fell backwards, startled by his swiftness. As fast as possible she found her footing and focused on the gem in his eye where a swirling mist cleared to reveal another vision.

The planet Hrenngen hovered before her, just like the three-dimensional image she had seen projected from the navigational platform in Gemdorin's treasure room. The scene zoomed in to the planet's surface where a massive group of people were under the control of Ghengat soldiers. A moment of observation showed the people being used as slaves, forced to mine caves dug into the sides of three joint volcanoes. The scene altered again.

An exhausted young boy worked alone outside the mines, hauling rock from the mouth of a cave to a dumping ground. Her heart ached for the abused child. When he turned, Eena recognized Jase's bruised and soiled face staring back at her. She was stunned.

"He's alive? Are you telling me Jase is still alive?" Incredulity drained her face of color as she dared to believe Gemdorin hadn't killed the boy. A lump caught in her throat as she continued watching, anxious for the scene to unfold.

383

Jase struggled to lift and dump a wheelbarrow full of rocks. It was plain to see he was drained beyond fatigue. At one point he collapsed, unable to push himself up from the ground. This attracted the attention of a Ghengat guard who yelled for him to rise and resume his labors. But the young man was too weak. The Ghengat marched over and dug his boot into the boy's ribs. Every attempt to rise after that was met with a swift kick that knocked Jase back down to the ground. What followed was worse.

A woman entered the scene, running to assist the boy. Despite a rough and grimy appearance, Eena recognized herself immediately. It was safe to assume she was also a prisoner on Hrenngen, working the mines alongside the others. She ran to Jase, only to have the riled guard swing his stick at her. He was stopped easily enough, shoved aside with a force provided by her glowing necklace. Then she turned to the boy and helped him up, offering a moment of compassion. Eena watched herself touch his chest and transfer a portion of her own energy to help him continue. But someone else was watching too.

Gemdorin approached from behind, visibly upset. The next thing she knew, he had grabbed Jase by the shoulder and was pulling him close. Her dreary image screamed as she witnessed a dagger pierce the boy's heart.

"See what happens when you interfere? The pest should've died a long time ago." These words were grumbled as justification for his evil actions.

Eena tore her eyes away from the prophecy, shouting at the dragon. "Noooo! This can't happen! Tell me this future can be altered! What's the point of showing me these things if there's nothing I can do about it? Or is that what you want? Do you want to see me suffer?"

Her attention was drawn back to the dragon's eye where a dark mist was erasing the first vision. There, another scene unfolded.

It began identically to the first, only this time she hesitated assisting the boy. Every fiber of her being longed to run to him, to save him, but for some reason she didn't. Instead, she stood helplessly by and watched a guard kick Jase again and again, beating him with a heavy stick as well. When she feared he would

384

die from the beating, Gemdorin's voice called out to the Ghengat, ordering him to leave the child alone. Eena peered over her shoulder to find the captain's gaze fixed on her. Jase was hurt, badly, but he was alive. At least he was alive.

"So it can be changed," she concluded. "That's what I wanted to know."

The dragon growled and reared his head—a distinctly threatening move. Eena understood he was preparing to spit fire. She called upon the necklace to form a shield of energy for protection, but as the necklace flickered in preparation, her protective dragon swooped down from the sky and dropped directly in her path. He stood as a screen, just in the nick of time. The beasts screeched at each other with comparable ear-piercing cries before flying off and disappearing in the darkness.

Eena woke up the next morning on a cold floor in the brig. Ian had failed to appear in her dreams, and she could only assume he had stayed awake, anticipating Derian's return.

Sitting up from the floor, she pulled her knees in and buried her face, burdened by guilt for all that had gone wrong. Ian would grow increasingly worried the longer Derian failed to show. Soon enough, she would have to explain why he was never coming back. Her stomach twisted up, knowing Derian's death was her fault. If only she had kept her big mouth shut and not breathed a word to Gemdorin. If only she had left with Derian and Sarii to begin with rather than going after that ridiculous emerald gemstone. Why was she so crazily drawn to it anyway? After all her efforts, she was without it and forever deprived of her dear friends.

Hours dragged by with no visitors. Hunger pains bothered Eena early on, but subsided as the morning passed. There was nothing to do but think—a torture, given her excess of guilt. Combined with a tendency to worry, it all sent her spiraling down an invented road of dire consequences in store. She resigned herself to whatever suffering lie ahead, believing she deserved far worse. Punishment was warranted for such absolute foolishness that had caused the deaths of her friends. Gemdorin was right. Harrowbeth was better off without her.

Eena thought back to the evening Ian had convinced her to put on the necklace.   She cried thinking about it, remembering how she had tried to tell him she was unfit for the calling.   She lacked the essential qualities of a good queen: bravery, strength, experience, wisdom…   Especially wisdom.

"I'm such an idiot," she condemned herself.   "I trusted the wrong person, made all the wrong choices, said all the wrong things.   I'm such a fool."

This train of thought made her cry even harder.   It was exactly what Gemdorin wanted, but she couldn't help herself. She was caught up in the agony of wishing over and over and over again that the hands of time could turn back for just a few hours. If only she had listened.   Her heart broke understanding no amount of remorse could undo the past.

"I'm sorry, Derian," she whispered as if speaking to his spirit. "I'm so sorry Sarii."

When a pounding headache set in, she pushed herself up and began walking a slow circle inside her cell.   For a moment, she worried about herself.

What would become of her?   Gemdorin would surely allow her to live for a while.   He had admitted to needing her help locating the dragon's eye.   And her latest vision had revealed a period of time spent on Hrenngen.   She felt confident this prediction would come to pass, which meant she would live long enough to see Jase again.   A tiny bit of comfort existed knowing she wasn't responsible for *his* death.   Not yet, anyway.

The afternoon came and went in solitude.   The only way to tell it was midday was by the return of compelling hunger pains. Eena pressed against her upset stomach, attempting to dull the ache.   She began to wonder if Gemdorin planned to starve her to death.   While it was true the necklace could protect her from a multitude of possible fatalities, surviving starvation didn't seem possible without some sort of sustenance.   Soon enough the hungriness passed, overshadowed by other grievances.

It was evening when Eena heard movement outside the brig. Her stomach told her it was dinner time, grumbling its complaints again.   The pains seemed prominent around mealtimes.   Eena looked up when a large Ghengat entered the room.   He said nothing, switching off the force field long enough to access her cell and slide a small tray toward her.   A single slice of bread slipped off the dish.   Eena was more interested in the cup of water.

As soon as the force field reactivated and the soldier left, Eena grabbed the cup, grateful for something to moisten her throat. She gulped downed every last drop and then broke the bread into small fragments, nibbling on one after the other to make the meal last longer.   Perhaps it would convince her stomach she was getting more than one measly slice.

After an inadequate dinner, Eena curled up next to the rickety bench, preferring the floor for a bed.   Resting her head on both knees, she tried blocking out unpleasant thoughts.   She was tired of worrying and wrestling with regrets.   Soon, she would fall asleep and have to face the unpleasant task of telling Ian the awful news.   As consciousness began to slip away, the door to the brig swooshed open.   Her eyes glanced in that direction.

Gemdorin was back.

Eena let her eyelids close.   He had already won; did he have to gloat yet again?   Why couldn't he just leave her alone?

She didn't bother looking up when his footsteps brought him to a standstill beside the cell.

"You know I don't want it to be like this."

Eena crinkled her brow at the sound of his voice, traveling to her ear like a secret confession.   She couldn't help but peek to be sure it was really him.

"I understand it was Derian who spoiled everything.   He purposefully tainted your view of me and forced you to go along with him.   I know none of what happened was your idea or your desire, Eena."

She didn't get up, but spoke from her curled position.   Her voice was weak, still heavy with despair.   "Derian didn't force me to do anything."

"But if he hadn't influenced you, we would be enjoying a pleasant dinner again, telling stories and laughing.   I'm sure that would be the case.   You would be happy......and so would I."

Eena chuckled without amusement.

"You have to admit we shared some very enjoyable evenings, didn't we?   There's really no reason we can't put this whole mess behind us and start from where we left off."   He sounded genuinely serious.

"You forget," she reminded him, "I heard your conversation

387

with the Ghengats. This isn't about Derian, it's about you."

"Alright," he admitted with an acquiescent sigh, "so I'm not everything you'd hoped for. But really, what man can ever live up to any woman's terribly high expectations?"

This got her attention. She almost stood up to face him, but decided it wasn't worth the effort. Leaning forward, she retorted, "Expecting a man to respect you, to be honest with you, and, oh yes, to not be a shameless murderer—I don't think those are overly high expectations!"

He shrugged, casually excusing his faults. "Nobody's perfect."

"What do you want?" she finally asked, exasperated.

He squatted to her level and stated his desire. "I want you."

Eena thought the expression on his face—the look in his weary blue eyes—appeared strangely sincere. But there was one thing she had learned from all this: never trust a master of deceit.

After a long pause she reminded him, "You already have me. I'm your prisoner, remember?"

"I don't want you to be stuck in there any more than you do."

Seeing the tiniest glint of opportunity, she immediately beseeched him. "Then let me go."

"You know I can't do that."

"Why not? For once in your life do something unselfish? Let me go to Moccobatra. Let me save our world and our people. What would it hurt for you to just let me go?"

"I have things for you to do."

She rolled her head backwards and laughed up at the ceiling. "Like finding that stupid dragon's eye?"

"Yes. I need it."

"To put an end to a war you've already won?"

"It's not over yet."

"Derian's gone! It's over!" Her face went back to her knees as she teared up again.

"Why do you choose him over me?" Gemdorin asked. She could hear the jealousy straining his voice.

"I never chose him. I chose you when I thought I knew you." She lifted her eyes to look directly at him. "It's not Derian's fault this happened, it's yours. And I don't know why you even stand there pretending to care about me when I know from watching how callously you spoke of me to your Ghengat friends that you don't. All you want is that stupid dragon's eye and my stupid necklace, and I'm sure when you finally get your hands on them you won't need to pretend to care for me anymore! In fact, you can just rip out my heart and watch it stop beating like you probably did with all those other girls you killed!"

"Fine!" he growled, rising abruptly. "Then just stay in there and rot!" He pivoted on his feet and marched for the doors.

"Now that's the real Gemdorin, isn't it!" she called out after him.

He turned back to her with burning eyes. She met his glare without surrender.

Then he left.

Eena curled up and drifted off to sleep in a matter of minutes. It had been one of the longest days of her life.

She realized she was dreaming when her stomach stopped aching. Out of a desire for something pleasant and familiar, she imagined her weeping willow tree high on the hilltop. Beneath its swaying branches she waited for Ian. It didn't take long for him to join her. He seemed upset and worried, as she had feared would be the case.

"Eena? Eena where are you?"

She stood up to face him, already crying. The enormity of her confession was a heavy burden to bear.

"I'm sorry Ian," she cried. "I'm so sorry; it's all my fault."

"It's alright," he assured her. "You don't need to be sorry. I just don't understand……why didn't you come back with Derian?"

She delved into a frantic explanation. Her words fell out as rapid, incomplete thoughts, attempting to spill everything at once.

"Gemdorin caught me—I wanted my mother's gem—it belonged to her—it belongs to me! I didn't realize there was a silent alarm. I mean, he had a lock with a combination, why would he need an alarm too? I didn't think when he stopped me—I told him I'd heard him say horrible things—then he pieced everything together. I didn't know he would figure out Derian was there—but he did!"

"Eena, wait, slow down." Ian was trying to interpret her

patchy story, but she wouldn't pause; she wanted to get it all out.

"No, you don't understand—it's my fault! I tried to help Derian get away! I tried to help Sarii and her boys escape because I knew they'd be in trouble if Gemdorin found out about Rhoen and.....and.....everything went wrong! I couldn't save them, Ian!"

She buried her face in her hands and admitted with a muffled cry, "Derian's dead. That's why he didn't come back to you. Gemdorin had his ship followed and destroyed. Sarii and her boys were with him. I'm so sorry, Ian, it's all my fault!" She broke down in a fit of sobs.

Ian took her firmly by the shoulders, jostling her so she would look up at him. His eyes carefully searched hers.

"Eena, stop." His head shook back and forth in disbelief, shocked she would assume any blame. "Eena listen to me— Derian's here. He arrived a few hours ago with Sarii and her boys. They're all here, alive and safe. What I don't understand is why YOU didn't come back, Eena. Why didn't YOU come back with Derian?"

"What?" Her brain struggled to process the information. "Derian...is.....alive? But Gemdorin said he killed them." Her head spun, hoping this was more than some ambitious dream.

"You don't think Gemdorin might lie to you?"

"He lied?"

She gasped when it hit her Ian was telling the truth. "He lied! Oh my gosh, he lied!" The tears fell again, this time raining for joy.

"Eena, where are you?" Ian was plainly concerned for her safety.

"I'm in the brig, but I'm alright. I'm so alright now. Derian's alive! Sarii's alive! Willum and Xander are alive! I didn't kill anybody!" She was bawling, her body trembling along with the sobs. She was euphoric.

Ian put his arms around her shaky frame and hugged her close. "Of course you didn't kill anybody. It wouldn't have been your fault anyway; Gemdorin's the guilty one."

"They're really alive?" she asked again, wanting reassurance of the truth.

"Yes. Although, Derian wasn't very happy when he got here,

390

I'll tell you that.   He didn't look so good either."

"Of course not."   She wiped at her tears and then explained. "I really messed things up.   I almost got him killed."

"What happened to him?"

"Gemdorin.   They got into a terrible fight.....all my fault."

"He looks pretty beat up.   It must have been one heck of a fist fight."

"It was, but at least he's alive."   She whispered it again just to hear the words.   "Derian's alive."

"Eena, why didn't you come back with him?"

"I wanted to get my mother's gem.   I didn't want to leave it behind.   I can't explain it, Ian, there's something that draws me to it.....draws the necklace to it.   I thought I could take it easily enough, but Gemdorin caught me.   Then he figured out Derian was aboard and went after him.   I got stuck here.   Derian had to leave, otherwise Gemdorin would have killed him."

"Well, the captain's pretty mad.   He had security escort Sarii and her boys to the brig the minute he landed.   You could see the horror on Sarii's face when he ordered her locked up.   She probably thought all those terrible things she had heard about him were true."

Eena pushed away from her protector.   "That's awful!   Why did he do that?"

"I don't think he meant to be cruel, he's just upset about not getting you back here.   In fact, I tried to ask him where you were and he about knocked my head off.   That's when I figured I might have better luck asking you."

"But Sarii didn't do anything—"

"Except end up taking your place.   At least that's the way Derian probably sees it.   Don't worry about her; she's with Rhoen.   They were reunited the second she stepped into the brig. I don't think they could be any happier than they are right now, whether behind bars or not.   I went up and talked with them before I came to see you.   They're extremely grateful to you, Eena.   And they're worried sick about you.   We're all worried about you.   I was concerned that maybe you chose to stay behind. I wasn't sure what I was going to say if that were the case."

"I meant to leave with Derian.   After what I saw and heard from Gemdorin......I don't want to be here.   I hate him."

"I'm sorry, Eena."

"No, I'm the one who needs to apologize. I'm sorry I didn't believe you in the first place. You were right about everything."

"I'm just glad you know the truth now. But there's still the problem of getting you back. Do you have any idea what he has planned?"

"He's taking me to Hrenngen, I'm sure of it. I overheard him talking to the Ghengats."

"Does Derian know this?"

She nodded. "We both overheard Gemdorin talking."

Ian frowned while calculating their distance from the Ghengat home world. "We're probably five or six days from Hrenngen if we take the Abbos One," he figured. "We'll get you back, Eena. But this time just come home with us, alright?"

"Are you coming too?" She yearned to see her best friend again, in person.

He gave her a warm smile. "I'll insist."

She returned the smile, grateful for his unmatchable friendship and the calmative effects of fading guilt. Taking Ian by the hand, she sat him beside her under the willow tree. No matter how bad things were in reality, the fact that no one had suffered tragically because of her carelessness eased the pain. Her head found the security of Ian's shoulder, and he naturally wrapped an arm around her.

"What am I going to do with you?" he groaned, mostly teasing.

"Just give me a second chance," she whispered. "If you don't, Gemdorin will. He came to see me tonight. He asked me to join him. He tried to convince me he actually cares. I swear the way he looked at me—I almost believed he was sincere."

"He's charmed women before, Eena. You aren't the first. I see you removed his pendant."

"I didn't know what it was, Ian, honest. If I had known, I would never have taken it. He told me it was his mother's. I thought it was just an old piece of jewelry."

"It's a promise pendant."

"I know that now. No wonder you and Derian reacted so strongly to it." She smiled up at him. "You thought I had agreed to marry your worst enemy, didn't you?"

"You had me concerned," he said honestly. "What did you tell Gemdorin when he asked you to join him?"

"I said no, of course. I told him I was looking for a little more in a man than some thieving, lying murderer."

"Ouch!" Ian winced.

"It's true!"

"You might want to keep from angering him, though. In fact, it wouldn't be a bad idea for you to consider his offer."

She wrinkled her nose and twisted her neck to gawk at her protector. "Are you crazy? Never!"

"Don't be so hasty, Eena."

"Ian, I don't care if he offered to make me queen of the entire galaxy, you know that's not what I'm after. You were right in the first place when you said he was only using me. I should've listened to you then. I'll never forget the callous way he talked about me to the Ghengats, like I'm some object to manipulate! I will not even pretend to be nice to him. Not ever!"

"Not even for five days until we come rescue you?"

"No!"

"Okay, okay. Talk about stubborn."

Eena settled down when he dropped the issue. Her head went back to his shoulder.

"Ian, will you please tell Derian something for me?"

"Anything," he agreed.

"Tell him I'm really sorry. When he calms down, I mean. I'm sorry for messing everything up. And will you also tell him……thank you."

"I'll tell him," Ian assured her. "I've really missed you, Eena. I was hoping to see you on the Kemeniroc tonight. I can't tell you how terrible it felt to watch Derian get off that ship without you."

"I'm sorry," she whispered. "Come get me. I won't hesitate this time."

They stayed together all through the night, neither in a hurry to go anywhere. Eena closed her eyes, listening to the rustling of scrawny limbs overhead. It was the most peaceful she had felt all day. "Derian's alive," she kept repeating to herself. It was confidence all hope wasn't lost.

When conversation picked up again, it centered around her

last few days on the Mahgshreem.   Ian wasn't happy to learn about her crush on their enemy, but he was relieved to hear how Derian had set it up for her to listen in on Gemdorin's eye-opening conversation with the Ghengats.   This brought them to the next topic of conversation—Gemdorin's past.   Ian told her everything he knew about the deceptions, the battles, the near-destruction of Derian's ship, up to the point where Eena had been abducted from the Kemeniroc.   He shared everything.   And this time Eena believed him.

"The guy is an expert at manipulating people.   Like I said before, you aren't the first woman to be swept off your feet by him."

"I wish you wouldn't put it that way.   I feel foolish enough as it is."

"Sorry.   What I meant was……there was another woman, a Mishmorat back on Moccobatra who fell hard for him when all of this began.   After my father avenged the deaths of your parents by killing Vaughndorin, that left the traitor's sons without family. People shunned the boys, doubting they were much better than their father.   Gemdorin and Derian weren't treated very well. The girl who was promised to marry Gemdorin—well, her parents immediately annulled the promise.   Everyone, including the council, agreed there was good reason.   Basically ostracized, Gemdorin turned to the Mishmorats for companionship.   He found a new girlfriend among them, a feisty young woman named Kira."

"What happened to Derian?" Eena asked.   "Did the girl he was promised to back out of her promise?"

"Well…no."

"Why not?   Did her family have reason to trust him?"

"Not exactly," Ian hemmed, reluctant to say much else. "You'll have to ask Derian about it."

"Okay," she shrugged.   The disparity between both situations did seem odd, but Ian went on talking before any further questions could be asked.

"Anyway, Gemdorin saw Kira frequently.   He eventually brought her to Harrowbeth where they were always together; you could tell she was seriously in love with him.   Most people disapproved of the relationship, her being a Mishmorat and all.

Some, however, felt sorry for them. They argued that it was our own fault Gemdorin was forced to turn to another species for companionship since Harrowbeth had callously turned its back on him and Derian, condemning them for their father's actions.

"Gemdorin used this division of our people to his advantage, and in time he developed a small group of supporters. The council publicly decreed that Gemdorin and Derian were not to be punished by any member of society for what their father had done. Opinions slowly changed, and they were no longer looked upon as threats but rather victims of Vaughndorin's actions along with the rest of us.

"All the while, Gemdorin was secretly planning his attack on Harrowbeth. He convinced Kira and his supporters that he would cleanse the land of all apparent evils. His real goal, however, was to use people to gain power for himself, just like he's using the Ghengats right now. You would think they could see how they're being manipulated."

Eena had her own opinion. "I think the Ghengats are too afraid of him to do anything about it. Besides, they believe he's going to help them find the dragon's eye."

"That's what he does," Ian agreed. "He charmingly promises whatever it is you want. But as of yet I don't think he's ever made good on a promise."

"So what happened to Kira, the Mishmorat?" Eena asked, curious.

"She stood by Gemdorin when he attacked Harrowbeth and overthrew the council. Then, when Derian chose to challenge him, she got in the way. Derian would have killed his brother that day if it hadn't been for Kira. He had Gemdorin cornered at sword point when she stepped in between them, begging Derian to spare his brother's life. Gemdorin took advantage of that split-second of hesitation and escaped. He and Kira stole off in a starship along with the majority of their followers. Since then, I've heard nothing more of Kira. I don't believe Gemdorin ever loved her the way she loved him. I'm sure she was disappointed when she found out what kind of man he really is. I sometimes wonder what happened to her."

"I haven't seen any Mishmorats on the Mahgshreem," Eena said.

Ian shrugged. "We may never know how her story ended."

After a period of contemplative silence, Eena pointed out the time. She cast Ian a tentative look. "It's morning."

"I know."

"Do you need to go?"

He could see in her face that she didn't want to be left alone. "No, I'll stay with you as long as you're here."

She laid her head on his shoulder again. "Thanks."

They sat side by side, gazing out at an ever-present sunset. In between the quiet moments they talked about other things—frivolous things. But the thought of Kira lingered on Eena's mind. She knew exactly how the girl must have felt.

After a few contented hours with her best friend, Eena was jolted back into reality by Gemdorin's commanding voice. Her dream image faded as she announced, "He's here, Ian. Thank you for staying with me."

Her protector automatically reached for her as she vanished. "Be careful, Eena."

CHAPTER TWENTY-ONE
Hrenngen

"Get up! It's past noon. Were you planning to sleep the entire day?"

Eena lifted her head from off the floor. She was freezing. Her hands automatically covered her cheeks as both arms pulled in close, seeking warmth. The oversleeping combined with a forced fast had left her weak and lightheaded.

"Get up!" Gemdorin barked again.

A low grumble sounded from her empty stomach as she rose. Her hands balled to rub at her eyes, trying to focus on what was happening. Looking past Gemdorin, she counted five armed Ghengats and three teenage boys. She recognized the young men from her frequent visits to the commissary. Their big eyes were locked on her, scared and confused.

"We've arrived at Hrenngen, your new home," Gemdorin informed her. "It's time for you to experience the joy of servitude. But before we go, let's review the ground rules."

She could barely tolerate his arrogance as weary and hungry as she felt. "I know the rules," she cut in, surprised by the frailty of her own voice. "I do what you say and no one gets hurt. I get it already."

Gemdorin's eyes scrunched coldly. "Don't antagonize me, Eena."

She held her tongue but returned his tight stare.

"Let's go," he growled.

After using his coveted remote to terminate the force field, Gemdorin yanked the cell door open and took Eena by the arm. The entire company marched her down to the docking bay where a glider waited to fly them all to the surface. Eena and Gemdorin boarded the ship first, followed by the Ghengats and their captives. They took off, able to view the approaching planet through a passenger window. It was exactly like in Eena's vision—a deep red world shrouded in heavy, gray clouds.

Once they landed, Gemdorin led her off the ship. The humid

air hit like a wall of fire; every inhale felt like a hot draw of flames. The first breath was the worst. Eena fell into an immediate coughing fit, as did the three teenage boys, suffering a scorched throat with each gasp of air. Though she tried, it was difficult to quit coughing.

"You'll get used to it," Gemdorin informed her. He didn't seem to have the same trouble adjusting to the harsh atmosphere.

The young men were hauled off to be orientated to their new positions as mining slaves. Eena was held behind by Gemdorin.

She took a moment to scan her surroundings. A steep, rocky summit towered high above their heads—the second of three consecutive mountains with steaming, semi-active craters. Her eyes squinted, attempting to peer through the clouds to the top.

"The three volcanoes," she whispered.

Her eyes dropped when they maneuvered down a slight decline. A multitude of people were gathered below, engaged in demanding physical labor. Some were carting rock and soil out of caves dug into the mountainside. Bulky equipment rumbled noisily, digging and sorting through the soil and debris. The dirt appeared an odd mix of red clay and black gravel. It had a strange oily sheen. Eena noticed that plant life was nonexistent. The few signs of flora consisted of dead, fallen timbers. Most logs littering the landscape were hollowed and sunken in.

"What is all this?" she asked, unable to hide the apprehension in her voice.

"It's a mining operation. They're removing quarrin from the caves. The Ghengats call this particular volcano *Avortacrec Crater*. The two smaller ones are *Atopit*—" He pointed off in the distance to the left, then to the right. "—and *Ozatsid Crater*. Do you remember the story I told you about the liquid metal discovered beneath three volcanoes on Hrenngen?"

She nodded while enduring another bout of coughing.

He grinned as if he had won a bet. "I told you it was a true story."

"There's no dragon," she managed to rasp.

"Not yet. That's where you come in. The dragon's eye is here somewhere. You will find it."

Eena grimaced, but said nothing.

Gemdorin continued guiding her down the dirt road toward a

398

central cavern.   As they neared the work area, both the Ghengats and the toiling Harrowbethians stopped to stare.   Eena tried not to meet anyone's gaze, but she couldn't help notice how gaunt and drained the workers' faces appeared.   What bothered her most was a shared expression—one of horrified shock.   She found the attention unnerving, a fact that didn't go unnoticed by Gemdorin. Amusement tickled his tone as he taunted her.

"Oh dear, what must they be thinking, Eena?"

"I don't know," she replied curtly.

"You can't read minds yet?   Pity.   Well, I know *exactly* what they're thinking.   Would you like me to tell you?"

"No," she hissed.   He was really beginning to irritate her. She walked on, eyes pinned to the ground.

He continued with his spiteful goading.   "They want to know why their precious Sha has let them down.   They're thinking that your presence here can mean only one thing—you're as foolish as your mother was, allowing yourself to be captured and subjugated. And because of your inherited lack of good sense, you will serve the Ghengats as a lowly slave, along with the rest of your pathetic onlookers.   Today you have shattered all hope of ever rebuilding Harrowbeth.   As long as you are a prisoner here, Moccobatra will continue to die.   This is a fact they know quite well."

Eena could feel her chest tighten, the anger mounting, tensing every muscle.   He was more than irritating, he was infuriating. She swallowed hard, fighting to control her emotions, but the harsh air scorching her throat was a reminder of how long she had gone without water.   Gemdorin waited as she suffered through another fit of coughs.

They approached the entrance to the central cave where work stalled; people couldn't help but stop to gawk at the young woman and her distinctive necklace.   Even the guards seemed distracted by her presence.   Gemdorin glanced about the crowd, thoroughly enjoying himself.   He wasn't about to let up on his fun.

Speaking aloud, he exclaimed, "Take a good look, all you dreamers.   I've brought you exactly what you wanted!   Your queen!   The long-awaited Sha Eena!"   His hands clapped together loud and long—a solo, mocking applause.   "Yes, yes, she has come to join you.   To work with you side by side!" Then he grabbed her arm and finished boldly, "And eventually, to die with you—right along with your pathetic Harrowbeth."

That was more than she could stand. The necklace reacted in a flash, sending an electric current zipping through her arms, striking Gemdorin where his fingers gripped her. The jolt sent him hurling backwards. She regretted the action immediately, knowing by the fury on his face there would be consequences. For a brief moment she considered striking again, but the surrounding guard might attack. There was no way she could hold off hundreds of Ghengats. Anxious and uncertain, she froze and watched in horror as Gemdorin yanked a metal bar from the hands of a nearby guard. At the same time, he grabbed the closest man by the collar, forcing the slave to his knees. The bar rose, threatening the innocent.

Eena screamed, "No! No, please don't! I didn't mean to— I'm sorry! It won't happen again, I swear!"

Gemdorin growled aloud and raised his metal club higher; it was an angry and ferocious picture.

"I warned you, Eena, their lives rest in your hands!" With those words echoing in the air, he struck his victim across the back. The man fell on his hands, groaning.

Eena begged further, tears flooding her eyes. "Please, please stop!"

The metal bar rose and fell again, knocking the man flat on the ground. His body lay motionless.

Gemdorin puffed out his chest, looming over the wounded. Right away, all surrounding company started back to work. The tyrant appeared satisfied that his message had been clearly communicated. Before marching over to the horrified queen, he dug his heel into the downed man's ribs—one last hurtful blow.

Eena could hear the victim's low anguished moans. Her tearful eyes wouldn't stray from him.

In a hushed yet daunting voice, her enemy warned her again. "Don't you dare turn those powers on me or I promise you, I will kill the next one."

She realized right then how imperative it was for her to control her emotions. No matter how angry or humiliated she was made to feel, she could not react to Gemdorin's taunting.

"Now then," he sighed as if nothing of any importance had occurred, "where were we?"

As Eena wiped at the moisture on her face, Gemdorin pulled her through the mouth of a wide cavern. It took a moment for their pupils to adjust to the dimmer interior and perceive the actual deepness of the hole. A faint light emanated from far within the shadows with no rear wall in sight. Machinery—drills and pumps—resounded from hidden pits, the sound muffled by distance. Thick, wooden supports kept the mountain from crashing down and crushing those laboring inside. Most of the workers were men or older boys, although a few females toiled alongside the others. It was exactly opposite of the Mahgshreem where Eena had spent so much time with mothers and their children. She now understood where all the men had gone. The few women condemned to Hrenngen must have really upset Gemdorin to have earned this death sentence.

They stopped before a pile of dark rock standing at waist height. Gemdorin released his prisoner's arm.

"You can start here."

She watched a young man struggle to remove a sizeable boulder from the pile and let it fall into a wheelbarrow. Once the barrow was full, he wheeled it outside while another one rolled in to take its place. A second young man worked to load it up with more black rock.

"If you want to stay alive, you will work," Gemdorin told her. "When you stop working, the guards will beat you….to death."

She bit her lip.

He leaned in and whispered in her ear so no one else could hear. "Your main priority is to find the dragon's eye. If you do that, I might consider lifting your sentence."

"And how do you suggest I find it?"

"That's your problem. But I would do it soon if I were you." Then he turned and marched outside.

Eena stood there for a moment, sucking in a burning breath. She was hungry, thirsty, humiliated, and still in shock over Gemdorin's recent performance. She remembered Roger, her earthly father, telling her more than once that *"a little humility never hurt anyone."* She regretted thinking of him. It only made her want to cry all the more.

"Get to work!" a gruff voice hollered across the cave. Eena twisted her neck to find two large Ghengats glowering at her.

401

She leaned over and put her hands on the nearest stone. Her muscles strained to lift it, but the chunk of rock was much heavier than it appeared.

"Of course," she groaned to herself. Why couldn't it be porous?

She struggled as best she could, searching for lighter bits of debris, helping fill wheelbarrows as they continuously left full and returned empty. No one spoke to her. Now and then brief eye contact was made before curious watchers quickly turned away. Most faces were miserable to glance at. She felt alone within the multitude—the outcast and betrayer guilty of bringing disgrace and apparent defeat upon them. Certainly her presence was cause for despair.

A large hand reached under her nose, taking hold of an extra heavy rock that she had attempted to dislodge. It was swiped from her fingers. Her eyes flickered up at a bearded face. A warm smile flashed behind the whiskers before vanishing. It dawned on her right then what these people were actually doing.

They were helping her.

It had taken a while to notice. She looked to both sides, finding the young men gone. They had been replaced by two of the bulkiest characters in the cavern—men with muscles capable of removing heavy boulders. They were leaving smaller debris for her to tackle, lightening her load literally. The gesture made her tear up.

"Thank you," she whispered. The man beside her nodded once in response.

Time passed in one long, monotonous stretch. No rest. No water. Her throat burned for a drop of moisture, inflamed by unavoidable coughing fits, while her body dripped with perspiration. It made the nightgown she was wearing cling to her skin. She wiped an arm across her forehead, brushing aside bangs matted with sweat. A few times her eyes caught sight of Gemdorin standing at the mouth of the cave, watching her. Then she would glance up and he would be gone. His presence was a reminder that she was to somehow find the red gemstone called the dragon's eye amidst all this mining rubble. How he expected her to perform such a miracle, she wasn't sure.

Eena tried to imagine where the treasure might be hidden, but her conclusions weren't helpful. Had it been her intent to bury a powerful gem for good, she would have destroyed it. If such was the case, she might be looking for a non-existent gem. If, however, it was simply buried, then the question begged, how was she supposed to locate one single stone amidst miles of compact rock and soil? She exhaled loudly, frustrated by her own thoughts. Someone remarked at her sigh from behind—a strong female voice.

"It gets easier as time goes on."

Eena didn't bother turning around. She didn't want to talk to anyone, nor did she care to make friends under the circumstances. Any potential friend would most likely end out getting hurt because of her anyway.

"I'm fine," Eena muttered.

She heard the woman laugh with real amusement. "I'm willing to bet this is the worst day you've ever had."

Eena thought about how Dr. Braxton had come very close to cutting open her skull back on Earth. With that thought in mind she replied, "No, actually, I've had worse."

The woman laughed again. She was the loudest person in the cave. Eena wondered if perhaps she was talking to a female Ghengat. Curiosity got the best of her and she turned around to look, surprised to find neither a Ghengat nor a Harrowbethian woman, but a Mishmorat. A striking, cheetah-spotted Mishmorat with straight lengths of charcoal hair and the most alluring dark eyes in existence. This bronzed female was the same size as Eena but observably more muscular. She appeared to be a mix of cheetah, Arabian princess, and gladiator in tight-fitting pants. Eena paused, dropping the stone in her hands.

"Kira?" she breathed.

"Hmmm," the woman grumbled. Her painted eyes scrunched with displeasure. The look was still stunning. "I see my reputation precedes me."

Eena gawked as if a legendary ghost had been resurrected. "You're alive?"

"Why wouldn't I be?" The Mishmorat strutted over to the pile of rocks, her hips swaying like a pendulum. "Where'd you learn my name anyway?"

"Uh…Ian. He told me about you. Just a little."

The two women faced each other, stationary for a few seconds too long.   This caught the attention of a Ghengat guard.   "Get back to work!" he growled, pointing his metal rod in their direction.

Kira stretched her neck to bark right back at him.   "Or what? You gonna come kiss me?"

The creature gave her a dirty look and then turned to bother the next slave.   Eena started on the pile of rocks again.   Kira stepped up to help.   One of the men moved over to the next pile.

"Aren't you afraid of them?" Eena asked, shocked by how Kira had spoken to the guard.

The Mishmorat cocked her pretty head.   "Why should I be? The worst thing they could do is kill me and end my miserable existence here."   She flashed a mischievous grin before adding, "But you better believe they'd have a serious fight on their hands if they ever tried."

Eena grinned meagerly in return.   "Is that why he ignored you?"

"They think twice before giving me too much trouble.   It ain't worth it."

Eena noticed how Kira easily moved the largest chunks from the pile, tossing them like pebbles into a nearby wheelbarrow. She didn't doubt the strength of this Mishmorat.

"So, girl, what'd you do to make Gemdorin beat up poor old Ben like that?"

Eena looked away, embarrassed and remorseful.   "Oh, you saw that.   You knew the man?"

"Yeah, I know him.   I know just about everyone in this hellhole."

"Is he okay?"

"Ah, Ben's alright.   He'll heal."

Eena asked the Mishmorat, "Will you tell him I'm so sorry for what happened?"

Kira wrinkled her pointed nose.   "Why?   You didn't do it, Gemdorin did!   And I can guarantee *he* ain't gonna apologize.   I just wanna know what you did to provoke Gemdorin."

"Nothing," Eena mumbled.

"Really?   Nothin' at all?"   Kira scrunched her gorgeous eyes, not believing a word of it.

404

"It doesn't matter; I won't do it again."

"Fine. Don't tell me then." The Mishmorat huffed indignantly, but didn't press the matter any further.

They worked quietly for a while, digging away at the mound in front of them, only to have it built up yet again by more debris deposited from the back of the cavern. Kira moved at least four times the mass anyone else did. Eena didn't try to keep up.

"You know," Kira started up after a period of silent contemplation, "everybody here is shocked as hell to see you." She chuckled. "Shocked may be a huge understatement in this case. We all figured if Gemdorin ever got his grimy hands on you, he'd slit your throat, you know, like your mom."

"You're better off not speaking to me," Eena said, bothered by Kira's words. "You'll end up getting hurt, like Ben."

The dark-haired beauty stopped working and planted her hands on her hips, almost accusatory with the gesture. Then she outright voiced her charge. "He's in love with you, ain't he?"

Eena's face contorted with incredulity. "What?"

"Gemdorin. He's in love with you."

Both repulsed and irritated, Eena exclaimed, "Absolutely not! Why would you even think that?"

"Because I know him. The man has feelings for you—that's why you're alive. I think he's punishing you because you don't love him back and he can't stand it." A crooked grin thinned Kira's cherry lips as if she found the whole thing amusing.

"You're crazy," Eena groaned. "He *needs* me, that's it. He's a selfish, horrible person, and once he's through using me I don't doubt my life will mean nothing to him." She could feel herself growing more upset and went back to shifting rocks.

Kira placed a firm hand on Eena's shoulder, forcefully turning her so they stood face to face. "You're wrong. He loves you. And if I were you, I'd darn well take advantage of it."

Eena hesitated with a response.

Kira swiveled on her heels and walked off—end of conversation. Eena was glad to see her go and went back to work, dismissing the woman's ridiculous theory.

The man who had continued on with the same pile of debris moved closer to speak quietly to the young queen. They were the first words he had uttered all day.

"I wouldn't talk too much to Kira.   She has a way of attracting trouble," he warned.

"I don't doubt it," Eena replied softly.   Then she asked, "Does Kira work for Gemdorin?"

He shook his head.   "No, not exactly anyway."

"What do you mean?   How can you not exactly work for someone?"

The man furrowed his brow, thinking carefully about his answer.   "She, uh… 'accommodates' him, if you understand my meaning."

"Oh."   Eena's face flushed.   "Oh."

He went on.   "Don't judge her too harshly.   She calls it self-preservation, and she's been able to influence him for our good at times."

Eena forced an uncertain smile.   "If you don't mind me asking, what's your name?"

"Millian."

She looked up at his tall, slender figure.   His clothes were soiled and worn.   Unkempt hair and whiskers gave him a wilderness look.   But it was the eyes she had noticed.   The gentleness in his soft green eyes reminded her of Ian.

"It's nice to meet you, Millian.   It would've been nicer under better circumstances."

They exchanged a friendly smile.

Eena noticed that all the workers had stopped and were forming a line before a square cart rolled in by a Ghengat soldier. It was obvious the crowd was anticipating something.

"Come on," Millian urged, stepping toward the others.

She started to follow when Gemdorin's voice echoed across the cavern.   He was parked at the entrance, watching her again. "Not her!" he hollered.   Everyone knew he was referring to the young queen.   She stopped dead in her tracks.

Millian flickered a glance at Gemdorin and then continued to the cart by himself.   Eena looked at Gemdorin whose eyebrows climbed high, daring her to protest.   She looked away and returned to work.   Everyone else in the cave visited the cart for a tin of water.   Millian was back at Eena's side in no time.

"When's the last time you had water?" he asked.

"Don't worry about me."

"How long has it been?"

"Yesterday," she said. "I'm fine. The necklace helps me."

Millian didn't say anything more. They continued their work, but Eena could feel the fatigue wearing away at her strength. No water, no nourishment, and no breaks….it was all taking its toll, even with the necklace's support.

After a few more hours, sunlight reached in from the mouth of the cave. Its low position in the sky colored everything a rich amber. Eena hoped the toiling would end with sunset. The thought of having to work into the night was demoralizing. Her tired mind focused on keeping her body moving.

Just one more rock, she kept thinking to herself over and over again. Just one more rock.

One rock too many had her stumbling, collapsing onto the ground. Her hands hit first, absorbing the impact. The exhaustion was too much; she wasn't as strong as the others. Her head dropped to the soil, desperate for a moment's rest. The ground felt cold and wonderful against her cheek. But her fall hadn't gone unnoticed. A Ghengat guard focused in on her immediately, shouting for her to get back up on her feet. Millian was instantly at her side offering a helping hand. She swallowed and coughed, pushing herself into a sitting position. That was as far as she could rise. Millian bent down and picked her up the rest of the way. The guard scowled, but said nothing.

"Your palms are bleeding. We need to take care of that."

"It's fine." She tried to free her hands from Millian's grasp, but he wouldn't let go. He was examining the cuts to determine how bad they were when an extraordinary thing happened right before his eyes. The wounds closed up on their own. Within a matter of seconds every trace of blood and broken tissue vanished, leaving no scars behind. Eena managed to pull her hands free as astonishment immobilized her rescuer.

"I told you," she explained, "the necklace helps me."

He was still staring at her in amazement when she fell to the ground again, this time screaming in agony. The same Ghengat who had yelled at her moments earlier had approached from behind while Millian was examining her hands. With lost patience he swiped his metal bar across the back of her legs, setting her down.

407

She cried out, taken by surprise. Her legs were on fire, burning more intensely than her lungs.

"I told you to get your lazy bones back to work!" the Ghengat growled.

Millian stepped away. He knew from experience that getting involved would only make matters worse, but his face was hot with anger as he watched Eena squirm.

"Stand up!" the guard ordered, prodding her with his stick.

She couldn't get up. Her limbs were throbbing, dead and useless. Tears streamed down her cheeks. The Ghengat swung his stick low, and Eena rolled onto her side, taking the brunt of the impact on her thigh. She whimpered, "Stop! Stop, I'm getting up!"

She turned her eyes on the monster, watching him raise his arm in preparation for another strike. It occurred to her that the only chance of ending his abuse was to engage him. Her arms stretched to grab at his foot. This took her attacker by surprise and his swing halted midair. He tried to step backwards and shake her loose, but she reached higher to take hold of his leg.

"Get off me!" he ordered, squirming like she had some infectious disease.

But she held on tight, using him as a crutch to pull herself up from the ground. When her knees could support her, she let go and the Ghengat stumbled backwards. His big eyes regarded her with revulsion.

Millian was quick to help his queen up the rest of the way, acting as a shield in case the Ghengat had some notion of engaging her again. Eena limped sideways away from the guard until she could lean on the pile of rocks. In her peripheral vision she caught a glimpse of Gemdorin standing in the cavern's mouth. Her head turned enough to catch his expressionless stare. He had observed the entire incident. She hid her face and hobbled back to work.

"Sha Eena…" Millian began in a whisper.

"No," she interrupted, "you need to leave me alone." She was concerned that his kindness would put him in jeopardy, and she didn't want to be responsible for another person's pain and suffering.

It took a little longer, but her legs eventually healed to where she could walk without limping.   Outside, a bare wisp of crimson defined the horizon.   The sky was mostly black now.   Light from the cavern's depths appeared more prominent without any incoming sunlight.   The weak backlights cast strange, long shadows on the ground.   Eena prayed their labors were near an end.   When a sudden glare of lighting switched on overhead, she almost gave in to despair.   She was ready to fall to the ground and let the Ghengats beat her to death.   At the same time, a siren sounded and she noticed how everyone stopped what they were doing.   She turned to Millian for an explanation.

"We're done for today.   We'll eat and sleep while the next shift takes over."

Eena didn't allow herself to feel any sense of relief. Gemdorin probably had intentions of forcing her to continue on with the next wave of workers, most likely without food or water, truly making this the most miserable day she had ever survived—*if* she survived.

As people began filing out of the cave, Millian motioned for Eena to follow, but she leaned against the rock pile instead, anticipating orders to remain.

"Come with me," Millian urged.   Gemdorin wasn't anywhere to be seen, but Eena was positive she wasn't supposed to leave.

When a guard smacked his stick against the stone behind her, she jumped and hustled over to Millian.   They left the cave together, following the crowd down a long dirt road that rounded the mountain's edge.   In the distance, a line of temporary housing stood in clusters—wide tents, a simple woodshed, two fire pits in use, and tables with benches protected by wide canvas coverings. They were halfway down the road when Eena was stopped by a heavy hand on her shoulder.

"Thanks for babysitting, Millian.   I'll take it from here." Gemdorin smirked at the man's wary regard.   He took Eena by the hand and started back up the road.

"One afternoon and you already have a new boyfriend.   I'm hurt, my dear."

"He's nobody," she said, attempting to minimize the man's significance in Gemdorin's mind.

"Yes, that I know."   His condescending laughter made her sick.

As he led her back to the cave where she had toiled away her day, her spirits plummeted.   The cavern appeared abandoned at the moment.   Gemdorin dragged her inside, headed for the furthest depths, their path lit by a far guiding light.   It was surprising how deep the tunnel actually turned out to be, the heat increasing with each step.   Eena wiped the sweat from her brow, coughing and choking on hot, gaseous air.   Finally, they came to a stonewall dead end.

"I believe the dragon's eye is here, somewhere beneath this central volcano.   This is the deepest cave dug so far."   He turned to Eena.   "Use your powers and see if you can sense it."

She stared at the rock wall.   If Gemdorin were to gain possession of the dragon's eye, there would be no hope for those who stood against him.   Derian and Harrowbeth would surely be destroyed.   But her rescuers were only five days from Hrenngen. If it was possible to stall for five days, chances were she would escape, and Gemdorin would lose the advantage of an unworldly tool.

"What are you waiting for?" he snapped impatiently.

She glanced at him over her shoulder but said nothing.   Even if she did attempt this, drained of energy, she doubted her ability to find anything.

"I'm tired and hot and thirsty," she complained to the wall.

"Try," he ordered.

"I'm exhausted."

"Find my gem and I will let you eat and drink and rest."

"I can't.   I have no energy."

"Do it now!"

A heavy sigh ended in an irritated cough.   It was a losing argument.

She gave in and approached the wall.   From the corner of her eye she caught sight of movement at her feet.   It appeared as if something was burrowing its way up through the dirt floor.   She scurried backwards, watching the ground burst, giving way to a centipede-looking creature.   It crawled from its hole—round and thick and more than two feet in length.   Beady eyes and active antennas darted about as the creature zigzagged across the soil on a plethora of scuttling feet.   It headed right for her.

Eena screamed, wasting no time seeking cover behind

Gemdorin. She grabbed at the back of his vest, keeping him in front of her like a shield. If this alien creature meant to take a bite out of someone, it wasn't going to be her.

"*What is that?*" she screeched, making sure Gemdorin stayed between her and the creepy-crawly.

His laughter told her it wasn't as dangerous as she imagined. Still, she wasn't interested in being near it. Her eyes followed the creature as it meandered past and toward the cave's entrance. Gemdorin pulled Eena out from behind him, still chuckling at her fears.

"It's not going to eat you, I promise," he said. "It's one of the few life forms that actually survived the mass destruction on Hrenngen. The Ghengats call it a trillot. It lives underground and only comes out at night. Get use to them; they're everywhere."

She groaned disgustedly. "Ugh, I hate bugs."

Now past the moment's entertainment, Gemdorin ordered her back to work. Eena stepped up to the stone wall again, steering clear of the hole from where the giant centipede had emerged. She was a little concerned others might follow. Placing both hands against the rock, she felt an immediate transfer of heat. It was bearable. Her eyes closed as she concentrated, using the necklace to sense what existed beyond the wall. The store of energy was tremendous. Vast amounts of liquid-metal quarrin were trapped within natural pockets in the rock.

Focusing, she sensed a separation between several veins of magma and the liquid metal trapped within the wall. Her attention turned to the quarrin. She could feel the energy contained in its chemical structure, substantial and concentrated. And highly unstable. Like a pent-up temper, it waited to lash out at the world. She realized the enormous quantity of this substance buried around and beneath these volcanoes needed only the right catalyst to blow the entire mountain to pieces. Thank goodness heat didn't seem enough to affect it. But the magma— that was a different story.

She recognized that if the magma itself were to come into direct contact with a pocket of quarrin, it would set off a violent chemical reaction. The unstable quarrin would discharge its energy and, without a directed path, explode where it stood—one large-scale release of massive power. That in turn would free other pockets of quarrin and magma, allowing them to connect, creating a chain reaction. It was a miracle it hadn't happened already. If the dragon's eye was actually buried here, she wondered, was this quarrin a security feature? Was it a trap purposefully set to keep anyone from retrieving the gem? She knew the dragon's eye was no good. Someone very powerful may have gone to great lengths to keep it from being recovered.

"Have you found anything?" Gemdorin was growing impatient.

"There's a river of magma not too far below this wall. And quarrin—huge amounts of it. There's so much energy."

"That's why the Ghengats sell it. It's a perfect power source."

"It's also dangerous," she pointed out. "It's not stable. If you were to set this off…"

"Yes, Eena, I know. They've been dealing with this substance for years now, long before you ever came around. Tell me, can you sense the dragon's eye?"

"There's too much energy. How am I supposed to find it with all the quarrin and magma?"

"Try!" he ordered.

Eena knelt to the ground and placed her hands flat on the soil. It wasn't as warm as the cavern wall, but it wasn't as cool as at the cave's entrance either. She closed her eyes and let her head fall forward in concentration. Deep underground stores of liquid metal were perceptible. In her mind she mapped out the layout—a river of magma with extended veins that ran over and under, encircling the natural pockets of energy-rich quarrin. As she slipped into a focused trance, the necklace shone more brilliantly.

She could see tunnels following the flows of magma where the trillots had dug. They thrived on the heat, needing it to stay alive. Her mind moved further into the heart of the volcano, deeper and deeper, nearing the molten reservoir. More trillots. She shuddered. That's when she sensed it.

It was a faint signal, unique from any other energy form. Her mind inched closer. What emanated from this small object wasn't a thermal power, not chemical, and not electrical. It was the fusion of something radioactive and responsive. What was it?

It seemed aware of her, virtually alive, but that couldn't be.   Yet she sensed it, an animate power.   It was unmistakable.

"Eena?"

She heard Gemdorin's voice behind her.   He sounded a million miles away as if calling her from a distant world.   A dream.   She blacked out wondering.

Ian was waiting beneath their favorite weeping willow, staring out at an autumn sunset.

"Oh crud," Eena moaned when she saw him.   "I must have passed out again."

At least she was getting some needed rest, and there were no rocks to be hauled around in her dreams.   After trudging up the hill, she took a seat beside her best friend.

He smiled, happy to see her.   "How are you doing?"

"Horrible," she groaned.

Her mood erased Ian's smile.   He draped an arm around her shoulders.   "Tell me everything."

Eena told him about the atrocities she had found on Hrenngen.   She told him about her day as a slave—the work, the intense heat, and the air that burned her lungs.   She told him about the lack of food and water and how she would give anything for one lousy carrot stick.   She described the guards and the terrible way they treated the people mining the caves. Gemdorin's behavior didn't take Ian by surprise, but he looked very angry when she described how much it hurt to be hit by a metal rod.

"We're on our way to get you, Eena, just hold on."

"How many days?" she asked, hoping they had found a way to travel faster.

"At least four more."   He sounded apologetic.   "We've got one day behind us, though, and I promise we're going as fast as the Abbos One can travel."

Eena forced a smile, trying to be grateful that at least they were coming.   "So, Derian let you go with him?"

"I insisted.   Two heads are better than one, right?   He didn't really want the company, so I had to be a pest to get him to agree.   But I did it for you."

"Thanks, Ian.   I'll be glad when you get here."

They sat silently for a moment until Eena remembered something.

"Oh! Ian, you'll never guess who I met!"

"Who?"

"Kira! Can you believe it? It was just the other night you told me about her and then there she was in all her exotic splendor. I can see why men are attracted to her. She's beautiful. Irritating, but beautiful."

Ian laughed. "I can't believe it! Kira's really there? Did she talk to you?"

"Yes, that's how I know she's irritating." Eena rolled her eyes to emphasize how much so.

"Kira was always a little feisty and opinionated. I think that's why Gemdorin liked her. Is she still in line with him?"

"No, I don't think so. Millian told me she wasn't."

"Millian?"

"He's one of the other people working the mines. He's been very nice to me."

"That's good. Wow, what a discovery—Kira...still alive!" Ian paused as if caught up in a distant memory. Eena wanted to ask him about the Mishmorat when she felt herself being drawn into consciousness. Her dream image began to fade.

"Ian, someone's calling me."

"Be careful, Eena. We're coming for you."

"Wake up, girl!"

It was a sharp female voice that jerked her into consciousness. Sitting up from a cold bare floor once again, Eena turned to face the woman. A row of metal bars separated her from the Mishmorat standing on the other side. Eena realized another cell with the same encompassing force field was keeping her prisoner.

"Kira?"

"In the flesh!" The dark-haired beauty added her unique feminine flair to the announcement. "Are you having fun yet?"

"That's a stupid question."

"You better be nice, girl. I brought you water *and* food." Kira pointed to a cup and sandwich resting on the table beside her.

Eena's mouth watered at the sight. "Did Gemdorin send you?"

Kira laughed—a sexy trill. "Hell no! Millian was concerned about you. He sent me so you wouldn't die of thirst."

"But if Gemdorin finds out..."

"No worries, I already put him to sleep." Kira flipped her charcoal lengths behind her. "He won't bother us for a good couple of hours."

"What about the Ghengats?"

"They're busy living it up. They like to drink at night, especially when the lovely Kira gives them a good spiked bottle of Krohn." The Mishmorat flashed a clever grin.

Eena shook her head. "Wow, you're really something else."

"Do you want the food or not?" Kira held up the tempting prize. Eena wondered if this woman enjoyed taunting her as much as Gemdorin did.

"Yes, please, but there's a force field. I can't get through it."

"Would this help?" The Mishmorat unpocketed Gemdorin's coveted hand-held remote.

"How did you ever—?" Eena busted out in awed laughter. "You're amazing!"

"Gemdorin'll never miss it." Kira turned off the force field and handed the water and food to Eena who downed the meal in gulps.

"Slow down or you'll get sick."

Eena paused briefly, a little embarrassed. "I'm hungry."

"I can see that."

When she finished, she handed the cup back to Kira. The two women stared at each other as if trying to find some level of mutual understanding.

"I could leave here right now, you know," Eena said. There was anticipation in the suggestion.

"No you can't."

"Why not? You could come with me."

"No way!" The force field buzzed back to life, preventing any chance of escape. Kira gracefully lifted herself onto the empty table, facing the young queen.

Eena was discouraged and perturbed by the Mishmorat's sudden betrayal. "Why do you want to keep me imprisoned?"

"Because. Look, believe it or not you're better off in here than out there facing all sorts of dangers, including a lack of food and water.   And besides, I'd be willing to bet my lousy life you don't know a thing about piloting starships."

"But *you* must know how."   Eena grasped at the bars between them.   "You could fly us out of here."

"And if by some miracle we did happen to outrun a swarm of Ghengat gliders, where would we go?   I'm sure you've heard all about my past.   There's no place I'm welcome anymore."

"You'd be with me; I'd protect you!"

The Mishmorat laughed out loud.   Eena was a little afraid someone outside might overhear.

"Get real, girl!   You can't even protect yourself!"   Kira jumped down from the table with an elegant hop and a soft landing.   She had such an alluring way about her.   "Take my advice: be nice to Gemdorin, and I guarantee he'll be nice to you."

"Never," the young queen grumbled under her breath.

"Good night, Sha Eena of Harrowbeth."

Kira left the room.

Eena sank to the cold floor, grateful for the gift of food and water.   She would have to remember to thank Millian.

CHAPTER TWENTY-TWO
Four More Days

Gemdorin roused Eena from sleep with an abrupt and voluble command. Her eyes flickered open to find him staring down inquisitively at her. Pushing up from a cement floor, she was surprised to have slept the entire night as soundly as the dead—undoubtedly from sheer exhaustion. The uncomfortable accommodations hadn't bothered her at all. In fact, the cool cement had felt good after toiling in the grueling heat of the caves. The captain started right in with a line of questioning.

"Are you feeling stronger this morning?"

Eena didn't bother giving him an answer.

"Did you happen to have another dream about the dragon's eye?"

She shook her head no.

He moved directly in front of her and asked, "Last night before your inconvenient black out, did you happen to find anything?"

"Nothing."

Gemdorin's jaw clenched as he scrutinized the girl behind bars. "Eena," he began, "are you *positive* you found nothing?"

She adamantly denied stumbling upon anything.

He made a few passes before her cell, his chin held thoughtfully between a thumb and forefinger. Eena followed his roaming gait with her eyes.

"You must be awfully thirsty by now."

Her head lowered in response.

"Find the dragon's eye for me. Once I have it, you can drink and eat to your heart's content. You won't be leaving these caves until you've located and recovered it."

"What if it's gone?" she asked, daring to meet his gaze. "What if it's been destroyed or someone else already found it?" She hoped he would at least consider the possibilities.

"It's here," he declared, utterly confident.

"How can you be so sure?"

"I *know* it," he insisted. His finger pointed at the ground, emphasizing his certainty. "I've spent over two years tracking it down. *I know* it's here somewhere."

She breathed a sound of aggravation. "Even if I did somehow sense it among all the other energy emissions, I don't know how you think I can retrieve it. You do realize that if the quarrin and magma located beneath these volcanoes ever came into direct contact…"

"—it would cause a catastrophic explosion!" He finished her sentence while rolling his eyes. "I know, Eena, we've been over this already!"

"Not just one explosion," she persisted. "The first would in turn set off the next pocket of quarrin and so forth like a carefully laid out track of dominoes! Don't you see?" She gestured toward the ground. "Whoever buried the dragon's eye meant for it to stay buried. It's not a good thing, Gemdorin, and it shouldn't be uncovered! You can't get to it without destroying yourself and everyone else in the process!"

He paused, his eyes big and eager. "You know where it is, don't you?"

She let her head fall forward, furious with herself for not knowing when to shut up. "Look, all I know is *if* the dragon's eye is down there it would take a miracle to negotiate that deadly maze and safely retrieve it."

Gemdorin stepped right up to the cell bars. "I believe in miracles, my dear. Dig up the gem, and I guarantee life will get a whole lot easier for you."

She knew she couldn't do that. "I don't know where it is."

"You're a poor liar, Eena."

He opened up her cell and pulled her out. She was surprised to find it still dark when they stepped outside the building. Just a hint of approaching dawn kissed the horizon—a mere suggestion of light outlining the mountains afar off. The fading night was still black enough she could see nearby planets shining in the sky, hovering over an ocher moon. These hours before sunrise were chilly even with a humid atmosphere. Eena wrapped her arms around herself and rubbed at her bare skin. The cotton nightgown she wore—her only piece of clothing—was too light for the crisp morning.

"Head toward the caves," Gemdorin ordered.

She took off at a brisk pace hoping to fend off the chill with exercise. A night's rest and the unexpected meal from Kira had restored her strength. No aches or pains lingered from the previous day's work—a benefit of the necklace. It was something to be grateful for.

As they scurried down a decline that led to the caves, Eena inspected her surroundings more closely. It was hard to imagine how the planet must have looked long ago, before it was destroyed by the Ghengats' world war. There was evidence of an ancient forest in scattered trunks withered by years of erosion. Most of what she assumed was once lush woodland now lied strewn as log corpses, the majority crumbled into heaps of brittle kindling. There was no indication that other flora had ever existed. Most indigenous life, both plant and animal, had long since died and turned to dust, leaving a terrain of mostly rock. This lack of greenery made large jagged boulders the scenic focus, all of it encircled by distant mountain chains.

Few people were up and around at this time, including Ghengats. Far to the right of the mountain, there was movement in the tented area where people were rising and preparing for another hard day of manual labor. Gemdorin stopped Eena before a cave located five hundred feet from the one she had toiled in the day before. He motioned for her to enter. Finding it pitch black inside, she halted, allowing her eyes time to adjust.

"Go on," he ordered, pushing her a step forward. She planted her feet, fearing what she couldn't see.

"It's too dark. What if those big bugs are crawling around?" The thought, and the cold, made her shiver.

Gemdorin reached along the wall and hit a switch. An overhead string of lights buzzed on, disappearing into the cavern. Eena followed the hanging lights, which led to a quick dead end. It turned out the cave was much shallower than the previous one.

With folded arms, Gemdorin leaned back against the cavern wall. "You know what to do, Eena."

She frowned. "And when I pass out from extreme lack of energy, are you going to carry me all the way back?"

"No, my dear, I will not."

She turned around to gape at him. "You'll just leave me

here?"

He laughed. "You worry too much, Eena. Have I ever let you out of my sight for long?"

Feeling semi-sure he wouldn't sacrifice her to roving trillots if she blacked out, she knelt to the ground. "You know this is a waste of time."

"Just locate my treasure, Eena, and pay attention to every detail surrounding it."

She was already well aware of the gemstone's hiding place, but in order to keep up the façade and prevent Gemdorin from attaining the powerful stone, it was necessary to make her efforts look believable. It seemed safe enough to expend a little energy visualizing the underground layout.

Eena pressed her hands against the grainy soil and concentrated.

She was eager to see if she could sense the stone's unusual signal more easily than before. Her mind raced to the very spot. The dragon's eye hovered in the heart of the Avortacrec Crater, suspended in a magma reservoir. Her mind moved closer to it, envisioning a spherical shape—a multifaceted scarlet ball glowing before her eyes. It seemed to beat with a weak pulse, drawing her in, untouchable for anyone else. Four more days and Derian would come. If she could keep Gemdorin busy for four more days….

"Sha Eena."

She heard her name grumbled from above. Her eyes flickered open to the sight of two Ghengats glaring down at her. One of them she recognized as Grah Raugh by the black sash worn across his chest.

Gemdorin's disgruntled face joined the others. "You passed out—again."

"Crud." Eena lifted up to her elbows. Her intent had been to preserve her energy, not waste it. But that peculiar stone was overly captivating.

Gemdorin offered a hand up which she accepted. He pulled her close where he could look directly into her eyes.

"Tell me you found my treasure."

She didn't hesitate with a reply. "Then I'd be lying."

He laughed out loud, and Eena wondered if he really found

her so amusing.

"Tell me then, what *did* you find?"

"I saw the crater and an abundance of quarrin. And tunnels dug by those trillots. There's a whole nest below here. Hundreds of them."

Gemdorin placed a thin computer pad in front of her. "Map out exactly what you saw, the entire layout beneath here."

"Why?"

"Just do it," he said. "It will give me a better idea where to dig for the dragon's eye. They'll be mining this cave shortly, so you can work outside."

The company marched toward a stream of daylight. As soon as they neared the exit, the subordinate Ghengat ran outside and doubled over, heaving up the contents of his stomach. A breeze carried the stench of vomit inside the cave. Eena plugged her nose, disgusted.

"What is his problem?" Gemdorin barked.

Raugh's nose automatically creased, flattening his notched airways. He was also put off by the smell. "I think they got a nasty bottle of Krohn last night. He's not the only one sick."

"Hangovers? I don't need this, Raugh! Take care of it."

"Yes, sir," the Ghengat grumbled. He grabbed his queasy comrade by the shoulder, and they walked off.

Gemdorin continued with Eena, seating her out in the open air on a sunlit boulder facing the caves. She went to work sketching the underground layout. It crossed her mind to create a false diagram to throw Gemdorin off, but she dismissed that plan, imagining mass destruction and the loss of innocent lives if they dug in the wrong place. So she created an accurate map, detailing everything but the sought-after gemstone. Even if Gemdorin did correctly guess its hiding place, he would be hard-pressed to exhume it without her help.

She drew a river of magma and its many veins, showing how the offshoots caged every pocket of quarrin. She even filled in the tunnels dug by the trillots, making use of her artistic ability to cartoon a fat, ugly centipede here and there. Gemdorin left her alone for a long while. Engrossed in her work, she failed to notice the many curious eyes continually flashing in her direction. It was nice doing something she enjoyed, even if the task was pointless.   It was definitely preferable to moving rocks all day.

Nearly two hours later the sound of approaching footsteps broke her concentration.

"Finished yet?"   Gemdorin's hand moved into her line of vision, stealing her art pad.   He examined her work interestedly. "A little more detail than necessary, but well done."

She was less impressed with his compliment than he was with her drawing.

Turning the screen toward her, he tapped on the very center and asked about a yawning pool portrayed there.   "What is this?"

"The magma reservoir beneath the volcano."

"And these?"   His finger circled what looked like fissure lines.

"Those are streams of magma," she explained.   "They extend around all those black pockets."

"I assume the black pockets are quarrin?"

She nodded.

"There's quite a bit more than I realized.   The Ghengats will appreciate this, no doubt."   His eyes tightened, studying her as he asked the big question.   "So, Eena, where is the dragon's eye?"

"I don't know."

"Okay, take an educated guess; tell me where you think the gem is buried?"

"I don't know," she repeated, unwilling to even pretend a guess for him.

"Of course not," he frowned.   "Very well then, you might as well hit the caves.   I can see your boyfriend over there waiting for you."   His head gestured toward the larger central hole.

Eena turned to catch Millian dumping a barrow of rocks outside.   He flickered a glance at her, keeping on task.

"Couldn't I work somewhere else today?" she asked.

"Nonsense, my dear.   Millian would miss you."

Gemdorin smirked crookedly, and Eena understood that any attempt to minimize her new friend's significance was hopeless. He had been marked.   Casting her eyes back to the cave, she caught sight of Kira effortlessly emptying a barrow after Millian. The Mishmorat also glanced her way.

Eena stood up from her boulder seat and casually shrugged it off.   "Fine.   I'll just go play with Kira."   She sauntered off, catching the collapse of Gemdorin's smugness. Intuitively, she knew he didn't like the idea of her and Kira comparing notes.

The day wore on tediously. Hunger pains came and went, less intense than previous days. She was getting use to fasting. The thirst was more bothersome, worsened by the irritating effects of the cave's hot, dense air. Her mouth suffered from such dryness, it made talking undesirable.

Millian worked by her side the entire day. Kira showed up now and then, putting a little panache into the hour. Eena longed for something to drink each time the watering cart rolled in, but Gemdorin was always present, making sure she found no relief. The second time the cart arrived he stepped inside the cave to stand beside his select prisoner. Everyone else lined up for a drink.

Eena leaned against the rock pile, stealing a break. "You know, I don't understand you at all," she said, wiping a layer of perspiration from her forehead.

"How's that?"

"You say you want me to find the dragon's eye, but you leave me no energy to do it." She turned to cough—a consequence of talking—and felt the burn in her throat. Gemdorin watched as she rubbed at her neck.

"My dear, you have a lot more strength than you give yourself credit for. Besides, you should know that the harder I push you the more your powers increase."

"So what doesn't kill me makes me stronger? Is that it?"

"I have full confidence in your abilities."

"Ohhh, why should I worry, so long as *you* have confidence…" She meant to finish her sentence but succumbed to coughing again.

He chuckled lightly at her cynicism.

"How can you be sure I won't die of thirst before I find your stupid gem anyway?"

Gemdorin tilted his head, looking mildly concerned by the question. "You would sacrifice yourself rather than help me?"

"No—but what if I can't do it?"

He resumed his sure composure. "I know you can, Eena. And as far as dying goes, the necklace keeps you alive."

"Not necessarily. It didn't keep my mother alive."

"Well, if you can't breathe, I suppose…." He let the thought trail, grinning maliciously.

"That's not funny," she snapped. "You're as horrible as your father was."

"I'm as *determined* as my father was," he corrected.

"Of course. How noble of you to continue in his reputable footsteps." Eena emphasized her disgust with her tone, again making Gemdorin chuckle.

"Your sarcasm amuses me."

"Is that what I'm here for? To entertain you?"

"No," he said, suddenly sober. "As a matter of fact you're here to work." He leaned in close to speak sternly in her ear. "Find the gem, Eena. Then you can have all the water you want."

She glared at his back as he walked off. Millian quickly reclaimed his spot beside her and resumed their endless toiling. The monotony of moving rock after rock after rock endured until late in the afternoon when shouting from outside the cave caught everyone's attention. Curiosity forced the young queen to a spot where she could see what was happening.

A boy lay on the ground near a dumping spot. He had collapsed from sheer exhaustion, much like she had done the previous day. An approaching Ghengat was shouting at him, demanding he get up and return to work. Eena watched the guard fall on the boy, impatient to dig his boot into the young man's side. The boy tried to pick himself up, only to receive another strike in the ribs. His face turned upwards to beg his attacker for mercy. Eena recognized her friend, Jase.

"Oh no," she breathed.

The Ghengat continued with his tormenting, making it impossible for Jase to rise. Anger drove Eena forward and out into the sunlight, but as she started after her friend, Millian grabbed her arm and pulled her back.

"Don't get involved. You'll only make it worse."

Her eyes widened as she turned to stare at the man. His words were a slap in the face, restoring to mind her recent, dreamed vision where she had run to Jase's assistance. Her blood went cold, recalling the consequence of her interference. Gemdorin had speared the boy with a dagger; he had murdered her friend.

Her eyes teared up as she watched the scene unfold exactly as it had in the dragon's red eye.   She stood helplessly by as the cruelest beating took place, scarcely able to stomach how the creature seemed to revel in the boy's pain.   Then she heard Gemdorin bellow from a near vantage point.   His commanding words were directed at the guard.   The Ghengat ceased his brutality at once—exactly as the second vision had foretold.

Eena twisted her neck to find Gemdorin standing tall and formidable, watching her.   She couldn't move.   Tears washed her soiled face as she thought of how close she had come to causing the death of her friend.   Her eyes went back to Jase. Millian was at his side now, helping him rise and limp toward an empty wheelbarrow.   She was thankful for this man who was putting his life at risk to be kind.   Her skin crawled as Gemdorin's shadow crept over her.

"You're learning," he said.   "It's best to stay out of other people's business.   I would hate to have seen the outcome had you interfered.   That guard might have turned his nasty temper on you."

She spoke quietly through her tears.   "You lied to me.   Jase never died; you sent him here."

"He's as good as dead anyway."

"Just go away."

She walked off, unable to forget her vision.   It made her sick knowing she kept a murderer's company.   Certainly she had known he was such before, but somehow this made it markedly real.   The images of that fatal prediction replayed in her head for the rest of the evening.   Her desire to protect Jase had nearly gotten him killed.   Knowing what the boy's fate would have been had Millian not made her pause—it solidified in her mind Gemdorin's depraved nature.

Eena finished out the day in a bleak trance.   She seemed a million miles away.   Millian and Kira both tried to draw her into conversation a number of times but without success.   She labored somberly until Gemdorin came to escort her to her cell.   There she collapsed on the floor, prepared to cry if only the tears could form.   Instead, her heart bled until sleep took pity....

Ian was waiting in her dreams.   She sat beside him under the

425

willow branches and rested her head on his shoulder.

"Another bad day?" he assumed.

She answered him with a nod.

Ian wrapped her up in his arms, understanding her desire not to talk. Huddled close, they watched the sunset in silence.

After a while, Eena whispered her only bit of hope. "Three more days?"

"Three more days," he confirmed, wishing by some miracle he could make it less.

"Eena! Wake up already!" The shouting broke through a deep sleep and startled the young queen back into reality. She opened her eyes to a spotted beauty squatting outside the cell bars looking anxiously down on her.

"By the Dirae!" Kira exclaimed. "You had me seriously worried, girl."

"Why?" The question came out hoarse. Her throat was sore. She tried clearing it, but it hurt.

"I've been here *forever* trying to wake you." The Mishmorat handed a cup through the bars. "Here. Drink this."

Eena's eyes lit up at the sight of water—the most precious substance in the universe. She gulped it down gratefully.

Kira shook her head in a disapproving fashion. "You gotta toughen up, girl. You're never gonna survive if you don't change that attitude of yours."

Eena ignored the criticism. "Thank you for the water, Kira." She turned back to the stone wall, seeking sleep.

"Thank Millian. Here, there's more." Kira held out a sandwich and refilled the cup with additional water from a canteen hidden inside her shirt. Eena went for the water first and then took the food while the cup was topped off a third time. After handing over another drink, Kira dropped her hip to the floor and started up conversation.

"You've really changed things around here, girl. A lot of dismal faces have found their spark again—a reason to hope. It's a first in a long, long time."

Eena mumbled through a mouthful of food. "What do you mean, hope?" She swallowed before declaring, "I'm nothing but a disappointment. I let everyone down."

426

"Are you freakin' kidding? The fact that you're here *alive* is a miracle! Do you know how many years I've listened to that man rant on and on about how he's gonna slit your throat someday? Gemdorin has forever been determined to rid Harrowbeth of the Shas. Yet here you are alive and well……or well enough. He watches over you like a protective crioness. On one hand you're his enemy, but on the other……he's seriously fallen for you."

Eena scoffed. "You're wrong. He's nothing but a vile murderer."

"Hell yeah!" Kira agreed. "So then why aren't you dead?"

"Because he needs me right now." Eena closed her weary eyes and laid her head against the wall. This was not a conversation she wished to have.

"No, that's not why. Maybe it started out that way, but something's changed. Somehow you've managed to pierce that stone heart of his like no one else ever has. Not even me."

It was quiet for a long time. Then a light tap—metal on metal—sent a resonating vibration through a cell bar. Eena opened her eyes to a full cup; it was the last of the water. She took it from the Mishmorat, drinking slower this time.

"I know he's looking for treasure," Kira went on. "That's why he's got us all searching those caves one rock at a time. A little inefficient for mining."

Eena said nothing, not denying or corroborating her theory.

"What I don't understand is why you won't cooperate with him a little. Lead him along, you know. At least make it *look* like you're trying to help out. He'd be a whole lot kinder to you."

"I don't care if he's kind to me or not," Eena said stubbornly. She handed back an empty cup.

"Well there's a good group of Harrowbethians out there who do care! There isn't one poor soul among them who wouldn't give his life to save yours, girl. The least you could do is try to show some interest in preserving your own sorry butt."

"What are you talking about?"

"Those tired and weary people have already started plans for your escape. I haven't seen this much spirit in them in years! They'll sacrifice whatever it takes to protect you. They need you. Hell, *I* need you. All my sisters back on Moccobatra need you.

You're our only hope, so why don't you stand up and at least *look* like you're trying!"

"I don't need anyone to save me..."

Kira cut her off with an eruption of laughter. "Oh, aren't you hilarious! Come on, girl, they're not saving *you*, they're saving *themselves!* By protecting their Sha, they save their future. Don't you get it?"

Eena stared at the Mishmorat, seeing her situation from an outside perspective for the first time. Kira was right. Her plight affected countless more lives than her own. She had sunk into a mire of self-pity, and yet strangers were willing to bear her burdens in order to save their planet and their future. She needed to be strong for them. To be an example. To be the sign of hope Kira claimed she was.

Eena forced a smile for the Mishmorat. "How'd you get to be so wise?"

The Mishmorat shrugged and winked. "Some people are just born great." She pushed her hip off the floor, hopping daintily to her toes. "So, girl, you gonna be okay?"

The young Sha nodded. "Yes. Thank you.....for everything."

"No problem." A static sputter brought the force field to life again.

"Wait, Kira."

A black waterfall of hair fell over the Mishmorat's shoulder as she pivoted back around. A thin eyebrow arched as if to ask, "What now?"

"Please, don't let anyone do anything, you know...heroic...for the next few days, okay?"

"Why not?"

"Just because." She wasn't one-hundred-percent sure this unpredictable woman could be trusted.

"Fine then, don't tell me." The beauty left with her usual sexy saunter. Eena considered Kira and Gemdorin a dramatic match. Too bad he hadn't turned out to be a better quality man for her sake.

Feeling stronger both physically and mentally, she dozed off to spend the rest of the night with her best friend.

The next morning was as crisp and dark as the previous one. Gemdorin awakened his captive early to have her search a few choice spots where he guessed the dragon's eye was buried. For some reason he believed it was encased in one of the larger pockets of quarrin. Eena was relieved it hadn't occur to him to seek within the heart of the volcano so she could truthfully say the gem was not where he anticipated.

"Eena!" he hollered, growing increasingly frustrated with her failed attempts.

"It's honestly not there, Gemdorin!" she hollered back. "Dig it up if you want, I promise it won't be there."

For the rest of the day she was sentenced to toil in the caves, a punishment she didn't mind so much. Derian and Ian were getting closer, and Kira's gift of water had helped significantly. She remembered to thank Millian for his part. The Mishmorat's words had proven a boon to her spirits, convincing Eena to exhibit some strength of character. As difficult and tiring as the work continued to be, her improved mood seemed to lighten the burden, a marvel that didn't go unnoticed by others. She caught a smile or two thrown her direction which she quickly returned. Millian and Kira were pleased to hear her respond to occasional attempts at conversation.

Gemdorin persisted in watching over her like a protective crioness, as Kira had put it, but he continued to refuse her any sustenance. She wondered if he thought the necklace was really keeping her alive without nourishment. It probably appeared that way.

Late in the afternoon, she realized Gemdorin hadn't shown himself for hours. The red sun was low enough to cast an amber glow into the cave when she finally caught sight of him hustling down the dirt road outside. His strides appeared brisk and determined. But worse was how he glared across the way directly at her.

"Oh crud," Eena whispered.

Millian looked at her with concern. "What's wrong?"

"Please, just stay out of it," she begged. Purposefully, she put some distance between herself and everyone else.

Gemdorin marched right up to the young queen, grabbed her by the arm, and dragged her up the incline to a large stone building.   She was shoved inside; a metal door slammed shut at her rear.   A crowd of Ghengats turned their large black eyes on her.

Eena scanned the room, noticing a number of blue-skinned creatures sprawled across beds aligning the walls.   Plenty of others stood over their sickly comrades.   The barracks looked like a military hospital housing several moaning, miserable patients.

"Yesterday I was under the impression that a few of these men got hold of a bad bottle of Krohn," Gemdorin began.   His voice was hard.   Angry but controlled.   "Vomiting.   Severe headaches.   Overall aches and pains.   All signs of a pretty bad hangover, which is nothing unusual for these cretins."

Eena didn't move a muscle.   She kept focused on the Ghengats glaring daggers at her.

"Now today I find even more men exhibiting the same symptoms, and I hear once again they've been drinking.   You can imagine my aggravation with their insistence to do this to themselves, making them useless to me in the caves.   Until I notice something odd."

He had circled the beds while speaking, stopping at one in particular.   "Do you remember this guard, Eena?"

She looked down at the sick Ghengat but didn't say anything.

Gemdorin screamed at her.   "*Do you remember him?*"

"No."   Her every muscle tensed at his loss of temper.

"Well, I'll tell you who he is then.   He's the guard who bruised your calves a couple days ago.   The one you latched onto and didn't let go of right away.   The one you *touched*."

Eena swallowed hard.

"He was the first to fall ill, Eena.   When I noticed who he was, it dawned on me that this had nothing to do with a bad bottle of Krohn—did it, Eena?   This is a virus, isn't it?"   He shouted the question a second time.   "*Isn't it!*"

She cringed.

He started toward her a step at a time, his anger boiling over until he was screaming at the top of his lungs.   "How.   Dare. You.   How dare you judge me for destroying those who stand in my way when you have taken it upon yourself to wipe out an entire Ghengat race!   You made them ill!   When you touched him that first day, you set this virus in motion.   *You!   The very girl who*

430

claimed she wouldn't kill anyone in this manner! Isn't that what you said? Answer me!"

Fear made her step backwards. Her fists balled up tightly at her sides.

"Don't you dare move," he warned, taking a great stride forward. She panicked and turned for the door, but he caught her. She was slammed against the wall, pinned by a strong hand at her neck. She gasped and the necklace glowed.

"I wouldn't do that if I were you."

The glow faded immediately. She feared the consequences.

"You will fix what you've done here, starting with the guard you first infected. And, Eena, if any of these men die from your virus, I will personally see to it that ten of your beloved Harrowbethian brothers die right along with him. Do you understand me?"

Her scared eyes blinked. "Yes," she breathed.

His fingers slipped away from her throat to grab at her wrist and drag the frightened girl to the sick guard.

Gemdorin pointed to the wheezing Ghengat. "Heal him now!"

Cautiously, she knelt beside the bed. The man appeared to be in a lot of pain, clutching at his stomach and sucking in shallow, laborious breaths. She reached over his chest, but he reacted hatefully, slapping her hands away.

"Let her heal you," Gemdorin ordered. The Ghengat laid his head back, struggling for air like a fish out of water. Eena cringed when her fingers touched him, affected by the pain transferred to her own senses. He kept still.

Closing her eyes, she called on the necklace to heal the very disease she had created—done in a moment of anger for the terrible treatment of her people and for the beating she had received from this particular guard. She had anticipated a longer incubation period for the illness, maybe three or four days before symptoms developed. Long enough for her to escape with Derian ahead of a plague contagious to Ghengats. Unfortunately, their immune systems had proven weaker than presumed.

She suffered the same misery felt by the infected, but endured as the necklace sent healing energy throughout his system, alleviating his sickness. As he improved, his breathing came easier.   She opened her eyes when finished and quickly removed her hands.

Gemdorin demanded to know if an antivirus now existed.

"He was too weak," she explained.   "I need someone stronger."

Gemdorin pulled her up, dragging her to the next ill patient. She knelt down and performed the same miracle, only this time altering the contagion to act as an effective antivirus.   It was powerful enough to destroy the illness, and being airborne, it would spread to all infected Ghengats.

She was tired when the necklace dimmed again, but Gemdorin hadn't finished with her.   Satisfied that an antivirus now existed, he marched her to a bare wall supporting only a row of shackles. He pulled her hands high above her head and fastened her wrists with the metal cuffs.   This left her on tiptoe facing the stone.   As she hung there he lectured her.

"I have told you and told you, Eena—cautioning you more than once not to interfere in the lives of others.   You were strictly ordered never to use those powers against me, and you were given fair warning there would be consequences.   Now, you will pay for ignoring me."

Afraid for her life, she attempted unsuccessfully to turn around.   She begged for mercy.   "Wait!   Wait, I healed him!   I did what you said!   He'll be fine now—they'll all be fine!"

"If you try to escape your punishment, I will take the lives of your new friends.   Do you understand me?"

She cried out in a panic, *"But I healed them!"*

"DO YOU UNDERSTAND?"

She pressed herself against the wall, whimpering.   "Yes."

A thunderous crack pierced the air at the same time a jolt of pain ripped across her back.   She screamed, arching in agony at the ruthless touch of a whip.   Before she could suck in a suffering breath, it happened again.   Five times Gemdorin allowed Grah Raugh to strike her with a heavy cord.   Each time she let out a shrill cry.   The strokes sliced through her gown and dug into her skin, spilling warm blood down her back.

When the Ghengat finally ceased his attack, Gemdorin approached her.   He touched the raw, open wounds.   Eena winced at the pain.   Then, every watchful eye witnessed a miracle as evidence of the beating completely vanished.   Slowly and flawlessly the gashes closed.   Purple undertones of bruised skin lightened until all that remained was the soft peach color of unblemished flesh.   No shadow of a scar existed.   The only indication that a lashing had occurred came from the shreds of blood-stained material hanging from Eena's gown.

Gemdorin turned to Grah Raugh.   "I thought I told you to give her five lashes."

"I did," the Ghengat growled.

"I see nothing to prove it."   Gemdorin ran his hand across her smooth back and then ordered that she be flogged again.

"No don't!   Please don't!"

Five more times the cord dug into her back.   She screamed with every snap, overwhelmed by the pain blitzing down her spine and through her legs.   Desperately she pled, but not with Gemdorin.   It was the necklace she silently beseeched.

"Don't heal me.   Don't heal me.   Please don't heal me!"

Gemdorin approached her again and watched as ugly gashes healed a second time.   The process took longer, but eventually her back appeared as clean as if no abuse had occurred.

"Do it again," he commanded coldly.

In her mind, she entreated the necklace.   "Don't heal me! You're only supposed to do what I want!   Don't heal me!   Oh, God, please help me!"

She couldn't help scream out loud as additional lashes tore her skin for a third time.   When it was done, Gemdorin came near. She could feel his fingers press against the raw wounds.   Her back heaved with every sore breath.   Salty tears streamed down her face as she anticipated more.

"You're not recovering," Gemdorin observed.   "No strength left?"

He leaned in close to her ear and breathed a stern caution. "If I were you, I would never cross me again."   Then he turned and ordered the Ghengats to take her to her cell.

They had to carry the exhausted prisoner.   She couldn't keep herself up—too devastated by Gemdorin's cruelty.   A couple of Ghengats dragged her across the way to a smaller stone building where they tossed her limp body onto the cold floor.   She was left alone in the dark where she crawled to the furthest corner and

433

curled up, weeping.

"Two more days," she bawled repeatedly. "Just two more days."

When Eena finally fell asleep she couldn't keep from crying in her dreams. Ian found her huddled against the willow tree. He begged her to tell him what had happened, but she wouldn't say a word. He held her tight, rocking her like a baby in his arms, worried sick about what could have caused such grief. The only time she spoke was to ask him to rub her back. He did so, tenderly, as she cried throughout the night.

The next morning Eena was awakened by the only person worse than Gemdorin.

"Get up!" Grah Raugh barked, kicking her in the thigh. He had turned off the force field and was looming like a hunter over his prey, watching her scramble to her feet. It was a nightmarish way to be pulled into consciousness. Eena cowered against the wall, frightened to find herself alone with the Ghengat leader—her assailant mere hours ago. The wounds on her back were throbbing. The bleeding had naturally stopped during the night, forming tight scabs over crisscrossed gashes. The necklace hadn't healed her because she wouldn't allow it.

Timidly, she asked about Gemdorin.

"You don't ask any questions, witch," he warned. "That fool may prefer you alive, but I don't." Raugh crowded her space, his face moving in inches from hers. His black eyes failed to blink. "Give me one reason to kill you while he's gone."

For that moment, she stopped breathing entirely.

The Ghengat retreated and pointed to the door. "Get your worthless carcass down to the caves."

She crept around him and hurried outside. The sun was already up, the entire area alive with workers. As she neared the activity, all eyes were drawn to her, both Ghengats and Harrowbethians. Based upon their expressions she guessed her wounds were a ghastly sight. She forced her gaze down, refusing to lock eyes with anyone, following the path to where Millian was already hard at work. It took less than a minute for him to shed his tattered vest and place it over her shoulders. His kind gesture was enough to make her cry. Without missing a beat, she slipped her arms into the covering and carried on, displacing one rock after another.

She didn't pause when the teardrops rained streaks down her soiled face. She was certain Millian was dying of curiosity as to why she had been beaten, and probably even more curious as to why the cuts hadn't healed like her hands had. Kira wasn't anywhere in sight, which was a blessing. The Mishmorat's inevitable questions were unwanted.

Eena hadn't imagined things getting worse, but with Gemdorin missing, the Ghengats grew bold in finding ways to make her life miserable. Grah Raugh assigned her to wheelbarrow duty, forcing an independent struggle with each load in and out of the cave. The guards made a point of walking past, taking every opportunity to swipe at her calves with their metal rods. After a couple painful blows, her anxious eyes remained constantly on watch for them. Millian did his best to position himself between her and the soldiers when they neared, turning the situation into an unspoken game of keep-away. She was again denied any watering breaks, and felt a pronounced thirst at having missed a drink offering from Kira overnight.

In the afternoon, the number of guards decreased and Millian took a chance at conversation. He kept his voice low and close.

"Why are they doing this to you?"

She kept right on working, ignoring the question.

"Sha Eena," he whispered, "why are they picking on you?"

She gave him one word. "Payback."

Millian looked confused. "For what?"

Their exchange ended when two Ghengats entered the cave, both eyeing the young Sha like hungry wolves. Millian picked up a large rock and timed his movements to put himself directly behind her as the guards strolled past. He had protected her for the moment. When the wheelbarrow was filled, Eena shoved the load forward, grunting, straining to maneuver it outside. The same guards followed her. Millian started after them when he felt a hand on his shoulder.

"Let me handle it," Kira said. She kept on their tails.

Eena had almost made it to the dumping point when her legs buckled under from a blow behind the kneecaps. She dropped her load and fell to the ground, smacking her head against a handle on the way down. Groaning, she reached for her throbbing areas. Spiteful laughter made her coil into a self-protective ball, afraid of being beaten.

"Get up!" barked a guard. He took a step forward, pivoting as if he would plant his boot in her hip. A seductive female voice stopped him.

"Boys, boys. What in the world could be so menacing as to require two big, strong, fearsome men to handle?"

The Ghengat hissed as he turned to face the female. "Kira."

"Gar." Her painted eyes glanced him up and down. "You're looking as fine as ever."

An irreverent smile crept across his scaly face.

Kira shifted her charm onto the next guard. "And Svrel, dear, how are you?"

"You're not wanted here, Kira," Svrel told her. She ignored him and traipsed seductively around the pair, ending up face to face with the young queen who was now on her feet again.

Kira laughed at Eena. "A puny excuse for a girl?" She glanced over her shoulder. "Are you two so starved for entertainment? How about paying attention to a real woman, gentlemen?"

"Kira, step aside," Svrel grumbled. "That 'puny girl' nearly killed a handful of our best men."

"Oh please." Kira rolled her eyes, swiveling on the balls of her feet to face the Ghengat. "You always over exaggerate, Svrel. So she caused them a little discomfort. They're tough; they'll get over it."

The Ghengat growled deep in his throat, offended by her nonchalance. He pointed a thick finger right past Kira's face. "That witch conjured up a sickness meant to destroy us! She's a threat, and she deserves to die!"

The Mishmorat's demeanor altered in a flash—from playful to deadly serious. She didn't appear even slightly intimidated by the monster whose nose she was rubbing.

"You listen to me, Svrel. Gemdorin may be gone for the day, but he will return tomorrow and I guarantee if any harm comes to Sha Eena, the person responsible will pay dearly for it. You may feel brave taking on that puny girl, but are you sure you're brave enough to take on Gemdorin?"

Svrel didn't back down. "He allowed Grah Raugh to give her fifteen lashes last night. I'd say he's grown less fond of the witch."

Kira rose onto her tiptoes, tightening her eyes into narrow slits. "That was by *his* order, not yours. She's his prize, and you both know it. She belongs to him. Now…you leave her alone or I'll be sure to tell Gemdorin exactly who harmed her today."

Gar entered their standoff. "I would think you'd want her dead more than anyone, Kira."

"Get out of here," she hissed.

They didn't challenge her further but made seething, guttural growls as they walked off, leaving the two women alone. Kira then turned her foul mood on Eena.

"You sure as hell screwed things up! I told you to be *helpful* to Gemdorin; instead you try to wipe out his entire army! Are you insane? Now you have not only *him* angry with you, but every freakin' Ghengat on this cursed planet wants to kill you! Sheesh, girl, could you have made things any worse?"

"I wasn't thinking."

"Major understatement!" The Mishmorat grabbed the waiting wheelbarrow and effortlessly dumped it. She handed it over empty and walked with the young queen.

"Thanks, Kira," Millian uttered when the women arrived back inside the cave.

Eena glanced at him, touched by his constant concern.

Kira started in on the pile of rocks when Millian stepped up to work beside her. He asked the Mishmorat why the Ghengats were being so cruel to Sha Eena.

Kira tossed a heavy stone aside, grumbling an answer. "Only because little Miss Stubborn-will-of-her-own tried her hand at exterminating them."

Millian looked to his queen, seriously troubled.

Eena defended herself. "It wasn't like that. Not exactly."

Kira's eyes grew wide and challenging. "So you didn't give them all a fatal virus?"

"It wasn't fatal," Eena muttered.

"Only because Gemdorin made you put a stop to it."

Eena huffed, exasperated. "How do you know these things anyway?"

The Mishmorat straightened up. She leaned forward, sticking her pointy nose into Eena's personal space. "I know *everything*, girl. And I know for certain that if you don't quit getting on Gemdorin's bad side, you're gonna get yourself killed!"

Eena stopped talking to them both. As irritating as Kira was, the meddlesome Mishmorat was probably right. She had screwed things up. But what no one else realized was that in two days Derian would arrive, prepared to rescue her from this awful place.

So there, she thought to herself. That pushy busybody doesn't know *everything*.

Kira stayed with Eena and Millian for the remainder of the day. It was highly unusual for her to work in one spot for very long. Normally, the woman came and went as she pleased. Eena noticed the Ghengats kept their distance so long as Kira was present. That was a plus. After a period of listening to Millian and Kira gossip, Eena interrupted them with a question.

"Why is Gemdorin gone?"

"He had a meeting with some old fool," Kira said. "He didn't say why."

Eena wondered.

It was late when the siren sounded all workers to a stop. The crowd made its way outside and down the dirt road toward camp. Eena was used to Gemdorin coming for her. With him absent, she started off alone, up the incline that led to her cell. Millian and Kira ran to catch up, offering to walk with her.

The room was dark and empty when they arrived, but before Eena could turn around, the door opened to Grah Raugh's shadowed figure.

"Leave her here," he ordered.

Raugh waited, still and silent, until Millian and Kira were a distance down the road. Then he grabbed Eena's arm and pulled her outside across the way. He shoved her into the same stone barracks from the previous night. One glance at a large group of angry monsters made it clear she was in serious trouble.

Her pulse raced with trepidation. "W..what's going on?"

Raugh gave her another shove, sending her crashing into the

waiting Ghengats. "I told you, witch, you don't ask the questions!"

Four strong hands took hold of her and ripped off Millian's vest. She protested, futilely. Slapping a heavy piece of tape over her mouth to subdue the cries, they secured her hands above her head in the same pair of shackles. She knew what was coming.

The Ghengats administered a brutal beating, whipping her over and over again. The fact that her wounds never healed didn't deter the severity of the assault. Had he not feared Gemdorin, Grah Raugh would have beaten her to death. By the time they finished, her tiny frame bled freely. She couldn't stand on her own. Two guards dragged her across the yard and dumped her onto the cell floor. They tossed Millian's vest next to the body.

Grah Raugh hissed a mortal warning before he left. "As soon as we get what we need from Gemdorin, you're as good as dead. No one threatens a Ghengat and escapes the consequences."

She passed out, bleeding onto the cold floor.

When Ian met up with her it was far worse than the night before. Nothing existed in her dreams but dead space. She was unresponsive, hugging her knees with clenched fists, rocking back and forth.

"Eena, we'll be at Hrenngen tomorrow. Do you hear me? Tomorrow." Ian lifted her chin but she wouldn't look at him. "We're almost there, Eena, you can't give up, not now."

She barely murmured a word of understanding.

"Okay, good, good," he said, "at least you're talking. Do you want to sit by the tree with me and watch the sunset?"

"No," she whimpered.

"Do you want to look out at the ocean?"

"No," she cried, "I can't....I can't......I can't even dream."

"Then stand up and come with me."

She shook her head, unwilling to move.

"Eena, maybe you can't dream, but I can. Come and see my dreams. Will you?"

She finally looked at him; he had found something that

appealed to her.

"I can do that?"

"Yes. Yes, you can. Come with me."

Taking her by the hand, he pulled her into his subconscious where new surroundings instantly appeared. Eena stood beside her guide and gazed at a breathtaking wonder of nature. They were standing atop a cliff overlooking the heart of Harrowbeth. Rows of two-story buildings stood clustered in the distance, the architecture both exquisite and decorative. These buildings encompassed a paved city center where a majestic tree stood directly in the middle of town, extending its shading limbs over a great amount of paved walkway. Beyond this district rose a guarded whitestone castle with towers pointing skyward at each corner. A large amount of grassy yard was fenced in clear around the castle. Outside the congested city, single wood-and-brick homes interspersed areas of farmland, orchards, and meadow.

Beyond the orchards a dense forest took over. The trees, both trunks and limbs, appeared twisted, reaching and tangling in every direction. Background to the woods stood a magnificent yet daunting chain of mountains. Eena could barely make out a fortress set near the top peaks. A warm wind brushed her hair aside, bringing with it a peaceful familiarity. She had been here before. This was home.

"It's Harrowbeth," Ian told her.

"I know," she breathed. "It's perfect."

"This is how it appeared before the war. This is why you have to return, so Moccobatra will thrive like this again." He looked down at her. "I used to bring you here when you were little. You always liked the view."

She leaned against him and their fingers intertwined. She couldn't take her eyes off of Harrowbeth. The clarity of Ian's memories made her wish she could stay in this dreamed world and never wake up.

"Eena." Ian squeezed on her fingers, daring a question. "What have they done to you?"

She didn't want to talk about it. She didn't want to think about it. "Just hurry and get me out of here. Come save me, Ian." The pain in her voice was heartbreaking.

It was at this moment Ian grasped how much she needed him and how much he needed her in return. The uniqueness of their relationship struck him hard as he acknowledged a mutual reliance on their special connection. Being in each other's dreams was an experience beyond description. It was an addictive indulgence no one else could possibly understand.

When Ian looked into her eyes he saw need crying out to him. Their hearts took over from there in a way only dreamers could fathom. They reacted to emotions equally strong, equally shared. Ian caressed Eena's cheek before bringing his lips near hers. He kissed her lightly at first, then again with more appetite. She responded longingly, embracing him. Two best friends finally expressed feelings they had masked for some time. It was fantasy and yet it was real—both aware of every touch and every kiss that made them want more.

Ian pulled Eena close, supporting her neck with his hand. She returned his advances, grabbing a mass of his sandy hair to keep him near. They couldn't get close enough, couldn't touch each other enough to express how much they wanted this, how much they needed one another not just for friendship but for a reason to breathe, to hope, and to dream.

Images swirled around them, changing constantly: shooting stars, rainbows shimmering in vibrant hues, a hidden meadow beneath their feet, a spraying waterfall, bright billows of color bursting in the sky. These and more fascinating images soared by as the two embraced, kissing, hearts pounding in harmony to their admission of much deeper affections than they had ever dared to confess. There was no way of knowing how long they stayed together this way, but when their lips finally parted they looked at one another in a new light.

Eena admitted something her heart had known for a long time. "I love you, Ian."

"No. No, you can't," *he breathed. He took a step back, shaking his head.* "I shouldn't have done this. I...I'm so sorry, Eena."

Her face tangled up, and she refused his apology. "Don't, Ian, don't say that."

"This can't happen, Eena, It's not..."

"Don't," *she breathed, stepping forward to cover his lips.* "I *don't care. Can't you just tell me how you feel? How you honestly feel?"*

He paused for a long, painful moment.

"Just say it," she begged.

"I love you too," he finally admitted. She fell into him, wrapping him up in a tight hug.

"Don't say anything else," she uttered, already aware of his thoughts. Keeping him locked in her embrace, she asked for one more thing. "Ian, will you please rub my back? Please?"

He rubbed her back and held her close. Inappropriate or not, for this singular night nothing else mattered.

CHAPTER TWENTY-THREE
The Dragon's Eye

When Eena felt a firm hand on her back, it immediately pulled her out of Ian's dreams. She woke up startled, hurting, jerking away to cower against the wall. Then she saw who it was.

"Gemdorin," she gasped, strangely relieved.

He looked at her, his eyes severe and angry.

"Who beat you?" he demanded to know.

She didn't answer.

His voice rose. "Eena, who slashed up your back so brutally?"

Her eyes burned at a rise of salty tears.

"Was it Raugh?"

She nodded that his guess was correct.

"Why hasn't it healed?" he asked. "The necklace is supposed to heal these things."

She didn't answer and wouldn't look at him.

Gemdorin decided it was no use talking to her. He was fuming as it was. Grabbing her arm, he yanked her up and away from the wall. She snatched Millian's vest from off the ground before being marched out of the building.

Red sunlight peeked from behind distant mountains. A few people had arrived at the caves, but not many. Ghengats outnumbered slaves. Gemdorin hustled Eena down the dirt road and sat her forcefully on a large boulder facing the mountain. She slid her arms through Millian's vest to cover her wounded back, embarrassed to have anyone see it.

Planting his feet apart, Gemdorin screamed out loud. *"Raugh! Get out here!"*

Every head in the vicinity turned at the daunting voice.

Eena dared a glance up and spotted Kira at the mouth of the largest cave. She was surrounded by Ghengats who were attentively focused on Gemdorin.

Again he screamed. *"Raugh! Show your ugly face!"*

Grah Raugh announced his presence as he appeared. He

approached the captain leisurely, seeming overly confident.   The Ghengat leader stopped just short of his angry ally.

"So, Gemdorin, you came back."

Gemdorin grabbed Eena by the shoulder and pressed her forward onto the rock.   He pulled the vest down to reveal her marred back.   She groaned but couldn't move, pinned to the boulder by his strong hands.   Every eye was watching.

"What's the meaning of this?"

Raugh barely glimpsed at her back.   "It's a reminder.   You said yourself she doesn't listen."

Gemdorin released Eena and moved in on Raugh.   They stood nose to nose, neither willing to back down.

"She belongs to *me*," he rasped.   "You had no right…..no authority to do this!"

Raugh came back at him.   "She attacked us!   My people have a right to fight back!"

"No—not with her!   I give the orders here, Raugh.   We need her to find the dragon's eye."

"She's not going to find anything for you.   She's worthless and dangerous!"   The Ghengat pointed to Eena as he exclaimed, "We'd all be better off with that witch dead!"

Gemdorin stood up taller, pulling his shoulders back to create a more intimidating presence.   Raugh responded in a likewise manner.

"So you're afraid—afraid of a measly girl."

"No, I don't fear that worthless wretch.   It's you who has me concerned.   You've lost your focus.   Five days she's been here and you have nothing to show for it.   You promised us the eye and still *nothing!*   She's made you soft.   I should've beat her to death last night and done you a favor."

Gemdorin snarled at the threat.   His eyes darted about, surveying the surrounding Ghengats.   They were all fixed on the confrontation.

"Is that how you all feel?" he shouted.   "Should I kill her now and forgo the dragon's eye?   Or do we wait one more day and have not only the most powerful gem in the history of warfare in our very hands, but control of the necklace's tremendous potential as well?   I have not come this far to throw it all away because of cowardice!"

It was obvious no one was willing to speak up for either side. Gemdorin turned to his challenger.

"You will not lay a hand on my property. *She is mine.* The necklace is mine, and the eye will soon be mine." He moved even closer to the Ghengat, leaving no room between them. "You will not challenge my authority again. And, as I've told you before, I will *never……be……soft!*"

With his last words, Gemdorin plunged his dagger—discreetly removed from beneath his vest—directly into Grah Raugh's heart. It was swift and unexpected. The Ghengat's eyes widened with disbelief before he fell at Gemdorin's feet, dead.

Eena gasped, horrified, and turned away from the gruesome sight. She was aware Gemdorin had taken many lives—countless numbers—but this was the first time she had witnessed it firsthand.

Kahm Gemdorin immediately addressed the remaining Ghengats.

"Does anyone else wish to question my authority?"

He waited and watched for movement. The crowd remained perfectly still and silent.

"I didn't think so."

He wiped off his bloody dagger and slid it into the sheath beneath his vest. Then he reached down and pulled the black sash off the dead body at his feet.

"Gar!" he hollered.

One Ghengat came forward. Gemdorin shoved the sash into his chest and grumbled, "Don't disappoint me."

"Yes, sir," Gar said. He was now the new commander of the Ghengats. The new Grah Raugh.

While this was taking place, Eena looked to where Kira had been standing. The Mishmorat was still at the mouth of the cave. She had seen everything. It seemed an awfully bold move for Gemdorin, but not for a man in love. Kira's eyes met Eena's, and she pointed at the young queen, mouthing the words "I told you." Eena looked away.

Gemdorin ordered his new Ghengat commander to oversee the work in the caves. Then he turned his attention to the rattled girl beside him. He pulled her up from the boulder and walked her uphill. He didn't stop at her cell, but stepped right past to another stone building in the rear. It looked much like the others but on a

445

smaller scale.

When they got to the door, he unlocked it and pulled her into the room.   He locked everyone else out.

"Sit down," he said, pointing to one of two chairs at a table. She sat.

Gemdorin went to a small cooler and removed a canister of cold water.   After popping the top, he took a long swig, staring at Eena the entire time.   As parched as she felt, she didn't care to watch him quench his own thirst, so she let her head fall onto her folded arms.   A moment later Gemdorin slammed the water bottle on the table.

"Drink," he ordered.

She looked up at him to be sure her ears had heard correctly and then grabbed the water and gulped it down before he could change his mind.

The next thing she knew, he had set a plate of food before her, insisting that she eat.   She was so hungry, the rations had an immediate effect, causing a wave of dizziness that made her grab at the table.

Gemdorin refilled the container with more water while she ate. When he gave it back, she emptied it again.   She downed the food in silence as her captor watched.   After a while he asked a question.

"Did you even consider defending yourself?"

She flickered a glance at him.

"Well?" he pushed for an answer.

She nodded, swallowing a mouthful of stale bread.   "Raugh wasn't alone.   There was a group of them.   I didn't have the energy to take them all on.   Once I passed out, they would've killed me."

"So you let them nearly beat you to death."   He simmered a disapproving growl in his throat.

"I figured they were too afraid of you to end my life."

Gemdorin's forehead tightened, tweaking the scar above his eyebrow.   "Why hasn't your back healed?"

She didn't answer.

"Why hasn't it healed?" he demanded louder.

She spoke between bites.   "There could be a number of reasons.   No food or water?   Working in the mines?   Healing those awful Ghengats?   Being beaten half to death?   Take your pick—I'm drained."

"Hmmm."

He continued to stare at her, but she really didn't care.   She was beyond pride or humiliation, just happy to have some actual nourishment.   As her stomach began to react to the food, her gorging slowed.   Gemdorin pulled something out of his pocket. He placed it on the table directly in front of her.

"This is yours."

She recognized the gold pendant.   He had found it.

"Put it on," he ordered.

"I don't want it," she mumbled.

"Put it on!" he commanded more fiercely.

She refused, bracing herself for his temper.   "No."

"You stubborn little.....*fine!*"

He grabbed the necklace and reached behind her, securing it around her neck before she could snatch it off.   She sighed with annoyance, but left it dangling.   It didn't matter anyway.   She would remove it later.

"Now get in the bed."

Her eyes shot up fearfully, but she saw no ill intent in his face.

"You need rest," he explained.   "Unless you'd rather sleep in the cell again."

That was a tough choice.   The bed did look comfortable. She scrutinized his expression once more, hoping his intentions weren't unscrupulous.

"Get in the bed and sleep," he growled impatiently.

She did.   The blankets were inviting—soft and warm and heavenly.   Gemdorin turned off the lights and left the room, locking the door behind him.   Fena fell fast asleep and was immediately caught up in another dream....

She was alone.   The surrounding area lacked any sign of living vegetation.   Only brown withered remnants of ancient trees covered the ground.   She glanced around apprehensively, feeling unreasonably nervous.   Then she realized why.   The red-eyed dragon was back.   He swooped from out of gray clouds, landing with a thunderous thud right in her path.   His taut wings stretched wide as he eyed her over.

447

Eena looked for cover, but saw none. It was just her and the glowering dragon facing off in the open. He cocked his head and watched his prey. When his wings folded, his muzzle reared and a terrible screech escaped his throat.

"What do you want?" the anxious queen shouted. Her mouth gaped wide with surprise when she actually heard an answer. It wasn't audible, but telepathic.

(I want you to leave me be.)

Her head shook automatically, confused. "What do you mean? I haven't done anything to you."

(Leave the gem buried,) he growled, (or I will have no choice but to kill you.)

"Stand in line then," she grumbled, rolling her eyes at yet another threat on her life.

The young dragon screeched once more, gaining her full attention. (Leave it buried!) The order vibrated in her mind.

"I don't want your stupid gem, but I may be forced to uncover it. Will you still try to kill me then?"

(You are not one of us. Only one of us can take the gem.) She heard how his words were tainted with hatred.

"Of course I'm not one of you," she agreed, annoyed by his statement of the obvious.

The young dragon raised his wings, spanning them. His red eye gleamed beneath an angry brow, and she met his stare with the same amount of spite. She watched him catch a breeze, lifting upward and out of sight. This was the first time he hadn't attempted to scorch her with his fiery breath. This was the first time he had spoken to her, even if the voice had come telepathically. She swallowed hard, reflecting on his warning, wondering if he was merely a dream representing danger or if he truly existed as the actual guardian of the dragon's eye. There was only one way to find out, and she had no intention of doing so.

The rest of her dreams were a mix of disturbing, familiar scenes—a jumble of the past few months intermingled in strange ways. She slept long, but not necessarily soundly.

Stretching her legs along the soft bedding, Eena yawned and opened her eyes. Her body felt refreshed, although the aching in her back persisted. She hadn't given the necklace permission to heal her wounds.   Uninterrupted sleep on a soft mattress had been a treat after so many nights on a hard floor.   A tranquil smile thinned her lips as she hugged the pillow beneath her stomach.

"Good—you're finally awake.   You slept most of the day away."

She rolled to one side to find Gemdorin lounging in a nearby chair, dampening her moment of contentment.

"Good afternoon," he grinned.   "Are you feeling stronger?"

"I've been better," she said.

He pushed himself up and out of the chair.   "Well, it will have to be good enough.   You have work to do."

"What kind of work?"   It was a pointless question.   His answer would be the same as always.

"Finding and retrieving the dragon's eye."

She groaned, sitting up carefully in bed.   Her tiny frame slouched forward, cautious of the headboard near her tender back. Gemdorin took a seat on the mattress' edge facing her.

"I'm not going to find it, Gemdorin."

"Hmmm.   I was afraid you might say that."

"I'm still very tired.   Maybe I should wait and try tomorrow when I'm fully recovered."

He laughed, amused by her attempt to procrastinate the inevitable.   "Nonsense.   The fact that you're holding a decent conversation tells me you're just fine."

Eena bit her lip.

"But I wouldn't want you to think I'm completely uncompromising.   We could negotiate for another hour of sleep— a give and take?"

She regarded him warily, less curious than concerned.   The impish curve to his lips hinted at a disagreeable proposition.   She didn't dare ask.

He leaned toward her and made a bold request.   "I'll let you sleep another hour for a decent kiss."

She shrunk away, staunchly refusing him.

"Come now, my lady, just one kiss?"

"No!"

"One small kiss for *two* hours of sleep?"

"No!"

"*Three* hours?"

"No—none—never!"   Her expression had altered into a greater look of horror with every appeal.

Gemdorin moved closer, causing her to inch backwards while trying to avoid contact with the headboard.   His face came so near hers, he could easily have stolen a kiss had he wanted.

"My dear, I recall you reacting very favorably to our first kiss. You were quite the temptress in fact."

She swallowed hard, very afraid he might try to touch her. He smirked before backing off, commenting with a bit of humor, "At least I have you in my bed.   That's more than I was able to accomplish the last time."

He laughed at the nasty look she gave him.   "Don't worry, Eena, work before pleasure.   I'll let you kiss me later."

She shuddered at the thought.   "You will never again get another willing kiss from my lips."

"Who said I cared if they came willingly or not?"   He waited for an anxious reaction; it seemed to amuse him.   "Relax, Eena. I'll save that challenge for another day.   First, I must get my hands on the dragon's eye."

Repositioning himself on the edge of the mattress, he completely changed the subject.

"Would you like to know where I was yesterday?"

She shook her head.   Despite her show of apathy, he went on to tell her.

"I had a very informative discussion with our newest ally. The old man agreed to meet me on the Mahgshreem in orbit around Hrenngen.   He was under the impression you would be present, and I must say he seemed awfully disappointed when you didn't show."

"You lied to him."   She frowned disapprovingly.

"Of course.   However, after I expressed my deepest regrets for your necessary absence, delivering a fair amount of quarrin to his ship as an apologetic gift from you, he was appeased.   My goal, Eena, was to get him to talk about the dragon's eye, but instead he chose to drone on and on about you and your ancestry. Fortunately, I still managed to acquire some useful information. The old fossil is a treasury of knowledge; I'm willing to bet he knows substantially more about that necklace than any of your predecessors.   During our conversation, he recounted a number of myths telling of incredible powers retained by that heirloom of yours. Now you and I don't have to question those rumors, do we?" He flashed a sly grin that got no response.

Eena began twisting her soiled hair around a finger—a nervous habit. Gemdorin watched her closely, lying down sideways on the bed to better see her face.

"Do you want to know the most interesting thing I learned?" She shook her head again. He told her anyway.

"The old man informed me that if someone were to fully utilize the necklace's powers, their senses would grow exceptionally keen. Such a person would find it a simple feat to distinguish between differing energy sources because, after all, that is what the necklace is designed to do—manipulate all forms of energy. If I understood him correctly, there's an unmistakable difference between the energy you would detect from, let's say, quarrin verses molten lava verses, oh, let's say....... the dragon's eye. Does that sound about right?"

His eyebrows arched critically, but her gaze was focused downward. She shrugged, still coiling her red strands of hair.

Gemdorin took Eena by the chin and moved her head until their eyes met.

"The necklace is designed to detect and manipulate every form of energy, isn't it, Eena? You tried to explain it to me once, remember? According to our ally, *you* not being able to find that gem is downright laughable."

"If that's true, then it must not be here at all," she suggested.

"Or, more likely, you're lying about its whereabouts." He waited for a reply, but she offered none.

"No big deal," Gemdorin sighed, sitting himself upright. "Sometimes all that's needed is stronger motivation. That's why I've enlisted the help of your very best friends. They seem eager to assist."

Eena let her finger slip from the ringlet of hair, entirely focused on him now. "No, you leave them alone."

"Fine. Give me the dragon's eye."

"But I can't; I don't have it."

"*Yet*," he corrected. "You don't have it *yet*. However, you will retrieve it by the end of today. Now get up. Your friends are waiting for you."

Grudgingly, she slid out of bed and followed him outside. They headed for the caves, the air unusually quiet for the time of day. The sun was barely touching jagged peaks on the horizon, yet all the workers had been cleared out early. Eena counted ten Ghengats positioned beside the entrance to the deepest cavern. What worried her more were the four figures on the ground with their hands tied.

Eena focused on the youngest—poor, unfortunate Jase. Millian sat next to the boy, holding his hand. She had warned the man to leave her alone; he should've listened. A frightened young woman was resting her head on Millian's shoulder. Eena's jaw dropped when she recognized a disheveled Angelle. Lastly, she spied Kira who appeared more put out by her circumstances than afraid.

"When did you bring Angelle here?"

"When was the last time you saw her?"

Eena gasped. "But why?"

"She was questioning my intentions toward you. I didn't need her filling your head full of unnecessary concerns."

"How could you?"

"Surely you aren't serious," he chuckled.

When they reached the waiting group, Gemdorin was straightforward with the young Sha.

"You have exactly one hour to find the dragon's eye, my dear. If one hour passes and you fail to locate it, your friend Jase will be executed. Two hours, and Millian dies. Three, and you can say goodbye to Angelle. Four hours, and Kira will no longer be able to play with you. Do you understand?"

"Gemdorin, I can't…" But she was hotly interrupted.

"One hour, Eena, starting now! Find my dragon's eye *now!*"

She glared daggers at him. "I will forever hate you."

Angrily, she stomped into the cave, clear to its core end. There, she paused, staring at a rock wall.

Locating the dragon's eye wasn't the issue; its whereabouts were no mystery to her. The problem was justifying imparting the information to Gemdorin. How could she rationalize granting him access to a tool that foretold the future? Derian would stand no chance against an enemy that knew his every move before it was made.

And then, as if that dilemma weren't difficult enough, there was her latest dream to consider—a death threat from that ill-omened, red-eyed beast.   Three out of three visions from the dragon's eye had come true, and now that very dragon had sworn to kill her if she dug up his gem.   She did not doubt his resolve.

It all came down to sacrificing someone.   But whom?   Four innocent friends or Derian and all of Moccobatra?   She had only one hour to decide.

Seconds ticked by as she considered her options, each moment growing more valuable than the last.   No Sha in Harrowbeth's history had ever faced a situation like this.   There were no memories regarding murderous evil foes.   There were no stored experiences making use of the necklace's advanced powers. Unsure of what to do, she turned to a medium taught to her on Earth.   Humbly, she whispered a prayer, pleading for divine intervention.

"Please, God, there has to be another way.   Please, please, show me."

The thought occurred to stand up and fight.   She felt confident in her ability to immobilize the Ghengats who were detaining her friends, but could she stop hundreds more who would come swiftly to their aide?   What if her energy were spent too soon?   If she passed out mid-battle, what then?   How many innocent lives would Gemdorin destroy to punish her?

Eena dropped her face into trembling hands.   Where was Derian?   Where was Ian?   They were supposed to have reached Hrenngen already—where were they?

It seemed like just minutes had passed when a shadow stole in from behind.

"Your hour is up, Eena."

"No!"   She rose from the ground in one swift move.   "It can't be!"

Gemdorin showed no sympathy as he excused his cruel intentions.   "Jase should've died weeks ago.   A soul can only cheat death so many times."

"You can't' kill him!" she cried, "because........because I found it!   That was the deal, Gemdorin, you said I had one hour to find the dragon's eye, and I did!   I found it!"   With big eyes she awaited his response.

453

"I don't see it, Eena."

"You didn't say I had to dig it up; you said I had to *find* it within the hour. Those were your exact words. And I have, I know where it is. That is what you said, Gemdorin, you have to keep your word!"

He laughed aloud. "Being precise in interpretation, are we? Alright then, Jase lives…. for now. Tell me where it is— precisely."

She breathed a huge sigh of relief, knowing it was most likely a short-lived victory.

"It's in the heart of the Avortacrec Crater, inside the magma reservoir."

"What? It's inside the magma?" Gemdorin looked genuinely surprised. "How? I was positive it was buried within the quarrin." He repeated a phrase he had read in a book. "'…*encased in a powerful liquid…*' I assumed it was the liquid metal…..the energy-rich quarrin. But you're telling me it's suspended in magma?"

"Yes. Heat is powerful too," Eena reminded him. "If you had guessed where it was, you would have realized there's no way to get to it. All this mining has been for nothing."

"No, no," he corrected her. "We have the valuable quarrin." His eyes tightened in stern regard, prepared to urge her forward. "Alright, Eena, let me be more precise with my words this time. You now have one hour to dig up the dragon's eye and place it in my hands. If you fail to do so, the Ghengats will execute both Jase and Millian."

"What? Why? That's not fair! You can't kill them both!"

"Why do you argue with me?" he exclaimed irritably. "Your hour starts now, Eena!"

"No, wait, Gemdorin!" She placed her hand on his back as he went to leave. He turned to her again, clearly unwilling to negotiate.

Her face was a tangled show of desperation as she admitted, "I honestly don't know how to get to it. You've seen the layout beneath this cave. There's magma all around the gem and then pockets of quarrin surrounding that. The veins of magma spread out everywhere, not to mention the trillot tunnels. I mean, if I were to accidentally pull the gem through a tunnel, the magma would spill inside and eventually hit a pocket of quarrin. The whole mountain would explode!"

"Figure it out," he ordered.

"But it's an impossible maze!"

"Eena, you have powers. Use them. Figure it out." He turned and marched off, leaving her to solve the problem on her own.

She was beyond desperate now. The last hour had slipped by faster than expected. Each second was costly. Finding the gem had been the easy part, but removing it safely?

And what about the whole dragon-threatening-her-life issue? If he wasn't just a figment of her nightmares, she wondered what would be worse, battling one huge dragon or hundreds of Ghengats? Somehow a single opponent seemed like better odds. Kneeling on the ground, she pressed both palms against the soil and closed her eyes tightly. Her mind rushed directly to the dragon's eye. She followed a multitude of possible pathways in her head, each ending with a volatile mix of magma and quarrin. Every pathway meant a deadly ending for the people on the planet.

"No, no, no!" she cried, frantic for a solution. "There has to be a way, otherwise that horrid dragon wouldn't have threatened me! But he just flies away and leaves me with no answers!"

She sandwiched her throbbing head between both arms. Then the very words that had crossed her lips hit her with new understanding. She stopped herself and replayed the last image in her mind—how the dragons always left her dreams in the same manner. They always flew away.

"Fly away.........that's what dragon's do, they fly up and away. That's it! Of course! I'm so stupid! I can't *dig* it up, I have to *raise* it up through the magma.......through the crater......through the air! *It has to fly!*"

She raced out of the cavern, unsure of her remaining minutes but positive now of what needed to be done.

"Gemdorin, I know what to do!"

He turned to face her as she ran from the cave. She asked how much time remained.

"Twenty minutes."

"Then you have to get me to the top of the crater—now!"

He commanded a Ghengat to ready a glider.

"Run!" Eena yelled, hoping to ignite a sense of urgency. She pled with Gemdorin as they waited, begging for the lives of her friends.

"There's no need to harm anyone, Gemdorin, I know how to get the gem. I know exactly what to do now, and I promise you I'll get it, just please don't hurt anybody."

He offered no reprieve. "You have twenty minutes, Eena."

She glanced over the dire expressions of her friends, unable to rest on any one face. She couldn't let them down.

"Where is that glider?" she grumbled impatiently.

As if in answer, a black ship emerged overhead, eclipsing the setting sun as it hovered. Gemdorin ordered everyone on board. They entered via a stairway that retracted behind the very last passenger.

It took only a few minutes to reach the crater. Eena was first to step off the ship. She didn't wait for a soul to follow, but ran to the brink of the steaming volcano. The heat was severe and the air more saturated with vaporous gases. It was difficult to breathe, immersed in noxious fumes. Eena dropped to her knees, coughing, and sensed the mountain's energy. Her focused mind found the dragon's eye—a faint, unmistakable pulse beating within the mountain's heart.

Using the necklace's more advanced powers, she began to pull the gem up through the magma. It rose slowly, dragged through the viscous liquid. She could sense every inch it climbed—perceiving each passing second it drew nearer to her. The gem felt heavy in her mind as she struggled to steal it from the grappling thickness. Finally, it surfaced. She stood up and placed her hands together, forming a waiting cup. Then she summoned the gem to her.

"Three minutes, Eena."

She comprehended the warning. It was enough time.

Gemdorin stepped up to the edge of the crater beside her. He watched as a glistening jewel appeared, floating like a ball of fire in the air. His hand reached out, seeking possession.

"Don't touch it," Eena warned, opening her eyes. "It's hot. Very, very hot."

"Bring it closer to me," he ordered.

She motioned with her hand and the gem drifted forward,

hovering above the ground between them.

"Well done, Eena," he crooned. His eyes gleamed, looking highly satisfied with her accomplishment. "You've proven friendship to be an effective motivator."

Their focus shifted when a tremor erupted beneath their feet. The ground shook with thunderous vibrations, breaking Eena's concentration. The dragon's eye fell to the ground, rolling forward in the soil.

Gemdorin demanded an explanation. "What is happening?"

The mountain quaked terribly, and Eena could swear she heard the faint sound of a…..stampede?

All at once, trillots burst through the surface, bugs burrowing up everywhere. Screams carried from the campsite below where more trillots were digging their way out of the soil. Gemdorin and the Ghengats fired weapons at the fat centipedes, killing and maiming one after another, but more emerged to replace the slain. Shots sounded in the distance, echoing up the mountainside. In a matter of minutes they would be overrun.

Eena now understood why these creatures still existed on an otherwise dead planet. They flourished near the volcanoes for a reason.

"They're defending the gem!"

Using her powers, she flattened a swarm encroaching upon her friends. Unarmed and cuffed, Kira and the others were huddled together using only their feet to fend off approaching bugs. A surge of energy struck two nasty trillots that threatened Angelle and Jase. They cast their queen a look of outright fear. Eena glanced all around, finding the entire area surrounded by vicious lava bugs. Her well-intended rescue efforts had turned disastrous.

Then a crazy idea came to her—a random fact she had learned in a high school physics class. The necklace shone bright as she used it to speed up a simple law of nature.

With one swift, forceful gesture Eena shoved her hands up high above her head. On the same cue, the air chilled to freezing temperatures. Frost crystals formed over the ground, running along the volcanic crust and far into the valley below. Moisture escaped every breath and vaporized in the cold air. But something else happened at the same time. The trillots stopped. Every last bug collapsed—all dead. Gemdorin looked around mystified, waiting for an explanation.

"They thrive on intense heat; they need it to live. Heat rises," Eena explained, shivering in the cold. "I just gave it a push."

Gemdorin chuckled warily at first, but then his laughter progressed into a boisterous display of amazement as he realized the threat had been eliminated. He grabbed the young Sha, lifting her into the air while twirling her around blissfully.

"That was brilliant!" he declared.

Everyone else breathed a huge sigh of relief.

As soon as he set her on the ground, he headed straight for the gem. Eena called the dragon's eye to her before Gemdorin could reach it. The crystal rushed through the air and into her hands, frozen like a giant, red snowball.

In her hold, the jewel's inner light began to grow. It seemed to pulsate with a steady rhythm as its brilliance gradually increased. She held on tight while crimson rays emanated outward in every direction, their glistening arms reaching further each second. A slithering line of vapor escaped the gemstone, climbing in the air. Trails of wispy gas particles ascended and spread until the form of a dragon appeared within the smoke. From out of the gas cloud, the creature came to life.

Everyone but Eena backed away to a safer distance. She clutched the gem, overcome by fear. The young dragon in his ghostly image hung overhead, straight from her dreams. He was a colossal, ominous figure with stretched wings that fanned the air, keeping him afloat. He communicated telepathically.

(You should have heeded my warning.)

(But my friends were in danger...) she tried to explain.

(I told you, only one of *us* can take the gem. Now you and your friends will die.) The dragon opened his mouth and cried aloud so that everyone could hear. All covered their ears but Eena.

(No! No, that's not what you said! You can't kill everyone! I'll put the gem back!)

(It's too late!) the beast hissed. His snout lowered near the ground. Both eyes burned red-hot. (No mortals can be allowed to abuse these powers!)

Eena was furious......and terrified. She would fight as best she could, unsure of how to battle a dragon.   The fiend threw back his head like a priming whip, expanding his chest and neck in a gesture Eena recognized all too well from her dreams.   In defense against a breath of fire, she called on the necklace to create a force field.   Instead, something entirely unexpected occurred. The necklace reacted independently.

In a blinding flash it emitted a light whiter than the reflection off fresh-fallen snow.   The whiteness increased in radiance, encompassing Eena and stretching outward.   All eyes turned away from the light out of necessity; its brilliance was worse than staring at the sun.   This stopped the dragon's attack.   He didn't turn away, but stared directly through the light at the young woman inside.   She could still hear his thoughts.

(You can't do this!) the dragon argued.   He flew backwards as if retreating.   A moment later his head bowed in grudging surrender.

In her thoughts she heard him say, (My stone is yours—for now.   But without the shield it will prove useless to you.)

As quickly as the light had expanded, the bronze necklace sucked in all the radiance.   The dragon glared at Eena and telepathically warned her, (I'll be watching you.)   Then he soared off into the sky, vanishing like the mist.

Eena sucked in a quivering breath.   She fell to her knees and sank down to the ground, passing out as the dragon's eye tumbled from her fingers.   It rolled across the mountain's surface, stopping directly at Gemdorin's feet.

The room was pitch black.   A chill kissed the air while thin moonbeams crept in through slender windows situated high on stone walls.   Only one woman could be seen, asleep behind cell bars.   A male voice called to her with hushed urgency.

"Eena!   Eena, wake up!   I'm here, Eena, wake up!"   He tried to rouse her, but she was too deeply unconscious.

A dead silence lingered as he contemplated what to do next. On a communications device he spoke quietly.

"Ian, come in."

"Yes, sir."

"I'm here with her but there's a force field.   I've searched for the remote to deactivate it, but I can't find it.   I can't wake her either; she's sleeping too soundly." He continued to speak softly so no one outside the walls could hear. "Ian, can you wake her up?"

"I can try. It may take a while, Derian, so you should keep trying too."

"Understood," the captain whispered. "Derian out."

The protector called out for his queen as soon as he entered her dreams.

"Eena? Eena, where are you?"

"I'm here," she answered. "But where are you? You said you would reach Hrenngen today."

"We did; we're here right now. Derian's with you as we speak, but he's having problems. He needs you to wake up."

"I can't. I'm too exhausted," she complained.

"Eena, we have to get you out of here tonight or we run the risk of being discovered. You need to wake up."

She nodded her understanding. "Okay, I'll try."

"Just listen for Derian's voice. Can you hear him?"

Eena focused her attention. "I hear him."

"Concentrate on the sound of his voice and you'll wake up. Just stay with his voice."

Her dream image disappeared. Ian's was soon to follow.

She woke to the frantic whispering of her own name.

"Eena, please wake up!" the captain pleaded. When she opened her eyes and looked at him he sighed with relief. "Oh, thank heavens."

"Derian?" Her voice sounded as weak as her body felt. Her eyelids were heavy, like stone shutters, difficult to keep open. The whole incident with the dragon had sapped her last ounce of energy.

Derian knelt on the floor outside the cell, as close to her as he could get. "Eena don't go back to sleep. I need your help. There's a force field around the cell."

"A remote," she breathed. "Gemdorin has it."

"I know. He had the remote with him when he put you in here, but when I went to look for it, I couldn't find it. Do you have any idea where it might be?"

"No."

"Eena, I know you're exhausted but you've got to stay awake. We need that remote…"

"You mean this one?"

Derian whirled around at a voice he remembered all too well from the past.

"Kira!" he growled. His eyes anxiously swept over the spotted Mishmorat.

She batted a hand, dismissing his obvious fears. "Don't freak out; I'm not going to turn you in."

He didn't look convinced.

"I assume you're here for Eena? It's about time. She wouldn't survive much longer around here as delicate and dreadfully stubborn as she is."

Derian held out his hand. "Give me the remote, Kira."

She pointed it toward the cell and turned off the force field. "Go ahead and take her. I'm not going to stop you. She needs to go home."

Derian didn't move but continued to extend his hand. "The remote, Kira," he insisted.

She smiled in her alluring fashion and sauntered forward, crossing into his personal space. One hand rested on her hip while the other dangled the remote in his face.

"You don't trust me? You think I might lock you in there with her?" She chuckled lowly, amused at the thought. "Now wouldn't that be a pleasant surprise for Gemdorin." Her fingers released the remote, dropping it into Derian's open palm. He immediately pocketed the device.

"Sit down and stay put," he ordered, pointing to the table by the cell.

Kira lifted herself onto the counter with ease, posing in a manner that would've enticed most men.

Derian scowled at her seductive ways. "You haven't changed one bit."

"On the contrary. I'm not at all the same person you once

knew."

"You're still manipulative and devious."

She sat up straight, reacting to the insult. "I can't change what happened in the past, Derian, any more than you can change your relations. But I am *not* the same naïve idealist I was twelve years ago."

"You're wasting my time," he grumbled with disgust.

Getting back to business, he entered the cell and knelt beside the young woman who had fallen asleep again. When he leaned down, he noticed the pendant dangling from her neck.

"Not in my lifetime," he growled. After removing it, he tossed the necklace into a far corner. Then he scooped Eena up in his arms, waking her in the process. Her weary eyes fell on her speckled friend.

"Kira?"

The Mishmorat addressed her in a softer, kinder voice. "Hey, girl. Derian's here to take you home. You knew he was coming, didn't you? That's why you asked us not to do anything heroic. How'd you know he'd come?"

Eena had to reopen her eyes repeatedly, suffering excessive drowsiness. She tried raising her head, but the effort proved too taxing, so she rested it against Derian's shoulder.

"I just knew," she smiled.

"Lucky girl. Your very own hero." Kira sounded jealous.

Eena tried feebly to reach out to her spotted friend. "Come with us."

Her request was denied by Derian and Kira simultaneously.

Eena whispered to her captain, "Kira's my friend. She's kept me alive."

"No, girl," the Mishmorat cut in, "Derian's right. I'm not welcome where you're going. My place is here."

"Not true; things will change," Eena breathed weakly.

The Mishmorat smiled. "Thanks for the offer, Sha Eena. I'll make you a deal though: you get back to Moccobatra and take care of my people, and I'll stay here and take care of yours. Besides, Angelle won't survive without my help. She's as fragile as you."

With effort Eena lifted her head in parting. "Thank you, Kira, for everything." She fell back on her rescuer's shoulder and let her eyes close.   It was too impossible to stay awake.

A proud and solemn Mishmorat looked up at her once sworn enemy.   "Don't you dare allow Gemdorin to bring her back here. He won't be so forgiving the next time.   You get her home, Derian.   I hold you personally responsible."

"I will," he promised.

The captain pressed on the band about his wrist and disappeared with Eena in his arms.   He followed Kira out into the night.   After hiking a few yards holding his queen against his chest, he decided it would be easier to cart her over his shoulder. As uncomfortable as it might be for her, he still had a long way to go.   He tossed her upward, hearing her whimper in her sleep.

"Sorry," he apologized.

They headed away from the volcanoes, taking an obscure path through what was once forested terrain.   Brittle twigs coated the ground and cracked beneath his footsteps.   The Abbos One had set down far enough away from the Ghengats to avoid exposure. Derian had cloaked the ship in order to approach the planet undetected, but after safely landing, he had used the wristband to go after Eena, leaving Ian behind to guard and to wait.   Under cover of darkness, they were relatively safe.   But daylight would leave them visible to patrols.

Derian was aware that Eena's absence might be discovered at any time.   He was nervous about trusting Kira, although he had sensed sincerity in her expressed desire to have the young Sha return to Moccobatra.   The fact that she had kept Eena alive on Hrenngen boosted his confidence.   He hiked hurriedly to the hiding place of the Abbos One where Ian opened the hatch to let them in.   Derian placed their slumbering queen in a passenger's seat closest to the wall, gently settling her head against the chair. An automatic strap held her secure.   He then rushed to attach his severed cloaking device to the controls.

"We're ready," he announced.   "Start her up and let's get the hell out of here."

"Yes, sir," Ian agreed wholeheartedly.

The engines fired, activating the cloak and the Abbos One. Ian steered them into the black night to rendezvous with the Kemeniroc which wasn't too far behind.   They encountered no patrols leaving the Elrah Gyan System.   Every moment that

463

passed uneventfully meant less chance of being followed by Gemdorin.

Derian and Ian manned the ship's controls, constantly scanning for signs of enemy vessels. They took turns checking on Eena who remained fast asleep. Ian knew the past five days had been a living nightmare for her, but he was a little disturbed by how much her appearance confirmed the fact. She hadn't looked so disheveled in her dreams, and it took him by surprise.

It was an entire day the young Sha slept before finally waking in a daze. She didn't remember boarding the ship but recalled a hazy conversation involving Kira and Derian. It all seemed like a dream. Scanning her surroundings, she recognized the interior of a battle cruiser. It was similar to the one used in her rescue from Earth. She assumed Ian was somewhere about.

"Ian?" she called out, her voice still too weak to carry.

She rose and stumbled to the narrow aisle leading down either side of the passenger seats. Turned around, she started toward the rear, meaning to find the bridge. Her wrong turn led to a room comparable to Jinatta's medical bay but on a significantly smaller scale.

"Jinatta?" she called. "Derian?"

It became readily evident her strength was in no way adequately restored. Seeking support, she leaned on a counter. Her back throbbed, suffering the worst pain.

"Somebody? Is anybody here?"

Lacking the ability to go any further, she slid down against a row of cabinets, curling up on the floor. Recent events flooded her memory—hardships forced upon her, the torture she had endured. It was overwhelming. Her trials had extended far beyond the realm of sane and practicable troubles. They had pushed her past her limits, but she had managed, somehow. Most likely because everyone depended on her. But not now. No longer. She was done.

The battered queen let misery have its way. "I can't do this anymore," she cried.

Her face fell into her hands where tears pooled and spilled over. Hrenngen was behind her; there was no need for a brave face. She let her grief flow freely, sobbing, remembering the pain and agony and fear. All of it she had suffered and survived. Her body ached as much as her spirit distressed.

Then her thoughts turned to those left behind. Feelings of guilt and abandonment crept in, fueling even more reason to grieve. Her friends would continue on in those horrible conditions. How could she help them now? What would they think when they discovered their queen had run away, leaving them all behind? Her despair was so potent as to be a physical claw tearing away at her insides.

On the bridge, Derian announced that the Kemeniroc was close by. They would prepare to dock soon.

Ian rose from his seat. "I'll go check on Eena—be right back."

Derian nodded over his shoulder.

Ian stepped down the narrow walkway, looking straight to the passenger seat where the liberated queen had been sound asleep for hours. She was gone.

"Eena?" he called out. Panic stricken, he imagined Gemdorin on board. This fearful thought drove him down the aisle, frantic for a sign of his best friend.

"Eena!"

Near the ship's medical room his ears picked up her muffled sobs. He rushed in to find her on the floor hugging the cabinets, head in hands.

He sighed, both relieved and concerned. "Oh, Eena."

Stealing a cloth from off the counter, he dropped to his knees and wiped at her tears. The hair around her face had soaked up moisture, and he brushed them aside until she leaned into him, seeking his shoulder to cry on. He whispered consoling words in her ear.

"It's alright, Eena, go back to sleep. Go to sleep and I'll be there soon. Everything's alright now."

He went to rub her back—the same gesture she had requested in her latest dreams. He thought the action might prove soothing, but when his hand brushed over her spine she jerked away from the touch. Curious as to why, he attempted to remove the tattered vest. She protested.

"No, Ian, don't."

This only made him more determined to see what she was hiding.

"Hold still," he said, constraining her hands. The vest peeled off. His jaw clenched at the ghastly sight. Her back was marred with striated scabs caked in dried blood. How could this be?

"What did they do to you? Eena, why didn't you tell me?"

She responded with harsher sobs, chocking on the tears as though her sorrows would be her end. Ian took her in his arms, careful to avoid the wounds.

"Go to sleep, Eena. Go to sleep and I'll be there. Just go back to sleep." Holding her possessively close he pressed his lips to her forehead and then laid his cheek on her hair and rocked her.

Meanwhile, Derian made his way to the rear of the ship, wondering why Ian had failed to return to the bridge. He stood in the doorway as the young protector consoled a sobbing girl, telling her to return to her dreams. Derian watched silently as Ian rocked their queen. Without a sound, he stepped away and returned to pilot the ship.

The Kemeniroc stood by with an open hatch. The captain guided the Abbos One inside and landed gently in the docking bay with barely a thud to announce their arrival. The mission had been completed safely, this time with Sha Eena aboard.

CHAPTER TWENTY-FOUR
Awake

The engines of the Abbos One powered down with a soft, descending hum. Ian felt the landing and realized they were back on the Kemeniroc. He scooped up his queen, holding her close as she slumbered peacefully again. He had lulled her back into her dreams where she could find relief. When he turned to leave the small infirmary, Derian stood in his way.

"I found her on the floor," Ian said, trying to explain why he was there. "She must have been looking for us and got turned around. She's very weak."

The captain stood silent and unresponsive, continuing to block the only exit. He seemed focused on the woman in Ian's arms.

Unable to get past, Ian kept on talking. "She was bawling. Sobbing. Her back…..have you seen what they did to her back?"

Derian finally managed a word. "Yes."

"They beat her! It looks awful! I don't understand why she didn't tell me. Why hasn't the necklace healed her?" Ian searched the captain's face for answers, getting barely a shake of the head.

"Maybe she's too weak," he guessed. "I don't know, but I've called Jinatta. She's on her way."

"Good, that's good." Ian was worried for his best friend; he felt confident the doctor would know what to do.

The captain stepped forward and held out his arms. "Give her to me."

Ian hesitated, fighting a protective instinct. Reluctantly, he handed her over.

Derian turned to exit the spacecraft with Eena sleeping soundly against his chest. Ian followed them down the steps into the immensity of the docking bay. They were approaching the elevator when it opened up. Jinatta and Leisha stepped out, guiding a hovering medical bed between them. The doctor rushed over to examine her patient.

Stern-faced, she scolded the captain. "She looks horrible,

467

Derian.   It's a good thing you got her back this time."

The doctor motioned for him to place Eena on the bed.   He positioned her on her stomach, mindful of her wounds.   The bed shifted down half a foot under the new weight and then adjusted, rising up again.

"Be careful with her back.   It's pretty bad."

The doctor immediately removed the vest to observe for herself.   She was met with an awful mess of dried blood and festered scabs.   Both women gasped.   Leisha covered her mouth and glanced fretfully at Derian.   Jinatta on the other hand moved in closer to examine the lacerations.

The scabs had naturally closed, trapping frayed pieces of material in them.   It seemed the necklace had done nothing to help.

"I'll have to get this gown off her.   Let's go."

They rode the elevator in silence, each wrestling with individual concerns.   When they reached the desired deck, Jinatta and Leisha guided the hovering bed into the medical bay.   Derian grabbed onto Ian's arm, halting him in the corridor.

"A word," he muttered.

Ian turned to face his captain.

"First of all, Ian, I want you to know how much I appreciate everything you've done to help retrieve Eena.   I understand it was a huge risk you took sharing your secret, but I don't think we would have tracked her down without your help."

Ian felt a little awkward receiving a compliment from the guy, but he appreciated the recognition.   "Thanks," he shrugged, shifting uncomfortably on his feet.

"I'm sure you're as eager as everyone else to see things return to normal.   It would be best if we helped Eena adjust to life as it should be.   Considering everything she's been through, I believe we owe her some sense of security and normality.   I think it best to start immediately."

Ian nodded.   "I totally agree."

"I'm glad to hear that.   Then you will no longer continue to visit her dreams."

Ian's face fell.   Shock drained his countenance of color.   He hadn't considered *that* not normal.   Realizing he had no real defense in this case, he set proper tradition aside and defended his

468

right to friendship.

"Wait, Derian, but she's hurt and frightened. She still needs me; I'm her closest friend."

The captain stood his ground, tall and intimidating as usual. "No, Ian. She has all of us to help her now. Your time for being in her dreams has passed. You told me before that your gift was for observation only. You shouldn't be a presence in her mind any longer, and you know it."

Ian huffed, his muscles stiffening in protest. He looked like someone had just taken away his right to breathe. "I won't stop," he insisted childishly.

Derian spoke more sternly now. "You are her protector, yet you've allowed yourself to cross a line of duty and get far too close to her. It's not proper."

"She's my best friend!" Ian hollered.

Derian echoed his tone. "I saw you *kiss her!*"

For a moment, Ian's thoughts returned to his dream shared with Eena. He thought of how time had stopped while they were consumed by a prolonged, passionate kiss. But that wasn't what Derian was referring to. He had no idea about that kiss, thank goodness.

Ian knew he was in the wrong, but his emotions wouldn't allow him to back down.

"I kissed her on the forehead because she was crying. It was an innocent, caring gesture."

"What about your promise to Angelle? Will you turn your back on that commitment?"

"That's not fair! I haven't seen her in over twelve years! Things are not like they were when our parents were young, Derian. These are not peaceful, normal times. Many promises have been torn apart by this war whether by death or absence or neglect.... Who's to say Angelle's even alive?"

Derian paused to take a deep breath. "I say she is. I saw her on Hrenngen with Eena."

Ian was stunned. "What? Wait a minute, you saw her there and you left her behind with those monsters?"

"Ian, our priority was Eena. You know what happened the last time I tried rescuing someone else along with her. I wasn't about to jeopardize the safe return of our Sha for anyone, not even for you."

"You coward!" Ian wasn't thinking anymore, allowing his emotions to rule his words. "You're such a selfish, arrogant bastard!"

"And you're a fraud! Eena can never be with you no matter how much you've allowed yourself to fall for her! The council would stanchly oppose even the mention of a union between a protector and a queen; they would never support it. Now stay out of her dreams—that's an order!"

"Screw you!" Ian growled.

Derian lost it. He grabbed hold of the troublemaker's shirt, slamming him hard against the wall. "I'll have you removed from my ship if that's what it takes," he threatened.

Ian grinned, a cocky expression. "So what? You can't stop me regardless of where I am. You have no power over us."

"I can make it so you *never* see her again."

Ian came back with a harsher blow. "And then she'll hate you more than she already hates you."

Derian couldn't curtail his anger any longer. He punched Ian hard in the stomach. Ian doubled over for a moment, laboring for a decent breath. Then his eyes turned up, filled with rage, and he charged his attacker, ramming the captain into the opposite wall. Fueled by ages of pent-up animosity and a long-lived family feud, they fought like enemies bent on destruction. Brutal punches hit their marks, ensuring the imprint of deep bruising. Each man suffered strikes to the face, both bleeding as a consequence.

"Stop this right now!"

Jinatta's shrill voice filled the corridor, but neither man gave heed. After hearing loud thuds against her wall from inside the medical bay, the doctor had rushed to see what could possibly be the cause. A desperate call went out on her PCD.

"Security, I need you now in the medical bay! Hurry!"

Mere minutes passed before help arrived, although the time felt like hours elapsing in slow motion. Derian and Ian were on the floor at this point, struggling to crush one another. Ian was pinned on his back, but managed to oust his rival, shoving against Derian's chest with a lucky foot. When the captain attempted to stand, Ian swept both feet out from under him. Taking the advantage, he pounced on his opponent, prepared to hit him in the

470

jaw when security stopped the punch mid-swing. They yanked the resentful protector off of their captain. Other security members put themselves between the combatants, preventing any further violence. Both fighters glared at each other across the way, hearts pounding wildly.

"Are you two completely insane?" Jinatta hollered. "Can't you get along for one lousy minute? Sha Eena's finally back with us and not in the best of shape, mind you. She doesn't need this reckless immaturity from the two of you!"

Leisha, who had come to see about all the commotion, watched from the doorway and joined in Jinatta's scolding.

"If you two kill each other, who will defend Eena when Gemdorin comes hunting for her again? What in the world is wrong with you guys?"

"That's enough," Derian barked. He headed inside the medical bay, wiping at a stream of blood along his temple.

Jinatta stopped him by clearing her throat, motioning with her head toward Ian who was still detained by security guards. The captain sighed heavily.

"Release him," he grumbled.

Ian yanked his arms free and smeared a line of blood near the corner of his mouth. Jinatta and Leisha shook their heads in disbelief, following the men inside.

Eena remained unconscious, lying flat on her stomach with a blanket covering her body. Jinatta and Leisha had moved their patient to the same secluded medical bed she had occupied during her initial visit weeks ago. The captain grabbed a chair and seated himself on one side while Ian planted himself on the other. Only glares were exchanged between the two.

"If you're going to stay here, you *will* behave yourselves," Jinatta warned. "I won't tolerate any mischief in this room. Understood?" Despite no response, she was certain they got the message.

Everyone watched as the doctor went to work. Leisha tossed cold packs to both men before stepping in to assist Jinatta. Derian and Ian placed the ice over bruises, thankful for the numbing relief from minor, throbbing injuries.

The medical monitors confirmed that Eena's vitals were decent. Her blood pressure was low and she was severely dehydrated.   Leisha went to wipe a liquid substance on Eena's arm when she heard the captain object.

"You know that stuff can be addictive."

"I know, but it will make her feel better."

"Didn't you give that to her back on Earth?" he asked.

"Yes."

"How many times?"

"Twice," Leisha told him.   "But she needed it.   She wasn't in good shape then either."

He simmered a growl in his throat; a clear sound of disapproval.

Jinatta settled the issue.   "Give it to her.   She'll be fine."

Leisha then started an intravenous injection of liquid before stepping in to assist with the task of cleaning and mending their patient's wounded back.

"You guys can go if you want," Jinatta said.   No one moved to leave the room.   "Very well, then.   This isn't going to be pretty."

Leisha cut around the gown and removed as much of the material as possible.   It took painstaking thoroughness to extract every trapped bit of fabric from the scabbing.   Significant signs of infection showed beneath swollen sections of bright flesh.   These areas were reopened and treated.   Once the cuts were cleaned, Jinatta used the regenerating device to suture the skin.   She worked on one small area at a time, mending each deep gash. The scars left behind were unavoidable, but they didn't appear half as ghastly as the original wounds.   Still, no one understood why the necklace hadn't cared for their queen on its own.

Jinatta straightened her sore back when the job was done, placing her instruments off to the side.

"Not quite perfect, but all mended.   Now she just needs a bath and some peace and quiet."   The doctor forced a weary smile for her observers.   "It's time for you two to go."

No one argued with her.

"I'm going to go check in on Marguay," Leisha announced out loud, making an excuse to walk the men out.   She wasn't about to risk another brawl in the hallway.   "Be back in a sec, Jinatta."

It was three hours later when the captain returned to the

medical bay.   Leisha, Jinatta, and Marguay were sitting around a slumbering patient, deep in conversation.

"Am I interrupting?"

"No, sir," Marguay said, rising from his chair.

Derian motioned for the man to sit, taking a seat himself. "She looks a lot better."

Eena was still on her stomach sound asleep, but Jinatta and Leisha had sponged her down and dressed her in a white medical gown.   Her face was clean and her hair glistening wet from a thorough washing.

"Has she opened her eyes at all?" Derian asked.

Jinatta shook her head.   "Not even for a minute."

"I'll stay with her tonight," he announced.   "You go get some sleep.   You've done what you can for now."

Jinatta informed the captain she would return in five hours to check on her patient.   Then she left with the others.

Once alone, Derian made himself comfortable by tipping back in his chair.   He watched his queen sleep, counting her slow exhales every few seconds.   His thoughts turned to the things he had witnessed on Hrenngen while invisibly watching and waiting for the right opportunity to snatch her away.   Her unkempt, anxious appearance had been a shock.   Her incredible display of power had alarmed him even more.   He had nearly grabbed her when the trillots attacked, but miraculously she had found a way to stop them on her own.   And then that dragon—simply indescribable.   The literal existence of dragons had never been a serious consideration, even though literature throughout the galaxy recorded tales of such creatures.

Derian reflected on how Eena had saved her friends, almost sacrificing her own life in the process.   Whether to call it sheer foolishness or grand heroism, he hadn't quite decided, but either way he realized she was someone to be reckoned with.   What concerned him most was what Ian had told him about Sha Tashi's warning.   He recalled Ian's words—'unspeakable consequences.' Had Eena gone too far with these powers?   He understood why she had used them—to survive Gemdorin—but was she tempting fate?   The next few hours he spent contemplating the things that would need to happen as soon as the young Sha awakened.

It didn't seem like five hours had passed when Derian heard

Jinatta approaching.

"How's our patient?" she asked, appearing from behind the dividing wall.

"She hasn't moved a muscle, but I imagine she's awfully tired after the hell she survived."

"I'm certain she'll wake soon enough." The doctor took a seat on the edge of her patient's bed before boldly asking a nosy question. "So, Derian, what was that little show of hostility between you and Ian all about?"

A note of irritation accompanied a curt answer. "Nothing." It was obvious he didn't care to talk about it, but Jinatta kept on him.

"Really? I'd hate to believe that bruise on your brow was for absolutely nothing."

Derian touched the area above his right eye. It was tender.

"What happened out there?" she repeated.

Again his reply was terse. "I told you, nothing."

"Derian, it's me. Look, I realize things have changed, but it's *me* you're talking to. I know you better than that. You two were bent on killing each other. Do I need to keep you apart? Because I'll admit I'm a bit concerned."

"Jinatta, we're fine." He rose from his chair, tired of her interrogating. His hand fell firmly on her shoulder as he told her, "You take care of your patient and let me take care of my crew." Then he started out of the medical bay.

"Well, at least promise me you won't hurt Ian," she called out behind him.

"I won't."

"And no more hitting," she added.

"Fine," he agreed.

"And no shooting!" she yelled.

"Okay, Jinatta, okay!"

The doors whooshed closed as he stepped out of the medical bay. The doctor sighed, shaking her head at no one.

Eena slept through the entire next day. Her friends came to see her, including Jerin who kept grimacing as Leisha and Jinatta rehearsed stories about Eena's unbelievable exploits. Derian had given them enough information to put together a good tale, even if

474

they did adlib here and there.   Jinatta noticed that Ian was the only one who didn't come by to visit.   It concerned her that he wasn't standing guard as expected, but given the skirmish he and Derian had had, she could only assume the two were keeping a healthy distance.   The captain stayed half the night in the medical bay again, watching Eena breathe.

Day three was similar, except Jinatta noticed Ian sitting silently by Eena's side for a while in the late afternoon.   She eventually approached him, observing the way he sat motionless, like a somber statue staring out at nothing.

"I see you have a bit of a nasty bruise there," she commented, leaning against the edge of her patient's bed.

Ian touched his right brow.

"You and Derian could easily be twins," she chuckled. Jinatta knew it wouldn't take much to heal their bruises, but since neither had asked her to do so, she figured it served as a good reminder for them to steer clear of another pointless fight.

"Where have you been, Ian?"

"My quarters," he murmured, looking highly disinterested in conversation.

"Eena hasn't stirred at all," Jinatta sighed.   Evidence of concern was in her voice.

"I know."

"You do?   You heard?"

"I….uh," he stammered, "uh….yes, I heard."

"So you aren't as indifferent as you appear to be."

"What?   Of course not!" he snapped.   Ian's brow furrowed as he shook his head at the floor.

"Well, you didn't show your face here at all yesterday.   This afternoon is the first I've seen you around.   I thought you were supposed to be her protector?"

"I am!" he barked defensively.

"I'm just saying—I expected you to be here.   That is unless Derian's ordered you to stay away for some reason?"

Ian scrunched his eyes.   "I know what you're doing, Jinatta. And if Derian hasn't told you anything, I certainly won't either." The statement was emphatic, but it didn't stop the doctor from digging a little deeper.

"Ian, two people don't try to beat the life out of each other for

475

no reason."

"It was a misunderstanding.   Let it go."

But she couldn't let it go.   "I've been thinking about it, and I believe there are only two reasons men get into such brawls. One—because of anger.   But you two have always been angry with each other, and you've never fought like that, so I have to assume it's because of the other reason."

Ian couldn't help but be curious.   "And what's that?" he asked.

"Jealousy."

"I am *not* jealous of Derian!"   He was clearly offended by the suggestion.

"I didn't mean you."

Ian's face twisted up, perplexed.   "Why would Derian be jealous of me?   He has everything—the power, the respect, the title…"

"But he doesn't have the girl.   Not her heart, anyway." Jinatta watched Ian's nonverbal responses carefully.   She didn't blink as he stared ahead expressionless for a good long moment.

"Eena and I are just friends, Jinatta," he finally insisted.   His eyes found the ground again.

"Good," she said.   "I know sometimes it's difficult to be *just friends*."

Ian rose abruptly.   "I wouldn't know."   He left the medical bay more upset than when he had arrived.

Back in his quarters, he threw himself down on a pillowed sofa and fell asleep….

"Eena?" he called out, glancing around.

Ian was in her dreams again at the foot of an all-too-familiar hill.   Looking up at the weeping willow tree, he caught her silhouette huddled against its broad trunk.   Three days had passed since she had made the decision not to wake up.   Ian had spent most of his time by her side while she had done nothing more than sit miserably beneath that tree, peering out with glassy eyes at a sunset that never rested.   Yesterday he had made things worse by trying to talk to her about their kiss.

Ian trudged slowly up the hill, wondering what he could possibly say to ease her troubled heart.   Standing over her

476

despondent figure, he tried to offer some hope.

"You know, Eena," he began, contemplating her ever-present sunset, "the sun also rises."

Her head inclined just enough to glare at him through red, swollen eyes.

"Not for me," she mumbled sulkily.

"Come on, Eena." He tried to sound optimistic. "Perhaps a change of scenery would do you some good."

She didn't say a word, but in a heartbeat their surroundings magically altered into a place unfamiliar to Ian. He found himself standing on a rocky cliff overlooking a wide river that ran deep down in the gorge below. The cliffs across the ravine wore striations of brown, apricot, and gold, pressed together, creating interesting crumples and bends in the rock. The setting sun had been replaced by a clear blue sky. A warm wind felt pleasant against the summer heat. Ian could hear seagulls calling overhead. These were surroundings from Earth. The only thing missing was Eena. Whirling completely around, he didn't spot her anywhere.

"Eena?" he called out. "Eena, where are you?"

"I'm over here."

He followed the sound of her voice over the cliff. Peering down, he detected a narrow trail leading to a ledge about ten feet below. Carefully, he descended the trail.

"This height doesn't bother you?"

She replied in a grave tone. "Not half as much as murderous Ghengats and dragons."

"Eena..." he began.

"I'm not talking to you, remember?" Her voice was sharp but sullen.

Ian chuckled without humor. "Okay then."

He sat beside her, peering down at the distant river. They were awfully high up which made his stomach turn. Then he saw what held Eena's attention. There was a boat race taking place far below. Ian observed two powerboats whipping across the water's surface, splashing up a thick shower of spray in their passing. After a period of silent observation, Ian tried again to lift her spirits.

"I spent the last couple of hours in the medical bay with you.

477

People are eager to have you wake up. They want to visit with you and welcome you home. Everyone's wondering why you're still sleeping."

"Let them wonder. I don't care."

Ian sighed. "You know you can't sleep forever."

"Yes, I can."

"Eventually you're going to have to eat."

"No, I won't."

"Well, I can't sleep forever, then. Life goes on you know."

She turned to look at him. "Ian, I never asked you to stay here with me."

"Why are you so stubborn?" His question communicated how difficult a time he was having with her behavior.

She didn't say anything.

Eena leaned forward on the brink of the cliff, legs folded. Her gaze crossed the river to run along the banks of a thin beach. She wasn't trying to be stubborn as much as she was trying to vanish altogether. Sleep was the closest thing to disappearing. As long as she remained asleep, reality couldn't bite her.

A tear slid silently down her cheek as she sat contemplating Ian's words—not only his present question, but their conversation from the previous day. She turned away from him so he couldn't see her cry. Trying to explain herself, she spoke to the wind.

"When I was on Earth, my biggest fears were that my dad would catch me coming in twenty minutes past curfew or that my mom would embarrass me by showing off family pictures to company or that I might never be asked to Homecoming. I feared not passing a physics test because either I hadn't studied enough or because no amount of study could make sense out of such confusing concepts. And I feared what would happen to our friendship once I graduated. Sometimes I even thought about attending whatever college you chose to attend, just to be near you. Those were my fears. Those were the concerns that made my stomach anxious." She turned to face Ian. "Now all those things seem meaningless."

Ian went to wipe a stray tear from her cheek but hesitated, reconsidering. His eyes remained fixed on her, swimming with compassion.

"My life is a nightmare now, Ian. I'm afraid people will die because of me—because of what I do or what I don't do.   I fear being tortured and killed.   I fear an entire planet will waste away because of my inabilities.   I fear that if I wake up, Derian will be right there saying, 'I told you so,' and lecturing me on how foolish my decisions have been.   Or worse, that Gemdorin will be there forcing me to choose between my life and yours.   I can't do this, Ian.   I mean, it's one thing to be asked or even told that you're supposed to be a queen; I wasn't sure I could live up to this calling.   But now—to be hunted by Gemdorin and the Ghengats? To have innocent lives resting in my hands?   I can't do this, Ian! I just can't!"

The tears soaked her face.   Ian felt horrible and went to wash them away, but she prevented his hand from touching her.

"And then there's you—the one person I have any feelings for at all; the one person who ties together my life on Earth and my life here; the one person I trust to call my best friend—and you tell me I can't be close to you?   I can't love you?"

The tears streamed, and she sobbed in between her words. Her hands wiped at her cheeks, only to have a new flood of sorrow wet them.

"You told me yesterday our kiss was only a dream, that it never should've happened.   You tell me it's not proper?   I don't buy it, Ian!   It wasn't just a dream!   We were both there and I know you wanted it to happen as much as I did!   I know you felt what I felt, and yet you tell me to forget about it?   Well I won't! I can't!"

"Eena..."   Ian tried to speak but he was forcefully interrupted.

"No—don't talk to me!"   She rose from her seat, looking down on him with a tortured countenance.   "I already know what you're going to say.   Angelle.....your promise.......all that dreadful tradition!   I hate these stupid rules!   You don't even know her!"

"You told me she was very nice."

"That's not the point!" Eena cried.   "She doesn't love you and you don't love her!   Why do you insist on keeping a promise your parents made to someone you don't even have feelings for?"

Ian looked up at her, his face as tortured as hers.   "Eena, someday you'll understand."

479

"I don't want to understand!" she yelled.   "What I want is to be with you the way I know you want to be with me!   If Harrowbeth won't allow it then let's not go there."   Her eyes glinted with frantic hope, and her tone changed as she begged him to consider her plea.   "We can leave together—go somewhere else.   Back to Earth, maybe, or another planet.   I know there's somewhere we can go…"

"No, Eena." Ian rose to meet her face to face.   "Harrowbeth needs you.   Our world needs you and I can't let my feelings take precedence over an entire world."

"I don't care about what Harrowbeth needs!   I need you, Ian!"   Her eyes begged for him to change his mind—to admit he loved her and needed her too.

"I'll always be your friend, Eena," he uttered softly.   "Your best friend."

She gave up.   With a broken heart she sank to the ground sobbing, her face in her knees.

Ian's heart was broken too.   He felt the weight of her sorrow as well, but knew he couldn't do anything to change it.   That would mean putting his own desires above the fate of Harrowbeth, and he had already done enough damage as it was.   Derian was right.   He had gotten too close to her.

"I never should've kissed you," he said.   "I'm sorry."

"You never should've been sorry for it," she told him.

Ian's dream image disappeared.   He woke up realizing his cheeks were wet.   He had been crying in his sleep.   There was nothing more he could do.   Being in her dreams was only making things worse, yet not being there was tearing him apart.

Derian sat beside Eena in the medical bay, counting her breaths as she slept.   Somehow he found it relaxing.   Then he noticed the steady flow of tears begin, forming an increasing damp circle on the linen beneath her cheek.   Curiously, he wiped his hand along her cheekbone.   It appeared she was crying.

He spoke into his PCD.   "Jinatta, get up here."

It took only minutes for the doctor to arrive.   Emerging from around the corner, she asked him what was wrong.

"Look."   He pointed to Eena.   "I think she's….crying."

"Did something happen?"   Jinatta sampled the tears as well, checking to be sure that's what they were.

"No, nothing happened. She's been asleep all this time."

"Huh. Maybe it's a nightmare," Jinatta guessed. "There's nothing else wrong with her; physically she's in perfect health. And frankly, that bothers me."

"How so?"

"Well, she's fit, she's rested, she's perfectly fine. There's no clear reason for her to still be sleeping. It's not a coma. There's no sign of head trauma, and I haven't detected any drugs that could be causing this prolonged unconscious state. I'm starting to worry something undetectable is wrong."

"Maybe it's the necklace," Derian suggested. "Perhaps it needs time to recharge or something like that."

"Well, maybe," the doctor sighed with little confidence.

The two stayed with Eena throughout the remainder of the night, talking and monitoring her for any other signs of stress. But nothing else happened that night or well into the next day. By late morning, Derian was beat. He left to seek some rest himself. He was sound asleep in his quarters when Jerin's muffled voice sounded from his PCD. It took a couple attempts before he replied.

"Captain, you're being hailed by the Viiduns. Please respond."

Derian reached in the darkness for his shirt. His hand followed the sound of Jerin's voice, half-heartedly feeling for his communicator.

"Kahm Derian, Shanks is hailing you. Please respond."

With a tired sigh, the captain reluctantly opened his eyes. He reached over the bed onto the floor, gathering up his shirt with the PCD attached. Pressing on it once, he answered.

"Jerin, I'll be right there. Derian out."

Falling back on his pillow he allowed himself a couple more minutes of rest. Spending all night worrying at Eena's side had left him exhausted. He had hoped to squeeze in a nap, but apparently luck wasn't with him. Knowing how impatient the Viiduns could be, he made himself rise, dress, and hurry up to the bridge.

"Put him on screen," Derian ordered as he entered the spacious command center. Like flipping a channel, the black display spanning the forward transformed into a close-up image of one big, burly warrior. The impressive figure was dressed in a short-sleeved leather shirt with matching gauntlets covering both forearms. A leather circlet held his long, blonde hair in place, away from bright violet eyes. He lounged leisurely in a captain's chair and beamed when he saw Derian.

"You look like hell! What's the matter with you?"

"It's nice to see you too, Shanks." Derian couldn't help but share a smile with the captain of the Triac 38.

"We're about eight hours from you," Shanks said, leaning toward the screen. "So what's the plan?"

Derian lifted a palm skyward. "I'm afraid you're too late. I already have her back."

Shanks bunched his bushy eyebrows. "Go on! Beat me with a bludgeon, Derian, you went off and rescued the damsel without me?"

"I couldn't wait. They weren't treating her so well."

"Ah, I see." The Viidun showed a little more serious regard. "She alright?"

Derian nodded. "Yes. She is now."

Shanks slapped the armrest next to him, and his exuberance returned.

"Fan-strikin'-tastic! Then we're just in time for the victory celebration! Get ready for us, Derian. We're a parched, starvin' lot, and I haven't danced a beat with a beautiful woman in ages! I can't wait to meet the lovely lady worth such efforts." He added an animated wink to his declaration.

"It might not be much of a celebration yet, Shanks. You see…..we're having trouble getting her to wake up."

Shanks frowned while rising from his chair. He was a giant of a man, generously endowed with thick muscles, as was all of his kind.

"Hmm. That could be a bit of a hobble. Do you think it's poison? Or perhaps Gemdorin put a curse on her." Shanks was being serious. The Viidun culture evolved around superstitions and legends of magical characters possessing formidable powers.

"No, Shanks, it's not drugs or spells. Honestly, I'm not sure, but I get the feeling she's just………tired."

"Then throw some ice down her britches," Shanks advised as

though they had overlooked an obvious solution.

"Shanks! Look, we've tried everything reasonable, but she won't wake up."

The Viidun captain approached the screen, filling up the frame with his big head. "Don't you fret it none, my friend. As soon as I arrive, I'll wake your sleepin' beauty. I've got just the right tools to help you out. Then we'll have our celebration!" He grinned wide, full of confidence.

The man was honestly trying to be helpful, but the whole idea made Derian more anxious to find a way to rouse Eena within the next eight hours. Otherwise, keeping a determined Viidun from a challenge would be next to impossible.

"I look forward to your arrival, Shanks."

The Viidun captain held up his right hand, his thumb and two consecutive fingers raised in a sign of parting. "Strength, truth, and honor, friend," he announced.

Derian copied the gesture. "Strength, truth, and honor."

The screen went black.

Derian turned to Jerin and ordered him to ready accommodations for their guests. "And let me know when they get close."

"Yes, sir."

On the way back to his quarters, the captain spoke to Jinatta over his PCD.

"Derian, I've run blood tests, done scans, and still I can't find anything wrong with her. There's no physical reason why she's not waking up."

"Alright, Jinatta. Just keep monitoring her. It's probably a simple matter of time."

"I truly hope you're right," the doctor sighed.

"Derian out."

Wanting very much to go back to sleep, the captain headed for his quarters, but something made him stop. There *was* one person guaranteed to know why Eena wasn't waking. He really didn't care to talk to the man, especially after their last encounter. But four days of Eena's unconsciousness and the Viiduns right around the corner was forcing his hand. Derian changed direction and headed for Ian's quarters. When he arrived outside the door, he paused for a few minutes, determined to keep his promise to

Jinatta.

"No hitting.   No shooting," he reminded himself.

"Come in," Ian hollered when a rapping sounded at the door. He wasn't surprised when the captain entered the room.   He didn't even stand up to greet him.   "I wondered how long it would take you to come by," he grumbled.

Derian got directly to the point.   "Why isn't she waking up?"

"What makes you think I know?" Ian asked wryly.   "You told me….no wait……..you *ordered* me to stay out of her dreams, remember?"

"And I believe you told me you weren't going to stop," Derian retorted.   He was trying hard to keep his temper in check.

The two men faced each other without another word.   The captain noted how disheveled Ian looked.   He didn't appear to have shaved or showered in the past four days.

"Sit down," Ian finally said.   Derian took a seat in the closest chair and waited for the man to speak.

"She doesn't want to wake up because she's afraid.   Nothing I've said or done has helped."

"Explain," Derian ordered.   His face showed no emotion, unlike Ian who couldn't seem to hide his anguish.

Ian leaned forward on the sofa and ran his fingers through a sandy mess of hair.   Sorrow colored his tone.   "She says her life is a nightmare now and she can't face it anymore.   She's afraid of Ghengats and dragons and Gemdorin.   She's terrified he's going to come after her.   She doesn't want to be responsible for the lives of our people or the fate of Moccobatra—she fears letting everyone down.   She's afraid she's lost control of her own life, and………she's afraid of you."   He looked up at the captain.

Derian raised an eyebrow.

"She's afraid when she wakes up you're going to berate her for making poor choices.   She's afraid of hearing you say, 'I told you so.'"

"I see."   A hint of discontentment crossed the captain's face. "Have you told her we're all here to help?"

Ian fell back into the sofa.   "Of course I have.   She won't listen to me.   Truthfully…...I don't think she likes me much right now."   He closed his eyes, resting his neck on the sofa's back.

Derian exhaled deeply, giving away the frustration he felt but hid so well. "I know things have been challenging for her lately, to say the least, but she's back in a safe place now. She's stronger, and we're more prepared for Gemdorin this time."

Ian laughed. "You're talking to the wrong person, Derian. I already know this."

"Okay then, Ian, what can I do?" The captain's tone was irritable. He felt uncomfortable and helpless.

"What can you do?" Ian's eyes scrunched as he thought. "Talk to her. Go and tell her everything. Let her know how you feel."

"But she's asleep. And unlike you, I can't get into her head."

Ian straightened up, meeting the captain's gaze. "Not true. She can hear you. If she wants to listen she can hear you, I guarantee it."

Derian's jaw went rigid. His back stiffened as he contemplated Ian's advice. He wasn't good at personal conversations. And as much as he needed to discuss things with Eena, he preferred she be awake to hear it. Sighing heavily, he rose and left without another word.

A few minutes later Jinatta was arguing with her captain, standing as a barrier between him and the medical bay exit.

"You can't just take her away! I haven't released her yet, and you know I have authority here." Derian was holding an unconscious Eena in his arms, trying to get out the doors.

"Jinatta, she'll be fine. You're overreacting."

"I am not. She needs to be constantly monitored, Derian."

"Then I'll monitor her."

Jinatta huffed indignantly. "You can't *force* her to wake up."

"I don't intend to. Now move!"

"Why can't you leave her here?" Jinatta tossed up an arm with the question. "Do whatever you're planning to do right here where I can keep an eye on things."

He hugged the unconscious queen closer to his chest. "I'm going to put her in a comfortable bed. Four days on a hard medical table has to be miserable, even for an unconscious person."

The doctor's eyebrows skewed with curiosity. "And you think that's going to make any difference?"

485

"I don't know," he admitted.   He tried to explain, "I just thought I'd talk to her for a while.   Alone."

Jinatta looked puzzled at first, and then interested.   "Really? Do you think she can hear you?"

"Yes, I do."   Derian stepped back, waiting for clearance to leave.

Jinatta gave in.   It seemed worth a try.   "Okay, fine.   But I'll be checking in on you, and you better be watching her, Derian."

She moved aside and let him take her patient.   Against her better judgment.

In his quarters, Derian tucked Eena beneath layers of heavy covers while Yaka wagged his tail excitedly, peeking over the bed's edge.

"Stay down," he warned the animal who looked depressed not to have permission to jump up and lick Eena's face.   It occurred to Derian that a friendly welcome from Yaka might be all it would take to wake her; however, he feared a volatile response if it worked.   Of course, it would mean she was conscious.

Last resort, he told himself.

When she was tucked in, Derian dropped into his sitting chair—a mahogany armchair placed at the end of the bed.   He reclined slightly, trying to get comfortable by kicking both feet up onto the footboard.   It was strange for him to feel so awkward. Attempting to talk to this woman was causing him more anxiety than a sword fight blind-folded.

"She's asleep," he muttered to himself, "but she can hear me. Maybe."

Recalling Shank's unsettling offer to rouse Eena Viidun style pushed Derian to try his hand at talking to her first.

He began by clearing his throat.   "Eena, I saw you on Hrenngen….on the crater.   I saw everything you did.   I was there using the cloaking device, waiting for an opportunity to get you away without your absence being noticed.   I was amazed to say the least.   The way you stood up to Gemdorin.   You were brave and admirably selfless.   You're a hero to those friends of yours.   Of course, if that dragon had done what I thought he was going to do……well, we'd be without…."   He stopped his train of thought. "Anyway, I still don't know what happened, why that dragon backed down like he did. But you were very courageous. Very courageous, Eena."

Derian sighed loudly. He wasn't expressing himself the way he wanted to. Tossing his feet up and off the footboard, he leaned forward in his chair and rubbed the sore, itchy spot on his brow.

"Eena, I know things haven't been very pleasant lately. Okay, things haven't exactly gone like I planned, that's for sure, but you've managed rather well. Granted, yes, I wish you would've come with me the first time I came to rescue you. That probably would've worked out better. But you're back here now in a safe place and that's all that matters."

He stopped again. He wasn't doing so well with the whole talking thing. So far he had delivered not much more than a softened "I told you so" and "wake up already." Glancing at the animal now snoring at the side of his chair, he wondered if Yaka might have better luck.

Derian closed his eyes and thought. He tried to put himself in her position. He tried to imagine how hard it must be to have such a heavy responsibility thrust upon her when all along her own desires had been so much simpler and less demanding. He tried to imagine how she felt, losing her family......twice. Then he realized, he did understand.

"Eena," Derian uttered, soft and sincere, "I know exactly how you feel. I know what you're going through right now. Oh, criminy, do I know how much easier it seems life would be if you could just run away and leave everything and everyone behind. I remember losing my mother when I was very young. Not as young as you when your mother died, but young enough. I thought for sure my heart would stop beating; there was no reason for it to continue on. I remember nights crying out for her, wishing I could hear her voice one more time. I wished I could hug her and hear her say 'I love you' just once more. Eventually, I started building a wall around my heart because I couldn't stand the pain of her absence. No child should have to bear that kind of pain. I know you don't remember, but I'm sure it was similar for you."

Derian could feel his eyes watering as he recalled the day his mother died, but he held back the tears with a few blinks.

"Then a blessing came into my life—your mother, Sha Tashi. My father dealt with your parents often because of our family's responsibilities. Kahm Vaughndorin was head of national security, and so it was necessary to meet with the council and your parents on occasion to discuss militant affairs. I was enamored with your mother right from the start. Not just because she was a beautiful woman, absolutely, but because she was so genuinely caring and giving. You could read it in her eyes. She couldn't hide her emotions, no matter how hard she tried. They were always there written on her face and especially in those sincere, green eyes. She took me under her wing before you were even born, like I was her own son. I was drawn to her, so thankful for her. She was the mother I had lost—the angel who healed my broken heart. I'd have done anything for her."

Derian sat in silence for a moment, trying to gain his composure before continuing. Poignant emotions were resurfacing, feelings he had buried long ago.

"When my father killed her...." He stopped again. No amount of strength could hold back his tears now. He remembered the day his life had turned into the nightmare that even now he continued to endure. He brushed his fingers underneath his eyes, pushing the tears aside.

"Eena," he whispered, "I lost my mother again that day. A second time." A mournful silence claimed the room for a while.

"I know you had a family on Earth. And even though you don't remember your parents from Harrowbeth, Earth was your second chance as well. You understand that it was necessary for us to remove you, but I know how painful it must have been—how painful it must still be. I'm sorry. I'm so sorry we did that to you."

Derian hung his head as he recalled not allowing himself any compassion toward her back when she first arrived. His mind had been set on the necklace and nothing more. He was truly penitent.

"The day Gemdorin decided to take over my father's failed quest, I was forced to make a choice. Either I could do nothing, and in so doing be counted as one of his followers because that's what everyone would assume. First my father and then my brother.....no one would've trusted me after that. Or, I could stand up and challenge him—prove my allegiance to Harrowbeth, to your mother and to you, Sha Eena.   I chose to fight.   Really there was no option.   I knew I had to do it.

"I almost killed him that very day, until Kira got in the way. I hesitated when she begged for his miserable life.   Gemdorin used that moment of uncertainty to escape.   You don't know how many hundreds of times I've thought back on that one mistake.   If only I had killed him then.   All the pain and suffering I could've saved everyone, including you.   We did manage to drive him away.   Others in Harrowbeth picked up arms and followed my lead.   Gemdorin avoided Harrowbeth for a while.   That day my fate was thrust upon me—a huge responsibility I have never felt adequate enough to shoulder."

Derian regarded how the sleeping Sha hadn't stirred.

"Eena, the one thing that has given me the courage to go on is my dedication to your mother, Sha Tashi.   When you were born, I promised her I would watch out for you.   I gave her my word, and my word has always been good.   Eena, I fight in behalf of your mother, for all that she gave her life defending.   I fight for you and to keep Harrowbeth alive.   And because of these things, I know I can't give up.   Even if it means I must die.   This calling has become bigger than me, and so I give all that I am to it because it *must* be done, and I *must* do it even if I feel inadequate or afraid at times.

"The calling that has been thrust upon you is likewise as demanding and daunting.   I understand how you feel, believe me. But we need you, Eena.   I would say I'm sorry, but......honestly I'd have no other woman take your place.   You are exactly what we need.   And yes, it does require a great deal of sacrifice, but you don't have to bear these burdens alone.   We are all here to help you.   And believe me there isn't one of us who wouldn't give his last breath to defend yours so you might go on to heal Harrowbeth.   Don't block us out.   Don't think you have to stand alone.   Please wake up and know that I understand.   And I promise I won't say, 'I told you so.'"

The room fell quiet.   Eena didn't move.   Derian could see how her breathing continued smoothly in and out just as before.

"I'll give you some chocolate if you wake up."   It was a last-ditch effort.   "I've got plenty of it, and I don't care for the stuff."

Derian fell back in his chair. Not knowing what else to do, he kept right on talking. He rambled on about his childhood, about Moccobatra and life in the villages of Harrowbeth. He had no idea how much time had passed when a knock carried from the front door. He rose to answer it. Yaka followed him out. It was Ian who faced him from the dim corridor, looking much better than he had earlier. He was cleaned up and appeared to be in good spirits.

"Well?" Ian began. "Why haven't you told anyone yet?"

Derian looked puzzled. "Told anyone what?"

"About Eena, of course." Ian sounded a little irritated.

The captain was utterly confused. "What about her?"

"She's been awake for over an hour now. Surely you were going to tell us."

Derian's face turned white. He whirled around and marched back into the bedroom with Yaka on his heels. Rounding the corner, he stopped and met Eena's bright eyes. She was lying on the edge of the bed smiling sheepishly up at him.

For a brief moment they felt a connection. He had unveiled a portion of his soul to her, and now she understood him better than anyone. Likewise, he understood her fears and sorrows better than anyone else could. The tie was quickly shattered by Yaka who jumped on the bed, eager to greet his mistress with wet, slobbery kisses. She pulled the covers over her head, screaming for assistance which was slow to come.

Eventually, she heard Derian's commanding voice. "Yaka, nrahk!" The attack ended, and Eena cautiously inched the covers down making sure it was okay to emerge from her place of refuge.

"Hi, Eena." Ian spoke tenderly, kneeling at her bedside. His green eyes twinkled, genuinely happy to see her. His kind smile was a reminder of how wonderful it was to have him as a best friend.

"Hi, Ian." Her arms reached for a hug. As often as she had hugged him in her dreams, this was better. It was satisfying to feel his actual arms around her.

"I missed you," she whispered.

"I missed you too," he whispered in return. Gently, he pushed away from her, not wishing to hurt her feelings but mindful of Derian's watchful presence.

490

"So you were awake this entire time," the captain accused.

There was a hint of guilt in her grin. "Long enough to know you owe me some chocolate."

Derian shook his head with disbelief. "I'm on my way." He winked and added, "Welcome back, Sha Eena. It's good to see you awake."

As soon as the captain stepped out, Ian scooted closer to the bedside. Eena looked in his eyes, her face aglow. He smiled his crooked smile for her.

"So, you'll wake up for Derian, but not for me?" he teased.

Her shoulder nudged innocently toward her ear. "He had chocolate. What can I say?"

"Chocolate!" Ian exclaimed. "You mean that's all I needed? It was as simple as that?"

She giggled at his mock offense and then sobered, prepared to share the truth. "No. Derian talked about Sha Tashi, my mother. He made her sound like a genuine angel."

"She was," Ian agreed.

Eena smiled, a touch of melancholy in her face. "He spoke of Harrowbeth too and how amazing it was to grow up there. I woke up to hear his stories. Honestly, I wish I could hear more."

Ian's hand fell gently on her lap. "Ask him. I'm sure Derian would share all he knows about your mother. She was an extraordinary woman."

"So I hear."

"And Harrowbeth, it's an extraordinary place as well. You'll know as soon as we get you there."

He heard her make a throaty noise of doubt. "*If* you get me there," she muttered.

"*When* we get you there," he corrected. His fingers squeezed firmly on her leg, emphasizing his certainty.

She frowned. "What if Gemdorin finds me again? What if the Ghengats manage to steal me away? They'll seek their revenge, Ian. They'll kill me given the chance."

Again he squeezed her leg, this time in a softer gesture of comfort. "They'll never get the chance. We'll have you safe in Harrowbeth soon."

Her trusting eyes locked on the man who was born to act as her protector.

491

"You'll look after me?"

"You know I will."

"And who will fight Gemdorin if he does come around?"

Ian grinned a wry grin.   "The same man who cheats death at every battlefront, who delivers one mean sucker punch, and also possesses the power to awaken sleeping queens."

They answered the riddle at the same time.

"Derian."

~ The End ~

You can capture this body of mine,
take away my freedom and enslave me.
You may even have the power to capture my soul
and sentence me to the realm of eternal darkness.

But my dreams you cannot touch.

They are my will—the very essence of who I am.
In them I laugh.   In them I cry.   In them I love.
And in them.....I live.

My dreams are untouchable and unceasing.

—Richelle E. Goodrich

ABOUT THE AUTHOR

Richelle E. Goodrich is native to the Pacific Northwest, born in Utah but raised in Washington State. She lives with her husband and three boys somewhere in a compromise between city and country settings. Richelle graduated from Eastern Washington University with bachelor's degrees in Liberal Studies and Natural Science / Mathematics Education. She loves the arts—drama, sketching, painting, literature—and writes whenever opportunity presents itself. This author describes herself beautifully in the following quote:

"I like bubbles in everything. I respect the power of silence. In cold or warm weather, I favor a mug of hot cocoa. I admire cats—their autonomy, grace, and mystery. I awe at the fiery colors in a sunset. I believe in deity. I hear most often with my eyes, and I will trust a facial expression before any accompanying comment. I invent rules, words, adventures, and imaginary friends. I pretend something wonderful every day. I will never quit pretending."

—Richelle E. Goodrich

BOOK TWO

The adventure continues in book two of the Harrowbethian Saga.

Eena, The Return of a Queen

The young queen of Harrowbeth, has been saved from the clutches of her enemy, only to fear prophetic nightmares of being captured by Gemdorin again. A red-eyed dragon haunts her dreams frequently, portending doom within his fortune-telling gaze. It is Derian and Ian's job to keep the beast's grim visions from coming true.

Joined by their allies—a large and warring race called the Viiduns—Captain Derian and his militia escort their queen across the galaxy toward home. An unexpected detour takes them to an advanced world where a quirky king might possess the power to rid them of their enemy for good. But is trusting the promise of a stranger a risk worth taking? It will require Eena to face her worst nightmare alone.

76112216R00271

Made in the USA
Columbia, SC
31 August 2017